An Appalachian Trail
Love Story

Richard Judy has breathed new life into the continuous march of books that perennially spring from thru-hikers' minds. Each has a story of conquest, sometimes defeat, but Judy's book, *THRU*, stands among the best. His characters and their interactions play on the reader's heartstrings like poignant symphony. A must-read for anyone who has hiked the Appalachian Trail, or who has the "Dream."

—J.R. "Model-T" Tate;
four times Appalachian Trail thru-hiker and
author of *Walkin' on the Happy Side of Misery*
and *Walkin' with the Ghost Whisperers*

What makes a thru-hike memorable is the people you meet on the trail. The characters in Richard's book show the diversity, richness and determination of the hikers you encounter on an A.T. thru-hike.

—Bob Almand
Past Chair, Board of Directors
Appalachian Trail Conservancy

The book captures the emotional and physical ups and downs of a thru-hike better than any other account I've read.

—Larry Luxenberg
Author of *Walking the Appalachian Trail*

An Appalachian Trail
Love Story

RICHARD JUDY

Published by
Appalachian Trail Museum
1120 Pine Grove Road
Gardners, PA 17324
www.atmuseum.org

Printed in the United States

10 9 8 7 6 5 4 3 2 1

First Edition

Cover design by Margaret Nelling Schmidt
Cover photo by Lorrie Preston
Back cover photo of author at Tinker Cliffs in 1973 taken by David Chandler

Visit Richard Judy's blog at www.thru-novel.com and his Facebook page at www.Facebook.com/THRUstory

ISBN-13: 978-0-9912215-1-6

Contents

Foreword   ix

1   Gathering   1

2   Georgia   13

3   The Bly Gap Gang   34

4   The Great Smokies, a Slug on a Treadmill, the Art of Yogi, a Bunion and Cell Phone Abuse   49

5   Slacking Toward Damascus, Trail Angels/Trail Demons   65

6   Digging the Highlands, Thru-hiker Tossed Salad and Damascus Redux   85

7   Shenandoah, the Return of Brave Phillie and the "Challenge"   114

8   Lost Love, Lost Weight and Them Pennsylvania Rock Blues   130

9   Bears, Delis, Clean Breaks and a Peek at the Emerald City   156

10   Dunroven in Connecticut, Meeting Prime Meridian and Porkies in Massachusetts   177

11   The Green Mountains, Skyhawk's Redemption and White River Immersion   192

12   Hanover!, Glencliff—Prelude to the Whites, the Joys of
Hut Food, the Agony of Descent   206

13   The Notch, High Peaks into Infinity and a Bit of Betrayal   236

14   Monson, the 100-mile Cooldown and Katahdin's Kiss   265

Epilogue   285

Acknowledgments   289

About the Author   291

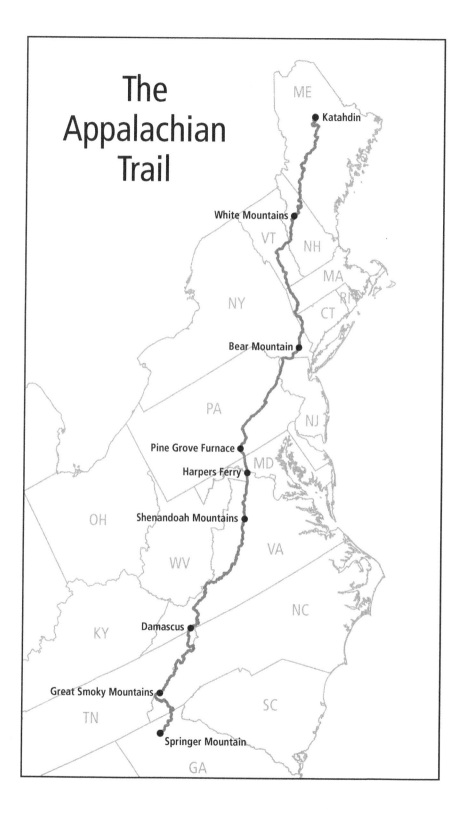

The Appalachian Trail

Katahdin

White Mountains

VT
NH
MA
NY
RI
CT

Bear Mountain

PA
NJ

Pine Grove Furnace
MD
Harpers Ferry

Shenandoah Mountains

OH
WV
VA

KY
NC
Damascus

Great Smoky Mountains
SC
TN

Springer Mountain
GA

Foreword

In a remarkably short time, less than a century since the initial proposal, the Appalachian Trail has become the best known hiking trail in the world and perhaps the most beloved. Millions of people have a special place in their hearts for the Appalachian Trail. Oddly enough, however, until now no one has written a love story about the trail.

Richard Judy, the author, was one of the early thru-hikers of the trail, hiking in 1973, the first year when dozens of people thru-hiked. Ever since, he has remained active in the trail community. His passion for the trail is so infectious that both of his children have thru-hiked as well.

On my 1980 thru-hike, with three-quarters of the trail behind me, one night I sat around a campfire near Dalton, Massachusetts, with a south-bound hiker. We talked about how hard it is to explain this experience to those at home. Some years later I wrote a book about the trail in part to bridge that gap. If I had this book in hand at the time, I might not have bothered.

Fiction at its best can capture the essence of an experience better than non-fiction. While this book is a novel and none of the characters—except for a few historical figures—actually exists, the book captures the emotional and physical ups and downs of a thru-hike better than any account I've read.

No two thru-hikes are alike and future thru-hikers will look in vain for these characters. But everyone sweats and strains, gets drenched and shivers, questions their own sanity and deals with the tedium, even boredom of endless steps as they head to Maine or Georgia. The beauty of the trail is that while each person has common experiences, they paint their own story on the 2,184-mile linear canvas.

Each hiker participates in the moving community of thru-hikers. They are also part of the broader Appalachian Trail community, peopled by Trail Angels (townspeople who befriend hikers) and the volunteers who build and maintain the trail.

For many years I've tried—and failed—to figure out why people are so intensely devoted to the Appalachian Trail. Thousands of people spend hundreds of thousands of hours working directly on the trail. That doesn't even begin to cover the efforts of the thousands of people in the trail maintaining clubs and unofficial volunteers.

I don't have any answers for this but I have observed this phenomenon for decades. People are intensely devoted to the A.T. They get married on the A.T., have their ashes strewn on the trail, turn to it for solace or euphoria. Many have wonderful trips on the trail. Others are miserable. But few go away without vivid memories and long-enduring changes in their lives.

The trail was first proposed in 1921 and by 1937 it was completed—there was a continuous trail from Maine to Georgia. Improving, preserving and protecting the trail has consumed even more work ever since. Not until 1948 did someone first complete the trail in a single season and in a certain sense, that brought the trail to life.

In these pages—or bits and bytes depending on your medium—readers will be introduced to a different way of experiencing the trail, through an informal group of a half dozen or more hikers who meet up on the trail. By nature, most thru-hikers are introverts and don't naturally take to groups. Most hikers come to the trail because they love the outdoors, want to experience nature and welcome the challenge of a thru-hike. What keeps them going through the many hardships is often something entirely different—their new friends in the A.T. community. Lifelong friendships spring up in a matter of days on the trail and this trail society is often what helps people surmount the physical and mental obstacles that are present in every thru-hike.

Blisters and mosquito bites, pain and injuries are part of the fabric of the Trail. So too are brilliant sunsets, close contact with animals, a profusion of wildflowers and engaging conversations with people from all over the world. What binds this society and shines through every page of this book is a buoyant optimism, a generosity of spirit and a thirst for adventure. And ultimately, an enduring love of the Trail.

As one who thru-hiked more than 30 years ago and has been part of the Trail community ever since, this book brought the Trail to life in a way that nothing else has. Do the Trail, read the book or better yet, do both.

—Larry Luxenberg

I may not have gone where I intended to go, but I think I have ended up where I needed to be.

—Douglas Adams

1

Gathering

March 22, Transcript of Captain Stupid recorded on the Approach Trail to Springer Mtn., Southern Terminus of the Appalachian Trail

What have I gotten myself into?

I emerged from a bus in Gainesville, Ga., this morning—predawn. Struck a deal with a hillbilly cabdriver to get me to Amicalola Falls. Jerk charged 10 bucks extra to take me to the top of the falls, thereby eliminating 700 vertical feet of climbing on the Approach Trail to the top. *How many times in months to come will I be willing to pay 10 dollars to avoid 700 vertical feet of climbing?*

Even after the 700-foot salvation, I still had miles of frigid slogging with my ill-fitted, overstuffed pack and my stiff new boots and my brand new official black Captain Stupid clothes. Captain Stupid—I have a trail name! All that way to Springer Mtn., and I never made it. Here I sit about halfway there at Frosty Mtn. tipping the scales in the ballpark of 345 pounds. I bottomed out six months ago way over the big three century mark and have been on an upward spiral ever since.

Yay!

What needs to be conveyed here tonight as I ooze in my sprawling hugeness—mini-recorder in hand—in my tiny little Hubba (a one-man tent not designed for a man the size of two, I'm learning) is how I would have quit—flat-out called it off—just over three miles into the Approach Trail if I somehow could have been transported away.

But isn't that the whole point? You are on your own with what you strap to your back. You can't take a break and go inside to reheat pizza and watch *Law and Order* reruns. You either keep going or collapse in a Self-Pitying Heap. Several times, I chose SPH.

I met an old woman. Her bespectacled eyes surveyed me from a glowering crone's face. Her straw-like legs, encased in tights, protruded like chicken bones from her baggy shorts. She gave me a critical once over and asked when I set out from the trailhead. I told her between two and three hours ago. "You've come about one mile," she said.

"You have some conditioning problems." No duh to a man of my standing, a lifelong spectator unable to finish the first quarter of the mile run in junior high, a committed advocate of inactivity who frequently brushes tortilla chip crumbs off his chest before collapsing into bed at night, a man who must rebel against his own tendencies.

So, a major decision was in order. As I sat contemplating the ups and downs ahead, I decided to separate useful wheat from extraneous chaff in my bulging pack. Extra flashlight and batteries gone. Sleeping bag liner—ixnay. Surplus food—outta there. Of course, cigarettes, a whole carton of filtered Camels. Insisting on a filter is my sole commitment toward a healthy lifestyle. I crammed all this—and more—into a garbage bag and attached a note reading, "all ye who get this far, help thyself to this bag o' goodies!" I suspended it from a tree branch, a swaying black pendulum left to the mercy of trail scavengers.

I wrestled the lightened load to my shoulders and carried on to the 3.5-mile point, where I collapsed once again, gazing to the heavens. Cold, but clear as vodka. No wind. I was ready to place tail firmly between legs, eat crow, wuss out, call it a day, cease, desist and get my fat white butt back to Akron to resume the computer recycling-business I'd left with great trepidation in the hands of Cousin Guilford.

There, the first of what will be many daily moments of truth occurred. An entity so soft and ethereal that it could scarcely be called a sound slipped past the cacophony of my raspy sobs. I wondered, was it the gentle click from flakes of frost falling from high branches and brushing past ice-hardened leaves? I held my breath to focus and concentrate the tiny bones in my inner ear as my heartbeat reverberated like trashcan lids colliding. Was this music? Was there a cadence, an instrument, a voice?

Stillness overcame the pain and stress. The threatening solitude of the forest became perfect peace. A bear emerging from hibernation, I labored to my feet and wrestled 50-plus pounds onto my shoulders and started upward, determined to isolate the source of this angel-voiced clarion.

March 22, Joint trail journal of Sky Writer and Bone Festival (Bone Festival writes)

So many details and logistics. We choose to dispense with discussion of gear, food, mileage, water bottles, polypropylene skivvies, mail drops and such. This will just be about poetry, music and people. Sky Writer was in good voice this morning—her clear soprano, so disciplined and practiced, but not overwhelmed by studied perfection. I strummed a little banjo cadence. She hummed, and then out came the words:

> Amicaloooooooooooola!
> Way down belooooooooow
> Amicaloooooooooooola!
> Goooodbye
>
> Bound for Katahdin
> So far to gooooo!
> We're the Northbounders,
> So Braaaaaave!

Letters on a page, but from her lips, the ideal. My banjo was accompaniment to an angel. Her crystalline voice ascended over still forest boughs to the cobalt blue of the North Georgia ether. I wanted to fall prostrate and propose marriage as she smiled at me from that angel's countenance—long blond hair, tall and trim, somehow never looking grubby and sweaty as we other mortals do. Man! I'm glad I didn't do that. What have I gotten myself into?

(Sky Writer writes)

Silly Bone. My little gnome with the twisted nose, the curly brown locks capped by a balaclava, and the wiry physique. He needs to think of today, a little of tomorrow, but nothing beyond. Isn't that why we're here? The freedom, the spontaneous lyrical perfection of each moment. On the Approach Trail. So far to go. And Bone Festival wondering what he's gotten himself into.

Here's what: no concern about jobs, taxes, marital commitments, toenail painting, oil changes, Power Point presentations, women without men, men without women, men without men, breath mints. He needs to not think and merely to transfuse the best part of himself into his tiny stringed instrument. Proper thought will emerge at the proper time, maybe a few hundred miles north. We've hiked before learning the basics. Now, equipped with necessities—his banjo and my voice— we stride forth with trail names and confidence.

So there we sat around an over-camped spot, the rock-strewn shoulder of Frosty Mtn. Suddenly, here comes a whale of a creature clad in a black fleece suit, black toboggan and ebony boots. Shrek-like, taking exaggeratedly short steps, counting them to reach a rest goal. He was Shamu the killer whale with legs and without the muscle tone. He sees me singing and Bone strumming, and his beatific smile transmits this message: "I am so ashamed to be what I am and what I must appear to be. I am an outrageous, morbidly obese pretender, here for what reason I know not except perhaps to escape a dismal life. I offer my sweet smile beaming out of my massive, blood-engorged cheeks, wrapped within my bulging jowls—a plea for you not to hate me on sight but to see the loving soul within all this, well, fat."

I stopped singing, and he staggered forward, collapsing in slow stages on a flat rock. Between gasps, he begged: "Please don't stop. You inspired me to get up this mountain." Gasping! Gasping! "The most beautiful sound ever."

March 23, First journal entry of Linda Bennett, Springer Mtn.

My parents never believed I'd go through with this, and I suppose that's why their protests were muted. It was only over the last couple of weeks, as the equipment pile grew and plane tickets were purchased, that my intentions became clear. By then it was too late to stop me. My mother settled for saying things like, "If you start out and don't like this, you can always call it off." Dad had the nerve to say, "People will admire you if you admit that this really isn't your cup of tea. That would take real courage."

None of this helped. Aside from Girl Scout overnighters, I have never camped outdoors. I intentionally did not ask advice, take shakedown hikes or do any more reading or preparation than I thought was necessary to buy functional equipment to get off and running. Except for a few tips from the guy at the outdoor store, I have sought no counsel, not even hints from trail blogs. I don't see this as stubbornness. For someone unaccustomed to failure, the risk is obvious but not intimidating.

Well before sunup, we toss my pack into the trunk. Mom wordlessly hugs me and shuffles in her slippers, sobbing back into the house. We cruise to the airport, my father's face dimly illuminated by the glow of the instrument panel. The quiet is not awkward. Dad and I feel no compulsion to chatter. He is sweet as we part near security, saying, "I hope this works for you. I hope you make it. I just don't understand it."

With my game face on, I fly to Atlanta. In the flurry of baggage claim I meet Gerald Hooper, a shuttler who drops me off 170 minutes later—after a barrage of one-sided, politically inspired conversation—at a gravel lot beside a primitive forest service road. I'm just one quick trail mile from Springer, much easier than the approach trail from Amicalola that I read about and decided to avoid. Then Gerald Hooper is gone, a vacuum of silence in his wake. I survey the path up Springer that I will hike in the opposing direction tomorrow morning, headed for something I suddenly realize I do not understand and am mildly terrified of.

Doodad, Caretaker on Springer Mtn., Southern Terminus of the Appalachian Trail

He was one of those well conditioned individuals, so thoroughly inured to a demanding physical way of life that his age was indeterminate. The longish hair and beard hid the incipient insults of time, except for smile lines at the edges of his humorous eyes. An inch shy of six feet, lean as a whippet, he was a man who spent so much time out of doors that his every move evinced economy and grace.

He was Jim Weathers, trail name Doodad, Springer Mountain Caretaker and teacher of thru-hikers, and this was the time of year that tested his patience.

Standing next to the rock slab placed in lieu of a monument on Springer Mtn., he scowled west of south at the spiky array of telecom towers on Mt. Oglethorpe. Then he turned to face Springer's flat summit and smile at the collection of sojourners interspersed among the gnarled oaks. Based on years of studied observation, he knew the aspiring thru-hikers with visions of Katahdin had maybe one chance in four of finishing. He also knew that the more he thought he could pick the winners, the less successful he would be. Who has it in them to walk 2,184 miles?

Life was better for thru-hikers than it once was. Improved equipment, better information, trail town support and enhanced trail maintenance had turned the one-in-eight success ratio of a few years before to a rosier 25 per-

cent. Of the couple of thousand starters this year, 500 would likely finish and count themselves among 14,000 or so who have reported hiking the whole thing. Doodad knew that the young stud—the one who had been everywhere as a rock and ice climber, a snowboarder, a marathoner and a long-distance trekker—was the very one who might go to pieces on his third day and stick his thumb out 30 miles north at Neels Gap looking for a ride back to suburbia.

On the other hand, a pair of fiftyish women who met on a hiking chat-room and had minimal experience outside their backyards and who looked like unlikely candidates to make it to the mailbox—these two might fool you. They would adapt to dirt, sweat, godawful weather, monotony, chronic foot pain, bugs, mice, sleet, days on end of precipitation, bone-penetrating cold, waves of sweltering heat, wrong turns, obnoxious shelter partners—all of this and much more. And after adapting and surviving for six months or so, they would find themselves at Katahdin Stream Campground ready to push five miles and 4,000 feet to the top of the A.T.'s northern terminus. They would be trim, triumphant, transformed and ready to return to a world that would never again be ordinary.

Thus, even after three thru-hikes and thousands of miles of additional foot travel, the venerable Doodad found the ability to pick winners and losers, or even define them, was elusive. He worked on contract with dollars scraped together by the Georgia Appalachian Trail Club. Part of his job was to protect the summit of Springer and the area around the trail shelter five minutes away on the flank of the mountain. "Leave no trace" education combined with unofficial enforcement.

He was a Jedi Master to the northbounders—the NOBOs—who passed over Springer like starry-eyed Alices through a white-blazed looking glass, bound for a dream they didn't understand with shiny new gear, fresh faces and resolve in their eyes. In several years of hanging around from early March through April, he had seen the traveling circus as it vaulted headlong toward Katahdin.

A few years earlier, he had met his favorite of all aspirants, the man he had personally voted least likely to make it out of Georgia, an affable middle-aged Aussie named Derek. Doodad met him at the Len Foote Hike Inn, a backcountry lodge a few trail miles south of Springer. Derek had taken the first possible wrong turn on the Springer Approach Trail, which led him staggering into the Hike Inn lobby an hour after dark. The inn had space that night, so he lugged his massive pack to a tiny bunk room and col-lapsed in a state of abject disbelief. How could this be so much more diffi-cult than he had imagined? What had he gotten himself into?

Doodad stayed at the inn on occasion and "worked for stay" by washing dishes and cleaning up after breakfast. The bemused manager introduced Doodad to Derek, and by mid-morning the next day, Derek's gear was strewn across four breakfast tables.

"Geez," Doodad gasped. "It looks like an REI store exploded."

"I tried straightaway to take everything I carry on motorcycle trips, and I'm guessing it's a bit much," Derek confessed.

Using kitchen scales, Doodad totaled Derek's load at just over 94 pounds. "You realize that just half this weight is a heavy load, don't you?" Doodad queried. He then established piles according to necessities, marginal items and outrageous stuff. In the outrageous pile went the complete SLR camera and lens system, the photographer's vest, and the tripod. A tiny backup digital camera went in the marginal pile.

Food was divided in half, some packaged to be shipped ahead. A large unleaded gas stove was deemed outrageous and replaced by a tiny alcohol model fashioned from a soft drink can, a freebie from the Hike Inn manager. Also in the outrageous pile went: a folding plastic wash basin, an entire third set of clothes, five cotton T-shirts (replaced by two polyester shirts bought at the Hike Inn), a poncho that was superfluous since Derek was carrying a serviceable, light-weight Gore-Tex rain suit, a fly rod (useless, as Derek would see only one marginal trout stream before hiking well into North Carolina), flies, fly-tying equipment, a nine-pound tent and on and on.

By late afternoon, Derek had scrounged cardboard boxes and tape and arranged with a staffer to ship the culled items home. At the nadir of emotional humiliation, he made a reservation to stay a second night. Doodad was waiting for him at Springer the next day, and as Derek labored tortoise-like to the summit with a pack pared to under 50 pounds, he seemed refreshed. After a brief chat, he stepped northward and disappeared.

Poor sucker, *thought Doodad,* He'll never see North Carolina.

Spring petered out, and Doodad headed for new tasks, ending up later that summer on a freelance photography assignment in Pennsylvania on the A.T. at Pine Grove Furnace State Park. As he tinkered with his tripod, he focused on a gorgeous young woman in her late twenties who had the telltale look of a NOBO from Springer. As she slipped out of his line of sight, a rangy male bobbed into view. Doodad adroitly twisted the focus ring for a clear view of the newcomer's face.

In slack-jawed astonishment, Doodad absorbed the shocking truth. The once-paunchy Australian was svelte as an otter. Derek had defied cruel odds and picked up a babe to boot. His trail name was Instrument of Pleasure, given to him by his new life companion, the comely Slinky Minx. His gear had been streamlined and was rarely above 30 pounds. He crested Katahdin 11 weeks later, trashing Doodad's prognostication.

So, as Jim Weathers surveyed the new crop of Springer arrivees, the only certainty in his mind was the uncertainty of eventual outcomes.

March 23, First journal entry of Doug Gottlieb

Wheels up out of Sea-Tac, a bank to the east, and the mountain is out—Rainier on a cloudless day. Big Tahoma, my first 14,000-footer at age 13. Dad took me up with the Rainier Mountaineering guides. We overnighted at Camp Muir and left for the summit at 2:30 a.m., storm clouds bristling above. A brisk, predawn front blasted through, pushing clouds to the east, and when we hit the peak it was slightly below zero with a 50-mph wind. I was terrified, exhilarated, pumped with pride and closer to my dad than any other kid in the world. Two years later, an aneurysm took him. I've spent the last 12 years trying to make sure Mom is okay and plodding along as a professional student.

I scribble in my journal, headed for an unlikely adventure for a guy who has always found refuge hiking and climbing in the Cascades— heading east for the Appalachian Trail. It's the allure of taking on the granddaddy of all trails, the one Benton MacKaye thought up from the upper limbs of a big tree on the crest of Stratton Peak in Vermont.

Five or six hours of flight taking me to five or six months of hiking. Time to ponder my terrestrial purpose. Maybe I'll get closer to God and benefit from the *New International Version* New Testament my Mom pressed into my hands just last night.

———

Aahh! A pleasant flight into Atlanta. I sit with my pack waiting for an undergrad buddy from my days at Stanford. We'll stay at his place tonight, take in a Hawks game, and resurrect decade-old memories of adventures involving girls, booze and a little redemption. I have a few doubts about my personal redemption coupled with a premonition that after this jaunt I no longer have excuses. It's time to quit studying and adventuring, time to apply myself to the "career," the true application of a meaningful trajectory. Since Dad died, I've felt stalked by death and unwilling to indulge in much beyond satisfying my curiosity and my appetites—the sacred "me."

Before Danny shows up at baggage claim, I've got that feeling, the one I always get when I light out on a new caper. My football buddies tell me that the apprehension of the big game dissolves when you take the first hit. It's the twilight before you get underway, when you question the sanity of leaving the comfort of your bed and air conditioning. Trading three decent daily meals for an endless array of substandard packaged crap. You question all this. A worm of apprehension eats away at your gut. You ask, "What have I gotten myself into?" But there is consolation in having been on the brink of adventure several times before and knowing that the grip of tension goes away. I'll bunk at Danny's tonight after fun and games and hit Springer whenever I get there. The worm will shrivel on its own.

March 24—Atop Springer

Doodad is busy, but he's used to it this time of year. The gathering picks up momentum day by day in all its motley glory. Springer is crowded—not just with picnickers and stray day hikers, but with some of this year's thru-hiking aspirants.

A guy with a banjo is entertaining the parents of Blue Devil, an 18-year-old black kid whose superior grades earned him early graduation from a Jacksonville, Florida, high school and time to take off for Maine before attending Duke. Bone Festival's miniature banjo is no toy, providing a sweet tone as the musician strums self-composed tunes, rich in melody and tantalizing in simplicity. His gorgeous companion sings a song with quirky lyrics describing a thru-hiker's dreams:

> *Amicaloooooooola!*
> *Sending us north*
> *Tumbling waters,*
> *So cleeeaaaaaar!*

On and on she sings, her angel's voice calm and confident. Propped against a gnarled oak, a sixtyish gentleman clad in navy blue polypro, trail runners and a Phillies cap covering sparse cranial terrain, looks on with a vacant grin. Nearby, gangly Blue Devil putters with his gear as his parents stand by awkwardly, awestruck by Sky Writer's intonations and Bone Festival's clever fingers. The Phillies fan watches approvingly as Doodad makes his way over to the kid and engages him in 20 minutes of casual conversation during which the nervous novice gets a primer in low-impact hiking and camping and a hint or two about what to leave in his parents' trunk before they vanish from the parking lot off the gravel road one short mile away.

Taking all this in is a raven-haired lass wearing cargo pants with zip-off legs, fresh-off-the-shelf Raichles and a green fleece anorak. Her pack is new, perfect, the result of hours of scanning through catalogs. It lies primly beside one of the twisted oaks near the summit rock, and she sits with her arms around her knees taking in the traveling circus before it begins the slow trudge north. Linda Bennett camped alone the night before at a secluded site 150 yards from Springer's crest. After a shaky night's sleep, she found fresh bear scat directly below her bear bag. Now I know why they say to hang the food, *she thought.* What have I gotten myself into? *Phillies cap approaches her with an engaging smile, which she cautiously returns.*

"What's your plan?" he queries. She ducks her head in thought and then makes clear eye contact: "I'm thinking Katahdin."

"I figured," he drawls with a Southern accent that clashes with his head gear. "This is my second time. I did my first one in three trips, but this time I'm going for the entire enchilada. I love this Springer Mtn. It's the startin' line for dreams."

Looking ready for CPR, a bulbous straggler clad in black fleece and producing rivers of sweat makes his way to the summit. The act of removing his pack and letting it slip precariously to the ground has the look of childbirth. He collapses in slow, stiff stages until he is gracelessly spreadeagled next to the summit plaque. Nearby, embedded in rock, is the metal-etched figure of an old-time hiker bearing an ancient rucksack, the kind of canvas torture device carried in 1948 by Earl Shaffer when he started at Mt. Oglethorpe, then the southern trail terminus, and headed north for the first thru-hike.

"Why am I not hungry?" the huge one asks the sky. "All I want is water. I've eaten nothing since I started." He empties the last two gulps from an Evian bottle and closes his eyes, his chest rising beneath his sweat-soaked fleece, a beached humpback. His shirt pulls up from his waist exposing a glorious gut, the product of a lifetime of determined sloth.

"We meet again!" Sky Writer calls out.

"Wasn't it Woody Allen who said that 90 percent of success is showing up?" he asks. "Well, here I am!"

Linda digs a full Nalgene bottle from her pack and places it next to the heaving hulk of squandered humanity. His big head swivels toward his savior. "I can't take your water."

"I'm going to the spring down next to the Springer Shelter," she replies. "Take it."

Leaning on one elbow, he tilts the bottle toward the heavens, and in an inhuman display of sight and sound, he empties the liter in seconds. "I don't want food at all. Just water. And I'd kill for a cigarette."

Blue Devil's dad sees a chance to make himself useful and ambles over to Captain Stupid to offer a pack of Marlboros and a light. "God Bless you," the Captain gasps. "I ditched my Camels to cut weight, but cold turkey doesn't work. I'll buy all the cigarettes you have."

"Keep 'em," says the dad. "I've got a carton down at my car."

"Where's your car?" the Captain queries.

"Less than a mile down to the Forest Service Road. If we see you on the way out, I'll give you the rest."

With glassy eyes, Captain Stupid ponders the vicious reality that he could have avoided the 7.5-mile Approach Trail if he'd convinced his cabby to go farther.

Phillies cap nudges Blue Devil's dad: "Banjo music sounds nice but it makes me a little uneasy. Know what I mean?"

Blue Devil's old man smiles. "Yeah, I saw that movie too."

Another soul approaches from the south. Compact and athletic, she wears running shorts and a long-sleeved polypro shirt, scant protection from the brisk mountain chill. In her nose, tongue, eyebrows and ears are a collection of rings and studs. Her cropped coif bristles red. Fair and lightly freckled, she's equipped for speed with a lightweight pack, trail shoes, and an emphasis on "less is more."

She approaches Linda and the Phillies cap man. "I see by your outfits you plan to be out for awhile. Father and daughter?"

"Actually, we just met," says Linda, now perched on a lower limb of one of Springer's signature contorted oaks. "But you're right. We're terminal northbounders."

The Captain, a little friskier after water and a smoke, chimes in: "Looks like we've all got the same disease. I'm betting this'll be a record year for crazy NOBOs."

"Well, welcome aboard the crazy train," says the spunky redhead. "I'm delaying my last semester for this—no rush—but I admit I'm wondering what I've got myself into."

Doodad smiles. He has heard a story—apocryphal he suspects—of a scout troop that scavenged Springer each spring to glean gear ditched by panicked hikers who quickly discovered how overburdened they were. One thing he believes about everyone starting from Springer: They have no idea what they're getting themselves into.

March 24, Springer Mtn. shelter register entry from Ultragrunge

The hike from Amicalola this morning was gorgeous. Subfreezing weather makes for great walking. I crave the uphills. I'm stopping here for water and lunch before lighting out for Katahdin. I feel arrogant stating my goal right here on Springer, but that's what I'm planning to do. Barring illness or injury, I'll do this. I've heard about Katahdin and seen the photos. Clearly, it trumps Springer. But I love Springer Mtn.—the summit and the gnarly trees and the ferns, a nice place to finish for a SOBO.

For now, my first big goal is to get through Georgia and up to Nantahala Outdoor Center in N.C., more than 130 miles. I'm bold; I'm pierced; I'm drug- and alcohol-free (mostly). I'm a skater, a climber, a boarder, a biker and a surfer. Now I'm a NOBO, and I'm feeling juiced.

Wowie zowie! I hope this weather holds—cold, clear, a perfect day for a perfect start. I even have a trail name—a NOBO in a baseball cap dubbed me Ultragrunge. Now for those first steps—I heard it takes five million to do the A.T. By the way, anyone reading this, if you found an orange University of Texas bandana back on the approach trail, hang onto it. If you catch me on my way to Katahdin, you will have the privilege of returning it and seeing the happiness in my eyes which, by the way, are a pleasing hazel hue. If you're a guy, you better be good looking, and not a smartass poseur! Be ready to submit to a superior being.

Georgia

MUDS AND PUDS

Whichever wag came up with the terms MUDS (Mindless Ups and Downs) and PUDS (Pointless Ups and Downs) was likely a NOBO. The Georgia section of the Appalachian Trail has no more ascents and descents than most other A.T. states, but when it's the first time a person has ever hiked long distance, it seems that way. The Georgia Blue Ridge is where you fear your heart will bang out of your chest cavity on the long uphills. It is where novice hikers discover the damage a long downhill stretch can do.

On the downhills, your feet slide inside socks and boots and jolt to a dead stop time after agonizing time—the genesis of blisters. If ignored, blisters turn from annoying hot spots into bulging, fluid-filled skin sacs. Untreated, they burst on heels, arches and toes. There are few prospects uglier than blisters turned into an oozing blight, a sight presaging a hike ending in its infancy.

Despite the hard work of volunteers who clear and grade the trail, untested NOBOs are shocked by the horrors of exertion. Often, to avoid a steep grade, experts engineer switchbacks allowing the treadway to wind back and forth upslope, sort of like a sailboat tacking against the wind. Climbing is also minimized at times by slabbing around steep crests. But there is still plenty of uphill exertion to sadistically abuse hearts, lungs and legs. A tyro is alarmed by how hard it is—nothing akin to armchair daydreams in the months leading up to the adventure. The trail may slip placidly by with a *profusion of native wildflowers; a diversity of mature oak, hickory, and conifer trees; birds of all persuasions filling the air with melodies and raucous squawks; small mammals and even bears going about the business of survival; and a hands-on geology lesson at every turn. But much of this goes unnoticed as the sad novice sucks wind and produces literal gallons of righteous sweat.* ▪

March 25, Transcript of Captain Stupid recorded near Hawk Mtn. Shelter

I can't stop shivering here in my Hubba at 5:30 a.m. I did nothing to train physically for all this. I remember one recent day having a choice between an elevator or one flight of stairs. Hey, which do you think I chose?

Yay!

In the depths of my most horrendous nightmares, I never imagined that this much pain, in so many places, could befall one pathetic mortal. I have a real throbber of a headache emanating from the top of my spine where it's hooked onto my skull and moving around the sides of my head until it ignites twin explosions in my temples. And speaking of my spine, there is spectacular pain and stiffness in my back starting at my ample pelvis and picking its way—vertebra by vertebra—all the way to the top where it quietly detonates into the aforementioned headache. The muscles attached to my ribcage emit a silent shriek of protest somehow connected to my inability to establish control of the little maze of straps which, rumor has it, can adjust my pack to ride painlessly on my obese carriage.

And my legs, God help them. My leg muscles are insulted to be part of a body containing a mind that thought they could carry out what they were asked to do. So vengeful is this musculature that each time I try to bend one leg or just roll over a little, a massive cramp jabs like a razor-sharp machete along the hamstrings. I get relief only by flopping like a sturgeon, straightening out my legs and flexing my toes upward until the pain subsides and lies in wait for the next assault.

But listen, fans, this is as nothing. I would take all I've just described in triplicate rather than face the sheer insane disaster of my feet. FEMA should be called in for this, plus the Air National Guard and a MASH unit of podiatrists and surgeons and EMTs. I cry when I look at what just two days have done. Blisters began on the Approach Trail to Springer. They demanded immediate attention, but I was so overwhelmed that instead of giving them first aid, I just kept slogging along and hoped for the best.

Today's hike was a lovely stretch of forest, but the ups and downs ate up my self confidence, and the pain sapped my spirit. From Springer to this shelter, my boots and socks formed a diabolical cabal dedicated to chaffing and stretching and ultimately ripping the pendulous little fluid sacs. Surprisingly, the pain wasn't that bad until I got to this shelter and found a nearby spot to set up my Hubba. A camcorder should have recorded the tragicomedy that was the prolonged process to erect my little home away from home. Bending at the waist or dropping to my knees was impossible, which meant the process of setting up a tent was interminable.

I wandered over to the picnic table beside the shelter with my little stove, my little pot and my little pouches of food. Then, I limped with a stiff-legged Frankenstein gait down to the water. I tried to kneel and fill up my water bottle, and my right leg cramped unmercifully. I went into a stuntman roll—if you can imagine a poorly conditioned man who weighs more than a Mini Cooper doing anything like a stuntman—and found myself on my back in mud and water, immobile. Frozen. The late afternoon air was in the 30s, and the water soaked inexorably through to my skin. My daily moment of truth. I assumed the Self-Pitying Heap position and cried out bloody murder. . . .

March 25, Shelter register entry from Ultragrunge at Hawk Mtn.

I'll be leaving this shelter soon for what looks like another primo day. I am sore, but thus far no hot spots on the feet. Modesty does not compel me to refrain from noting that my rock-hard calves are looking, well, rock-hard. Yesterday was my first NOBO day, and I loved the stretch between here and Springer—gorgeous streams, a waterfall, mile upon mile of hardwood forest and other hikers as happy as I was. I dined on sardines wrapped in a flour tortilla topped with mustard at Three Forks, where a mountain stream had attracted a group of college kids with Oreos.

I tried not to overplay the drama of leaving Springer, but I think all of us headed north had a personal moment of self doubt as we took first steps. But the trail was not very difficult, and my gear is so light it feels like cheating. I love it!

I spent the day passing, getting passed by and repassing the gang of NOBOs I met on Springer a couple of days ago. We all congregated here, cooked together and compared notes. The great weather has everyone on a big high, and the short day to Hawk Mtn. left us full of piss and vinegar—except for the guy in the black fleece who calls himself Captain Stupid. He got here late, amid the huge NOBO crowd, and the drama began. He gripes and moans and staggers around. But he is so funny and so likable. No sane person believes he'll ever make it, but we root for him.

He disappeared as dusk approached, and although his good humor was intact, it was clear he was in misery. Soon, we heard heart-wrenching screams coming from the water source. I scampered down there and found him sprawled in mud and water. I couldn't keep from exploding in laughter at the sight of this huge man, a prisoner of his own fat, splayed like Free Willy while water pooled around him.

He is such a self-loather that my inconsiderate laughter didn't faze him. He explained that he had to keep his legs straight, which kept him from rolling over, and eventually go through whatever lengthy process it took for him to stand erect on two feet. He seemed resigned to staying there all night.

About that time, Sky Writer strolled up. She knelt beside the Captain and gently patted his big jowly head—Shirley Temple petting a Saint Bernard. He whined and apologized for the trouble he was causing, and she cooed that everything was okay. She motioned for me to help, and we managed to position ourselves beside him, get very low to the ground and do a barrel roll to free him from the water. Then Sky Writer worked his left hamstring, and I massaged his right. It was like kneading big lumps of dough. Soon he could bend his legs without setting off a four-alarm hamstring disaster, and we were able to assist him to his feet and back to the picnic table at the shelter.

Then Linda coaxed him out of his muddy fleece pullover. I rinsed off mud while Linda twisted off his boots to find the sweaty, bloody carnage inside. Sky Writer and Linda worked skillfully, removing his socks, washing his feet with Dr. Bronner's peppermint soap and cold water, and spraying disinfectant on them. Before long, he was in his size 13-Crocs and back to what we all assumed was his old self.

The old guy in the baseball cap told the Captain that the first paved road was at Woody Gap with a straight hitchhiking shot down to Dahlonega if he was thinking of calling it quits. That put Captain Stupid into a sad mood. "I'll take the pain to be around people like you," he said. "Why would I want to quit?"

Blue Devil, the skinny kid, suggested the Captain should sleep on it, and maybe he'd have clarity in the morning. I suspect his feet will make his decision for him.

March 26, Journal entry of Linda Bennett north of Woody Gap

What have we done to deserve this weather? Maybe it was the Habitat for Humanity project I organized in my dorm last year or the Hunger Walk a couple of months ago. The weather out of Hawk Mtn. shelter yesterday was sublime. Much of my Springer trepidation has given way to elation. I keep forgetting about all those miles ahead and just concentrating on getting through Georgia day by day. I write this in the first stillness of March 26. Already so much to tell.

We decided to hike past Woody Gap yesterday and camp where I am now, an area on the ridge before the climb up Big Cedar Mtn. I hiked alone most of the day, but I often saw the rest of the group I stayed with at Hawk Mtn. last night as we randomly rambled along. A consensus developed to camp here. The assumption was that Captain Stupid would get to the highway and call it quits. He started before dawn yesterday. He loomed in front of the shelter and quietly pledged to see us later. Then, he was gone, and I lay in the subfreezing stillness of 6 a.m. nestled between Sky Writer and Bone Festival, listening to mice rustling around the rafters and across the floor.

I woke up in the shelter the night before last and was horrified at the rodent racket. I developed one of those middle-of-the-night feelings of anxiety cured only by getting up the next morning. I was certain a mouse would get in my hair. I pulled the drawstring on my sleeping bag until there was a hole the size of a silver dollar to breathe through, which made me feel comfortable that mice would not molest me. Still, I worried about mice chewing or wiggling their way into my pack and feasting on my food. The shelters have strings knotted to the rafters with tin cans attached to baffle mice. Not one soul believes they work.

Now it's early morning, with no wildlife sounds, no wind, only the occasional snort or rustle of exhausted trekkers in deepest slumber. I marvel at how much happened yesterday. So many people heading in both directions. The Springer group did not travel as a unit, but we saw each other a lot during the day. Sky and Bone sing as they hike. Her voice is indescribable. It carries through the forest and seems to pass through the canopy as if it will carry on forever. I imagine giant radio dishes on distant planets picking up the timeless sound of her voice, causing some little green gentleman to pause and grin. And Bone, although his voice is little more than serviceable, is wonderful on the banjo. They sing everything from "Wildwood Flower" to "Yesterday" to "I'll Fly Away" without missing a beat.

As I pulled up to Woody Gap, the first paved road, Sky and Bone were entertaining tourists in the parking area. Her singin' and him pickin'. The man in the Phillies cap was there, and within a few minutes, Ultragrunge came trucking across the highway with that swagger of hers.

Bone ate a sandwich supplied by the tourists, and Ultragrunge wound up with grapes and cookies to share. Then the question: Where is Captain Stupid? We couldn't believe he could have made it this far, so where was he? No answer emerged, so Phillies cap man started north, and the rest of us joined him after filling our water bottles at a nearby piped spring. In less than a mile we found a place with tent spots and went about the business of establishing camp. A pall hovered over us as we wondered about the Captain.

Soon I was in my tent with visions of Neels Gap in my weary mind. Then, I jolted awake in inky dark. If I had not heard Sky and Bone murmuring, I might have been totally disoriented. I heard eerie, distant sounds—moaning and cursing. I knew it was the Captain stumbling in with all the subtlety of a pack of snarling pit bulls.

March 26, Transcript of Captain Stupid recorded at Neels Gap

Yesterday and today have been the LSATS, Lent, boot camp, spring finals, waterboarding and the Iron Man all in one big miserable bundle. I have done what every law of God and physics clearly states is undoable. I have expended more cumulative physical exertion in the past 48 hours than in the last couple of years combined. I managed to get more than 12 miles to Woody Gap yesterday—12 miles of ups and downs, and then more ups and downs, and as if that were not enough, more ups and downs. The ups ravage my heart and lungs, and the downs are razors and sand paper doing their damnedest on my feet. As I whined to southbound hikers, they laughed and offered me food.

"I don't need food," I cried. "I'm not hungry!" These words sounded hollow from a blubbery hulk, but I simply am not experiencing hunger—just overwhelming thirst.

What about me is always so freakin' funny? A lard-butt man suffering through an overwhelming life crisis should not be the subject of ridicule.

How did I keep going on legs powered by muscles with the resilience of limp pasta, hamstrings bent on revenge and feet with oozing sores? I established what I call the pain focus mantra. I set my mind on the next step. I understand that the step will cause pain to shoot out the tips of my fingers and toes and out my ears and nostrils. I neither ignore the pain nor set it aside. Rather, I concentrate on it. It's unavoidable. Why not just look it in the eye and demand respect?

This is what I did all the way to Woody Gap, and there I faced the daily moment of truth. I stuck out my thumb and headed to Dahlonega, surely a town large enough to supply medical care and dispense drugs. That is how I met Sarah Minderbinder, a native of nearby Suches headed for the Super Walmart and absolutely thrilled to see my big torso jammed into the passenger seat of her ancient Ford pickup.

I guess she's about 40, a good 10 years my senior. She exhibited no comely traits, seeing as how she was overweight (not in my class, but a contender), had horrid frizzed-up hair, teeth only an orthodontist could love, and a physiognomy that encouraged me to constantly look out the window at the beautiful mountain scenery and avoid eye contact. But Sarah was a winner. She took me to the Smith House, where I indulged in the traditional family-style Southern feast. Sweet tea, meats galore and all manner of vegetables, and believe me, they don't say "veggies" here. But I could hardly put a dent in the plateful. No hunger!

Sarah took me to a hilltop clinic and sat beside me as I got prompt attention, because even though I do not have health insurance, I sure as hell have a Visa card. A doc who looked too young for a learner's permit heard my grousing about pain and muscle failure and did a remarkable job of cleaning, medicating and binding my feet.

"How are you handling the pain?" he asked.

"Mind-control techniques," I replied.

"He's sumpin," Sarah chimed in.

The little guy came through big time in the pharmaceutical department, prescribing pain killers, anti-inflammatories and topical ointment. Before sending me out the door, he suggested I come to my senses and return to Akron. All the while, just as everyone does, he laughed. He brought other doctors by to see me, and they laughed as well. Good God! What's so funny about this?

Yay!

I hobbled into the Super Walmart pharmacy to load up on drugs while the not-so-lissome Sarah burdened her shopping cart with my kind of goodies—bacon, candy bars, chili, ice cream. Her husband passed on three years back and left her with money and a house. If I wanted to stay with her for a few days, it would be okay. She told me all this as we careened on a sinuous backwoods two-lane toward Woody Gap, and I swear she gave me a sidelong leer. She was flirting! This happens rarely—like never—so I probably wouldn't miss it. I thought about her offer for about two seconds. "No," I said. "I guess I better get back on the trail."

She dropped me at Woody Gap in the gathering gloom and zipped off in a bit of a huff. It was so quiet. The temp was plummeting, and I knew I needed to stumble nearly a mile to where my newfound compadres might be. I went into mantra mode, cursing and shuffling on my bandaged dogs and moving at half a mile per hour. When I stumbled on the little encampment, I woke them all—Sky Writer and Bone Festival, Linda, Ultragrunge, the guy in the Phillies cap and Blue Devil. But they were glad to see me! I was part of something.

NEELS GAP—THE 30-MILE OASIS

For years the old stone structure built by the Civilian Conservation Corps at Neels Gap has weathered blasts of winds sucked through this low spot in the ridge where a winding highway tops out and squeezes through. Known as the Walasi-Yi Inn, the place gets its name from a native American reference to "the place of the big frog." It is the first spot for NOBOs to get a taste of luxury right on the trail, a rarity while hiking the first few states of the A.T. This is the one spot where the trail goes under a roof, and even in this case, just barely—an open-air breezeway connecting the two major structures of the inn.

Here a savvy hiker has a mail drop waiting at the Mountain Crossings store. There is long-term resupply, up-to-date gear, experts to check out and lighten your pack, and pints of Ben and Jerry's. Up and down the trail, thru-hikers learn that pints are convenient, albeit insufficient. One pint normally whets the taste buds for a second and even a third. Cherry Garcia and Chunky Monkey are most popular.

Neels is the first spot with showers and bunks, even laundry, comforts not available on-trail for another 100 miles. This is where SOBOs blow *through quickly, taking just enough time to fuel and freshen up before blast-ing up Blood Mtn.'s easy switchbacks, eager wings on their trail shoes for the last 30 miles to Springer. NOBOs are another story. Thirty miles is a tri-umph. Neels Gap is a victory. They hobble in feeling an ill-earned sense of entitlement to the goodies within.* ▪

March 26, Journal entry of Brave Phillie at Neels Gap

I don't believe in the Apocalypse. I saw a little bit of Armageddon in Vietnam, and so did my daddy (God rest his cantankerous soul) when he got shot down somewhere near Dresden in his war. The old tail-gunner took a quarter-pound or so of flak before bailing out. When he slammed into terra firma, he broke both legs. But by God's grace and the com-passion of a kindly nun, he stayed alive in a German hospital. He got his Purple Heart, and so did I, but both of us were reluctant to discuss it much.

Still, I don't buy into an Apocalypse—manmade or otherwise. Nuclear destruction, climate change, melting polar ice caps—I accept none of it no how, no way. I never understood Faulkner. But he was right when he said mankind will not only endure, we will also prevail. I've seen how technology can destroy people, property and natural resources. It's discouraging. But I've made a good life for myself and spread a little good will in the process by combining my wits with tech-nology. I've made my little fortune, and I believe if I can be positive, all of humanity can—and will!

Now I plan to shake the sadness of my past and keep on enjoying the best the world has to offer. These days the best is out here on the A.T., and for the first time since I hauled my old carcass off Springer, I'm writing something down. I am 63 years old and enjoying a frigid breeze on my bare toes at Neels Gap after hiking 30 miles from Springer over the last few days with a group of nice people I met there. All are headed to Katahdin. I'll stay in this little group as long as it holds, because I'm always impressed when people a third my age treat me like something other than a fossil.

I have hiked the entire A.T. already, from Harpers Ferry to Springer. Later, I hiked from Hanover, NH, to Harpers Ferry and wrapped up by doing Hanover to Katahdin. Ever since, my urge has been to do a thru-hike. I lost my wife to cancer a few years back, and since then I have buried myself in work. I live in Gainesville, Georgia, and have my own business as a systems designer for retail inventory. It has made me pretty wealthy, but it's even more boring than it sounds. It's time for a hike.

My trail name, Brave Phillie, came about like this. Most of my adult life I have been an Atlanta Braves fan. But back in 1988, I had a six-month contract in Philadelphia and lived near the old Veterans Stadium. I ended up going to a bunch of home games and wound up as a fan of the Braves *and* the Phillies. I wear the Phillies cap because I like it better than the Braves version. My old Marine buddy Slezack calls it "sports bigamy," particularly heinous because the Braves and Phillies are in the same division. I tell him that if that's the worst crime I ever commit, then I'm a frickin' saint.

So, here I am at Neels Gap, the first exciting mile point for NOBOs. The weather's primo—frost at night, 40s most days. I'm sitting outside the old Walasi-Yi Inn to soak up rays. This crowd I'm with was so excited to get here you'd think we're at Times Square. The hike this morning took us along a typical up-and-down ridge walk until we passed the turnoff to the Wood's Hole Shelter, named after a sweet lady named Tillie Wood from Roswell, Georgia, who operated a nifty hostel up in Virginia before she passed on a while back. Not far after that you switchback to the top of Blood Mtn. Great view of the A.T. ridge to the southwest and the Track Rock Valley and Brasstown Bald (Georgia's high point) to the north and northeast.

Even though it has always been notorious for skunks, the refurbished CCC-built Blood Mtn. shelter is one of my favorites. I stayed there one icy January night in 1971. I woke up freezing in the morning and heard a helicopter landing outside, Army Rangers on maneuvers who let us jump in and drink hot coffee from their thermos. The summit has more vegetation now, so a copter landing is a no-go.

The old four-sided shelter on Blood has two rooms, a dusty floor and a wood sleeping platform. No water here and no telling how much good old-fashioned human waste was deposited in and around this old stone rat trap over the seven or so decades before a moldering privy was installed nearby. Somehow, people managed to keep on crappin', and the mountain managed to keep on absorbin' it. My drill sergeant used to say that there is only one certainty in life: "You eventually have to take a dump." I love watching greenhorns come to terms with that unavoidable necessity.

My new friends are checking this place out and eyeing all the lightweight gear. The outfitters here do a pack-weight evaluation, and I'm sure a few changes will be made. Linda, Ultragrunge, Bone/Sky (they go

pretty much together), and Blue Devil are coveting gear and resupplying. It tickles me to watch how thrilled they were to submerge in the
first little patch of civilization. The only one without a trail name is
Linda. I tagged a trail name on Ultragrunge right there on Springer, and
she bought it.

Captain Stupid is appropriately named. He has no clue. He complains and whines constantly, and for some reason, everybody but me
seems to think he's funny. I'm sure when he makes it to this place he'll
call it quits. Everyone will be staying at the hostel here tonight. It's
early to be jumpin' at the chance to do laundry, get a shower and sleep
in a bunk, but what the hell. Take it when you can get it.

March 26, Journal entry of Doug Gottlieb at Stover Creek Shelter

I left the Len Foote Hike Inn this morning and hotfooted it to
Springer immersed in shame. I have been a very bad boy. After Danny
picked me up, we did exactly the kind of stuff I try to avoid. The Hawks
game was perfect. The Thunder (my old Sonics) trounced Atlanta by an
effortless 17 points. Then, Danny and his buddies and a few of their
girlfriends took me bar hopping in Buckhead, Atlanta's party center.

It was way too easy to drink and drink and drink some more. I woke
up next to Wendy on Danny's couch. Except for a black silk thong,
Wendy (last name still unknown) was, well, unclad. She wasn't at her
most enticing with tangled hair, smeared makeup and a string of drool
trickling down her chin. I had to ask her name when she woke up,
which embarrassed me and absolutely put her in a fine mood.

Soooooo, I quickly coaxed Danny to drag his hungover self out to his
Miata convertible. Despite brisk temps, we sailed top down from Buckhead to Amicalola Falls in a cool 90 minutes, which took seriously wild
lane changes, defying all laws of mechanical dynamics, along with
insane backroad speeding. Then Danny was gone, and I was on the
Approach Trail. I did the Hike Inn thing last night to ease into the
process of living outdoors. I got my money's worth and got lucky by
running into a Springer caretaker named Doodad who gave me expert
info.

The hike to Springer was uneventful—a nice way to transition into
the A.T.'s parallel universe. After a little prayer and meditation, inter-
rupted intermittently by other thru-hikers and their friends jabbering
away, I stole away a few miles north to Stover Creek, where I found a
little shelter space among three other NOBOs—a husband/wife team

named Winken and Blinken, and their yellow lab named, of course, Nod.

Here I lie, the worm still gnawing at my gut. It's not as if I've taken the first snap from center. There is something about waking up with a woman whose name I could not recall that I find unamusing and more than just a little depressing. I feel toxic. I need to forget the Buckhead craziness. I settle inside my bag, writing by the light of my head lamp. I think of Mom. What a macho man! I miss my Mommy.

March 27, Journal entry of Bone Festival at Mountain Crossings

Any NOBOs chasing after us just to hear the songs should be forewarned that there might be bonus music. Sky was snoring last night. Everyone was griping. Her snoring—guttural and harsh—is such a contrast to her gorgeous voice. When we woke her, she laughed and went right back to ripping logs.

The glories of showers and laundry so close to the beginning seem like cheating. I examined my feet and cleaned toe jam before donning fresh socks. Sky and I wandered to the parking lot to sing and pick for tourists. Phillie Cap grinned from the picnic tables. Linda already wonders if she should ditch her conventional Dana Designs pack and consider lightgrading to something like Phillie's Granite Gear pack at less than half the weight. As for me, I have cheap, heavy stuff. Just keep my banjo dry, baby.

This morning, Brave Phillie is antsy and trying to get everyone up and at it. He's been cranky since Captain Stupid blundered in last night after dark. Brave Phillie, as nice as he is, just can't seem to see past the Captain's whining and see the kind heart beneath. I think he wants CS to crash and burn so he won't preoccupy the rest of us. I see the Captain as sort of a mascot.

When the Captain arrived at Mountain Crossings, huge and blustery in the black fleece, black hat, black pack and black boots, he dropped his gear and cried a little when we told him we'd saved a cozy spot for him. He can't understand why people go out of their way to help him. Linda had kept a pint of Cherry Garcia for him, and the frigid outdoor air kept it firm. Ultragrunge knelt before him like Mary Magdalene, removing his boots, peeling off his stinky socks and working on his swollen dogs.

Sky coaxed him to cover up in his bag and remove his sweat-stained fleece and underwear, not to mention those vile socks, and loaded the whole thing in the laundry. I picked the banjo beside him. "To soothe the savage beast," he said. Soon we were all in a state of intermittent sleep, disturbed frequently by Sky's snoring. Wide open spaces by day and close quarters at night, an odd dichotomy.

I write this morning still struggling with my feelings for Sky. I am just a puppy dog she can't live without. But things are so different for me. We hiked a few weeks together last year and got comfortable as chums—even created trail names for ourselves and became a musical team. But my feelings grew deeper. She knows it. Everyone sees it.

March 27, Journal entry of Sky Writer at Low Gap shelter

Today I followed the Georgia Blue Ridge north from Neels Gap, my mind so at peace that I believe I'm hitting my groove—at last. My voice was a little raspy yesterday, but today the mountain air purged the little burrs. We hiked over a couple of lovely mountaintops. Brasstown Bald with its little tower on top was prominent to the northwest, much closer than it seemed from Blood Mtn. I love the way we trace our progress as we watch landmarks come into view and float past, day by day.

The trail is barren. Few leaves on the trees and only the beginnings of new green growth from wild flowers or grasses. Precious few animals—the occasional skittish squirrel, a phoebe, a few sparrows. A thrill occurs a few times each day when insane pileated woodpeckers blast out their staccato call. Mates stick together. Spot one, and you'll likely see the other—miniature pterodactyls holding dominion over the sky.

My feet and legs have adjusted, as have my lungs. I'm adapting. Maybe the actual terrain is about the same, and I'm a little stronger.

Poor Bone. If we keep traveling together, he must understand that our bond is based on music and friendship, not romance. I am not looking for love. I expect it to show up someday, but I don't think it will ever be directed toward Bone. He no longer keeps a joint journal with me. Maybe we need to have a talk.

Ultragrunge and Linda are great friends. I can see hiking all the way to Katahdin with them. It's glorious to have girl talk. I've always been a guy's girl, and close girlfriends have been rare. The thought of spending months with close female acquaintances is so inviting.

I worry about Captain Stupid. He seems committed to this little traveling band, but he struggles so. Linda, UG and I work on his feet, but I wonder how many layers of skin he can destroy before he finally has to take time off or just quit.

There is a nice shelter here at Low Gap. Good water, too. Cold tonight. My 20-degree bag does not quite cut it on these bone-chilling nights. I'll huddle up among Bone, Ultragrunge and other assorted NOBOs and hope for the best.

> Halfway through Georgia,
> Blue Ridge ahead
> Blisters are healing
> Time now for bed.

March 28, Journal entry of Linda Bennett at Unicoi Gap—Hwy. 75

Cloudy and cold today. The core group is intact, and everyone agreed this morning to head about 15 ambitious miles to Montray Shelter. Grunge and I left just after sunup and knocked off this first 10 miles to Unicoi Gap. The temptation is to hitchhike down to Helen, an ersatz Swiss Alpine tourist mecca. Instead, we're layered up and using a pickup truck as a windbreak as we catch up on our journals.

The Captain left in pitch black, well before us, but we passed him at the five-mile point this morning at Chattahoochee Gap. He informed us that if we spit to our right, the globule would work its way into the Chattahoochee River and possibly reach the Gulf of Mexico via the Appalachicola River. If we spit to the left, the droplet would take a different route to the sea. You have to love this man with the super-sized belly and the overtaxed circulatory system and the feet like raw hamburger. Will he escape Georgia?

So, here we sit, cars whizzing by and a tempting lunch trip to Helen not happening, because Ultragrunge is preparing to hit the trail up over Rocky Mtn. and down and up again to Tray Mountain, a spot everyone raves about. The clouds are gathering into a black mass, and the temp is in free fall as gale after gale blast through this gap. My fingers are numb, and writing is a chore. I'll call a halt and follow Grunge's disgusting self-discipline. She's got a hard shell—the cockiest female I have ever known—but I can imagine hiking with her for months on end. She's always ready to help, quick with a laugh and endowed with a sailor's vocabulary.

I think of Mom and Dad. I guess it's common for a person just out of college to see her parents as leading dull, unexamined lives. I hope they find some inspiration in this trip, but I suspect they will just count the days until I'm back home. Then I'll find a job and move out, and they'll just worry about that.

Now I steel myself to knock off better than five tough miles to the shelter on the other side of Tray Mtn. It's gonna be bone-chillin' tonight.

March 28, Journal entry of Momma Llama at Montray Shelter

I'm lonely. Rough weather is poised to rampage over this mountain. I ate early, got my stuff straight, even have my food bag hung on cables, safe and sound. I'm all tucked into my down bag and wondering if I'll have this place to myself tonight.

I started in late February with an old high school friend, Jackie Christie. She's divorced and I'm single, so at the common ages of 59, we were both free, retired and as footloose as two women could be. We struck out from Chicago loaded for bear, although neither of us had ever done any long-term backpacking other than a shakedown hike in Wisconsin last fall.

The first few days on the A.T. were hell for Jackie. The weather chilled her to the core, and she could never get comfortable. The weakness from the chill cascaded throughout her body. When we pulled into Neels Gap late on the fourth day, she arranged a ride back to the Atlanta airport and sat sobbing like a child, inconsolable that the dream was dead and that she was forsaking her best friend.

I was so busy comforting her that I didn't think about suddenly being alone. We camped near Neels Gap, and I waited until her arranged shuttle came by the next morning. More tears. Then I struck out north and hiked hard to Cowrock Mtn. I brushed the dust of snow off a fallen tree and took a seat there to let the sudden solitude penetrate. It didn't feel good. I was scared. But as I pushed on to Low Gap Shelter, I knew I'd be fine. I knew I had the strength—until the next morning.

Lighting out into four fresh inches of snow, I felt an old enemy sneaking back into my life—Plantar Fasciitis. If you aren't familiar with it, imagine an electric ice pick jabbing the back of your heel. I had worked hard in preparation for this trip and was rewarded by not having muscle aches or blisters over the first few days. The foot pain blindsided me, and I was furious. I made it to Blue Mtn. Shelter—just over seven miles—after nine hours of hiking. I knew I was screwed.

That night was the windiest, coldest night I've ever experienced. I thought Georgia was subtropical compared to Chicago, but this was arctic. At dawn the foot pain was unchanged, maybe even worse. It had been a cool 20 years since this demon had visited, and I had ignored the possibility of a relapse. Just over two miles later, at Unicoi Gap, I could deny it no longer. I hitched down to Helen, the little Alpine wannabe town, and got a room at the Comfort Inn. The next afternoon, I was in Chicago getting surprisingly good news from an orthopedist. The condition—painful as it was—was not likely to be debilitating long-term. With a shot, some rest, inserts in my boots, and some skillfully applied tape, I could be back on the trail soon.

After the hassle of flying and shuttling from Chicago back to North Georgia, I ended up back at Unicoi Gap this morning and hoofed it to this shelter. The heel feels good, and I'm ready to instill a little optimism into what was looking like a fiasco.

A couple of terrific girls just walked up, a sweet one named Linda and a ball of fire named Ultragrunge. The latter is decked out in studs and rings and seems an unlikely partner to the former, but from what they tell me about the rest of their group, the diversity has just begun. I feel good here, but this weather, from the looks of the wind and the clouds, is getting ready to work up into a pretty good lather.

March 29, Journal entry of Blue Devil at Montray Shelter

I am freezing my young butt off this morning and catching up on my journal with headlamp assist from within my sleeping bag. Brave Phillie (we call him BP, which he doesn't like because he says it makes him sound like an oil company, but we don't much care because it's easier and he needs to get gigged from time to time cuz as nice as he is, he's one smug dude) checked his thermometer well before daylight and said it was all the way down to 22 degrees, not surprising considering we're over 4,000 feet above sea level here, so, my sleeping, bag which is rated to 15 degrees, just doesn't quite hack it, despite the fact that I have on fleece and polyester layers.

Every time I think I'm going to go solo, something causes me to hang around, and I wonder if maybe I just like it with these nuts or I'm nervous about being all by my lonesome? They are fun, I have to admit, particularly Captain Stupid, the black-clad standard-bearer of lardbutts the world over. Last night was classic. Everyone had straggled in by late afternoon except the Captain, and as usual, we all made odds about when he'd arrive, and he surprised us by emerging earlier than expected from the gloom of the latest part of dusk. Like the rest of us, he got no views from Tray Mtn., because the sky was slate gray all day, and by the time CS arrived, there was a ton of white stuff coming down, a cross between snow and sleet.

BP found wood and started a fire, not a good habit for thru-hikers, but on nights like this there's a tendency to just say "to hell with it" and go for comfort. We wound up hovering over the flame and treating our backsides to a little thaw while our front sides chilled; then we turned around to reverse the process. By the time CS arrived, we were packing ourselves in rather snugly. The Captain proclaimed that despite the mileage and rough terrain, he was in a state of what he called "slightly suspended pain due to increasingly successful mind-control techniques."

Linda filled a milk jug of water for him, saving him a trip to the spring, and he decided to skip dinner and cook in the morning. "I'm not hungry," he said for maybe the 3,000th time since I met him. "I thought about thumbing to Helen to wolf down town food, but I wasn't hungry."

By this time, everyone had cooked, cleaned up and retreated to the sleeping bags—except for BP and CS, who hung around the fire. "You gonna rack out, man?" BP asked. "I don't think I can bend my legs to get in the sleeping bag," CS replied. "The hamstrings would go into a seismic cramp."

Then a very sweet-natured gesture occurred, and amazingly it was directed from Brave Phillie to Captain Stupid. Everyone has picked up that BP has a low regard for the Captain and is tired of all the attention everyone lavishes on his big pneumatic butt, so it was surprising to see the old guy help the Captain get out his sleeping bag, set up his inflatable pad and assist him in working it over his legs and torso while poor old Captain kept his legs stiff and toes pointed up to make sure the cramps didn't savage him as they seem to do each night. After gasping and moaning and cussing from both parties, not to mention a ton of giggling from the rest of us, including this nice new lady named Momma Llama, the Captain was on his back with the sleeping bag about halfway zipped up. "This is the first night I don't cramp. I just know it," he said.

With that, BP stood silhouetted, impressive in the dying glow of the fire, leaning on one of his poles and listening to precip clicking on the roof. A cozy moment snuggled into our bags, 20 or 30 magic beats until we noticed that familiar rustling heard in each and every shelter on the whole A.T., a pitter-pattering mouse. BP clicked on his head lamp, and the tiny rodent appeared—oblivious to the spotlight—gamboling along as if he owned the place, which I think it is safe to say, he did.

This was a pivotal moment in A.T. history. BP could have minded his own business, and we would have drifted off into that half-sleep, half-lucid dream state that occupies most backpackers during darkness. But no, BP had to meddle. He had to casually lift his hiking pole and with one deft flick he just had to make contact with the mouse. We all saw it, the way the mouse—illuminated in the headlamp—described a perfect arc through the frigid shelter air (Sky Writer later said she was certain she heard the mouse screaming "EEEEEEEEEEEEEEE!" as it plummeted through space toward its legendary rendezvous, and as I write this the morning after, who am I to disagree?) and landed just at the spot where Captain Stupid's sleeping bag was open.

In other words, I am telling you that the mouse, the Captain, and his ginormous sleeping bag became one. The rodent vanished into folds of fabric and fatty flesh, and the Captain, in a paroxysm of panic, attempted to get out of his bag. I don't need to tell you—do I?—that when he bent his legs, he went into hamstring cramp arrest, meaning that even if he wanted to, he was going nowhere; he was sprawling in communion with a mouse having the worst night of its life. The sounds, the movement, the manic sense of 50 different emotions being given voice all in one series of explosive moments is something I will sit back and meditate upon in years to come.

Captain was screaming, BP was shouting, and the rest of us were just going absolutely ape excrement with laughter until after a few minutes, Linda and I squirmed out of our bags and managed to unzip CS enough for him to roll away from the bag. Then, still giggling like kindergarteners, we sifted through the bag while CS probed his body looking for the mouse. It was nowhere to be found. Somehow, it had dematerialized out of sheer fear. Either way, it was 20 minutes before we got the Captain settled down and we were securely ensconced in our bags, even Brave Phillie who showed no remorse for instigating this Armageddon.

As with all momentous occurrences, this one still had legs. An hour after midnight, a healthy gust zoomed past, and we were awakened by a huge tree branch cracking, splitting and crashing to earth. We jolted out of whatever state we were in and lay there. A scurrying sound came from above, and BP clicked on his headlamp to search for the source, and there went our little mouse buddy again—it had to be the same one. He ran along a crossbeam with one minor change: He had a definite limp. Everyone just guffawed, even the captain, and Sky Writer said, "Aww, poor little thing!" I never would believe I could have so much fun with a bunch of backcountry caucasians.

March 29, Transcript of Captain Stupid recorded at Hiawassee, Ga.

BP flicked a mouse into my sleeping bag. He swears it was an accident. I'm not so sure. I don't think BP much likes me. If that mouse had not ended up in my bag, I may have had my first night without horrendous leg cramps. Regardless, I slept well and felt good when I started out this morning.

Dawn broke really cold but clear. Crunching through the snow on the side trail from the shelter back to the A.T., I came to a rock outcropping where Linda stood gazing to the south. "Look, that's Atlanta way out on the southern horizon," she told me. Sure enough, there were Downtown and Midtown and Buckhead sparkling in the clear air last night's gale left behind. Linda had a sweet smile on her face, and I know I will eventually fall in love with her, as I already have with Sky Writer. They are kind to me, and I'm a sucker for a pretty face. I have this dream that the trail will whittle me down to fighting trim, that I will find the real me inside this big blubbery vessel I occupy, that one of these women—or maybe another I'll meet on a remote bend in the trail—will see a new Prince Charming version of Captain Stupid and love him back. That's how I allow myself to think. If I can hike all the way from Springer to here, who knows? Everyone has a right to be loved. Up to this point, I can safely say only my mother loves me. But maybe the story of my trip can be a love story.

Temps stayed down today, so the snow stayed dry without soaking our boots. I braved 11 miles with a general emphasis on the downhills to Hwy. 76. Most everyone was staying at Blueberry Patch Hostel a few miles down the road where they had mail drops. Blue Devil and I hitched into Hiawassee, picked up our mail drops at the P.O. and splurged on a Holiday Inn Express and a steak dinner. I ordered a small steak and ate half. What's happened? I left part of a baked potato and half my salad. I drained four beers and an ocean of water. It's all about thirst, not hunger.

Now I'm soaking in a tub, wondering if my appetite will ever return. I called Mom, and she tells me everything is fine, but one thing concerns me. Guilford hasn't called Mom since we last talked, and he isn't answering the phone at the recycling shop. I called the office, and his cell with no luck. This makes me nervous.

We have a ride set up back to the trail in the morning. With snow still on the trail, everyone likes the idea of hiking a little less than 11 miles to Muskrat Shelter. If I can make it tomorrow, I will have hiked the entire A.T. in Georgia. The hot tub bath is nirvana for my poor legs and feet. Knee and back pain are holding steady—not getting worse. I love these people. I'm keeping up with them. They're being nice. This is so unaccustomed to a man who has spent a lifetime running from his own bulging silhouette. God help me heal and get strong. Let me carry out this ambitious task that just a couple of days ago seemed unattainable. What a shot of optimism a fat man can get from a few beers and a hot bath. Blue Devil hollers for me to quit hogging the tub.

Yay!

March 30, Shelter register entry from Ultragrunge at Muskrat Shelter

OK, NOBOs. The greatest hiking contingent on the continent has conquered Georgia and is heading hell-bent into North Carolina. We are: Linda, Sky Writer, Bone Festival, Blue Devil, Captain Stupid, Brave Phillie, me (Ultragrunge) and now Momma Llama, who is recovering from a trick foot.

Today we battled snow and basked in sunshine from State Route 76 to this place, a decent little shelter that will be forever blessed by having had us here. I carried in a Nalgene liter of homemade blackberry wine given to us by a fellow traveler at the hostel last night. Bone, Blue Devil, and I are getting enough of a buzz to make us entertaining for the rest of the troops. There was a group of five Boy Scouts and two leaders filling up the shelter when we got here, but they gave way and set up tents when they heard we were mighty NOBOs. Yield to the almighty thru-hikers! We are entitled!

We have been in a pack since the beginning, and we all fear the glue will eventually fail, leaving us to mutate into something different. But as of today we are together. We are one. We are mighty. And we have dubbed ourselves the Bly Gap Gang. Oh, what a lovely spot Bly Gap is, set on the GA/NC border—not far south of here. We climbed into various limbs of a big oak tree and got a passing hiker to photograph us together. It was cold today, but the sky was a deep royal blue—a splendid day to be out here and part of all this. Everyone felt mutual karma, and Sky proclaimed us the Bly Gap Gang. Then she sang and Bone picked:

> Passing through Georgia,
> Bone-chilling cold,
> Brave walkers trudge on,
> Lovely and bold.

> We're the Northbounders,
> So far to go,
> So long, sweet Georgia,
> Goodbye.

The greatest day of the trip. Captain Stupid says he has never felt more alive. Brave Phillie snorted that if the Captain knocked off another 100 pounds, he'd feel like a freakin' marathoner.

3

The Bly Gap Gang

TRIUMPH!

ess than 80 miles in, NOBOs hit the first state line—GA/NC. This results in a little healthy arrogance and—for those who have stayed injury-free—a sense of inchoate self-confidence. Georgia, despite its switchbacked trails and comparatively moderate weather, has plenty of ups and downs, putting stress on the muscles, ligaments, all parts of the feet, and the overall respiratory and circulatory systems.

Getting to Bly Gap means you made the first cut. You weren't one of those unfortunate souls so totally unprepared that they bailed out at a lonely highway crossing and returned home with two things on their mind: (1) How do I save face? (2) What do I do with the next five or six months now that I've ditched the dream?

Most everyone arriving at Bly Gap poses for photos in the big oak with low-to-the-ground branches just begging climbers to enter its embrace. Then it's time to walk north. It's hard for the next few days and harder still after that. For those who have held up to this point, it's okay, but the ones whose knees and ankles and lungs have been on the razor's edge of shutdown, there is no relief. The A.T. has no mercy.

The Bly Gap gang has developed a traveling core of support and friendship. A comparison can be made to the "Band of Brothers" camaraderie common to wartime experiences. Although thru-hikers are not under battle conditions, they do suffer physical pain for hours on end. Sleeping conditions are less than ideal on thin sleeping pads and makeshift pillows. Bad weather is inescapable. Unlike a torturous training run back home, a day of hiking usually does not end with a hot shower, clean clothes and tasty chow. It ends with a gloppy substance eaten from a pot. Hygiene amounts to washing up with biodegradable camp suds, brushing teeth, and living with the stench of sweat-encrusted clothes slept in at night and hiked in the next day.

The Bly Gap crew are early standard bearers for the NOBO spirit. The ones behind them are intrigued by what they read in shelter logs or hear from other hikers. Those who pass them later stare into space and wonder how they are doing, this diverse conglomeration of NOBOs, dreaming of that great summit photo at Katahdin. ▨

March 31 Journal entry of Brave Phillie at Carter Gap Shelter

Well, the Bly Gap contingent was feeling mighty good last night. But today knocked the wind out of our sails. The day dawned cold and overcast but good for hiking. Our sights were set on Carter Gap Shelter, and even though we had serious terrain to contend with—including up and over Standing Indian Mtn.—everyone seemed fit and ready. Everyone except Captain Stupid, who sucks sympathy out of every person, tree and rock. I must admit, the big bozo is still putting one foot in front of the other.

I feel bad about the mouse incident the other night. I caught the mouse in my headlamp, my stick was in my hand, and I gave the little bugger a quick flick with the tip of the pole. I couldn't have put that rodent any more perfectly into the Captain's bag if I had placed it by hand. Even though it started out funny with all the rolling and thrashing, I felt bad that it triggered one of his spasms. *Somewhat* guilty—not that much.

I'm not sure what to think of this Momma Llama character. She's hooked on to our group, and everyone appears to accept her, but she comes on a little strong for my taste. She was watching me cook the other night and told me I wasn't using the simmer on my stove properly. I politely asked if she could do any better, and she apparently took affront at my tone, because she said, "You don't have to be so defensive."

She came over and started messing with my valve control—damned presumptuous if you ask me. I almost took her by the shoulders and steered her away, but I'm enough of a man of the 21st Century to know that mule-headed women don't take kindly to unsolicited touching. I watched what she did, and sure enough, there is a very sensitive spot on the far end of the valve knob that provides a real fine adjustment to the simmer. We worked together on it for a few seconds, with her hand twisting my fingers. I had to admit that with a little practice, she showed me that fine touch to get it just right.

God, though, she is a cantankerous and independent soul. Midwestern women don't have quite the same edge as East Coast women, but they sure have more crust than Southern women. She doesn't hesitate to say what she thinks, and she's mighty free with advice. The other gals cotton to her, and Captain Stupid loves her advice. I admire the way she overcame her foot problems and got right back out here. And she's a fine piece of horse flesh. Strong and lean. Like me, she's run marathons and mountain-biked. Time will tell if her hard edge will wear thin.

Anyway, we all took off in high spirits and then ran into the worst kind of weather. The wind, fog and rain got increasingly bitter the higher we got up Standing Indian. Our first peak over 5,000 feet, and we can't see from blaze to blaze. Cold enough to chill you to the bone but not cold enough to freeze the precip. Perfect for hypothermia. I watched everyone to make sure they were layering up and keeping as dry as possible.

Before we started up the Indian, I pulled over to the Standing Indian Shelter and heated water so that the group could get out of the wind and get some hot beverage in their core. Sky and Linda were both shivering when they got there, and I loaded them up with hot chocolate and convinced them to take a break and wrap up in their sleeping bags. Everyone else seemed to be doing okay, especially Momma Llama, who helped me keep the hot water supply going.

When we straggled into Carter Gap, the shelter was filled with NOBOs and short-termers. We squeezed into tents and tarps and got hot water going for food and drinks. We were one wet, miserable bunch, although nobody made a big deal out of it. Sky said the last six miles from the peak of the Indian were the toughest she's ever walked, due to the penetrating chill.

I write by headlamp, and everyone is stripped to their skivvies, dry and cozy in their sleeping bags. Maybe tomorrow morning will bring fresh attitudes if this mess blows through. I'm bone tired.

March 31, journal entry of Doug Gottlieb at Deep Gap Shelter

I humped it up over Tray Mountain today. No views, just eddies of mist, lots of rain half a degree from transforming into ice, and wind out the wazoo. Eagle Scout that I am, I was prepared with a layer of polypropylene underwear, a thin puff jacket and a Gore-Tex rain suit—the perfect ensemble. Still, when I hit the shelter, I was soaked through. You can't exercise vigorously and keep sweat from drenching you.

I crashed in the shelter on the north shoulder of Tray for a couple of hours all cozy and nearly naked in my down bag before heading out to Deep Gap Shelter. At Tray, I read in the register about a group of NOBOs a couple of days ahead of me whose antics I've followed in shelter logs since Springer. Some character named Captain Stupid wound up with a mouse in his sleeping bag, and the person writing in the register, a newcomer to the group named Momma Llama, thought it was the funniest thing she'd ever seen. I gotta meet this bunch, particularly the females. Their entries are filled with intrigue, and I have to admit, this trip needs all the spark it can get.

Thus far, these Southern Appalachians don't do for me what Western mountains do. Give me the High Cascades any day—above tree line, spectacular vistas. Here in Georgia, minimal views and wildlife, and wildflowers haven't peeked out yet.

What I enjoy is interaction with other hikers. I passed a Katahdin-bound guy the other day who had a trumpet strapped to his pack. We chatted for a few minutes, and he offered to play something, suggesting I pick a genre or a specific tune. I remembered an old Leroy Anderson tune called "Bugler's Holiday" from middle school band days and assumed he wouldn't know it. But after running through a couple of quick scales, he was triple tonguing like a madman and nailed it. I love this guy!

I ran into an elderly couple. She told me she was 73, and he was older. The husband had on a small day pack, and she wasn't carrying anything. They were in a remote area, a 14-mile stretch between two paved roads. I asked if they were concerned to be exposed to March weather with no extra clothes or shelter. She just laughed: "We've been married 49 years next month, and we've been hiking like this for 40, so don't you worry about us. If we get in trouble, it won't be the first time."

Tomorrow, into Hiawassee for resupply. I'll either crash in a hotel or do extra miles. I can't kid myself. I'm dying to meet those chicks in that crazy group up ahead.

April 1, journal entry of Linda Bennett north of Winding Stair Gap

BP was calling for clear weather today. He predicted a Blue Norther bringing clear skies. He was right, which he typically is. We heard all about it during breakfast. What BP forgot was what the rest of us remembered. This was April 1. And if anyone needed to be fooled, it was Brave Phillie, the self-proclaimed expert in all things.

Most of us were terrified to attempt trickery on this old boy. Momma Llama is the only one who is fearless in BP-related matters. The rest of us—particularly Captain Stupid—are uneasy messing with him. Momma conspired with Captain Stupid to do the old "rock in the pack" trick. The Captain found a serviceable three-pounder. When BP took off for a call to nature after breakfast, she broke the big taboo— messing with someone's pack. She carefully removed items such that she could be assured of putting them back as she found them, nestling the little boulder on the bottom. Then she repositioned everything as only a female could. The caper was on!

We all discussed the day ahead. Normally this doesn't happen, but there seemed to be a communal urge to light out in this clear weather and put in a big day. Grunge suggested we hike to a campsite the other side of the big highway that comes up through Winding Stair Gap— more than 16 miles, the biggest mileage day to date. The thing no one was comfortable bringing up was whether Captain Stupid was up to it. We watched his reaction from the corners of our eyes, and he seemed okay with it.

We rolled along for over five miles and then came to a steep climb up Albert Mtn., the most severe gradient we've seen. Up top was a fire tower. We couldn't get to the upper platform, so we gathered on the higher steps to ogle the valley to the east and the ocean of big mountains to the north. All except Captain Stupid.

We went up and down for 10 miles to the other side of Winding Stair Gap, U.S. 64. It was late in the day when we reached our campsite, and by the time we set up tents and cooked, it was dusk. I was exhausted and worried about the Captain.

It comes down to this: I have never been anywhere doing anything that feels more right. I have great faith in humanity. My parents worry about my trusting nature, but I have met no one out here who didn't seem to have anything but good tidings for the trail and me. Even grumpy people, self-centered ones, obnoxious ones rise above their frailties and share the spirit of this big imaginary line running along the ridge crests seemingly forever and ever.

Captain Stupid, this obese, whining mammoth, is my favorite. Despite his groaning, he has kept up with people who are in infinitely better physical condition than he could ever hope to be. So as I lie cozily in my bag, I wonder: Will he catch up tonight?

Just as I click off my headlamp, I hear what we've been waiting for, the torrent of curses from Brave Phillie who just discovered his April Fool's "gift." "It was that fat lard!" he hollered. I can see Momma Llama going toe-to-toe with him, making it clear that she knows who put the rock in the pack and that it was not the Captain. BP is really angry, but I, conversely, end my day on a note of humor. But I hurt for the Captain.

April 2, Journal entry of Brave Phillie at Burningtown Gap

A tough hike today with a shadow over it because of Captain Stupid. I think we would be better off if this guy would throw in the towel and let us get on with it. But as much as he pisses me off, I can't imagine what kind of discipline he must have to keep pace. Just the same, I found a little April Fool's surprise in my pack last night—a damned heavy rock—and I'm betting he did it. I hate practical jokes, and I don't like people messing with my pack. I also didn't like the smirks while I was venting my spleen.

We got up this morning in clear weather, and the plan was to get about halfway to Nantahala Outdoor Center and the pleasures of that little paradise. We hiked all day to this clearing at Burningtown Gap. No water here, but with the recent rain, we were able to fill up not far away. It's dark and clear tonight, and my head's poking out of the end of my tarp so I can look right up at the stars. I am not a formally religious man, although I can't escape my Southern Baptist roots. In combat, there were times when I lost faith and times when I clung to it. On this night, I'm just amazed by the mystery of it all. I look up at those bright pinpoints and say a prayer for the Captain.

As glorious as the day started out, there was gloom before we took off. Blue Devil was thinking of hiking south to look for the Captain, but I suggested we hike on up to Siler Bald and see if we could rouse him on a cell phone. I hate the damn things, but I know Blue Devil, Momma Llama and Ultragrunge are equipped with them, as is Captain Stupid. I thought we could figure something out there. The hike is a long uphill but nicely engineered. At the top, there's one of the great 360s in the Southern Appalachians. It was cold but windless, so we lounged in the dry grass while Momma tried to call. No luck. Either his phone was not turned on or the battery was dead. We kept going with the thought that we would connect with him later.

We booked it to Wayah Bald, and despite a load of climbing, we made it by early afternoon, everyone at their own pace. The tower up there is another 360 with views up to the Smokies and all the way back into Georgia. The hike to where we are tonight was pretty easy. Sadly, we never managed to hook up with CS, and everyone is irked at me for talking against waiting. The plan is to take it in to NOC tomorrow and enjoy a zero day. Damn, I hate a situation like this.

April 2, Transcript of Captain Stupid recorded at the Microtel in Franklin, NC

Frickin' disaster at every turn! I fear that my friends are way ahead, and I'll never see them again. When we pulled out of Carter Gap on April Fool's Day, I knew I couldn't keep pace. I have been having a lot of knee pain, and my right Achilles tendon is inflamed and throbbing like a snare drum with every step, even with a double dose of Vitamin I. (That's Ibuprofen, for you rookies).

I fell way behind. I got on my knees right on the trail and cried. I said a prayer: "God, I have been a pretty good man. I have looked after my mom and avoided booze and bad language most of the time. But I never knew happiness until I met the Bly Gap Gang. Now I am about to lose them. How do I make this work? Help me." I was Saul on the road to Damascus, except God wasn't giving me a sign. Just as well, seeing as how, as I recall, Saul got struck blind.

Ten minutes later, I tripped on a root and this blimp-like vessel in which I reside and all the attached paraphernalia went crashing down like a palletful of feed sacks. Hard impact. An inelegant face plant. My glasses flew off and got scratched and bent. My face was scraped and bleeding. My left knee was bruised and so painful I thought I might get a second look at my breakfast. This was God's answer: "I gave you a fine body to occupy. You spent a lifetime turning into Jabba the Hutt's first cousin, and now you expect to hike 2,000 miles on a rugged mountain trail. I don't think so, child. There's only so much I can do."

The climb up Albert Mtn. was the toughest part of the trip thanks to the pain and the steep grade. Then I shuffled and sobbed to Winding Stair Gap. I gave up and stuck out my thumb. The 43rd vehicle stopped. Here was a possible miracle, my sign from God: *A Krispy Kreme Doughnuts* delivery truck! The driver let me sit in the back amid the sweetest aromas imaginable, and took me to the Microtel in Franklin. He opened the back door, and I toppled out like a stack of cinder blocks, absorbing the fall with my right arm and my upper right torso. My pack cushioned none of the fall—just added to the impact.

I lay wondering if I would ever get up again. The driver was inconsolable and knelt next to me, saying, "You're okay. You're okay, buddy." Miraculously, I was. A man my size should have wound up with multiple fractures, but I came through with just scrapes, bruises and blood. The driver helped me schlep my stuff into the Microtel lobby and handed me a box of one dozen glazed doughnuts. Oh, the irony!

Yay!

I showered, doctored myself, recharged my phone and called home. Mom's news landed like a haymaker. Guilford has disappeared. Mom went by the shop, and my inventory was gone—liquidated. Mom went online to check out my cash balance, and he had taken everything. I'm busted. I am on a manic-depressive roller coaster. A couple of days ago, I was as happy as I have ever been in my life. Now I'm flatlined.

Mom said to keep on. She would pay my credit card bills, and then we could check to see if maybe Guilford was planning to set things right. Mom is on a teacher's pension, Social Security and a little nest egg. I came along when she was 40, out of wedlock, her only child. She continued teaching under the stigma of raising a child whose father was absolutely out of the picture. I never met him. I sweetened the pot by being a fat, whining, precocious brat—too lazy to get past an associate degree at community college and surely no source of pride for her. Despite that, I can't count the number of times she has smiled at me and said, "Honey, you are my pride and joy!"

No, I can't let this sweet woman support me. I'm finished. I'm done.

April 3, Journal Entry of Ultragrunge at Nantahala Outdoor Center

We have trudged more than 130 miles without a zero day. Now's the time. We're bunked at the famous Nantahala Outdoor Center. The hike from Burningtown Gap was another one of those perfect days. Easy, easy hiking for NOBOs, with a long, gradual drop down to the Nantahala River Gorge. The river has chiseled out a gorge so deep you have to look for a sunny spot. None of us know where to start with laundry, showers, restaurants, an outdoor store, all next to this fine river. A perfect spot to vegetate. Sky, Linda and I are painting our fingernails and toenails green. Blue Devil—all buff and freshly showered—came sashaying by, and we're doing his toenails. "I'm one lucky trail gangsta," he mused as Sky worked on one foot and Linda on the other.

News on Captain Stupid grows curiouser and curiouser. After disappearing for a day and a half, he has now been located. Apparently, our frantic efforts to reach him via cell phone from the high ridges were a bust, because his battery was dead. He recharged, and BP got him from a land line here at NOC this afternoon. BP thinks everyone is mad at him for convincing us to keep going and not waiting for Captain Stupid back at Winding Stair. I told him not to worry. We all have free will. Anyway, he reports that the Captain is in dire straits physically and financially. Within 10 minutes of hanging up, BP had paid an NOC staffer who allowed the use of his truck to go to Franklin and rescue the Captain. Momma Llama and BP headed off together in the tiny pickup. "I'm damned if I'll get blamed for this," BP muttered. Momma just looked at him with a big grin. Boy, she's got his number.

Wowie zowie! Sky and Bone and Linda and Blue Devil and me. Well fed, clean clothes, our first zero day tomorrow, great weather and the Captain Stupid recovery effort underway. Chunky Monkey!

April 4, Journal entry of Momma Llama at Nantahala Outdoor Center

WOOOOHOOOO!!!! Zero day, and what a great place. The girls are mellow, even Ultragrunge, who often needs watching. Blue Devil showed a sign of immaturity last night. He snagged a sixpack from some rafters and drank it all. He's an unpleasant drunk. His cocky personality went sour, and he almost got ejected from NOC by the management after getting hostile with a group of college boys who wanted to look tough to their dates. Sky and Linda calmed him down and interceded with the NOC guy to make sure BD could hang around. Booze will do it to you every time.

The best news is that Captain Stupid is back. BP finagled a pickup truck to drive to Franklin on a rescue mission. God, what a mess! The Captain's body was falling apart. His cousin fleeced his business. He was broke and could never catch up with us.

Brave Phillie let his loving side emerge. Riding back to NOC with the three of us in the cab was out of the question, so I sat serenely in the back willing myself not to get nauseated on the winding backroads. Back at NOC, everyone had a tearful reunion with the big, lovable Captain. He moaned that the trip was over for him but that he would never forget us. BP sat us down and detailed a plan. "Hell, I'm single and a millionaire a few times over. That's what money's for," he said. He'll ferry the Captain around in the pickup to hike from Winding Stair to NOC. The rest of us take *two* zero days at NOC to accommodate the Captain. The Captain needed only to comply with this plan to let us help him out for the time being while he figures out if he can continue the trip.

Captain Stupid was obviously touched. "I thought you didn't think much of me," he said to BP as a tear ran down one of his florid cheeks.

"There is a way to thank me," BP replied thorough narrowed eyes. "You can come clean about putting the rock in my pack."

The whole group went rigid. I got nose-on-nose with BP—Eskimo style—and said, "I put the rock in your pack lover boy. What're *you* gonna do about it?"

This whole scene playing out next to the river caught the attention of not only our group but a few passersby to boot. Brave Phillie gently pushed me away and muttered, "Don't worry. We've still got 2,000 miles left." Then, he walked calmly away, freed of his burdens.

Meanwhile, the Captain got his toes painted green, and we all got a pretty good night's sleep. Today, BP is riding herd on Captain Stupid and seeing to it that he does his "makeup mileage" today and tomorrow. Wow, what next?

April 5, *Journal entry of Bone Festival at Nantahala Outdoor Center*

I feel lazy taking a second zero day here, but it's for a worthy cause. Sky and I have been popular with the tourists, hikers and rafters. We have a repertoire of old favorites plus a few songs we've cooked up since we left Springer, and we can draw a crowd without much effort. A guy with a hammer dulcimer hooked up with us, and we vamped a little bluegrass. The dulcimer dude had a whiny backwoods tenor. Before long, people started throwing coins and bills into the dulcimer case, and we dedicated the money to the Captain Stupid Maintenance Fund.

The Captain is putting in a long day today—packless. Sky, Grunge, Momma and Linda went rafting, and I've been relaxing, nursing my sore knees and strolling through the outdoor store. I had some damage to the tip of one of my hiking poles, and one of the guys replaced the whole thing for free with a part he scavenged from an old pole. He said Sky and I could pay him back by singing.

Last night, I went into one of the common areas of the hostel and found Captain Stupid and Sky snuggling on a bench. CS was leaning his big shaggy head against Sky's shoulder. She was stroking his hair and singing a quiet ballad. He looked so grateful and submissive. I smiled and left them alone feeling a little jealous, although I can't imagine romance between those two, can I?

Pulling out of NOC in the morning, we gain just short of 3,500 feet up to Cheoah Bald—a really long climb—but the good news is that Brave Phillie has a buddy who will slackpack us from here all the way to Fontana Dam. Two really tough days will be made much easier thanks to this guy, Orville Slezack, an old hiking buddy of BP's who lost his left foot last year to diabetes. But he can still drive, so he'll pick up our gear and meet us at Sassafras gap tomorrow. Oh boy, we must be living right lately.

April 6, Journal entry of Blue Devil at Hike Inn Motel

God bless Mr. Orville Slezack—honorary trail name, Monopod—because the poor sucker lost a foot 10 months ago to complications from diabetes. He and BP are lifelong buds, and he showed up at dawn this morning at NOC in a tricked-out Dodge Grand Caravan to pick up all our gear, with the exception of detachable summit packs, to carry rain gear, snacks and water, thereby transforming what could have been one of our toughest days into slackpacker's paradise.

This young stud is feeling mighty bold after resting two days. Without a pack, I got into a nice cadence and passed a couple of NOBOs laden with heavy loads—misplaced yaks—and left them in a light covering of trail dust as I blasted ahead of the crowd and paced along at something just short of a slow jog all the way to the peak of Cheoah Bald. On the way, there was a stupendous view down into the Nantahala Gorge with the road and train tracks and the rafts in the river—everything looking like an electric train set, and the view beyond of Wesser Bald, which we came down a couple of days ago, is just awesome, with level after level of tree-covered elevation. I think this was my favorite view of the trip, even more than Albert Mtn. or Blood Mtn. down in Georgia.

I needed to bust out today, because my pals were all pissed about me getting lit and starting a fracas with a bunch of frat studs from Clemson. It didn't get racial—if it had, I surely would have thrown a few punches—and I have to admit it was my fault for talking Clemson down, because I guess I'm pretty impressed with myself for getting accepted at Duke. But if my old man ever taught me anything, he taught me not to look down my nose at anybody, not to judge them on where they're from or what they look like, and somehow four or five beers put clear thinking on hold. Mamma Llama took me aside and let me talk it out without giving me a well-deserved lecture. I've let this trail thing go to my head and convinced myself that I'm some sort of young conquering hero who deserves to have his butt kissed just because he's been out in the woods a long while and gotten his nails painted green.

I got past all that when I reached Cheoah peak and breathed deep, deeper than my lungs have ever held, pulling all the pure alpine air into my chest to nourish my heart and my brain and my soul, expunging my bad behavior and exhaling out all the dumb things I've ever done in one glorious moment of young black male fervor.

The descent into Stecoah Gap where Monopod was waiting with cold drinks, Little Debbies, Snickers, tortilla chips and salsa was murder. It was as if I had blown out the elation of the peak and was left a little empty, like making love to the most beautiful woman you've ever fantasized about and then feeling voided afterwards. The others straggled in, commenting on the difficulty of the hike and rhapsodizing about slackpacking. We crammed into the van for a ride to the Hike Inn Motel—no connection with the Hike Inn just off the Approach Trail—and, since there were seven seats and nine people, the Captain and I wedged into the luggage space in the back. It's a good thing Monopod dumped our packs at the motel, because CS takes up a lot of room, and for whatever reason, he was bodaciously flatulent, making me glad the ride was a short one with him floating air biscuits and all. The Captain was on the pensive side, and I get the feeling he's bearing more than the weight of his pack.

When hikers are confined to a vehicle for more than just a few minutes, they get stove up, and it takes a few minutes of walking to warm up and get back to normal. As we headed for our rooms and the sacred showers within, we did the "town trot," a stiff-legged gait accompanied by a slight spinal hunch.

Monopod had arranged with the hotel owners to commandeer their kitchen, and he welcomed them to join us for a feast of spaghetti, fresh-baked bread, Caesar salad, and unlimited ice cream. BP and Monopod grew up together and served in the Marines, and the stories they tell of their military service and their hiking experiences are a riot. Monopod said that the trail up over Cheoah Bald used to go straight up the mountain, no switchbacks as there are now, and he and BP went up the north side in a rainstorm back in the late '60s. The trail was more river than footway, and the two of them were covered in silt by the time they had climbed the steepest part. "You young bucks have it made these days," he told us. "Enjoy the hard work these volunteers did, and do some trail maintenance yourself."

Before we headed for our rooms, Captain Stupid told us he is down to his last $75 and that it's decision time for him—keep going and hope for the best, or return to Akron to see if he can pick up the pieces. His mother has arranged for Visa to assign a card under her account with his name on it to be overnighted to Fontana Village, where he can pick it up tomorrow, but he's thinking that's wrong.

A long silence set in, and BP spoke first: "Something special is happenin' with this group. We may or may not stay together all the way to Maine, but for now, Bly Gap Gang is family. I think you can hang in here, Captain. You can scrounge hiker boxes when we get into towns, and we can share with you, too. Your equipment should hold up okay, and you can take your Mom up on her offer and pay her back later. I've come to think enough of you that I'll front you some cash now and then. I have no doubt you'd pay me back. A lot of good will come out of this for us if you stick with it."

Momma Llama kissed BP on the forehead. Sky burst into tears, and said, "If you leave, I leave." And then, and man, it sounds so cheesey, but if you had been there brother, you'd understand: She sang "Amazing Grace," one verse after another, and Bone's banjo quietly blended in, and even I began to cry.

April 7, Journal entry of Linda Bennett at Hike Inn Motel

Nearly 16 miles today, all the way to Fontana Dam. This is considered a rugged portion of the A.T., but with Monopod around for the second day, it's so easy. Monopod met us at a road crossing in the middle of the hike, and he had set up a propane camp stove. We feasted on pancakes, eggs, grits (I passed on those), bacon, sausage, orange juice and hot coffee with real cream. I told Monopod I was coming back to Georgia after Katahdin and marrying him. He said that was the best offer a 63-year-old, one-footed diabetic has ever received.

The last half of the hike had lots of ups and downs, with a long pull down to the dam. I was hiking with Bone, and as he looked down through the trees at the big dam in the distance, he said he felt like a commando in a World War II movie moving in to place dynamite charges and blow the thing sky-high. Leave it to a man to think destructive thoughts out in the middle of nature. To me, the dam is a silent manmade disruption that forced the destruction of untold acres of hardwood forest and human history. But just after World War II, I imagine the people working on this Herculean project were justifiably proud that they were supplying electricity to fuel the baby boom.

At the Fontana Hilton, we officially filled out self-service backcountry permits for the Great Smoky Mountains National Park. Fontana Hilton is the Tennessee Valley Authority's effort to provide the best shelter on the A.T. A fair number of NOBOs have already passed through; a few are intermingling with us; many more are following behind. The Smokies shelters will be bursting at the seams.

Monopod made a run to Andrews to supplement our mail drops. Heavy packs for the big climb up Shuckstack tomorrow. Monopod and Momma Llama cooked steaks, baked potatoes, and steamed broccoli with melted cheese. Sky Writer, the vegetarian, feasted on side dishes. Dessert was a phenomenal apple pie. Captain Stupid seems stable, and the Bly Gap Gang remains intact. Bring on the Smokies.

April 7, Journal entry of Doug Gottlieb at NOC

I felt so lazy here yesterday that I took a second zero day. I will displace the guilt with the pleasure of reading and talking to other NOBOs. I hiked for a couple of days with a Kathadin-bound fellow from Oregon out for a second time after a thru-hike back in the early '80s. His favorite of all thrusies is an Oregonian named O.d. Coyote, "the fiercest thru-hiker of them all." Coyote penned a book about his hike titled *Chained Dogs and Songbirds*—something of a collector's item among trail aficionados. It tells the story of the longest thru-hike ever in terms of the number of days from beginning to end—at least the longest for its time. He started in February and finished, illegally, at Katahdin in November snows. He got thrown out of Baxter State Park by rangers on his first summit attempt and sneaked back later.

The stretch coming up gets high marks for difficulty, so an extra day of recuperation might be a blessing. The downhills are chewing my knee up real good.

Still checking log entries of the Bly Gap Gang. Judging from the followup entries of other hikers, the Bly Gappers are a sensation, particularly the musical duo. They slacked out of here, so I may not see them soon if the slacking helps them eat up a ton of miles. Tomorrow, I'm up with the roosters to attack Cheoah Bald.

4

The Great Smokies,
a Slug on a Treadmill,
the Art of Yogi, a Bunion
and Cell Phone Abuse

THE GREAT SMOKY MOUNTAINS

W̱alking over Fontana Dam is a time-altering experience as you imagine yourself during the post-World War II era, taking in the construction of the greatest technological achievement to date in North Carolina (with the exception of Wilbur and Orville's little project). The place was a beehive of heavy machinery and Lilliputian mortals swarming over a deep narrow spot in the valley. Now it is silent, Sphinx-like, as it performs its triple duty of forming a lake, creating electricity and controlling floods. Many a hiker rests a day or so at nearby Fontana Village, built in the mid-'40s for the huge labor contingent needed to build the dam. Now it comprises a quaint vacation attraction, a mid-20th century tourist camp that has somehow survived into the 21st. Other hikers are content to lounge in the luxurious confines of the "Fontana Hilton."

Aside from the arduous climb up from the dam and out of the river valley—cumulatively more than 4,000 feet in a day—the 70-mile A.T. walk through the Smokies is surprisingly easy in terms of terrain. Easy, at least, compared to what the NOBOs have seen in the 160 miles leading to the park. The trail follows the ridge along balds, knobs and gaps, and despite a few substantial elevation variations, it is easier than most of what NOBOs have experienced.

Hiking up from the valley, one passes through hardwood forest that changes rapidly with the elevation until, at the higher reaches of the park,

the trail passes through laurel hells on Thunderhead and conifers on Cling-
man's Dome. You may see a bear or a boar or hear the wails of bobcats and
the howls of coyotes at night.

Over decades, the old stone shelters in the Smokies were dank and cave-
like, with chain-link across the front to prevent bear encroachment. In
recent years, the Smoky Mountain Hiking Club and the Park Service have
upgraded shelters by building out rooflines and removing fences. The results
are large protected areas in front of the sleeping platforms, with benches and
tables for cooking—a haven in rough weather.

Unlike section hikers who reserve shelter space through the Park Service,
thru-hikers register on a self-service basis as they approach the park at
Fontana to the south and Hot Springs to the north. A few spaces per night
are reserved at all shelters for thru-hikers. Unfortunately, during the peak of
the traveling circus's northward surge, hordes of thru-hikers appear, making
for a situation where tents are necessary—not the best way to prevent wear
and tear on campsites in high-altitude settings in use for decades.

Thousands of people have tales stored in their trove of personal lore
about bears, weather, crazy people, wild boars, mice, coyotes, owls and bob-
cats. Recollections of the Smokies have intensity and color. Thru-hikers feel
a tingle when they get to the border of the park and begin the ascent that
delivers them to that glorious cloud walk. ▪

April 8, Transcript of Captain Stupid recorded at Spence Field Shelter

I'm crazy to think I can do this. And crazier still to aspire to the blis-
tering pace of this Bly Gap Gang. The Shuckstack climb is a legendary
rite of passage for NOBOs, and I was a slug on a treadmill, falling
quickly behind as we ascended to the famous vista looking over cloud-
covered Lake Fontana and the Nantahalas to the south.

Monopod said goodbye at Fontana dam early this morning in your
basic pea-soup fog, and we hiked up out of it into sunshine pretty
quickly. When I reached a viewpoint, the Nantahalas jutted up out of
the fog, craggy dunce caps nestled in soft cotton candy. My aching feet,
my tender tendons, my exploding knees, and my storied hamstrings
aside, I realized why it's worth the excruciating agony.

The plan was to reach Russell Field Shelter. It took me 10 hours to
get there, and a note informed me that everyone else had hiked three
more miles to Spence Field. It might as well have been 30 miles. I knew
I'd be lucky to make it in two hours.

But that's not the half of it. The temperatures had been okay during the day, almost balmy at the dam and comfortable low 40s up higher. But an arctic rush from the Northwest raged across the ridge, and the temperature did a swan dive. I checked my thermometer at Russell Field—low 20s. On the way to Spence Field a blizzard kicked up, and when I got to the shelter after dark, someone noted that the temperature was 19 in the shelter. No telling what the windchill would be.

Yay!

The shelter was packed with thru-hikers who had snapped up the reserved bunk spaces, leaving us to survive in tents. Sky and Bone decided to sleep on the floor of the shelter, a lousy proposition considering all the dangling packs and middle-of-the-night stumblers getting up to take a pee. Linda and Momma crammed into Momma's Flashlight—a tiny two-person tent—figuring they'd share body heat. Blue Devil and Brave Phillie are sharing BP's tarp. Those two could set up a circus tent in a wind tunnel. I found a spot in the lee of the shelter for my Hubba. I was fagged out—in the first stages of hypothermia. I got into my bag without cooking and noshed on Snickers bars.

I'm zipped up tight, muttering these final few words. I just heard some frat boy, tipsy on cheap wine, blowing chunks. I hope Sky and Bone weren't in the trajectory. Frickin' April man, and I can't stop shivering. Don't look forward to hiking in this crap tomorrow. Brave Phillie just walked up to my tent door to see how I'm doing. I said my uncontrollable shivering is yielding to mind control. Here BP, speak into my recorder.

BP: *"OK, you big hulk. You're a freak of nature, a bumble bee. By all laws of aerodynamics, you can't fly, but somehow you do. You're the toughest SOB I've ever known, and I'm a Marine, dammit!"*

Soon we'll finish 10 percent of this trek. I'm feeling borderline okay in single digit cold—just thinkin' about my friends.

April 9, Journal entry of Sky Writer at Double Springs Gap Shelter

Bone and I had an awful night. Spence Field shelter was slammed, so we slept on the floor. By huddling close, we stayed just on the right side of warm.

It was clear and gelid when we woke this morning. I put on every layer, boiled water for herbal tea and scarfed down granola. I left first, bulling along the access trail back to the A.T. through seven or eight inches of perfect snow. Blazes were hard to pick up, because the trees were frosted. The trail led through bald meadows and wooded areas before heading up Rocky Top. Oh, what a view—my favorite moment of the trip so far. Rocky Top is a 360 of the Smokies—a sea of ridges buried in snow. Bone came up behind me, and without his banjo, we vamped into "Rocky Top" as if the University of Tennessee had scored a thousand touchdowns. I hugged Bone and told him that I was glad he could share my favorite moment of the trip. Then, he told me loved me and wanted to be with me forever. Like uncorked champagne, he finally burst out with what I hoped I would never hear.

Poor Bone. It was time to tell him he was my musical soul mate, my sweet hiking companion, my little elfin buddy—but good God, not my lover or (I cringe to write it) my future husband. "Can you still hike with me knowing that?" I asked.

"I already knew it," was his answer. "Why should anything change? But do you always want to be alone?"

I told him I would confide in him if my feelings changed. This settled nothing. I walked up the peak of Thunderhead, at more than 5,500 feet, the highest spot we had seen. The rest of the day was a combination of emotional and actual ups and downs through laurel, hardwoods, and firs. We saw a few birds—titmice for the most part—and our first fox. We followed his tracks. Occasionally, the little guy stopped and stained the snow with an amber trickle of urine. We continued along, embracing the cold, and there he was—a little statue 25 yards ahead, staring us down. We had the presence of mind to freeze, only breath clouds from ours mouths and noses to distinguish us from trees. The fox lost interest. He peed again and went on his way, prim and perfect.

We hit Double Springs Gap Shelter, where there were only two others joining us. One was a man in his sixties out for a few days. The other was a thru-hiker headed north at a 20-miles-per-day clip. He had read about us in shelter logs, and we had fun swapping stories. He had the best trail name yet: *The Hiker Formerly Known as Phil.*

Momma Llama said hiking into Spence Field yesterday was her worst moment since she got knocked off the trail in Georgia. But today was her best day. "Isn't that what this is all about?" she asked. "Literal and figurative crests and chasms—day after day."

The Captain still has moments of truth each day, often several crises in 24 hours. But he's coping. "I love all of you," he said. He was right next to me. I unzipped my bag a little and scooted close to him. I put my arms around him and placed my cheek next to his big shaggy face. Then I kissed him. Not some sisterly peck. I *kissed* him if you take my meaning. We're both still wondering where that came from. That was just an hour ago, and not one word has been spoken since. What was I thinking?

April 10, Journal entry of Bone Festival at Icewater Spring Shelter

Good miles today, arriving first at an architectural eyesore atop Clingman's Dome. At 6,643 feet, it's the highest spot on the A.T., right on the border of Tennessee and North Carolina. There's a spiral-shaped monstrosity at the tiptop of the mountain. A paved trail ascends from a parking lot below, but there were no tourists up at this high altitude due to the blizzard. The tower took us above the fir trees and gave us a clear view in all directions of this endless mass of mountains—the highest, thickest part of the Appalachians. Mt. Mitchell to the Northeast is higher, but the massifs around Clingman's Dome comprise the master chain of the Eastern U.S.

We were strung out today, with Momma Llama and Brave Phillie out in front. Blue Devil and I lagged a little behind them and enjoyed passing time at Clingman's. We lamented the passing of the Fraser firs in the park. An exotic aphid-like beastie—the wooly adelgid—has invaded them, making them susceptible to disease. Experts think acid rain has contributed as well. All that remain are tall, gray, dead spikes—sentinels observing their own funeral. And if that's not sad enough, a blight a century ago wiped out all the majestic chestnut trees across America. Although chestnut saplings still grow out of the stumps of their dead ancestors, the blight eventually gets them. The Smokies are a lesser place for their absence.

From Clingman's, it's a breeze to Newfound Gap, the only road crossing in the Smokies. The road between Cherokee and Gatlinburg had reopened as temperatures rose and melted snow. RVs, vans, trucks and cars gathered, and tourists braved high winds whistling through the gap to see the views. This is the most visited national park, and an amazing number of visitors never leave pavement. Long-distance hikers are a curiosity, and clever ones never turn a snobbish nose away from tourists. We gravitate to them, feed their curiosity, and indulge in a practice called the "Yogi." Like the animated bear who pilfered picnic baskets, a hiker learns to Yogi food.

Blue Devil, the ultimate charmer, was working the crowd when I arrived. Middle-aged women adored him and worried that this lanky picture of African-American young manhood was underfed. He was bantering away with a sandwich and an orange in his hand. He soon headed north, but I stayed behind and plotted my own Yogi.

Linda, Grunge, Sky and the Captain soon appeared. Without being told, Sky set up beside me. It was too cold for the banjo, but crowds, and food, still gathered around the singing. It was like the parable of the loaves and fishes—food appearing from nowhere. Camera phones clicked, iPad HD camcorders digitized, and we got fed. After all, we'd just walked out of the wilderness, and were starving for food and maternal attention.

The mostly uphill hike to Ice Water Spring was easy. There was plenty of daylight left by the time we cooked and hoisted our food bags up the bear cables. It's not so frigid that we can't layer up and sprawl on the ground on the open area in front of the shelter where the sun has melted the snow and dried things out. A NOBO husband and wife—Chewing Gum and Baling Wire—are with us tonight. They need to hit Katahdin early, because Baling Wire has business in early August. This will likely be the only time we see them. They are entranced by Sky's voice, while, as usual, I'm strictly supporting cast. I'm not on the long-term Sky Writer play list.

April 11, Journal entry of Brave Phillie at Tri-Corner Knob Shelter

That freak storm the other night chased away the spring breakers. Even though there is still a little snow on the ground, the weather has been perfect the past couple of days. I'm getting my best look ever at the Smokies. With only a dozen easy miles today, we had time to burn, starting with the Bunion. This area was heavily logged years ago and then hit by a fire, leaving a scarred spur with a big rock outcropping called Charlie's Bunion. Momma Llama and I sat there and solved the world's problems. She has lots of opinions, and she can hold up her end of a conversation. But she has an easy manner that never gives the impression she's a chatterbox.

Momma says the Bly Gap Gang remains "cohesive" despite the independent spirit of each member (except Captain Stupid, a dependent soul if ever there was one). She says they all have a little fear of me, similar to what they might feel for their dad and that I have a gruff, "authoritarian" streak. I surprised her by agreeing that I sometimes come across as being what she calls "autocratic." The U.S.M.C. has its side effects.

Captain Stupid brought up the rear as usual, reaching the shelter this afternoon with Sky Writer as company. He doesn't lag as far behind as he used to, and though he still has pain, his feet look almost normal, and his hamstring miseries have vanished. I think he's lost over 20 pounds in the three weeks we've been out here. He's still a fat pig, no other way to say it. But if he keeps this up, who knows?

Tonight there were two hotshot executive types in the crowded shelter, guys in their mid thirties. They started up a stir with their smart phones, and to my credit, I put my "authoritarian" tendencies on hold and just watched the fun.

It is no secret among us that Momma Llama, Blue Devil, Ultragrunge and Captain Stupid have smartphones. There is an unwritten rule that they are for calling home or for logistical assistance, like calling ahead to check mail drops or to verify a rendezvous. This is done unobtrusively, and rarely in a shelter or around others. Playing games or sending and receiving text messages is okay, if the person does it without making a big deal about it. Calls home to friends and family are private. Ringtones are switched to vibrate even though it often leads to missed calls. There are those who think a cell phone on the trail is bad news, a distraction that creates a false sense of security based on the belief that if you get in trouble, the phone will magically get help. Reliance on cell phones creates more trouble than it solves. At least our group has the etiquette angle worked out.

One of the hotshots called his office and spent 10 minutes barking orders to some poor schmo in demeaning terms. This put us all in a sour mood. Then the other guy got on the phone with his broker. He talked even louder, and he wanted everyone to know he was a high roller. This went on for half an hour, and when it ended, he started dialing another number. Momma Llama and I held our tongues, and Grunge filled the breech. "Hey, do us all a favor and deliver your next butt-reaming somewhere else," she said.

Hotshot gave her his "withering glare." "If you have a problem, take yourself somewhere else," he barked. "I've got business to transact."

"Fine," said Grunge. "Take it outside and quit acting like a horse's ass."

To his credit, the guy's buddy began chuckling. "I see her point, Jared," he said. "We have been sorta obnoxious." Jared glared at his friend, then at Grunge and finally at all of us. No one blinked. He walked out in defeat. I had learned a lesson in self-control compliments of Momma Llama.

April 12, Journal entry of Ultragrunge at Standing Bear Hostel

This morning was awkward at Tri-Corner Knob. Yesterday, I got into it with a poseur who insisted on making loud phone calls yesterday to his broker. I called him on it, and the atmosphere was icy this morning. Actually, at 28 degrees, it was pretty icy anyway. So screw him!

We hiked about 17 A.T. miles today, out of the Smokies to the Pigeon River. Linda and I tried a side trip to the summit of Mt. Guyot, but we got lost halfway up and decided bushwhacking was not our order of the day. We added more to the 17 miles by taking a side trip over to a restored 1930s-vintage stone firetower on Mt. Cammerer—a great look north at Snowbird peak and beyond.

This was the longest day yet, but there was an easy, gradual down-hill to the Pigeon River that made it downright cushy, although rough on the dogs. Linda and I hit the road next to the river at about 3 p.m. We burned trail. Thru-hikers talk about a three-week rule, which says it takes 21 days to hit your stride. Today ends three weeks. I hit my stride this morning and kept it all day. Linda feels the same. Maybe the long climb up Snowbird tomorrow will take the starch out of all this confidence.

When we hit the road at Pigeon River, a kid in a pickup pointed the way to Standing Bear Hostel. We practically had to pour cold water on him to make him leave us alone—one randy hillbilly who had problems taking no for an answer. Linda told him we're nuns on a sabbatical, and dating is not allowed. The little hayseed looked us up and down, and said, "You don't look like no nuns!" Thus was born a phrase to be repeated many times.

Standing Bear is a haven after conquering the Smokies. There are a bunch of other NOBOs here, so it's full of the kind of good cheer stimulated by showers and junk food. I got heavy into Coca-Cola to satisfy my high-fructose corn syrup Jones.

Big news! Linda's parents are driving from Columbus to meet us in Hot Springs in two days. We'll do a zero day. Then they'll slack us all the way to the Nolichucky River. Wowie zowie! We have 19 miles tomorrow to Roaring Fork Shelter and then another long day into Hot Springs. Linda, that fabulous little Buckeye, is coming through big time. She don't look like no nun neither.

April 13, Journal entry of Momma Llama at Max Patch Mtn.

God help me, the climb up Snowbird was a bull bitch this morning. It took the spizzerinctim out of me. Despite high clouds, I could see back to the Smokies—even the firetower on Cammerer. I took a nap under a covered area next to a telecom control building to sleep off indigestion from the garbage I ate at the hostel. After six decades, my body is giving in to acid reflux.

I was dogging it en route to Max Patch Mtn., suffering stabs of heel pain and emotional depression. Then, north of Groundhog Creek Shelter, I was in the presence of a sow bear and two cubs. The cubs headed off the trail, and mom reared up on her hind legs to sniff and look around. I froze, 40 feet away. She was glorious and thin after the long winter. My first bear! She went back on all fours and was quickly and silently gone in a patch of laurel. Adrenaline coursed through my body, my soul, my psyche. I trucked hard to the grassy summit of Max Patch. The sun burst out. My foot was free of pain. Nothing like a thrill to do your body good.

Oooohhh, Max Patch! Several groups have wandered past me as I sprawl in the grass. A couple made reference to the Julie Andrews scene at the beginning of *The Sound of Music* where she sings the title song in gaudy alpine splendor. This summit is huge and grassy, and the view in all directions is like ocean waves of peaks, frozen in place, silent for the ages. I said a prayer: "Thank you for this freedom. Thank you for this place. Thank you for these friends."

Blue Devil and Brave Phillie came along with big smiles. "Is this the best yet?" Brave Phillie asked. I didn't respond. I just got up and threw my arms around Blue Devil and then surprised myself by hugging BP and kissing him long and hard and exuberantly, the first kiss I've exchanged with anyone in quite a while, and it was good. He backed away with a look of surprise and exhilaration, and said: "Where I come from, if a woman kisses a man, he can kiss right back." And he did.

"Oh, Gawd!" Blue Devil moaned. "This is as bad as watching my parents."

"If your parents like kissing, good for them!" I said.

"Right on!" Brave Phillie yelled. "Watch and learn!"

April 14, Journal Entry of Linda Bennett from a cabin near Hot Springs, NC

A spate of emotions today—all good. I haven't seen Mom and Dad for three weeks, but it seems like half a lifetime. Everyone wanted to hit Hot Springs fast today to get started on tomorrow's zero day. I was up before dawn, pulling out of Roaring Fork shelter with Grunge and Sky just behind. The place was crawling with NOBOs, so I tented. I've never broken camp this early. We booked it all morning to cover the 15 or so miles to Hot Springs.

Mom had done her internet homework and was aware of a little info center in the middle of Hot Springs housed in a red caboose. We were to gather there. So about 2:30, the three of us hiked triumphantly down the main street—rockin' our boots and sticks and bruises—and there they were, standing beside a huge van Dad rented for the occasion.

Mom sprinted down the sidewalk, tears streaming down her face, and grabbed me as if I were a G.I. returning from Afghanistan. Dad hung back shyly, but he was beaming. "You must be Sky Writer, and you must be Ultragrunge," Mom cried as she gave them big hugs. "Your moms aren't here, so I'll hug you for them." Mom held me at arm's length. "Goodness! You're skinny as a waif."

Dad threw open the back of the van, and food appeared. Homemade cookies, cold drinks, chips, dip, sandwiches. We attacked. They had rented two cabins on a mountainside just outside of town—with hot tubs! We waited for the rest of the gang, and Mom identified all by trail name on sight. She hugged indiscriminately. Throwing decorum to the wind, Brave Phillie, a dozen years older than Mom, swept her up in his arms, spinning her around. She squeezed Captain Stupid, and said, "They should call you Teddy Bear. Captain Stupid sounds so mean."

We ignored faint drizzle and took in the vibes of this mystical little town on the French Broad River (BP and Dad agreed that French Broad is the best name ever for a river). Everyone moseyed down to Bluff Mountain Outfitters and checked out whatever else there was in town. Dad offered to treat everyone to early supper at the Smoky Mountain Diner, which came well-recommended by the locals.

But before we dispersed, we noticed someone else had appeared, a thru-hiker from his looks, who went to one knee next to Ultragrunge. "I think I can identify all of you by trail name," he said. "But first, I officially offer this bright orange University of Texas bandana to this lovely young woman. I believe you're Ultragrunge."

For once, cocky Grunge was speechless—for a couple of seconds, anyway. "You brought that all the way from the Approach Trail?" she asked.

"I did," he replied. He then pointed to each of us in turn, correctly guessing trail names, saving me until last. "You are Linda Bennett, the only member of the Bly Gap Gang without a trail name. I'm in the same dilemma. Just call me Doug Gottlieb."

In an unsubtle parent whisper that could have been heard two counties over, Mom blurted, "This one's a keeper!" She made things worse by inviting him to join us for the next few nights. He declined, thank God, saying he was staying a block away at the legendary Elmer's Hostel. He did agree to join us for a few days of slackpacking. Just like that, this Gottlieb character effortlessly insinuated himself into our midst. Sky, Momma Llama and Mom gazed at him as if he were some tasty delicacy, and Grunge—totally out of character—mooned like Hannah Montana. He is a real fox, but there's something about the way he manipulates people that I find a tad annoying.

After cramming meat and two veggies, sweet tea and corn bread down our gullets at the Smoky Mountain Diner, we jumped into the 12-person van and headed for showers, hot tubs, ice cream, beer and comfort. Mom and Dad were finally on board with what I was doing. They also got an introduction to A.T. perfume, that fabulous aroma emitted from people who have been hiking for days without showers. As she rolled down her window, Mom said, "I'm doing laundry! This van reeks."

THE ZERO DAY

A treasured tradition among thru-hikers is the zero day. The smart NOBO dispenses with guilt and takes an occasional day off. It's good for the soul, restores vigor and cures some of what ails you. NOBOs revel in the time off and spend the day doing as they please. Food and beverage are central to the plans, but some people go rafting, catch up on journals or indulge in personal relations of a most private nature.

Hot Springs is a prime zero day venue. There are good restaurants (one features decent jazz), a P.O., stores for resupply (average at best) and a great outfitter. There's even a spa next to the river for the authentic hot spring treatment. Bly Gap Gang is experiencing parental largesse—free luxurious accommodations, hot tubs, endless food and the promise of slackpacking north to the distant Nolichucky River.

Gottlieb, meanwhile, has been quickly embraced by the group, and though he does not have Bly Gap credentials, he has the charm and masculine grace to gain acceptance and enjoy certain rights and privileges.

The Bennetts' concerns about Linda are assuaged. They have met the gang and realize how safe they are in each other's company. Grunge and Blue Devil scored points by buying a gift for Mrs. Bennett at Bluff Mountain

Outfitters—a tee shirt stating, "I have hiked the entire Appalachian Trail" in big block letters. But there is a twist. Between the words "entire" and "Appalachian" are three words in small print—"width of the." Jenny wears it with pride. ■

April 15, Journal entry of Doug Gottlieb at Elmer's Hostel, Hot Springs, NC

First zero since NOC. I'm staying with Elmer who has run a hostel near the main drag of Hot Springs for decades. Good organic vegetarian food, friendly confines—a dandy place to hole up. On this damp, lush day, Hot Springs is ethereal, as if it materialized out of the mist for just this day—a sort of Brigadoon. I could never just hike past without spending at least one day. Besides, there is another attraction: the Bly Gap Gang at long last! I saw them in the distance as I walked along the sidewalk and identified each one. I dropped my pack and fished out the orange bandana for Ultragrunge, the Texas Longhorn, and managed to sneak up and blend in. I Yogied lunch and scoped the Bly Gappers.

I am astounded at how closely they correspond to my vision of them:

- *Brave Phillie:* Lean, wiry ex-Marine. An old timer who has kept in the game by biking, running, climbing, hiking and obsessing on diet. A good heart lurks behind the gruff façade. He feels a proprietary leadership responsibility, which the rest of the group indulges with amusement.
- *Momma Llama:* Yankee female counterpart to southern-fried Brave Phillie. Matriarch to his patriarch. Pushing mid-fifties—maybe more. Her ironic smile tells you not to try to slip anything past her. Incredible legs. I suspect she's Mom's age, but she's easy on the eyes. No sag in those shorts.
- *Bone Festival:* A leprechaun with skinny legs, a sparrow chest and the face of a nebbish. His imposing nose is set ungracefully in a weak-chinned countenance. What beard he has is a goat's tuft. He lives for music, and his songs are wrapped totally around Sky Writer. I get the feeling his obvious adoration of Sky Writer is unrequited, and he seems resigned, if not satisfied, to bask in her bright talent.
- *Captain Stupid:* Why is it that this fat slob (no other way to say it) has such an irresistible persona? He resembles Comic Book guy

on *The Simpsons* minus the haughty erudition. He clearly loves people and wants to be liked back. How can he muster the internal grit to carry this load of flab over this demanding trail? My favorite underdog.

- *Blue Devil:* This kid fits right in. African-Americans are rare out here, but this tough customer seems unfazed about being a *rara avis,* despite being just out of high school. Tall and lean, a prototypical thru-hiker physique. We compared notes about academia. He had considered Stanford—my alma mater—before settling on Duke. These months on the A.T. will leave him with a different world view for a terrific life journey.
- *Ultragrunge:* Compact, athletic, sensational musculature, pierced here and there to maintain a punk aura. Flaming red hair recovering from a burr cut. Despite the hard shell, she can't disguise standard girlishness and occasional giggles. The rigor comes effortlessly to her, but bravado may be a coverup for self doubt.
- *Sky Writer:* Not impossibly beautiful, but she doesn't miss it by much. Long, wheat straw hair. Clean limbs with minimal muscle definition. Effortless grace in movement and voice. Watching her walk with trekking poles is sheer poetry. Not my type exactly, but it is difficult to take my eyes off her.
- *Linda Bennett:* Her mother digs me—probably kiss of death. But in the midst of the chatting and sniffing around, Linda was checking me out while trying to make it *look like* she wasn't. Still waters run deep with this one. A face made to stand alone without makeup. You would never tag this Buckeye as an epic hiker.

What are the odds that one group would have the most beautiful female NOBOs? No wonder I see shelter register commentary from wistful guys wishing to be part of all this. But the Bly Gap Gang has a no-stick quality that subtly discourages additions. Perhaps I'll be accepted as an occasional hanger-on. For now, I'm so in with Jenny that I'm guaranteed a slack to the Nolichucky.

April 16, Journal entry of Momma Llama from a cabin near Hot Springs, NC

Up with the freakin' chickens this morning for early breakfast, compliments of the Bennetts. Always thank trail angels at least three times. Grunge and I headed down Bridge Street to cross the French Broad.

Captain Stupid skipped breakfast, observing that the only advantage he can get over the rest of us is time.

Doug Gottlieb was on the sidewalk in front of Elmer's fiddling with his gear. We invited him to join us, but he smiled longingly down the street in the direction we'd come and said he wasn't quite ready. Grunge laughed as we walked away and hinted that Doug's interests lay somewhere other than her. "Is it Sky or Linda?" she wondered. I'm twice his age, but I'd sure share shelter space with him.

When we hit the bridge over the French Broad, Grunge stuck her tongue out at me. When I asked what I'd done to deserve that, she said she'd ditched her tongue stud. "It's tough enough to keep your teeth fresh out here without that thing. It's goin' in the drink." She lobbed the trinket into the river.

We left the bridge, hiked upriver and up a series of rocky switchbacks leading to a ridge overlooking Lover's Leap and across the river to Hot Springs. It seemed that with a good running jump I could make it all the way to the river. "I'll be a sculptor and return here to live," Grunge mused.

We crossed a highway later, and there were the Bennetts with goodies. Jenny had taken a jaunt back into the woods and found lady slippers and wild azaleas. We told her the woods have slowly come to life as spring builds momentum. Captain Stupid had come through an hour ahead of us and rubbed petroleum jelly on his chaffed inner thighs—not an area any of us want to think about. He calls it Hiker's Diaper Rash.

Then, the rains came. We hiked through buckets of raindrops and lots of ups and downs all the way to Allen Gap, where the Bennetts were waiting again. For the first time ever, Captain Stupid finished first. We found him emptying his heart about his aches and pains to Jenny's sympathetic ear. When Mr. Bennett drove what we now call the "Bly Gap Express" back to Hot Springs, we showered up at the cabins and headed back to town. We serendipitously stumbled onto what is known as Trail Fest, a celebration of a long-term love affair between Hot Springs and the A.T. We browsed exhibits and talked to people from the local maintaining club and the A.T. Conservancy. I saw Brave Phillie in deep conversation with a lady from the Conservancy giving her an earful about things that needed to improve. She was gave him an earful right back on how someone with his talent should be involved in his recommended solutions.

What really captured our attention was the spaghetti dinner. For the first time, Captain Stupid has an appetite. After the day he just put in, the big whale needed to replenish his energy. My God, did he ever! He skipped green stuff and bread and concentrated solely on spaghetti and sauce. He looked happy, as if things may take a good turn for him in the days to come. When NOBOs discovered the Bly Gap Gang, their eyes lit up. Sky and Bone organized a jam session that drew a sax-man who wandered up and joined in. Sky is singing "Girls Just Want to Have Fun."

Linda's angelic next to her dad. I heard her say, "See, Dad, I'm just trying to have fun. What's wrong with that?" He watched and listened with utter bemusement, trying to figure out how a ragtag group of musicians could come together with this unlikely song in this unlikely place with a decidedly unlikely audience and somehow make it fuse in the most unlikely way.

April 17 Journal entry of Blue Devil in a cabin near Hot Springs, NC

I'm out of the hot tub luxuriating in clean shorts at the kitchen table. Mr. Bennett brought his favorite DVD, *The Gods Must Be Crazy*, and there is a lull while everyone sprawls on chairs, the floor and the sofa to take it in. Everyone loves it, except Jenny, who says it makes no sense but doesn't care anyway since she's with her beloved Linda who seems content to lean her head against Jenny's shoulder and munch Cheetos.

We hiked together all day, setting a slightly slower pace to accommodate the Captain. The plan was to be on trail before 6 a.m. to put in over 20 miles to Devil's Fork Gap, a bit of a challenge seeing as how the day started all wet and grungy and we knew the terrain was nothing to sneeze at, starting with a long, long uphill and then mudding and pudding along with no views (thanks to the clouds and rain) and finally getting us to the "Bly Gap Express" by 6:30 p.m., meaning we averaged way under two miles per hour. But, hey baby, we made our longest day yet. Jenny grilled steaks (Sky got a stuffed Portobello) along with baked potatoes, a huge bowl of salad, ice cream and a big chocolate birthday cake for Linda who today turns 22.

We all called for Linda to decide on a trail name, seeing as how it's her birthday, and she is one year into adult accountability and all. She demurred and promised to attempt to resolve the issue by Damascus, if not before. My suggestion has always been Sunshine, which fits her sweet disposition. She may fall back on Buckeye, due to her illustrious Psych degree at Ohio State that would give us two college nicknames in one group, though, and she thinks that's unfair to me, which I assure her it is not.

Anyway, today we passed some Civil War graves with a sad story attached. Brave Phillie took the opportunity to observe that he had several descendants who fought in the Civil War—or as he jokingly called it "The War of Northern Aggression"—and after years of thought, he thinks America would be better off if the South had prevailed. "We would've too, if Lee hadn't had a brain cramp at Gettysburg," he lamented.

I disagreed with this audacious line of reasoning by noting that if things had gone his way, I wouldn't be calling him Brave Phillie. Instead I'd call him Massa and carry his pack along with mine—a truly unjust state of affairs from my point of view.

"But don't you see," he objected, "the industrial revolution was going to make slave labor obsolete soon anyway. Slavery would have died on the vine economically."

We all get along well enough that there really was not an uncomfortable moment at that point, despite the provocative and profoundly stupid nature of BP's remark. "Well, now, I'm just a humble pickaninny, and I wouldn't question yo' authority, but if you believe that then you also believin' pigs are gonna fly out of Captain Stupid's butt."

BP—for once—seemed content to shut up and keep his stupid opinions to himself, but I'll give him credit: For all his tone deaf bullheadedness, he treats me as a friend and an equal, and I am stone amazed at the way that old guy—in his sixties, mind you—can sprint uphill with a full pack.

I'll skip the rest of *The Gods Must Be Crazy*. I need major shuteye.

5

Slacking Toward Damascus, Trail Angels/Trail Demons

SLACKPACKING

He who would travel happily must travel light.
—Antoine de Saint-Exupery

Define slackpacking however you please. Expect vociferous differences of opinion. Most long-distance hikers view slackpacking as having someone support you by vehicle so that the main part of your gear stays in the car while you carry snacks, water and rain gear in a day pack or a detachable summit pack. Some purists sneer at slackpacking, but most trekkers enjoy a few days free of a heavy pack. Most thru-hikers who get "slacked" view it as an opportunity to put in long days with minimal effort.

One must look back several decades to discover the first recorded use of the term "slackpack." Then, it meant something entirely different from the conventionally accepted definition. Long ago on the A.T. in Virginia, a fabled thru-hiker known as O.d. Coyote was hiking with a group known as the South Georgia Heathens. One day, the group was waylaid by some tasty pies at a roadhouse café. This caused a major delay, preventing the group from putting in the miles they had hoped to make that day. Frustrated that the group had allowed itself to get slowed down, one of them—Baha Heathen— said that they weren't backpackers so much as "slackpackers."

According to O.d. Coyote, everyone laughed at the play on words and acknowledged that even though they had not made the desired distance for *the day, they undeniably had enjoyed the afternoon. This is a discovery all hikers should make when they get carried away with making big miles day after day at the expense of enjoying the journey.*

Years later, when Dan "Wingfoot" Bruce provided a definition of slack-packing in his popular The Thru-Hiker's Handbook, *it corresponded to the more conventional one about merely hiking without a pack. In later years, after correspondence with O.d. Coyote, Bruce gave the following definition:*

> *Slackpacking is a hiking term coined in 1980 to describe an unhurried and non-goal-oriented manner of long-distance hiking (i.e. slack: 'not taut or tense, loose'), but in recent years has been used to refer simply to thru-hiking without a backpack.*

It has been suggested that hiking without a big pack could be called "lackpacking," but that term has not become part of the trail lexicon and likely never will. Trail culture dictates that hikers use whichever definition they choose, but it would be nice if more hikers would think about slack-packing in the original tradition of Baha Heathen who created a more whimsical and instructive use for the term. ■

April 18, Transcript of Captain Stupid recorded at Uncle Johnny's, Erwin, Tenn.

Yay, oh yay!

To Sam's Gap today—18 miles. Everyone watches me, wondering when my body will go into vapor lock, collapse, inertia submission, metaphysical free-fall, outright coma—what a hopelessly obese man experiences when he matches well-conditioned outdoors people stride for stride. But hey, we have the "Bly Gap Express" providing support, so there is an urge on the part of my compadres to use the opportunity to pile up mileage.

Here's what's weird: I'm succeeding! Inventory time:

- *Feet:* Serviceable. Discolored from burst and infected blisters, but the skin around the balls of my feet and the heels is heavily calloused. But—like career ballet dancers—our feet always hurt.
- *Hamstrings:* Last cramp was during the infamous Tray Mountain mouse incident. 'Nuff said.
- *Back and Shoulders:* The other day, Brave Phillie asked me why I hunch as I walk. Tinkering with my straps, he said, "Aw hell,

Captain! Your load-lifters are out of whack." He adjusted them, and the pack rested lightly, settling more weight on my waist belt. I told him this cancels out the mouse incident.

- *My appetite:* Growing. I have lost plenty of weight since Springer. I might as well admit that the main reason I lit out on this quixotic exercise was that I dreamed of losing pounds and redeeming my health.
- *My overall mental, spiritual and emotional state:* The carrot dangling in front of my snout is the Bly Gap Gang. For such independent spirits to hang together and embrace a big slob is a 21st-century miracle. I remember when I prayed for support somewhere south of Albert Mountain and then took a tumble that sucked the last fading helium from my shriveled emotional balloon. I recall the way the least likely of the Bly Gappers busted his buns to keep me on board and the way all of them hugged me when I reappeared. That keeps me strong when I contemplate a 2,200-foot ascent.

I am far luckier than I ever could have imagined—tackling the toughest this trail has to offer. Feeling more fit with every step. Financial worries eat at me, but I can handle all that. I'm getting smarter too. In Hot Springs, I traded my seven-pound pack for a used ultralight, which forced me to pare back on gear. I feel the difference step by step. The whole exchange cost more than I should be spending, but Brave Phillie, after adjusting the load lifters, told me it was a long-term loan. Wow!

Cosmic stuff aside, I am settled in a chair at Uncle Johnny's Hostel on the banks of the Nolichucky. Linda and her parents are at the Holiday Inn Express. Everyone else is here at Johnny's, right on the trail.

April 19, Journal entry of Sky Writer in Erwin, Tenn.

When I read this years from now, I hope I don't see myself as a having a rose-colored worldview. But how wonderful it all was today, even if it did begin on a doleful note. With the Bennetts headed back to Ohio, the "Bly Gap Express" made its last run. They hauled us up to Sam's Gap, where a freeway has cut a massive gash out of the ridge. We thanked the Bennetts and looked on shamelessly as Mom and Dad and Linda shared a tearful three-way hug. Jenny was forlorn behind the rain-splattered window, taking a little piece of all our moms with her.

We had arranged to meet Uncle Johnny just over 13 miles away, at a road crossing at Spivey Gap, an easier day after pushing it lately. We entered the woods in a downpour and ascended toward Big Bald about six miles away. About a quarter of a mile from the summit the sun brightened the mist and rain, and we broke out of a thick puree of clouds into dazzling sunshine—the kind of sunlight I've seen only one other time in my life, while traveling through the Greek Isles. I looked up and there was the top of the big, treeless hill just a brisk walk away.

We converged at a cairn, sprawling on the sun-dried crest. Bone softly strummed, casting a spell as we surveyed a flat plain of perfect white cloud cover. A few other summits poked out in all directions. We were the only people on the planet. No whisper of wind. No sound of a voice—just Bone's banjo. We had entered a zone, a place earned only by those willing to hike for months in the mountains with the promise that such moments occur just a few times.

Brave Phillie was on his back, his head on Momma Llama's shoulder, with that endearing vacant smile. Captain Stupid put his arm around me. Grunge, Linda and Blue Devil were on their backs with feet and ankles intertwined and eyes half-shut. Bone's fingers stilled. This occurred in an incalculable interim. All things temporal froze. Across the windless summit, a solitary hummingbird moved toward us in that odd, uneven perfection of movement common to its breed. It went directly to Momma Llama and hovered inches from her nose, then Brave Phillie, then Bone and Grunge and Linda and Blue Devil. Last it lingered before the Captain and me with an elegance and effortlessness that makes me cry as I write. I whispered the old song: "Hummingbird don't fly away."

Then, after bestowing its blessing on Doug, it vanished. No one spoke. No puff of wind. No sound from below the clouds. We inhabited a region of time and space that poets and thru-hikers and—I presume— lovers are privileged to occupy.

April 20, Journal entry of Ultragrunge at Uncle Johnny's, Erwin, Tenn.

Asian paradise last night at a place in Erwin called the China Kitchen. Sometimes you just want standard Chinese, so we asked a local to haul us into town for a dose of meat that was fried and sweet and sour. Egg rolls and rice. Soy sauce. Hot mustard. I drank a couple of quarts of water to attain equilibrium within my digestive tract. Blue

Devil, Momma Llama, Brave Phillie and Captain Stupid all agreed that Big Bald was supernatural—a door opening between physical and metaphysical planes. Even BP, curmudgeon that he is, agreed that we had been witness to something other-wordly.

Back at Uncle Johnny's, we got into a discussion of what we were taking away from the trail experience. "When SOBOs come through here later in the year, they have a clearer idea of what it's all been about," Momma Llama speculated. "They're almost finished, but we're not a quarter done yet, haven't worked out why we're here and what we expect from it."

We carried light loads this morning after Johnny shuttled us to Spivey Gap. We knew heavy packs awaited us later in the day. We're blue that slackpacking is over. But the weather was cool and clear, a day to pause and check out wildflowers. We followed a roller coaster route before riding a long switchbacked descent to the Nolichucky River where we picked up our packs at the hostel.

As we crossed the bridge over the Nolichucky, we were a balky string of pack mules, saddled up again with spine crushing loads as we hiked upstream and then up a steep ascent to Curley Maple Gap. Even though we pulled in early, the shelter at Curley Maple was packed with NOBOs. We pushed on to a nearby clearing to camp.

This day was never in sync, a backlash from losing the Bennetts and returning to the familiar drudgery. Our life since Hot Springs has been sweaty luxury. I intend to settle under my tarp and read Sky's beat-up copy of *Doctor Zhivago*. I swapped *Life, the Universe and Everything* for it. Momma Llama is reading *Emma* on her smartphone.

April 21, Journal entry of Doug Gottlieb at Ash Gap

I'm back on my own tonight with mixed emotions. I might as well admit, they're not mixed at all. I miss the Bly Gap Gang. But this morning, I was determined to get to this spot knowing I would be ahead of them, probably from now on. Piggybacking on the slackpacking gravy train was irresistible, and everyone seemed perfectly happy to let it happen. The gang was happy to have me around, but it was clear that Linda was struggling with sharing the group with me and maybe sharing me with the group. So I've moved on. Nearly 26 miles today to Ash Gap, the longest I've hiked in years.

I said my goodbyes last night and was on the trail way early with a headlamp. I came to Beauty Spot, a ridgetop field with a view into the river valley and massive mountains all around. In a gravel parking lot below a couple in a little RV saw me and waved me down for coffee. Rhonda and Bill Agee, a retired California couple taking a yearlong tour of America, decided I looked hungry. Unoffended by my funky aroma, they set me up with bacon, eggs, toast, juice and coffee. I explained that I was a thru-hiker and suddenly realized that they did not understand they were parked next to the A.T. They interviewed me on a camcorder. Trail angels unaware, oblivious to where they were or who they were helping until I told them.

I headed out as the mist burned away, making my way through wooded trail and open meadow before ascending Unaka Mountain. I'd read Earl Shaffer's *Walking With Spring* and recall his bleak assessment of Unaka, which had been burned over in the 1940s and was in lousy shape when he hiked through in 1948. Now the place is magic. A regal stand of red cedars dominate the summit, a carpet for my throbbing feet.

The rest of the day was hard work, but all these weeks of hiking coupled with the recent stretch of slackpacking had me brimming with stamina. The last climb halfway up the flank of Roan Mtn. was tough, coming after 25 miles, but I set up camp with plenty of daylight. A family of two energetic boys and their parents shared apples and cookies—a complement to my chicken and rice. The dad warned that the water source was contaminated by wild boar, based on all the rooted up soil. Oops! I should have been more fastidious when I filtered my water.

So I'm headed to Katahdin on my own again. No doubt I'll have withdrawal from my newfound friends, particularly Linda. There was something there, but an undefinable impediment made the situation untenable.

WATER

A list of necessities for any A.T. hiker includes a way to treat water. Forty years ago, a thru-hiker could hike the entire trail drinking untreated water and never get sick. It was risky behavior to be sure, but rarely a problem. If a hiker attempts that today, there would not be trouble most of the time. But most of the time isn't good enough. If you fail to account for the purity of your water, you will get sick—sometimes, very sick.

The ATC provides information about the location of water sources all along the trail route, but they warn people to filter, boil or chemically treat water. Fastidious hikers will both filter and chemically treat. Most will select one or the other and probably do fine as long as they carefully follow instructions. Few boil their water (except for cooking), because it wastes fuel.

There are many brands of filters and chemical treatments. Read up on the topic before committing to a method. Consider water purity as a life or death matter and never neglect to treat it as prescribed. The sickness one can get from bad water tends to be violent and debilitating. Why risk it? ■

April 22, Journal entry of Brave Phillie at Overmountain Shelter

I drank a beer or two too many in Hot Springs and Erwin. I've spent the past few days sweating stale alcohol out of my system and remembering my philosophy about hiking successfully after age 60: "Know your limitations." Momma Llama agrees. An older person can sometimes walk circles around people a third their age. The key for geezers is to maintain discipline. The kids—just about every one of them—squander the advantage of youth at least one or two days a week. Then they look at me in awe when I out-hike them.

If I had what they have, knowing what I know now, I wouldn't just hike over these mountains. I'd by God move 'em! But when you're older and you have a glitch in your carefully planned routine, it hits harder. That's why I pulled into Overmountain Shelter last behind Captain Stupid, about half sick.

What perks me up is being at one of the top two or three shelters from Maine to Georgia, and probably the biggest. Overmountain is a barn converted to a trail shelter. Since there are so many NOBOs, the place is loaded. Momma Llama and I squeezed on one of the platforms looking over an open meadow, a grove of evergreens and a basin of mountains. It's still daylight, and I'm scribbling and checking out a couple of wild turkeys strutting in a field down below us.

These days headed north out of the Nolichucky Valley have been grueling, but I felt the last of the poison drain from my pores as I climbed up and over Roan Mtn. where the eventual explosion of rhododendron color is weeks away. I miss Doug. We'll follow his progress in shelter registers—all the way to Maine, I hope.

April 23, Journal entry of Bone Festival at Apple House Campsite

Linda was out of Overmountain quickly this morning. Blue Devil and I were hot on her heels. This is a fun stretch—one bald after another with eyepopping vistas. As we crested Little Hump Mtn., where dry grass was waving in the wind like little ocean currents, we saw Linda sitting in it, smiling off into the postdawn countryside. Gentle zephyrs disturbed the blade tops, creating the illusion that Linda was levitating.

Later, we ascended Hump Mtn., a less attractive summit, but one with a great view plus the bonus of longhorns grazing in the meadows below. Then a long downhill toward Hwy. 19E. This was shaping up to be an easy day, but we didn't account for a major complication. About a half-mile from Hwy. 19E is the Apple House campsite, much too close to the road, particularly since this highway crossing is smack in the middle of an area where some locals have treated hikers badly—even criminally. But the problem at Apple House had nothing to do with that.

Before the clearing came into view, we heard the distinctive sound of an adult male retching his guts out. "Geez," Linda said. "Sounds like a cataclysmic hangover." Blue Devil's gigglebox turned over. Aside from the sound of resounding flatulence, nothing is funnier than the sound of some wretched jerk hurling—as long as it's not you.

Our amusement faded when we got to the campsite and saw Doug on hands and knees, tossing his cookies, one mighty heave after another. Before we got to him, he rolled away from his puke puddle sweating like a summer mule.

Now there has been plenty of speculation among the Bly Gap Gang as to whether there was chemistry between Doug and Linda. Momma Llama asked Linda point-blank about it and received an uncharacteristically rude rebuff from the normally even-keeled Linda adding fuel to the speculative flames. Linda's reaction to Doug's embarrassing situation left no doubt that she cares about this guy. She poured water onto her bandana, mopped off his face and wiped detritus from his mouth, chin and chest. Then she ordered Blue Devil and me to pick him up— "be gentle"—carry him to a flat spot, lay out a ground cloth and place him on his sleeping pad.

"I'm sorry guys," he mumbled. "Bad water at Ash Gap. I got this far yesterday and got real sick. I wish I could just croak."

Linda borrowed BD's phone to call a cousin, a doctor in an emergency room in Columbus. When she got resistance from the other end about connecting her, she revealed a steely side. "I want him on the phone in 60 seconds. I guarantee Dr. Bennett will be extremely upset at your lack of cooperation."

Within almost no time, he was on the phone. She hit the speaker so Doug could answer questions. Doug said he drank from a spring he later suspected was contaminated by wild boar. The doctor established that his symptoms began within 24 hours after ingestion, which probably eliminated Giardia or E-Coli.

"There are a few things it could be," the doctor speculated. "If you're lucky you're probably through the worst of it. You need to get something for the diarrhea and bland food for your stomach—broth, pudding, stuff like that. Count on being weak once the nausea, vomiting and diarrhea stop." Then, came the yadda yadda yadda of telling Doug to get rest and above all, "drink lots of fluids, stuff like Gatorade and such." As doctors normally do, he suggested going to a town for medical care.

Then, as any relative would do, he peppered Linda with an onslaught of questions about her hike. She put up with it briefly, then unceremoniously signed off and established a game plan. The gang began trickling in, and Linda managed to come up with beef broth from her pack, vanilla pudding from Mamma Llama and Gatorade from Sky. Captain Stupid pulled Imodium A-D out of his first-aid stash. "This'll put the squeeze on a dam break," he said. What had looked like a long day was cut short. Everyone wants to help Doug. Lots of NOBOs came through, but our gang is setting up tents for the night. Linda's in charge of TLC for Doug. I can think of worse things.

April 24, Journal entry of Ultragrunge at Johnson City, Tenn., Medical Center

I'm cross-legged on a waiting room couch fighting waves of fatigue as we careen toward midnight. Linda and Mamma Llama are with me, and everyone else is at Kincora Hostel staying with Bob Peoples. Everyone, that is, but Doug, who is laid up here at Johnson City Medical Center. Wowie zowie, what a freakin' day! Thank God for friendship, quick thinking, loyalty and old-fashioned good luck.

I'll try to get this down on paper with input from Linda and Momma. Even though the events are only hours old, it's tough to process them on the written page.

Our plan was to put in a huge day out of the Apple House site. Doug said he would not go far, but everyone else was thinking crazy thoughts—like getting all the way to Dennis Cove Road and the comfort of the Kincora Hostel we've heard so much about—nearly 24 miles over not-so-easy terrain.

We shot out early in the gray period when the birds just stir and deer get in their predawn browsing. The first miles were sublime, woods interspersed with high meadows and curious horses sidling up to nose at our packs—past recipients of handouts. Doug and Captain Stupid whined about feeling puny. Doug has the lean thru-hiker look, and the illness left him downright gaunt—an anorexic Matthew McConaughey.

A few miles in, meandering down switchbacks, we peeked through the trees and saw a cemetery. As we got closer, we saw one of those giant macho pickup trucks—red with a club cab. Momma Llama, BP, Linda and I were in the lead, and as we came into view, we heard someone say, "I like the one with the red hair. Hey, Porter, I'll take her and you take the tall one." Shivers ricocheted down my spinal column. Who were these jerks?

"That skinny ol' bitch has tight buns. I'll settle for that. I like antiques," another one said. Four punks in their early 20s and a skanky girl in a tank top and jeans smirking back and forth between us and her mouthy friends.

"Look straight ahead—keep going," Brave Phillie mumbled. "No confrontation."

We kept moving—never getting within 50 feet of them—and they kept lobbing comments. "Ditch that old fart and come with us! Hey, you with the red hair, I like those muscles!" We made it around the cemetery and headed back into the trees as the sleazeballs hopped in their truck and peeled off, leaving empty beer cans and showers of gravel in their wake.

"OK," said BP. "We wait here and bunch up. We have two road crossings comin' up in short order, and I'm thinking we haven't seen the last of those losers." I was scared enough, but something about BP's pessimism shook me even more.

We waited for everyone to catch up, and a game plan came together. BP said this stretch of trail was known for trouble—mostly trash on the trail, vehicular vandalism and verbal harassment. But sometimes it was worse. Years ago some women hikers were raped not far from here. "If these snakes try to find us, we need to be ready to fight," he said. "I don't mean just pushin' away. I mean breakin' bones. This is nut-cuttin' time."

As the Bly Gap Gang assembled, we filled them in on the problem. A paved road was minutes away, so we headed on and paused as it came into view. Sure enough, the weasels were parked at a tiny church where the road crossed, slouching around their truck and swigging beer. As bad luck would have it, one of them spotted us. "Come on out y'all," he hollered. "We got beer enough to get you in the mood." They erupted in a rumble of drunken guffaws.

"We don't need this," Momma Llama said. "I say we call the cops and wait until they get here." Just then, the little mob crawled back into their truck and headed down the road, stopping to look us over as we stood back in the woods. "Looks like there's more of 'em," one of them yelled. "I still want the redhead."

Brave Phillie left the shelter of the trees, and walked up to the driver's side. A few words were exchanged, and then the driver stuck a pistol out the window aimed right at BP's nose. Sky gasped and sobbed, and we all looked in disbelief as the old Marine stood his ground and looked right down the barrel. His voice was loud and clear: "You better use that or leave little man! I don't see no middle ground here."

Slowly, the truck pulled away, and in a display of manhood, they threw beer cans out the windows. They rolled to the edge of the road as the truck disappeared.

"Blast, I can't get a decent cell signal," Captain Stupid said. "How about the rest of you?"

Mamma Lama, Blue Devil and I all tried. I got a signal but couldn't sustain a call. "We need to move," BP said. "We have one more road crossing before we get to a roadless stretch. These slugs aren't much threat if we can get where they can't drive." We were only a few minutes' walk from the last paved road for many miles.

"You men take the lead," BP barked, a platoon leader in an old war movie. "My guess is they're watching and plan to meet us whichever direction we go. I'll jog down the road and meet you at that crossing. If you get there first, haul ass across the road, and keep your eyes wide open. Don't go pacifist. That Glock'll put .45 slugs in you as fast as he can pull the trigger."

I hated this kind of talk. For the first time in my life, I had an obligation to ditch my peaceful inclinations. We headed past the lonely church back into the woods at full stride. A grim group moving wordlessly while Sky sobbed in a state just short of hysteria. I held my folding knife tight against my hiking pole handle, the pitiful two-inch blade ready for action.

Too quickly, Campbell Hollow Road loomed ahead closer and closer. I prayed we would cross over into the security of the wilderness. But just as we all expected, just as we reached blacktop, just as we were ready to make our sprint for safety, the truck roared up and screeched to a big redneck halt. The punks—along with their bad-haired slut—tumbled out into our path.

The leader had his gun tucked in his jeans right where his Dale Earnhardt memorial "#8" tee shirt was tucked in. He and his friends blocked our path. We stood our ground.

"Ooooh, I like the blond best of all," said the gangliest and youngest looking of the crew. "Let me have her, Porter."

"Naw, I get first choice. She beats out ol' red and her little black-haired friend. You guys can fight over the others. Hell, Sean, that old one looks like a buckin' bronco." Porter, the bandy-legged man with the gun was sure of himself, swaggering like a barnyard rooster. "You girls just drop them big bags and hop in the truck. We'll take you where your friends won't bother us."

The little gunman walked over to Sky Writer and grabbed her arm. At this point, I really can't record all the things that happened in amazingly rapid succession, but Momma Llama's here, and we'll try to list the sequence in order:

1. Doug stepped between Porter and Sky Writer and took an awful hit on the side of his head from the butt of the pistol. Blood was all over.
2. Captain Stupid—a dirigible in fast forward—enveloped Porter, and their bodies hurtled to the ground. Porter released a combination scream and moan as the impact of all the weight squeezed the air from his lungs in a big vocal explosion. He was putty in the Captain's hands.
3. I dove for and clutched the handgun that flew out of Porter's hand.
4. Brave Phillie was suddenly on the scene with one of his hiking poles tight against the neck of Sean, the skinny one.
5. Momma Llama was beating holy crap out of the redneck girlfriend.
6. Linda and Bone ganged up on another punk, a fat kid who had little zest for battle. Soon enough, they were twisting his arms with the savagery of people who've been living in the woods for too long.
7. Then the fourth punk spoiled the positive momentum. He was pointing a big revolver right at Blue Devil and me.

We had reached an impasse.

He had a big shaggy head, a torn filthy tee shirt, greasy jeans, and perhaps the worst teeth I've seen outside of a concentration camp film. "Well, Red," he drawled. "The difference between you and me is I'd just as like blow your little head off as look at ya. You and Sambo and me all know you ain't never gonna shoot back."

My feet were wide apart. I had the gun extended toward him with a two-hand grip. "I didn't catch your name," I said.

"My friends call me Tracker."

"OK, Tracker," I said. "My daddy's an accountant down in Houston. He used to be in the Army, and he developed a real keen attraction to guns. He loved to take me and my sister to the range on weekends, and we got to shoot all kinds of pistols and rifles. I even shot an Uzi. I loved it. Daddy always told me, 'Honey, don't ever pick up a gun unless you know you're ready to use it.' I took that to heart."

Judging from his squint, I could tell I had Tracker's attention. Everyone else's too. Captain had Porter in a constrictive bearhug, applying excruciating pressure on his sternum. Brave Phillie was nearly choking skinny Sean to death. Mamma Llama had the floozy in a professional full nelson, and the girl's tattooed boobs had popped out of the halter for all to admire. The fat kid was well-tended by Linda and Bone. Except for heavy breathing and birds twittering, it was dead quiet. Just Tracker staring down Blue Devil and me.

"I like Glocks, Tracker," I said. "Daddy was dead on. I'm ready."

Whatever Tracker had in mind became moot. He was on the ground getting his head pounded with a short-handled shovel. I kept one hand on the gun and used the other to pull Sky away while Blue Devil picked up Tracker's revolver. I saved the life of the man I had been willing to shoot to death moments before. Sky slumped to her knees clutching the shovel in a death grip, quietly hysterical. If Blue Devil and I had not pulled her away, Tracker's head was on the verge of becoming buzzard lunch.

April 24, Transcript of Captain Stupid recorded at Kincora Hostel

My mom took me to a specialist years ago. He thought I was a "little professor," a borderline-autistic type with Asperger's Syndrome. He said I could absorb tons of knowledge and couple it with a pretty fair intellect, but would have trouble processing and applying it in a socially advantageous manner. People would avoid my precocious personality, because the manner in which I forced my knowledge on them was irritating to the extent they'd knock over lamps getting out of the room.

Time proved the diagnosis wrong. I was "normal." People found me funny and self-deprecating. I interact well socially and professionally, but something has always blocked my path to success. I was restrained by stress or worry or just a wretched fear of failure. To compensate, I ate, drank and smoked to excess and failed to succeed in school or elsewhere. I wound up living with Mom, limping from job to job before attempting to run a computer-recycling and resale business out of a rustbelt warehouse in Akron, saddled with failure—uncomfortably resigned to it.

Today was an epiphany. I no longer accept failure. We clawed our way out of cruelty and violence and discovered how decency can materialize in the wake of a nightmare.

Now I sit at a picnic table on the porch of Kincora Hostel run by Bob Peoples, who has dedicated his retirement to maintaining the A.T., preserving its reputation and providing a place to shower, cook, wash clothes, sleep and commune. He's always available to tell a story, provide advice or help out with a shuttle. All he asks in return is a modest voluntary cash donation to cover his costs, which most right-thinking travelers are happy to provide. He doesn't maintain this little log cabin haven just a five-minute walk from the A.T. to get rich. He does it for love of the trail and trail people. He's a diminutive man with an elfin sparkle in his eyes and unconditional love for the life he's created here.

Yay!

It's late now, and aside from one of Bob's dogs who occasionally noses around my boots, I'm the only creature stirring. Sky Writer is next to me, sleeping atop the table. At times she moans and cries in the midst of her snoring, but a couple of gentle pats reassure her before she comes completely awake. I told her all day she was a heroine, but I wonder if she will ever get over the emotional strain of intentionally harming another human being. While all the action was taking place, she crawled around the side of the truck, peered into the bed and found a shovel—a pretty good weapon as it turned out. Now she's facing the scorching realization that she inflicted all that pain—never mind that she was inflicting it to protect friends from a lowlife felon.

God, what a day! We became statistics, one of those rare hiking groups on the A.T. assaulted by criminals. When the dust settled, we came out of the melee alive and with just one injury. As if puking his guts out yesterday wasn't enough, Doug is in the hospital with a concussion.

After we fought off the scuzzballs and got them under control, we flagged down a friendly retiree to drive Ultragrunge to a place where she could make a cell call. The rest of us stayed behind and kept the band of troublemakers subdued. Ultragrunge called 911 and got response from the county sheriff (three cars) and local EMT. While on the phone, she provided the tag number of the truck, which really caught the attention of the law enforcement people. It had been stolen two weeks before in West Virginia.

As the sheriff's cars drove up, BP placed the guns on the ground and waited calmly. The cops figured out who the good guys and bad guys were, but we all ended up getting a ride in sheriff's vehicles to the county seat. Wouldn't you know it? All of them—except the girl—had outstanding warrants and were in violation of parole. Porter and Tracker met in prison. They were driving a stolen vehicle, carrying unregistered firearms and had been on a small-time crime spree. This bunch was in a world of trouble. Our cause didn't need much help, but it was useful that a couple of the deputies were ex-Marines who dug Brave Phillie.

Meanwhile, Doug and Tracker got a free ride to the hospital in Johnson City with a deputy to keep Tracker company. After the cops were through with us, they took Ultragrunge, Momma Llama and Linda to stay with Doug at the hospital. Later, a kind soul took the rest of us to Kincora after a stop by a grocery store to resupply. Sky was in shock. She held my arm constantly, never letting me out of her sight. I practically had to pry her loose to take a shower.

Tomorrow we go back to the sheriff and give statements. Processing this bunch will involve back and forth between the judicial systems in West Virginia and Tennessee. The law-enforcement people we talked to were irritated that the malfeasances of a bunch of West Virginians are being visited on the A.T. in Tennessee, where progress has been made in recent years to improve the relationship between hikers and locals. We may be asked to come back as witnesses in a trial. That could be months from now, assuming they don't get extradited. They know how to find us, so we'll worry about that later.

For now, a zero day at Kincora. This story has been picked up by the regional press and will be national news by tomorrow. Brave Phillie talked to the Appalachian Trail Conservancy, and they're taking calls on our behalf. The sheriff is disgusted that these outsiders caused trouble in this particular neck of the woods. There have been no problems with locals of late, and the bad publicity is not at all useful.

A Johnson City TV news crew found their way to Kincora, and Brave Phillie agreed to do the talking to what he calls "those media pukes." Basic message: We subdued some bad guys bent on causing us harm. No more than that. The Conservancy is giving the basic truth: The world is a dangerous place, and the A.T. is part of the world. You just need to use your head to be as safe as possible.

I put my sleeping pad on the porch to sleep out here with Sky. I'm more worried about her than Doug.

A DOSE OF REALITY

It's not all peace and tranquility and people loving and sharing. Sometimes it's dangerous and threatening—just as any place on earth is. Over the years, there have been assaults, rapes, thefts and murders on the A.T. Sometimes crimes that occurred near the A.T. and had nothing to do with hiking on the trail got mistakenly related to the trail due to sloppy news reporting. But the fact remains: People have done awful things to other people right smack dab on the trail.

Experts say you are probably safer from crime on the A.T. than you would be walking down the main street of a conventional American city. But nearly everyone has heard of the Appalachian Trail, and when something dramatic happens out there, the media love to grab it, manipulate it to make it as lurid as possible, and fling it up on the wall for all the world to see. The sad result is that many people get the idea the A.T. is especially dangerous, a truly fallacious notion.

Any hiker who bothers to read a trail guide will learn common sense rules: Don't hike alone. Make sure someone knows where you are and where you are headed. Approach strangers with friendly caution. Learn to identify weirdos and thugs. Never camp near a highway, as troublemakers rarely stray far from their vehicles. Don't draw attention to yourself with odd clothes or kooky behavior (this rule is laughable to many, but not a bad idea). Don't carry firearms. Protect your pack, credit cards, money and I.D. with your life, as your trip will likely end if they are stolen. Leave a paper trail of your trip in shelter logs and other trail registers. Virtually all hikers break some of these rules, because adhering to convention is one thing they are trying to escape.

Best advice: Trust your instinct. Keep your antennae out. If someone asks too many questions and takes too much interest, "disappear" yourself. It's easy. After all, you're in the wilderness. ▪

SUBJECT: **The recent unpleasantness**
DATE: **April 25, 7:24 p.m.**
FROM: **Linda Bennett** < LindaBennett98Z@yahoo.com >
TO: **Jenny Bennett** < JenBenchick@gmail.com >

Just a followup to yesterday's email and phone call. I know you're hearing about all this on the news, and I want to tell you we're safe and taking a zero day at Kincora. It's raining cats and dogs and racoons, a perfect day to be inside. Doug did not receive life-threatening injuries, but because of all the attention and excitement, the hospital kept him overnight. His concussion is minor, but he'll have a scar on his temple from the 15 stitches.

Stop worrying!!! The odds of this happening again are next to zero. So don't bother coming down here. We're not stopping, and we're triumphant that we defended ourselves and gave that bunch what they deserved. The only one who will walk away is that girl, Gini. We heard she caught a bus back to West Virginia.

The story on these guys is that they're from Charleston, W.V., have criminal records and are in violation of parole. They stole that truck, and the law-enforcement people are piecing together other crimes they've committed, including armed robbery, assault and who knows what else.

My biggest concern is for Sky Writer. She's filled with angst about hiking on. Her solace is big old Captain Stupid, her safe haven. Otherwise, all of us are fine, even Doug with the big bandage on his head.

Brave Phillie is annoyed that the punk named Porter had on a Dale Earnhardt shirt. "Dale deserves more respect than for that pissant to be wearing a Number Eight shirt."

Tomorrow Bob will ferry us back to where this all took place and we'll go 20 trail miles back here to Kincora and spend one more night here. Then on to Damascus! Spaghetti's ready!

April 26, Journal entry of Doug Gottlieb at Kincora Hostel

If Bob didn't exist, someone would need to invent him. He picked me up at the hospital this morning after dropping the Bly Gap Gang at the very spot where the hoo-ha occurred. I spent the day resting up and feeling relieved that the headaches from the bonk on the head are dissipating. I might be back hiking tomorrow. I insisted that the rest of the crew hike today, and I'll see them tonight. I'll catch them later.

While I was racked out in ICU, I spent some time with the New Testament Mom gave me. Nothing like near death to give you a spiritual jolt. I'm not jumping to the conclusion that God spared me for any "special purpose." But I got knocked deeper into the way I approach prayer and introspection—not doing them differently, just experiencing them more profoundly.

When I catch up, I can be a member of the Bly Gap Gang. I didn't help much, but I stuck my neck out. I couldn't let them take Sky, Linda, Grunge and Momma Llama away without a fight. I got a conk on the head, but it was worth it.

Linda was my self-appointed hospital angel. Every time she walked in the room to help me, I got tears in my eyes, not so much out of gratitude, but more because I couldn't imagine how awful it would have been if the scene had played out worst case.

April 27, Journal Entry of Blue Devil at Iron Mtn. Shelter

We were ready to make up for lost time today—24 miles to this place. The falls and Laurel Fork Gorge early in the day were dynamite after all the recent rain. The air was charged with mist and cool fresh air. No doubt the falls are the best on the trail. Bob suggested we take the high-water route, but all of us took the river-level trail and paid by wading in knee-deep water—pretty stupid way to start a long day.

Bone and I hiked together, and he's blue on two major counts: (1) Slight damage to his banjo in the altercation. (2) He is dying slowly from the knowledge that not only has he lost Sky Writer, the woman of his fantasies, but he has lost her to the most unlikely of characters. Captain is a great guy, but let's face it, he's pretty hideous, right?

It isn't as if Bone resents the Captain, seeing as how Captain Stupid never made a play for Sky Writer, but what hurts ol' Bone is that right in Sky's hour of need, the very time when Bone wants most to console and comfort her, she turns to another guy.

Bone is considering splitting off from the Bly Gap Gang and wonders if I want to tag along. I got over the idea of going solo long ago and figure to stay with these crazies until the mood strikes me differently. I feel a strong bond with these people. I'll never forget standing next to Ultragrunge and her Glock while that cracker stared down the barrel of his stolen Smith and Wesson—all of us wondering second to second how this was going to resolve itself and knowing all the time that somebody might go toes up. You don't go through something like that and not feel closer to your friends later; I mean how could I hike away now?

And get this: Grunge—the real star of the show during that altercation—was bluffing like some deadeyed card sharp. She told us later, as a casual afterthought, that she'd never shot a firearm in her life, her dad wasn't in the army and her classy two-handed pistol stance—legs wide apart—was an imitation of what she'd seen on TV. Wow!

I never thought I'd be glad to be back full pack. But it was nice having a normal day, ending with the familiar simultaneous hiss of our stoves, my titanium pot filled with noodles/mushroom-soup mix/tuna/powdered cheese to go with fresh-filtered spring water and a Twix bar for dessert. It made the long hike worthwhile, baby.

Sky is smiling. At the Captain's gentle urging, she walked over to Bone and coaxed him to sing a couple of new verses of the Amicalola song:

> On to Damascus,
> Clear trail ahead.
> Destiny's children,
> Safe now, not dead.

April 28, Journal entry of Momma Llama at Abingdon Gap Shelter

Half an hour after I pushed out of Iron Mountain Shelter this morning, I reached a melancholy landmark, the burial place of old Nick Grindstaff, a solitary mountain hermit. A flat stone monument is embedded in an aging brick-and-mortar structure to bear testimony to this forlorn fellow. Orphaned at age three, Nick led a life of poverty and was robbed and nearly beaten to death at age 26. Bitter and weary of a world that held no happiness, he moved to a cabin on Iron Mountain and became a recluse.

A poem by Adam M. Daugherty recalls the solitude of a loner's life:

> He roamed up there for forty years,
> Under the heavens' chandeliers. . .
> And thus he slept within his rights,
> Fourteen thousand, four hundred nights. . .

His stark monument reads:

UNCLE
NICK GRINDSTAFF
Born
Dec. 26, 1851
Died
July 22, 1923
Lived alone, suffered alone, died alone

When they found Nick's dead body in his remote cabin, his little dog so ferociously protected him that it had to be killed so that Nick could be carried away. I guess there must have been some goodness in a man who could have inspired such loyalty. Sadly, I doubt they were buried together.

Over 16 miles of easy hiking today, I had Nick on my mind, jumbled with all the combined physical and emotional baggage of the last few days. I finally know the meaning of "dog tired." I cooked and ate fast and settled into my bag before sunset. We'll take a short day into Damascus tomorrow, the equivalent of a zero day. This shelter is packed with NOBOs tonight, tents all around, lots of talk about Damascus and, of course, the Campbell Hollow incident.

I'm monitoring the Bly Gap Gang and beaming with a sort of parental pride in the way none of them is crowing. We agreed on the story, and we're sticking to it. You can't ignore the dangers of long-distance hiking, but you also can't *not* do this.

Brave Phillie is next to me as I write this, as beat up as I am. I think seeing so much of what you care for dangling over the abyss takes the wind out of your sails—more so for seasoned adults such as BP and me and less for the kids. He normally shaves and stays neat and fresh, but tonight he is scruffy. He smiled that distant smile: "I need that short day tomorrow. Let me buy you lunch."

I can't hide my heart's truth. I'm slowly falling in love with this man. A long lifetime of disappointment and bitterness is thawing very, very slowly—an icicle in a late April thaw. I am terrified of being hurt, and I know he is too. But we need to talk. I hear that Buzzard Rock near Whitetop Mountain, just a few days away, is a lovely spot. Maybe I'll make it a point to arrive there early and wait for him, a perfect time and place to force the issue. Why wait until we both qualify for Social Security?

6

Digging the Highlands, Thru-hiker Tossed Salad and Damascus Redux

DAMASCUS

*A*n old thru-hiker was seeing his son off a few years back as the lad started an end-to-end hike of his own. Dad was brimming over with unsolicited advice, but he boiled it down to a simple thought: A SOBO owes it to himself to get as far as Hanover, N.H., and a NOBO should feel the same about getting to Damascus, Va. Either way, you've seen about as much as the trail can throw at you. Either way, you have nearly the first quarter of the trip under your belt. Either way, you will truly know if a thru-hike is the thing for you.

A NOBO enters Damascus with confidence and elation. You're in Virginia now! No longer is there a need for the faux cockiness you felt at the first few big landmarks. At Damascus, you continue northward with the certitude that unless you get sick, hurt or just become a victim of existential panic, you're going to make it.

Damascus has all a thru-hiker needs: a couple of outfitters, good restaurants, B&Bs, hostels and a grocery store. NOBOs often return in mid-May for the famous Trail Days Festival. They see it as the gateway to Virginia, the longest state on the trail. Damascus is a sort of Mayberry peopled by kindred spirits who are glad you made it to their town and decided to lay your head and a few dollars there. ∎

April 29, Journal entry of Sky Writer at Dave's Place,
Damascus, Va.

What must Captain Stupid think of me? Or I of myself? He's my
haven as I work my way out of the dark depression and despair that
has come over me since Campbell Hollow Road. How many times have
people told me I did the right thing? I remember seeing what was about
to happen—an evil man with a gun trained on brave little Grunge who
stared back without batting an eye. My soul spoke to me. I crawled on
all fours to the back of the truck and grabbed a shovel from the bed.
The rest is a gray blur, but I can't kid myself into not remembering the
way I hammered him in the head so hard and so many times that
Grunge and Blue Devil had to pull me away. Since then, my Captain is
where I go for sanctuary as I reassemble my serenity.

Day after day of hiking has seen me through. In and out of rain,
through temperature fluctuations, wrapping myself in the loving
comfort of Kincora and all the shelters. Finally I emerge from my
funk here in Damascus at a hostel called Dave's Place. A short day into
Damascus—a sweet little trail town too cute to be true. Time to do laundry, shower and talk on the phone with my mom, reassuring her again
that we're fine. As we feasted on Italian food at Sicily's on Main Street,
we captured the ears of two musicians, one of whom had a contact in
nearby Abingdon who was willing to take a look at Bone's broken banjo
and arrange its repair. Bone was ecstatic.

We also talked to a gentleman who wants us to come back to Trail
Days in mid-May so that Bone and I can perform some of our original
music. He might even arrange for us to rehearse with a professional
bluegrass group to do one of our songs for the crowd.

Walking into Virginia was cathartic. As I tossed my trash bag of
empty food pouches and dirty Zip-Locs into a garbage can on the out-
skirts of Damascus, I pretended I was shedding the sorrow and depression deep in my guts. Now I'll sit next to Captain Stupid, whose off-trail
name I still don't know, nor he mine.

April 30, Journal entry of Brave Phillie at VA 601

Eighteen miles today out of Damascus with lots of ups and downs
and a level stretch where the A.T. and the Virginia Creeper Trail
merged. The Creeper is a railroad right of way converted into a bike
path that runs through Damascus. We shared it with hikers and cyclists
all in the same good mood.

While in Damascus we were approached by a reporter from the *Roanoke Times* who tracked us down for the in-depth scoop on the Campbell Hollow donnybrook. Momma Llama and I had breakfast with him and recounted our experience. We made it clear that we did what we had to and went light on the specifics. We said we still feel safe on the trail and that this incident should not serve to scare people away. As far as I'm concerned, the media circus ended when I paid the check. Enough!

What's interesting is that the media pukes never picked up on the details. Momma Llama thinks if they knew how Ultragrunge bluffed her way with the handgun and how Sky Writer used a shovel to play Ping-Pong with old Tracker's head, the story would get made into a movie. Never mind that Grunge knows zip about firearms.

Anyway, we're on the edge of a dirt road in a field, and everyone has tents and tarps up due to likely rain tonight. We cooked quick to beat the precip, and everyone is stoked for tomorrow—heading into the Grayson Highlands with an expectation of clear weather. For some the stretch ahead is a favorite along the entire trail.

I hiked with Momma Llama a lot today. I can't kid myself that she's not the best part of this hike for me. I still have trouble dealing with that Midwestern toughness of hers, but I'm growing fond of it. Can a man my age fall for a woman the way young guys do? When my wife, Marina, died in 2000, it was after she got beat to a pulp by ovarian cancer—two major operations combined with chemotherapy and radiation. She fought and fought, but the truth we tried to avoid over the several years she battled was that she was not going to make it. After it got into her bones and killed her, I buried myself in work just to keep from turning into a drunk. It worked—barely. But since Marina faded away, I haven't had so much as a cup of coffee with a female, unless you count my sister—and I don't. I can't fool myself. I just don't know if I have the guts to stick my neck out.

May 1, Journal entry of Ultragrunge at Old Orchard Shelter

Wowie zowie, was today the best yet? I think so. It started weird, though. I took off late, trudging the long uphill to Buzzard Rock with a thru-hiking couple from the Czech Republic. She was a ballet artist, and a couple of times she stepped off the trail, removed her pack, planted one foot, bent sideways at the waist and pointed her other foot at the sky holding the position effortlessly for a few beats. Such a gorgeous sight!

When I gave her the goggle eye, she flashed a big Slavic smile and said, "This is how I stretch the moosles and leegaments." She and her husband are attempting 30 miles per day, and after commenting about how shocked they were at obesity in America, they disappeared up the trail.

I reached Buzzard Rock, a crag with grassy spots to relax on after the climb. Momma Llama was stretched out with her hands behind her head—pensive and disengaged. I left her alone with her thoughts, booked it over Whitetop Mountain, and scurried down to the road crossing at Elk Garden. A mob of scouts was about to head north from the parking lot. I stayed long enough to Yogi chocolate chip cookies—eager to pass the brats and enjoy the Highlands in solitude. From there, I walked through woods and ancient orchards to a junction with Mt. Rogers Trail. Mt. Rogers is the high point of Virginia, but I avoided the side trail, because the summit had no view.

Bone Festival caught me, and for 10 or so miles we shared the Eden of the A.T. I've hiked in Montana, and this place with its rocky peaks and open areas has that look. It even has herds of wild ponies, who nosed into our packs looking for handouts. Bone fed a quarter pound of gorp to a few of them. What a dolt—wasting calories on ponies! Miles flew by over rocky ridges down through wooded valleys and back over open mountain again. A 21-mile day that seemed half that.

When we got to Old Orchard Shelter, there was a puff of breeze wafting through, enough to dry sweat and discourage bugs. Bone and I cooked in his clunky aluminum pot: noodles, cheese, the last dregs of some liquid butter, 'shrooms, salmon and my personal potpourri of spices blended in—with liters of powdered fruit punch to wash it all down. I got sweet and washed Bone's pot for him. Later, as we stargazed in the grass near the shelter, Captain Stupid brought cigarettes. "I'm down to three a day," he said. "I'd quit altogether, but Gawd, they're good."

Bone and I are members of an elite international clique who smoke one cigarette a week without wanting more. Nicotine mingled with sugar, protein and fish fat. Divine decadent pleasure! I went to sleep with my head propped on Bone's leg. He woke me and gently steered me to my bag to write this and crash.

May 2, Journal entry of Bone Festival at Partnership Shelter

Maybe this is heaven. A clear sky with puffy clouds drifting like wisps of angel hair. No bugs. Temp is a dry 74. Nearly 25 miles today to Partnership Shelter, and we hustled so we'd have extra daylight. The shelter is overflowing with thru-hikers and section hikers, and there are two major bonuses:

1. We're a couple hundred yards from the headquarters of the Mt. Rogers National Recreation Area. From a phone there, hikers can order pizza to be delivered from nearby Marion. Brave Phillie bought pizza for all, and it must have cost him 150 bucks.
2. The shelter has a heated shower. I showered with my clothes on and then changed into town clothes while the trail clothes dried in the breeze.

I called the banjo guy in Abingdon, and he hopes to have it ready in a week or so. He said when it's finished he'll drive it to me. Sky has slipped away from me, but the worst of the pain has dissipated into numbness. She's excited about returning to Damascus to perform at Trail Days. I'll see that through and decide what's next.

May 3, Transcript of Captain Stupid recorded at Relax Inn in Atkins, Va.

Cruise control today—12 miles to Atkins, right on Interstate 81. A stretch of grassy hill walking with the Interstate popping in and out of sight and truck growls beating time to our silent strides. Most of us had food drops waiting at the Relax Inn, so the consensus was to cram into four double beds—one room for girls and one for beasts. Three showers in a week. We may get skin conditions from unaccustomed soap and water.

Yay!

Today a miracle occurred. I straggled in at the end of the pack and noticed Momma Llama and Brave Phillie at the motel in an animated conversation with—of all mortals on earth—Cousin Guilford. "Hey, Captain," BP drawled. "Your legendary cousin is here, and from what he tells me, I won't have to whip his double-dealing butt."

Guilford is a dumpy dweeb who couldn't hold his own with a miniature schnauzer. He was cowed by BP. He looked me over and gasped, "Man, there's a lot less of you."

I took my pack off and laid it next to the office door, fully aware of the drama and ready to use it to my best advantage. I tinkered with my gear, took my time and then stood tall and squinted at Guilford. "I see you have my Toyota," I noted.

His lower lip trembled like a three-year-old. I had no sympathy. Sputtering and snorting, he said Mom had tracked him down through my Aunt Matty (Guilford's mom). The two retired school teachers laid a guilt trip on Guilford that scalded his ears. They made him spell out the state of my finances. He had spent part of my hard-earned coin, but he still had more than $12,000 left, plus my old Corolla.

"I did what they told me," he whined. "I put all the money in your checking account, and your mom arranged to get you this debit card." He handed me the plastic. "I owe about $3,000, and Mom is going to make me live with her until I pay it back. They said to tell you I was sorry, too."

I have had the upper hand so few times in my life that it didn't occur to me to tie Guilford up in knots and toss him in a ditch. Instead I told him to go home, sell the car, and put the money in my account. I told him to get lost, and off he went.

Now I can hit an ATM and restore the bucks I've cadged from BP. I can continue this trip without relying on anyone else for cash, and restart my life. "You should've had that little turd arrested," Brave Phillie barked. I told him Aunt Matty got the job done for me. I didn't want to cause her additional grief. She'll see that Guilford flips burgers and slowly restores my stash.

Thirty days ago, Guilford's appearance would have been a revelation, a watershed, a sign from heaven that life was finally taking a positive turn. Today it wasn't all that big a deal. I can't gainsay a certain warm glow about being in the black again, but I didn't need this to know that I can make things work out for myself—things like finishing this trail, getting healthier, loving my friends and restarting my life.

Sky and I bask in late afternoon sun in the grass outside the ritzy Relax Inn. Later, we'll wander down to the C-store near the freeway ramp, and tomorrow, at a nearby restaurant, I'll treat my faithful companions to the biggest breakfast ever.

May 4, Journal entry of Linda Bennett at Chestnut Knob Shelter

Some voyager once said, "Travel is only glamorous in retrospect." Retrospect alone could find glamour in this day—24 miles in relentless rain to this four-walled mountaintop shelter. We gorged this morning on western omelets, pancakes, bacon, sausage, biscuits and grits with butter, syrup and white gravy—compliments of Captain Stupid's replenished coffers.

What we didn't know was that a perfect confluence of warm, wet air from the Gulf and a blast out of the Arctic were crashing together above us, producing high 40s with buckets of frigid rain. My theory on Gore-Tex is that it keeps you dry about 15 minutes longer than normal rain gear. Today was proof. We wandered through meadows and forests for hours, and the layers underneath our rain gear were soaked in sweat and rain that found its way down the backs of our necks and through badly sealed jacket seams.

When we kept moving, we stayed warm. When we stopped, our fingers were so numb it was difficult to undo waist buckles and sternum straps. The terrain was tame, and we made good time here to this mountaintop meadow called Chestnut Knob. Grunge and I squeezed in with the mob, but others were forced to perform that most miserable of all backpacking ordeals, setting up a tent or tarp in driving rain and unrelenting wind.

Now we're crammed in with other hikers—gear dangling from every peg and nail—everything dripping wet with a combined stench of sweaty bodies, mildewed clothes and gear, mouse urine, ramen noodles and whatever canned chicken or fish parts are blended with them. With this is a lullaby of tired voices, sibilant stoves, pounding rain and the rustling of damp fabric. I was hypothermic, so I asked the guys to be gentlemen and turn their backs while I got into a clean tee shirt and panties and hopped in my bag. In my old life, I would never have done that. I'll eat what would have been tonight's dinner for breakfast in the morning. No way I get out of this bag. Grunge and I are jammed together pointing in different directions to maximize space. A mouse scampered over my forehead. I was too tired to scream.

May 5, Journal entry of Blue Devil at Big Walker Motel in Bland, Va.

Section hikers at the shelter last night told me they're staying in Big Walker Motel, just off I-77 close to the A.T., and that they had a big church van parked at a road crossing 21 miles away and offered to ferry us to the motel tonight and slack us tomorrow and *they did not have to ask twice*, so I hooked up with the hotel on my cell phone and got their two remaining rooms, guaranteeing a dry roof over our heads after a long, wet hike under unrelenting precipitation causing flooding and washouts in the valley below.

Easy today—undulating at first and later following a road bed to the road crossing, although we had one stretch along a creek and through a rhododendron tunnel still gloriously in bloom where the trail was awash under the burden of six more inches of rain. This was not clear water. No, this was mud glopping in over our trail runners and turning feet into shriveled, muddy, moldy disaster areas.

Before we got to the Big Walker, the church guys dropped us at a Dairy Queen to gorge on burgers, rings, fries, cheesedogs and ice cream. I've got a major jones for the watermelon-flavored frozen drink. Captain Stupid warned that I risked a black stereotype, and I eyeballed him real hard and said, "Who are you, Paula Deen?" Captain caught the reference and guffawed.

We got the last rooms at the Big Walker. The place is crawling with NOBOs. No laundry, so everyone used the tub to rinse shoes, underwear and clothes, creating a gelatinous residue that may contain the primordial key to creation. Now I sit writing with one eye and keeping the other eye on CNN, which reports from time to time on the unprecedented rain settled in over the Appalachians. More days of misery ahead.

TRAIL WEATHER

hru-hikers will tell you that weather falls into a 50/50 friend and foe category. Few life experiences are more memorable than awakening in a dry shelter, packing your gear, having coffee and emerging onto a sunny trail right out of an old nature movie. A deer scrutinizes you from behind a will-o-the-wisp while a squirrel chatters from a treetop and a wren blathers mindlessly and gloriously. The sky is blue beyond blue. The clouds are swirling instruments—God's calligraphy. All's right with the world, and miles fly beneath your feet.

Here's the flip side: You awaken from a cold, wet night after a day of cold, wet hiking. You suck in your guts and put on cold, wet clothes that put you into the tooth-clicking shivering of hypothermia. Deciding it's too damn cold to boil water, you eat a vapid energy bar while you pull on soggy socks and spongy boots. You brace yourself to emerge from your tiny tent into a vicious rainstorm made more horrific by morning temps hovering in the mid-

40s. You strike and stuff your tent, but not before it gets plenty wet inside after you take off the fly. You walk down a trail saturated by days of rain, knowing your feet will soon be marinating in a witch's brew of rain, mud, newts and whatever else slops in. One or two days of this is bad enough, but when it goes on for days on end, morale begins to crack and erode. Many a long-distance hike has been killed by a ruthless rainstorm that continues for days. ■

May 6, Journal entry of Momma Llama at Dairy Queen in Bland, Va.

Our friends from the Methodist Church in Falls Church are so kind to lug us to the Big Walker for a second night of waiting our turn for showers, watching cable and scarfing bushels of junk food at the DQ. The Methodists have one of those vans that swallow 15 people and their gear. We repay by answering trail groupie questions. There are five of them—two adults and three teens. One of the boys has fallen for Linda, and she is sweet enough to show him attention and feed his puppy-dog fantasy. Today it rained harder. After 18 miles of wet foliage, slippery ridgetop rocks, and fresh blowdowns, we came to a suspension bridge over Kimberling Creek. The water rushed below like a freight train, with sufficient sound and fury to make me feel shaky.

I sit in the DQ in silent contemplation, soaked and muddy from the long day. Hunger pangs forced us to stop here before we hit the motel. Despite the distance we have managed over the past few days under the worst possible circumstances, I still feel like a wimp. I can't get Buzzard Rock off my mind. I can't bring myself to be an adult woman and face up to my aching heart.

May 7, Journal entry of Brave Phillie at Doc's Knob Shelter

I think I'm going to pray to new gods, even though I don't believe in them. I'm going to ask Zeus or Neptune or the Great Spirit or some such to stop this infernal rain. My regular "Father, Son and Holy Ghost" version is so worn out from making all this rain that He won't notice me taking my prayers elsewhere to turn off this faucet.

Our buddies from Falls Church dropped us off this morning before they headed home, and we stepped into steady rain. Except for a pretty good climb up Sugar Run Mtn., the terrain was easy. But when you're soaked to the bone and can't see the views, it just sucks. I saw Sky

Writer in tears when we stopped for lunch at Wapiti Shelter. The shelter kept the rain off, but given the cool air and the wet clothes, we ate fast and started walking again just to warm up. I've changed into my dry polypro skivvies and I'm settled into my bag after shivering through cooking dinner. I try to eat a candy bar before going to bed after a wet day to generate heat while I hunker down in my bag.

Momma Llama is nearby. It seems I'm on her mind as much as she's on mine. A few days back, I strolled up to her at Buzzard Rock ready for a little cheerful chat. I held my tongue when I saw her face. She looked thoughtful and had tears in her eyes. I'm the last guy to figure out a woman's mind, so I asked her what was wrong.

"I'm what's wrong," she said. She was up fast, donning her pack and heading like a bat out of Hades toward Whitetop Mtn. Suddenly I felt tears in my eyes too, but I had nobody but myself to ask why they were there. I didn't know for sure.

SUBJECT: **Jack and Jill take a tumble**
DATE: **May 8, 11:35 p.m.**
FROM: **Sky Writer** < singinghiker@yahoo.com >
TO: **Clara Spangler** < claraathome@att.net >

Oh, Mom, an awful day for the Bly Gap Gang. It should have been so nice—a short hike into Pearisburg and a zero day tomorrow. You know what they say about the best laid schemes of shelter mice and hiking men and women: Things often go totally awry.

We left Doc's Knob this morning—again in rain—headed for the Holy Family Catholic Church Hostel in Pearisburg. After all this rain and the big miles, we're physically and emotionally trashed. The forecast was for one more day of rain and then a big, dry front to push the clouds east and return cheerful spirits.

We were in tents last night. The shelter was mobbed. We had eight miles to Pearisburg, and we hustled to a long downhill where there was a dreary view of the little river city from a crag known as Angels Rest. I just wanted to clean up, dry out and rest for an entire day. I thought of pleasant things—food of course, but other things, like how much I wish you and I could talk into the wee hours, and whether or not I'll see Dad this year. Will he come ever back from Europe? He never emails.

Maybe that's what happened to Momma Llama—like me, spacing out on being through for the day and not watching her step. She's so strong that sometimes I forget she's older than you! (No offense, but she'll turn 60 soon.)

She and Brave Phillie were descending from Angels Rest, a steep downhill pitch planing off into switchbacks and leading to a paradise of showers, food, clean clothes and food . . . you get my drift. Momma Llama was on BP's heels in an area where the rainwater was running down the trail like a stream. She hit a slick spot and gravity threw her into a rotating fall. She glanced off BP, and he tried to catch her, but missed. The two of them tumbled like a human snowball until crashing to a stop, with hiking sticks and arms and legs and packs all intermingled—thru-hiker tossed salad.

They lay there with water flowing over and around them and silently took physical inventory. She was the first to get up, and except for a pretty good gash in her leg that later merited a big butterfly bandage, she got off with scrapes, bruises and lots of mud. BP stayed down, his right leg pulled up underneath him, and his foot hyperextended. She rolled him over to disentangle his sticks and his pack. He slowly stood up and attempted to put weight on the right foot. She said the moan he gave out and the look on his face told it all. His hike was severely waylaid—maybe trashed.

I've filled you in about how we think Momma and BP are in love but unable to articulate it. That all ended. Momma helped BP sit down and then they just put their arms around each other and cried and poured out all their feelings. She said the accident was all her fault, and he refused to accept that. He said he loved her, and one stupid fall would never change that. She said she loved him, and she'd see him through. They sat in the middle of a trail river embracing next to a cascading water bar.

When we found them, it was bittersweet. Brave Phillie, the grand poobah of the Bly Gap Gang, was on the disabled list. Our immediate concern was getting help for this seemingly invincible character who suddenly couldn't walk. Captain Stupid put BP's pack on his head and balanced it against his own pack. Off he went. Blue Devil and Bone put Brave Phillie in a cradle hold and toted him right down the trail, no easy task considering they were burdened by their own packs and dealing with slippery footing. Soon we muscular females insisted they shed their packs so we could carry them. All the while, Momma Llama flitted like a katydid in a futile effort to make things better.

At the first paved road, Captain Stupid successfully called the Holy Family Catholic Church hiker hostel for help. They said a retired parishioner would pick us up and help BP. After 20 minutes in the drizzle, sharing Powerade and lamenting our crummy luck, here came a minivan driven by Dr. Paul Podlesney, a retired physician, trail enthusiast and devout Catholic. We helped Brave Phillie into the van, and Momma hopped in with him. "I'll get them to a good doctor," he said. "Then I'll come back and get you. We've heard about the Bly Gap Gang!" Now we're at the hostel, showered and chauffered around like VIPs. Campbell Hollow has made minor celebs of us. I'll call tomorrow.

May 9, Journal entry of Doug Gottlieb at Holy Family Church, Pearisburg, Va.

I pulled into Pearisburg early after a 10-mile pull from Woods Hole Hostel. They were getting the hostel up and running for the NOBO surge, and I stopped by, seeking company. Tillie Wood from Roswell, Ga., used to run this place until she passed on, but family and volunteers keep it running.

When Tillie's husband, Roy, was doing an elk study for the government back in 1939, the Woods stumbled across this Virginia property and made it theirs. Some years back, they turned it into a haven for A.T. hikers. This morning, five other NOBOs and I enjoyed homemade biscuits, scrambled eggs, and bacon—all for a nominal contribution.

Tracking shelter registers, I figured to meet the Bly Gap Gang in Pearisburg today. What I couldn't predict were the long faces. Brave Phillie is down and out. Doctors can't provide a clear diagnosis until swelling subsides to allow an MRI, but even best case will have him off the trail for a while. He and Momma Llama were sitting on a bench outside the hostel when I arrived, and they hugged me like a prodigal son.

Everyone else is having a typical, albeit cheerless, zero day. BP and Momma Llama called a meeting to tell us there had been a meeting of minds and hearts between them. Now that they understand each other, they're blissful, despite the injuries. They've decided the Gang should continue, Momma Llama included, and that Brave Phillie will return to Georgia for rehab. He'll get back when he can. After we hit Katahdin, Momma Llama will go back with him to the section he missed, and they'll hike it together. That sounds simple enough, but continuing without BP won't be easy. They had to have a serious accident to figure out they're in love.

I have a problem of my own. My high school basketball knee injury is flaring up. Ibuprofen helps, but I need to take a zero day and ice it.

Linda was surprisingly demonstrative when I arrived, giving me a big hug and acting thrilled to see me. When I told her I would not be leaving with them tomorrow, I could see her disappointment. It's almost enough to make me skip the zero, bad knee and all.

May 10, Journal entry of Ultragrunge at Pine Swamp Branch Shelter

I was a lean, mean struttin' machine as I hiked out of Pearisburg and assaulted the climb up Peters Mtn. Blue sky, dry air. Rested and recharged. I broke into a trot up the mountain—not smart, but I was in the zone. The farther I went, the more I wanted it. At the top of the ridge, I assaulted the level crest until I reached Rice Field Shelter and took a breather after jogging full pack for nearly eight miles.

This wasn't enough, so after rehydrating and eating a Power Bar and jerky, I double-timed to Symms Gap. I understand the attraction of trail running. I devoted all my mental and physical faculties to the constant cadence, the ebb and flow of dovetailing my moving body with the obstacles of the trail—climbs, rocks, roots, blowdowns, descents—a new element in my inventory of trail experiences that I would not tell my friends about. They'd scold me for taking chances.

I couldn't stop. The trail always had something waiting as I glided along with the forest looming up, bobbing beside me and falling behind—ageless, triumphant, resounding with the glory of song birds and the explosive appearance of startled deer.

After more than 20 miles, I pulled into Pine Swamp Branch Shelter early in the day, first person there. I disappeared in the woods with bio-suds and canteen water to get naked and thoroughly clean and rinse. I washed out my nylon shorts and my Mt. Rogers Outfitters tee shirt and put them on to air-dry.

Before the Bly Gap Gang and other NOBOs began to arrive, I cooked a special meal with chicken, pimento, ramen, my personal spice mix and a couple of wine coolers I carried for the first day. I felt guilty having fun in the wake of the Brave Phillie letdown, but when Momma Llama arrived hours later looking serene and rockin' a beatific smile—hey—it's okay for a girl to have fun.

May 11, Journal entry of Bone Festival at Laurel Creek Shelter

You never realize how much you love something until you lose it and get it back. Perry Shellenberger, my friendly banjo repair guy, showed up at Holy Family Hostel with my pride and joy perfectly repaired. As I played, he seemed so pleased that he refused money. Just the same, I paid him with cash freshly puked from a Pearisburg ATM. So much trail magic! I decided to name the banjo "Twangin' Perry."

Sky and I crooned a medley of favorites. The Bly Gap Gang, other hikers and a few parishioners gathered to listen and join in. Sky sang a Ferlin Husky classic, "Wings of a Dove."

Since leaving Pearisburg in perfect weather, we've stopped countless times to sing. We'd forgotten how much Twangin' Perry added. Brave Phillie promised to come in a week or so and take us back to Damascus for Trail Days, so Sky and I are anxious to see if we can knock 'em dead with our sound.

After a few miles, we had a long climb up to a typical Virginia ridge walk. It took us to Wind Rock for a leisurely lunch and more music. The view was special, because there is so little haze. Linda sang an old Beatles tune, "Blackbird," I'd not heard in forever. Her voice was clear and unselfconscious, causing me to wonder why I hadn't heard her sing before. Maybe she's intimidated by Sky's talent.

Tonight I mixed precooked pouch hamburger with wild rice. Captain Stupid, king of freeze-dried, shared raspberry crumble, a gloppy mess in a pouch. We passed it person to person, one sporkful at a time.

May 12, Transcript of Captain Stupid recorded at Audie Murphy Monument

Momma Llama knows who he is, and Brave Phillie would be all over the whole Audie Murphy thing, seeing as how Audie was the most decorated combat hero in WWII. I know who Audie Murphy is, too. A lazy lard who lives with his mom and goes rubberkneed at the thought of female company spends countless hours wearing out a La-Z-Boy and watching Turner Classic Movies. Audie Murphy is no stranger to me, although he is to the younger members of this group, except for Blue Devil who vaguely remembered something about the movie *To Hell and Back.*

Yay!

Anyway, poor Audie died somewhere nearby in 1971 when the plane he was in—lost in fog—crashed into this very ridge. We hiked 18 miles to get here and set up a bootleg camp. A little monument is off on a side trail. If you have to die violently, this is as good a place as any, a quiet Virginia ridgetop.

After all the recent wind and rain, there's a surfeit of blowdown wood, and Bone collected a few healthy armfuls. We've stuck with "leave no trace" ethics on this trip, but we found a nice little fire ring and will make the best of it. I'll emcee a fireside trivia challenge this evening.

May 13, Journal entry of Linda Bennett at McAfee Knob

I've seen intriguing pictures of the Knob, so I was off and running this morning to get there this p.m.—over 20 miles. Typical Virginia hiking with a few climbs to stretch your legs, past field and farm and a little level ridge-walking. I think of motorists below looking up at the long ridges and wondering what it would be like to be walking them as I do.

I hiked with Bone today. If he's not singing, he's talking. If it's solitude you have in mind, he's not your man. It's like minding a frisky Labrador pup. Everything's a revelation! Each bend in the trail is not just more mileage—it's an *opportunity*! Blue Devil is much the same. For a recent high school grad, he has a vast store of knowledge and a compulsion to share it. So diverse is his brilliance that he can't decide whether to major in engineering, literature or poli-sci. He is eminently informed. Unlike Bone, Blue Devil has blessed spells of brooding silence.

By design, most of my hike has been alone. I know my trees and flowers, and I've gotten better with birds. I keep my eyes open. I dig being *totally alone*. I talk without moving my lips. I pretend to be a reporter interviewing novelists, philosophers, Henry Thoreau, Fiona Apple or Barack Obama. I make up dialogue for movies and create characters. I walk with a blank mind and rest my brain. When I finish, I'll long for the luxury of aloneness. Surely I will rarely have this many more times in my life.

Bone and I used our early start and the pleasant cloudy day to move fast to Dragons Tooth. Leave it to Bone to whip out his banjo and start working through melody and lyrics for a ditty called, of course, "Dragons Tooth." I climbed up it as high as I dared.

Then a scramble down through a farm valley and an unintentional sprint to the Knob. I say unintentional, because some days you don't try to hike fast. It just happens. McAfee Knob is a big rock slab jutting straight out of a cliff where I was photographed dangling my legs over the void. We idly waited for our friends and dug the view. I carried water in, so it was easy to toss together an early supper and relax with *Unbroken*.

NOBOs, including Bly Gappers, clowned for photos. A couple of NOBOs we'd never seen, Skeeter and Gnat, clasped hands and leaned over the edge, sheer lunacy. Everyone straggled off to Pig Farm Campsite, as camping is taboo at the Knob. I stayed behind, gambling on a rainless night. I'll sleep illegally under the stars and watch lights twinkle in the valley. I write by headlamp, and a few minutes ago I heard that most thrilling of all sounds—a screeching bobcat!

SUBJECT: Livin' high on the hog
DATE: May 14, 4:30 p.m.
FROM: < chunkyhiker@yahoo.com >
TO: < Lizcopeland754@aol.com >

I notice from today's ATM receipt that my balance has gone up. I guess ol' Guilford is sticking to the plan to restore my vast wealth. Mom, because of you, I'm lifting myself out of a self-dug pit of personal shame. By the time I get home, you'll be proud.

As for here and now, we're suffering cable/fast-food/hot-shower/laundry deprivation, and this interstate crossing is one of the best places on the A.T. to indulge our most obscene appetites. I walked off the trail near Interstate 81 and proceeded right to the Hojo to clean up and head for the swimming pool—just opened!

Yay!

I remain self-conscious about my body. But in less than two months, I have gone from morbidly obese to a run-of-the-mill fat guy with muscle tone in my legs. Blue Devil and Bone Festival joined me in the full bloom of their sculpted physiques and roared approval as I nearly emptied the pool with a bodacious cannonball. The girls came jogging out in shorts and sports bras and caught the attention of every red-blooded male HOJO customer in sight.

Big news! Brave Phillie and Monopod tracked us down and will slack us over the next few days and then take us to Trail Days back in Damascus. BP's physical therapist has him on a rehab that should have him back on the trail about a week into June. He and Monopod flew up from Atlanta to Roanoke and rented a giant van. When BP limped up to poolside, Momma Llama left no doubt about the authenticity of what's going on between them, when she jumped his bones and laid a big smack right on his lips.

Today we followed ridges early to Tinker Cliffs and wandered along an escarpment. Sky Writer and I stopped on a ledge and gazed like contented sheep into the farm valley. It was one of those days when cloud cover and barometric pressure do magic things to sound. We heard a brother and sister squabbling about who was supposed to do chores around the farmhouse. They were a mile or two away, but their voices carried with uncanny clarity. I hollered deeply and with perfect diction: "Divide your duties fairly!"

There was a long, comic interval. The brother said: "Did you hear that?" I responded: "This is God. I command you to cooperate."

Again, a hilarious pause. Then both kids went screaming into the house crying, for their mom. The final sound was a slamming screen door from far below. I thought Sky was going to rupture her obliques she laughed so hard. Ah, Mom, there is nothing sweeter than the sound of Sky's laughter.

May 15, Journal entry of Momma Llama at the Hojo in Daleville, Va.

My upcoming birthday is a secret, but everyone knows I will soon hit 60, long since eligible for AARP membership, but not for Social Security or Medicare. I am in amazing health (great body weight-to-fat ratio), and I am independently wealthy thanks to a law degree from Northwestern and 35 years of shrewd investing.

Could a woman be more carefree and self-assured than I? Who am I kidding? I have lost control of my heart, my feelings and my carefully established plans. I have proclaimed my love for a man so overwhelmingly divergent from myself that my head spins. His politics are career-military, free-market, pull-yourself-up-by-your-bootstraps right-wing, whereas I cut my teeth as a Gene McCarthy Democrat. He believes in multiple use of public lands; I am committed to federally designated wilderness.

But this cold, feminist heart has opened up to the fact that love finds a way to ignore politics, ideology, gender friction and just about every other prejudice. I still am independent in my mind and my soul, but I love Brave Phillie as much as ever. And it is clear that this jaded jarhead loves me, too.

Content in this life vision, I joined my friends this morning back on the trail and slacked 20 miles to a predetermined spot on the Blue Ridge Parkway where Monopod and BP met us and zipped us back to the Hojo. Brave Phillie treated us all to Tex-Mex just across the highway!

Then, while Monopod and the youngsters enjoyed hot showers and HBO, BP and I sat in pool chairs, speaking freely and openly past midnight. No commitments, no conditions. The only plan is that he will rejoin us when he can and hike to Katahdin. Then we'll return to Pearisburg and finish up his thru-hike. After that, whatever. He said that after we fell, and after we looked each other in the eye and owned up to the truth, he can let go of the pain of Marina's death and allow me in.

May 16, Journal entry of Sky Writer at Hojo in Daleville, Va.

At Hojo, basking in Brave Phillie's largesse for the third night. Slacking by day, grazing on the lush life by night. We managed a score of miles today, despite rain and mist. Bone hiked with me, and we *reeeaaally* communicated. I mean we have been talking and singing and getting along okay, but today he asked about where I'm heading and how he factors in. I told him our music still hangs together. He thinks that musically, he is nothing without me—a silly notion that I tried to dispel. We really look forward to singing for the crowd in Damascus at Trail Days.

Then he asked what's going on with me and the Captain. I told him what I've told no other soul, not even Captain Stupid: that I love the Captain very deeply. For a while, I thought it was because he helped pull me out of my depression after Campbell Hollow Road. But now it goes way beyond that. I can't imagine such an unlikely match. Captain Stupid has never so much as hinted that we could have a life together. He is terrified of rejection due to a life overwhelmed by turndowns.

Serious climbing today on graded trail. Slackpacking doesn't eliminate the drudgery from the 3,000 feet of climbing it took to crest out on Apple Orchard Mtn. Not far from there was a classic spot called the Guillotine, where a big rock is wedged in a crevice right over the trail. How many pictures have been taken here of hikers looking up at the big boulder as if it's destined to crash down on them? Bone and I took exactly this shot and then walked to the Parkway, where BP and Monopod took us to the overwhelming luxury of Hojo. Momma Llama and Brave Phillie remember when Howard Johnson was a national restaurant chain known for offering multiple flavors of ice cream. We Millenials think of it a place to shower and sleep.

May 17, Journal Entry of Ultragrunge at Buena Vista, Va., Hotel

Tonight we're in a mom and pop motel in Buena Vista (pronounce that first word Beeyoona) and planning to hit a local barbecue joint later. Since we're taking a couple of zero days to go to Damascus, we decided to do a real ovary buster today. We went so far—nearly 26 miles—that we actually passed four shelters, stopping near mile point 51.7 on the Blue Ridge Parkway. To me the parkway is an annoying chunk of asphalt designed for lardbutts to see the mountains from the comfort of air-conditioned gas guzzlers. The only good I see is that it makes slacking more convenient.

We didn't see much for the second day in a row—rain and fog. We're closing in on June, but I still get cold on windy, rainy days. We had a long descent down to the James River, where we crossed on a footbridge and came to the realization that we are way past one-third of this little outing. The water swirled muddy and murky, and we braced for a long, wet slog back out of the river valley. It's great to get slacked in the rain, knowing that BBQ, beer and showers are at the end of the day, instead of pre-packaged sludge, soggy sleeping bags and inquisitive rodents.

I hiked with Blue Devil, who wanted the scoop on my post-trail plans. I told him I have one more semester at UT. I love Austin, but I won't stay there forever. I did the A.T. thing right before wrapping up college to avoid making abrupt decisions. He has lost much of his enthusiasm for Duke and wants to do the Pacific Crest Trail next year. I told him to relax and just start Duke. With his keen mind, he'll love the intellectual discourse. The PCT will still be there.

I'm blah about going back to Damascus. Taking time off blurs my karma.

May 18, Journal entry of Blue Devil at Damascus, Va.—Trail Days

It was surprising how long it took to drive back to Damascus seeing as how it's only been a couple or three weeks since we hiked out of there, and when you travel back by car, it's astounding to contemplate the sheer number of steps we've taken to get so far up into Virginia, away from the Tennessee border and Damascus. It was cloudy today, and we hiked in and out of mist until getting to a forest service road before noon, where Monopod and Brave Phillie were smoking stogies and sharing spirits—two old coots swapping dirty jokes and lies about the conquests of their misspent youths.

Doug caught us. He knew from the grapevine that we were slacking and doing town time, but he just kept hiking full pack until catching us to grab the Damascus Express. He's one of us and a hero to boot for taking a gun butt across the head. On the road to Damascus, we made two stops, one to converge on a laundromat and another to resupply with goodies to get us to Waynesboro after we start hiking again.

Trail Days got into full swing this morning, and our main goal was to cram into Tent City by dark, check out the lay of the land, and allow Sky and Bone to locate the people they'll be singing with tomorrow night. This place is packed and pretty squishy, seeing as how there has been wet weather, but we're no strangers to scraping mud off our footwear before crawling into our tents for the night.

Momma Llama says Tent City is the hiking community's version of Woodstock Nation—like-minded freaks oblivious to mud and rain and ready to share community before going back to the "normal" life. She and I took in the displays, free food samples, lectures, and finally the spaghetti dinner at the firehouse followed by hand-churned ice cream. Momma can totally ingest.

I watched a peppy country band and then broke away to stretch out under my tarp. It is loud and crowded here, and I miss my hip-hop. I feel a bit excluded. Regrettably, thru-hiking is—with few exceptions—a caucasian-centric activity. People eye me as a curiosity. One guy cluelessly asked, "What made you think you would enjoy this?" I did what my Mom taught me and just smiled and said, "I guess the same thing that made you think you would."

Trail Days is an unaccustomed cacophony. So much noise! Such a jumble of odd foods mixed in my belly! I liked Damascus better the first time.

May 19, Journal entry of Doug Gottlieb at Damascus, Va.—Trail Days

My tarp didn't set up well in the muddy spot I picked. Wind and rain blew through last night, and I wound up with my sleeping bag exposed to rain. I slept as best I could and finally got up to wring out the water. Linda stirred nearby in her Zoid. I offered to escort her to the free showers down at the Baptist Church and treat her to breakfast. I speculated that the Baptists were surreptitiously using free showers to baptize us—a chance I was willing to take in exchange for the pleasure of hot water and soap. Linda said she was Episcopalian and had been "sprinkled" as a child, obviating the need for further ritual. I told her I was Presbyterian and had been similarly spiritually inoculated.

Linda emerged with her wet hair loose and unkempt. I once saw an old publicity photo of Grace Kelly in water up to collarbone level with her hair wet and plastered against her scalp. Few women have the facial features to withstand such scrutiny. Linda has an unspoiled, unaffected face and figure that look good effortlessly. I felt proud walking down Laurel Avenue with her by my side. I treated her to a breakfast biscuit and coffee at the Dairy King and sat outside on the curb with a couple of NOBOs, Manatee and Margaritaville, both from Florida.

Such guiltless pleasure to roam around this carnival of hikers and not have to *hike*. We found ourselves at an A.T. slide presentation set to music and narrated by Warren Doyle, who set a speed record for the trail in 1973 and then went on to hike it umpteen more times in umpteen different ways. Doyle is a man with strong opinions who draws more than his share of controversy. He laces his remarks with homespun advice such as "Flow with the trail" and "Leave your emotional 'fat' at home."

Trail Days is a moveable feast. We grazed through free food at several sponsored exhibits and activities, culminating in hot dogs and lemonade. Then we went to the parade, which Linda likened to a "poor man's Mardi Gras." Hikers had scrounged dayglo costumes, psychedelic hats, moonshiner outfits, giant clown shoes. Hikers and spectators pelted one another with howitzer-sized squirt guns. Sky, Captain Stupid and Blue Devil clobbered us with water balloons. Our only consolation was the absurd awareness that all this was happening in a light rain!

We wandered back to Tent City and lounged beneath my tarp with free energy bars, free peanuts, free saltwater taffy and free beverages. With her legs scratched by brambles, her odd tan lines and her hair casually unkempt, Linda had absolutely every excuse to look terrible, but she was as beautiful as ever. I decided to take Warren Doyle's advice and "flow" with the moment. No dumb remarks, no effort to be clever, no attempt to be smooth, glib, erudite or urbane. I just hoped she wouldn't vanish. She did not.

May 20, Journal entry of Bone Festival on the road back from Damascus, Va.

A listless crew heads back to where we left off near Buena Vista—a little hungover, ready to mosey north. Monopod drives wordlessly, and everyone else but me is dozing. Sky and I rehearsed yesterday with The Blue Grass Smokers—authentic bluegrass artists with reverence for the Bill Monroe legacy. They loved Sky and were thrilled to use her superb talent, and my modest skills, in the middle of their long set.

They embraced "Amicalola," and "Wings of a Dove." They taught us an original song—"Damascus Breakdown"—a chance for my banjo skills. They claimed it was a pleasure to have authentic heroes on stage with them. We were introduced as "the members of the Bly Gap Gang who heroically defended the integrity of the trail at Campbell Hollow Road." The crowd roared.

Before the evening gig and after the parade, we performed at the talent show. I picked and Sky sang "White Horse," a little something pieced together over many trail miles:

> Bring me eight white horses as pretty as you please,
> right up to my front porch! Bring those eight white steeds
> to try to please me. You could sure do a whole lot worse.

> Bring a string of pearls as pretty as you please,
> white as the moon up high. Put 'em round my neck
> in the the thin moonlight and see love light in my eyes!

> Bring a white Cadillac as pretty as you please,
> folks'll come from near and far just to see how hard
> you try to please me with a fluid-drive Cadillac car!

> Bring a sweet, dewy peach as pretty as you please,
> sliced up with sugar and milk. Just watch and see,
> 'cause I'll be more pleased than if it was diamonds or silk.

> Bring me your fine self looking pretty as you please,
> you know how fine you be. And 'cause you know
> how you stop 'em in their tracks you'll never be the one for me.
> Yeah, it's 'cause you know how you stop 'em in their tracks,
> you'll never be the one for me!

The only extraneous sounds were birds singing, a car horn or two, and some generators in the distance. The A.T. Nation gazed adoringly while listening to her show-stopping voice. I can never have her, but at least I get to accompany her.

Blue Devil did standup. He went into his urban persona and played up being a thru-hiker of color. "Never mind y'all that I've never been to Africa. Never mind that my dad is about one-quarter Seminole. Never mind that my mother has a ton of cream in her coffee an' a little Far East. And never mind that I haven't actually thru-hiked yet. Chillen, I am still an African-American thru-hiker, and you better show me respect, cuz after I get to Katahdin, I'm going to Duke University and learn how to be an African American *in-tel-lec-tu-al*! If that doesn't work for ya, I'll bitch slap you from here back to Hump Mtn." Then he did a riff on privies. Someday I'll be his warmup.

May 21, Journal entry of Linda Bennett at Priest Shelter

Two days off have recharged our batteries. We kicked off early from U.S. 60 with a 2,000 foot climb—not to mention a collection of PUDs all the way to Priest Shelter—around 21 miles. We cruised through our first day back in full packs with true aplomb. Pain is at a minimum, and Doug's trick knee is behaving.

Bly Gap Gang was charged with emotion as we bade farewell to Brave Phillie and Monopod. BP promises to get back soon, noting that he is walking almost normally with minimal pain. He hopes to meet us at Harpers Ferry. What stood out today is how good it is to be back after two zero days. I spent time with Grunger, lazing at Spy Rock. This may be one of the last days with weather so cool and clear. As we bear down on June, the haze will get worse and worse.

Priest Shelter is full tonight, so I'm under the stars. A man and woman appeared at the shelter not long after we pulled up, and we suspected they were day hikers. They were dressed in crisp outfits fresh out of a Land's End catalog and carried tiny packs. After closer inspection, we saw that their trail shoes had seen action similar to ours. They were indeed thru-hikers—trail names Stick Figure (her) and Bilbo (him). They started 18 days after we did and are burning up trail. We tossed a ton of queries at them such as: How do you stay so fresh while moving so fast? How much do those little packs weigh?

It turned out that they have a system that allows them to share lots of equipment. They have a half-pound tarp and a tiny ground cloth, no sleeping pads (leaves under the ground cloth suffice, they say), alcohol tablet stove, hardly any extra clothes (they wash their clothes once a day and wear them as they air-dry) and nylon shells—no sleeping bags. Minus food and water, their loads are about seven pounds apiece. He shaves nearly every day, and she washes her hair about the same. They plan to do the Pacific Crest next year and the Continental Divide the next. Averaging 25 miles per day, including zero days, comes easily to them. They kept going past the Priest and headed for Harpers Creek. Since they started this morning at Brown Mtn. Creek Shelter, that means they were putting in 30 miles for the day. I am humbled.

May 22, Transcript of Captain Stupid recorded at Maupin Field Shelter

With incalculable pride, I acknowledge the reputation as the laziest thru-hiker of them all. I know that anyone hiking 15 miles per day is not lazy per se, but there are degrees of reticence among our ranks. I proclaim myself the champion of that most popular of the seven deadly sins (except maybe lust), and that would be sloth.

Yay!

How did I garner this hard-won status? Simple: I do not walk one step more than necessary. I am determined to hike the entire trail, mind you, but when others will go a mile or two offtrail to see a waterfall, I stay on the straight and narrow of the A.T., always eschewing side trips. I often get water at trailside sources to avoid the trip to springs at the end of the day. Some shelters are located right on the ridge, meaning the nearest spring may be a quarter mile or more away and a couple hundred vertical feet down, *which must be reclimbed*. I avoid this whenever possible.

A good example came today, after we descended to the Tye River. Where the trail crosses the Tye, a side trip is available to a swimming hole. Everyone else headed for it, but Sky and I freshened up where the trail crossed the river and kept going. We ascended about 3,000 feet over six miles, with nice views over the valley back to the Priest, finally reaching the highest of the Three Ridges, where we looked down on a vineyard in the Tye River Valley. Then we hiked downhill toward Maupin Field Shelter.

Just before we got to the shelter, we met an eccentric chap in baggy jeans, a filthy tee shirt commemorating a 2005 tour by Judas Priest, and shoes that looked like Salvation Army culls. His pack was seedy, as was the rest of his gear. He had a goatish beard and long, greasy hair—an unsavory customer, but his need to talk was compelling. He had started at Harpers Ferry, and said that most people he meets don't like him. "Hike your own hike," Sky said. "Find some peace. Resist the anger."

From some, this would have sounded condescending, but Sky exudes sincerity. The fellow seemed honored that such a woman would show empathy for him.

He told us he was subsisting on peanuts and water. Sky warned that this diet was a recipe for disaster, and she explained some of the basics of carbs, protein and fat. He gazed at her—falling in love as most men do when they meet her—absorbing little of what she said. He said when he caught up with hikers, he often got off the trail and walked beside them for long periods, crashing through the underbrush while keeping pace. "It seems to annoy everyone," he said.

I noted that his behavior might be construed as creepy. I suggested he politely ask to pass. That would make people friendlier. He thanked us for making his outlook brighter, but we were dubious as we watched him walk away with an eccentric, jerky stride.

We arrived at Maupin Field Shelter and discussed the possibility of a side trip to Rusty's Hard Time Hollow. Sky was for it. I—in my typical state of lassitude—was against the idea. Rusty's is a fabled spot off the trail near the Blue Ridge Parkway rumored to have a sauna, a hot tub, showers and handmade signs with homespun witticisms. The argument ended when Sky scoped the shelter register and noted that Hard Time Hollow was shut down while Rusty handled personal business.

Rusty's sounds like a hoot. Fans describe it vividly in the register. It features an outdoor trough urinal with a bullseye for male-only target practice. It has a hand-painted wooden cutout profile of a little urinating boy in a feathered cap next to a sign stating:

> Piss Here—Not In The Yard.
> It Kills The Grass.

May 23, Journal entry of Momma Llama at Paul C. Wolfe Shelter

Maupin Field Shelter was crammed with a youth group last night. We tented nearby, with all the disadvantages of the ill-supervised brats and none of the advantages of the shelter. When we broke camp at our customary early hour, I chuckled at Bone and Doug, who kept strolling over to the shelter where the rabble-rousers from last night were sleeping late. "Hey guys!" Bone shouted, "Have you seen a left-handed handball glove? In all the confusion last night, I think I left it in there." Long pause, and a response: "What's a handball glove?"

"Oh, never mind," Bone said. "It's in my pocket."

Before we pulled out, Bone and Doug stood in front of the shelter and sang: "Many brave hearts lie asleep in the deep!" It was blissful watching the slack-jawed kids gaping out of their sleeping bags at what turned out to be pretty decent two-part harmony.

I felt a little pain in my heel today, never a good sign. Then, magic. The last time I felt serious heel pain was south of Max Patch in North Carolina when I made the first bear sighting of the trip. It made my pain vanish. It happened again. Five or six miles in, not far from a fine view at Cedar Cliff, I had a premonition that I was under scrutiny. I turned slowly to my right, and there was a yearling bear whose head turned in concert with mine just in time to meet my gaze. Startled, he vanished in the late-spring greenery. Another solitary sighting, another rush of dopamine, another emotional high—just like last time. When I made it to the cliffs and was enjoying the view, the pain was gone. Bears do that for me. I am Momma Llama, sow queen of the bear women.

Tenting at the crowded Paul Wolfe Shelter tonight. Bone and Blue Devil continued to Rockfish Gap for a zero day tomorrow. Oh, this weather is so fine!

SUBJECT: Blue Devil's Conquest
DATE: May 24, 4:28 p.m.
FROM: < banjomania@yahoo.com >
TO: < prettylittlething22@gmail.com >

Linda: How's my most favorite and onliest sister, and how are things in Boulder? Mom says your final semester is going swimmingly and that you soon will match older brother in earning a college degree. My business major is much more marketable than yours in education. Look how rich I'm gettin', baby sis!

I'm online at the library in Waynesboro. Mom says things are cool in Denver and that you were home last weekend carousing with Jeff. She really likes Jeff, so you must hate him now. She also said Molly McMahon has been inquiring about me, so you can bet she'll be getting my next email, a major signal that things with Sky Writer remain Platonic. I still love to sing with that girl, I'm telling you!

Mom and Dad remain as detached as ever. I don't claim to be some conquering hero just because I'm hiking this trail, but you'd think they might show a tad more interest. They act like I'm doing an internship with Walmart or something.

Blue Devil and I hiked long and hard yesterday to make it into Waynesboro, a comfy trail town. After a quick hitch to the Post Office, we found new shoes among the letters and packages. Since we wear the same brand of trail shoe, we called the company 800 number a week ago and told them we were A.T. thru-hikers whose shoes were wearing out. The result: brand-new footwear waiting at the P.O. I could stand on a mosquito in my old shoes and identify its gender. I was showing sock.

We checked into a church hostel and got spiffed up like rose buds before strolling to Kroger. We met Indu Patel, a checkout girl, and I'm telling you, this chick is a blossom of young Indian female pulchritude. The pheromones were interacting big time. In about two seconds of conversation, it was clear that she likes hikers and she truly digs Blue Devil. He thoroughly reciprocated. Indu's shift ended in 15 minutes, so we hung around and were rewarded by her smiling face, delightfully accented perfect English, and her ratty Civic, which she placed at our disposal. She's going to the University of Virginia next semester and is rooming in cheap digs here in Waynesboro—working at Kroger in the interim. Since three was a crowd, I came to the library. I'll eventually hit the hostel and watch movies, but first, I'll send a provocative email to Molly McMahon

May 25, Journal entry of Sky Writer at Waynesboro, Va.

We followed Blue Devil and Bone this morning and had no trouble getting rides into Waynesboro. I got my business handled and wound up at the hostel where Bone was on part two of the *Godfather* trilogy with a couple of NOBOs we've seen a few times, a man and a woman named Chewing Gum and Baling Wire. When we met them in the Smokies, they planned to hike fast to Maine. Now they've decided to savor the experience and hike slower.

This brought up the topic of trail names, those little tags we pin on ourselves to identify our varied personalities as we walk north from Springer. It has been a heretofore unspoken rule with the Bly Gap Gang that we don't share our real names unless we want to. Obviously, Doug and Linda have not yet tagged themselves. Linda hinted in Hot Springs that she would come up with one by Damascus. Now she says she'll try to decide on one in Harpers Ferry, and we all made it clear that one will be chosen for her if she isn't careful. She is well aware that Brave Phillie loves to pick trail names—Ultragrunge for example—so now's the time to take action. Anyway, *The Godfather* Part II ended, and the topic of trail names and real names began. Here's what I know:

- Bone Festival's name is Charles "Charlie" Crown. No one else knows that.
- Only Bone knows I'm Joy Spangler.
- Momma Llama told us that she and Brave Phillie want to keep on a trail-name-only basis. I guess their real names will emerge on Katahdin.
- Captain Stupid has told only me that "the name of that fatter and uglier person is unimportant."
- Ultragrunge and Blue Devil ain't sayin'.

We tried to come up with the consensus favorite trail name, and surprisingly we agreed on one. Back north of Pearisburg we caught a middle-aged NOBO who had started a week ahead of us. His trail name was Three Weeks and Four Days. When his wife dropped him off at the Approach Trail to Springer, her last words to him were, "Three weeks and four days. That's how long before you quit."

"I'm showing the old broad how much she knows, don't you think?" he asked.

TRAIL NAMES

Who knows where they started? Possibly with Earl Shaffer's "Crazy." Some are predictable and derivative. Since the '60s, J.R.R. Tolkien has inspired a boatload of Bilbos, Frodos, an Orc or two, and, of course, Striders. A slew of hikers have chosen Mountain Man and Bear. Another, carrying forth an old nickname, is known as Catfish.

Others allude to a trail experience: Tortilla Tosser, Bag of Tricks, Bustace, Gallopin' Trots. And because hikers are underfed and poorly hydrated, food and beverage factor in: Swiss Cheese, All You Can Eat, Spork, Miller Time, and Big Maguro (Japanese for tuna). Still others come from school or pro team names: Blue Devil, Brave Phillie.

Erotic suggestion often plays into the selection of trail monikers. Instrument of Pleasure, Slinky Minx, Sexy Beast, Bone Festival and the immortal Orgasmatrail.

Some are inexplicable, or ethereal: Sky Writer, Crazy Uncle. Two names are the basis for a great A.T. chronicle, When Straight Jacket Met Golden

Sun. *One hiker named himself after an old Transformers toy, Optimus Prime, while another was dubbed Steady to characterize the even keel of her personality. Place of origin is common: the legendary and beloved Baltimore Jack. A veteran back from Iraq was Free Hugs.*

Trail names are whimsical. They equip travelers with an alternate persona as they enter the portal into the parallel universe that is the Appalachian Trail. ▪

7

Shenandoah, the Return of Brave Phillie and the "Challenge"

May 26, Journal entry of Ultragrunge at Blackrock Hut

Butter, pancakes, sausage, orange juice and coffee this morning. I even ate grits. God Bless Weasie's, the type of little café we adore. I stayed away from biscuits and gravy, which seem unusually unhealthy. Momma Llama says don't believe people who say a hot oven burns any fuel. Her credo is that no matter how many calories you burn, you still need nutrition in addition to the high-calorie town crap we eat. She says a lot of things.

Anyway, late start out of Waynesboro, but we didn't have to hitch. Blue Devil's new squeeze, Indu, took us up to Rockfish Gap in two loads. We witnessed a sappy farewell between BD and Indu with unabashed rudeness and a couple of old-fashioned wolf whistles from the Captain and Brave Phillie. She promises to reappear in Front Royal.

We self-registered before entering Shenandoah, which means we have an itinerary for five days. I packed light, assuming I can get that rarest of delights, town food on the trail. Easy grub is convenient at a few spots in Shenandoah.

No shock we're tenting tonight. After 20 miles, we found Blackrock Hut packed to the gills. The trail is nicely graded, making for unnoticeable climbs. Tonight water is close and plentiful. We finally met Flautist, who's been ahead of us for weeks. He broke out his flute and jammed with Sky and Bone.

So what about this Shenandoah Park? All the national forests are amazingly free of roads and tourists. Suddenly we have more than 100 miles in a national park distinguished by its long, narrow trajectory on a beautiful ridge bisected by Skyline Drive. The Blue Ridge Parkway provided more road crossings and access than I would have preferred, but for the most part, it was no problem. But Skyline Drive crosses the trail about a quadrillion times, and I feel like a sideshow for the mini-van and SUV crowd.

Junctions in the park are marked by concrete stakes wrapped in metal bands indicating places and distances. I cluelessly wandered off the A.T. at one point and spent half an hour tracking a lovely, grass-covered lane—all downhill. When it occurred to me that this idyllic thoroughfare was blazeless, I had to face the frustrating truth that I was cursed to a long uphill back near the ridgecrest to rejoin the A.T. I examined the well-blazed intersection where I took the wrong turn and had to admit I had nobody to blame but my dumb self.

Tonight we're tenting near an old guy who hikes here a lot. He says we'll love the trails, the tame deer, and all the amenities, despite Skyline Drive. His grandfather worked for the CCC back in the 1930s as a crew supervisor constructing the road. "I have mixed feelings about that," he told us. "But back then, people needed work. Besides, if the Shenandoah project had never happened, this parkland would not have been restored to the pretty decent shape it's in now. It's all a big compromise, isn't it?"

Linda told me to take the park as it is and enjoy it. I told her to clam up and concentrate on picking a trail name before I started calling her Pollyanna. And then, after nearly 900 miles of hiking, it happened. She was tagged. If ever anyone was a Pollyanna, this sweet-natured chick who always smiles in the worst weather, takes up for all her companions regardless of how obnoxiously and boorishly they behave and who never ever has a negative comment about a soul—it is Linda. She submitted, realizing that Pollyanna she is and forever more will be, even unto the end of the age.

May 27, Journal entry of Doug Gottlieb at Hightop Hut

The weather took a cruddy turn today, wet and windy, which suited my sour mood. How can I feel morose when I have every reason to feel free, ecstatic, unencumbered? I know what's at the root of it. Ever since I watched Mt. Rainier glide by on the flight east, I've committed to two things. First, hike from Georgia to Maine. Second, climb Katahdin knowing where I'm headed next. So, where to?

This morning, most of the BGG diverted to the camp store at the Loft Mtn. camping area, eating and drinking tons of junk. I broke ahead of the pack, and the sugar high ran out after a few miles at the Ivy Creek Overlook, where I crashed to regather what Momma Llama calls "spizzarinctim." A window of calm had hit, and the wind and rain were in abeyance. A scout troop from D.C. appeared, 11 boys ranging in age from 12 to 16, and a couple of adult leaders who had their heads screwed on straight.

I told them I'm a NOBO and an Eagle Scout. The dads asked me to give the boys a rundown on my background in scouting and what led me to the A.T. So I began talking and experienced that magic I've felt so many times when I'm around kids. I have the ability to help them rise above the need to display their smart-ass tendencies and—for a little while—let their curiosity take control. I talked of scouting, of climbing and backpacking in the Cascades, of using my journey to become an Eagle to learn about all kinds of areas I would never have otherwise, of how I managed to take my studies seriously enough to get an academic scholarship at Stanford, and how it all led to what I'm doing now: exploring the world on foot and looking for what to do next. I talked about long-distance hiking, leave no trace and respecting the wilderness.

Later, I walked alone, musing about what I've always known. I'm drawn to adolescents and have always had a knack for gaining their higher levels of maturity and respect. Pondering all this is what put me in my dour mood. I need to face it. I'm born to be a teacher. But I had always hoped I could slay a bigger dragon than this.

After a few hours of hiking alone and meditating, I realized I am among a select few people on earth who possess the leisure, the strength, the abundant good health, the limited (but adequate) funds and the courage to take off on a trip like this. I acknowledged the hardwood trees, the wildflowers, the bees battling the occasional wind and rain as they prepared for a long summer's work, insouciant squirrels, the river valley to the west and the verdant farm country to the east. I asked God to grant me some measure of appreciation for what I have and a degree of common sense and humility. And then I decided to do what I know I can do best.

A doe and fawn appeared on the trailside ahead. I approached within five yards and stood wordlessly. The mother's head nodded. I believe you take meaning where you find it, and I really got the sense that this lissome doe was telling me: "It's okay, dummy." When they realized I was not going to provide goodies, the pair ambled away and vanished silently, as deer do.

Tonight turned out funny. Sky and Captain Stupid bought hot dogs at Loft Mtn. We set up near Hightop Hut, and built a fire for the weenie roast. The wood was wet, and there was still drizzle, but Bone and I managed a cheerful blaze. By the time we munched down the dogs, chips and candy bars, the western sky cleared to reveal a blazing sunset. My heart was light as I dozed off. I was determined not to forget this day, nor to allow myself back into the soul-killing rut of dour self-doubt.

THE BOY SCOUTS OF AMERICA

What an enormous impact the Boy Scouts have on the lives of fine young men and the adults who lead them. Also, what an equally huge impact the Boy Scouts have on the A.T. and the people who share it with them. Normally this influence is positive, allowing the hiking community to share wilderness experience with young people. At other times, scouts and leaders are clueless, boorish, loud, destructive and grace the A.T. only by their absence. This writer tempers his criticism by noting that he is an Eagle Scout, as are his father and son. This writer was also part of a well-supervised troop who used the A.T. many years ago and was reasonably respectful, though not perfect.

What it comes down to with Scouts is leadership—from both adults and the older scouts themselves. As long as courtesy and order are maintained, the Boy Scouts deserve a place of honor on the A.T. ■

May 28, Journal entry of Pollyanna at Big Meadows Campground

An active weather system blasted away the clouds last night. My Zoid vibrated in the high wind. When I switched to a 40-degree bag at Waynesboro, I never dreamed I'd shiver in late May, but last night's chill penetrated my core.

I hiked with Doug today. Yesterday he was in a dark mood. I guess he shook it off by this morning, because throughout the day he kidded me about my transformation into Pollyanna. I dug back at him for being devoid of enough imagination to cook up a name for himself. "I'll come up with one before Brave Phillie nails me," he promised.

We covered about 20 miles, and this is the first time I hiked with someone all day. Miles flew by on easy Shenandoah trailway so well-graded we never broke stride. The kind of day a hiker adores, the kind where you motor for long stretches. We pulled into the public campground at Big Meadows by mid-afternoon and went about the languid business of setting up, and then grabbing showers.

Ultragrunge discovered a climbing tree and scaled it like an Appalachian chimpanzee. She located a note written in a little girl's scrawl on lined notebook paper: "I am on vacation with my family. My name is Kendra Murphy, and I am nine years old. My brother is Phillip. He is 11. My Mom is Linda and my Dad is J.P. We camp everywhere we go. I like Shenandoah Park better than any place we have been, and I want to stay in Big Meadows for a long time. I saw 11 deer today and one of them was a fawn with spots on it. A ranger told us not to feed the deer. If you find this note, please send me a letter at 245 Collinsbury Street, Roswell, Georgia 30075."

Grunge wrote a letter to the little girl describing our hike and insisted we all sign it. She scrounged an envelope and stamps at the lodge and mailed the letter to Kendra with an A.T. bandana she bought at Neel's Gap. "I've had two bandanas since Doug returned my UT rag in Hot Springs," she explained. "Who needs two?" So off went the best letter Kendra Murphy will ever receive.

Doug felt penitent for making fun of me, so he took me to dinner at the lodge—town food and beer and just talking. Doug said he'd never seen me drink beer, and I informed him that despite my Pollyanna reputation, girls sometimes wanna have fun. We returned to the campsite and talked on into the dark. Doug is landing on where to go after Katahdin. He wants to teach. "I need to walk around inside the idea a couple more months and see how I feel," he said.

May 29, Journal entry of Blue Devil at Pass Mtn. Hut

Ohmigod! It finally happened! Vicious bear attack! Well, not really an attack, but at least now everyone but Ultragrunge can finally add a bear sighting to their lists. Grunge was up and out early today, so she missed out. Everyone else was strung out over the first couple of miles this morning, with my fine self in the lead, and as I hit a level area on the ridge coming around a corner of the trail—totally blanked out to reality and deep in thought about whatever it is I groove on for hours on end—I was suddenly face to face with a massive ol' black bear.

This big ursine was clawing at a dead log, sucking up dead insects for breakfast, and I was up close and personal all of a sudden, causing him to stand erect and go "Huff!" at me and making all the hairs stand up on the back of my neck and all my bodily orifices pucker. Listen up, y'all, this big old furball was 20 feet away, and I reacted by lifting my hands over my head and screaming, "Yaaaaaahhh!!" which worked, I'm guessing, because he went to all fours, and after giving me a disdainful glance, ambled into the woods. I finally checked off the bear box, and it felt so good! I can't wait to tell Indu.

So—the story goes on—when everyone else caught up to me later, they told me that as they passed the same log, which must have been an arboreal goldmine of six-legged goodies, Yogi kept returning, each time yielding territory reluctantly. Sky and Captain Stupid said he hissed and looked really annoyed that they were so presumptuous as to invade his big old bear space.

Coupled with Bearapalooza, we had great weather, hiking past Hawksbill, Stony Man, Little Stony Man, the Pinnacle and Mary's Rock—big stone cliff edifices. Best day in Shenandoah.

I switched to a lighter bag in Waynesboro and ditched a couple of items of my royal hiking raiment and packed really light on food due to all the eating opportunities in the park, and the end result is more spring in my step. I'll see Indu tomorrow—not that I'm counting the hours or anything.

May 30, Transcript of Captain Stupid recorded at Skyline Motel, Front Royal, Va.

Don't ask me what's cookin' between Indu and Blue Devil, but after putting in over 20 easy miles today, we met her in the afternoon at a spot on Skyline Drive. She was in a borrowed minivan, clad in tight jeans and a lovely blue tank top with all that black flowing hair cascading around her shoulders. Blue Devil is a love slave.

Yay!

These two should get married and produce spectacular offspring combining the best of East Indian, African, Native American, and whatever else makes up Blue Devil's ethnic and racial heritage. But they haven't even gone to college yet—plenty of time to contemplate that stuff later.

It rained all day, and the best part was finishing. We're almost out of Shenandoah, and for the most part we had decent weather and easy trails. My food stash coming out of Waynesboro was half what I nor-mally carry. I dumped packweight by trading out for lighter stuff and sending some home. As we left the hostel in Waynesboro, a guy hooked up a hanging scale, and my packweight, even with a liter of water, was 23 pounds! Compare that to what I started with (maybe 60) and what I actually ended up with at Springer after ditching cigarettes, surplus food and other non-necessities—low 50s I'm guessing. Switching to an ultralight pack in Hot Springs and refining the whole system has been an education for the collection of urban fat cells designed for watching television and subsisting on transfatty acids that left Georgia back in March.

So, what have these fat cells turned into? Time for inventory:

- *Feet:* Calloused. No discoloration. They still detonate with pain every night, but so do everyone else's.
- *Aches and pains:* Headaches, muscle aches, backaches, ham-string miseries, and general physical malaise of the first few hundred miles have receded to a level similar to what my hik-ing mates experience. I take Vitamin I about once a week, always at recommended dose—not the daily doubles and triples I scarfed earlier.
- *Fitness:* I am on the Official A.T. Guaranteed Weight-Loss Regi-men, jettisoning massive amounts of weight day-by-day. My legs are mighty from hundreds of climbs. And even though town food has not been the healthiest, I have managed lots of fruits and vegetables. The on-trail regimen—in my case, lots of freeze-dried—is high in sodium, but I sweat and drink it away. Hiking poles work on my trunk, shoulders and arms. I possess infinitely more cardiovascular capacity than the most optimistic personal trainer could ever imagine.
- *Personal finance:* I can get to Katahdin and return home free of debt and with enough stash to get back on track.
- *Relationships:* For the first time in my life, people accept me for no more or less than what I am. And, dare I say it, I am in love.

I'll sleep on the floor tonight as always. No sane human shares a bed with me. Bone, Blue Devil and Doug can fight over the solo second bed. Meanwhile, I watch cable and remember the little old lady on the Approach Trail to Springer who said, "You've got some conditioning issues." She should get a load of me now.

SUBJECT: Nothing can stop me now!
DATE: May 31, 6:51 p.m.
FROM: < ATMommaLlama@charter.net >
TO: <Jackiechristieqt@aol.com >

Here I am in Front Royal, looking at being out of Virginia before long and seriously close to halfway. And yes, I am still in love and giddy that the object of my passions will be back with me soon—probably at Harpers Ferry. I just talked with him, and he is rehabbing his way back into my life.

Jackie, you'll love him, too. He's a gentleman and a gentle—though hard-edged—person. Not bad on the eyes for a dude his age. Keeping a hard body into your sixties ain't easy. I am flummoxed that I've fallen for a man so totally removed from my ideological sphere. Love is not only blind, it is apolitical.

Blue Devil fell in love with a ravishing Indian checkout girl in Waynesboro, and she is shuttling us around. She ferried us to the trail this morning, and we knocked off the distance to U.S. 522 really fast. The trails are nice in Shenandoah, not to mention mostly downhill today. Part of the way was an abandoned fire road, and I walked alone through mature hardwoods and ferns that gave me the feeling I was back in a distant century before we "improved" the wilderness with vacation homes, subdivisions, shopping malls, etc. An easy day with a luxurious night ahead in Front Royal.

I notice that Doug "I still don't have a trail name" Gottlieb—my, what a foxy young stud this kid is—and Linda "I guess my new trail name is Pollyanna" Bennett are off together for German food tonight. Linda brooks no discussion of anything between them, but they get closer by the mile.

I still have flare-ups of fasciitis. It helps when I tape up and if I know where we will be stopping for the night, so I can combine stretches of hiking with rest and treatment stops throughout the day. When I try to pin down the rest of the Bly Gappers in the morning as to where we will stop, I sometimes get blank stares and traces of annoyance, as if I'm a mother hen setting an agenda. This is a problem I'll work out as best I can. These kids don't know what you and I do—approaching 60 ain't for sissies.

June 1, Journal entry of Bone Festival at Dick's Dome Shelter

Off late this morning due to histrionics between Blue Devil and Indu. Fifteen miles to this ramshackle dome long since spoken for by other NOBOs. A nice night for tents and tarps, although it's kind of rocky around here for setting up. As we started this morning, we paralleled the boundary of the National Zoo's Zoological Park. Grunge and I spotted exotic horse-like creatures—sort of half-horse/half-something indeterminate. On this quiet morning, with mist still covering the meadow, we gawked past the fence like visitors to Jurassic Park attempting to identify captive denizens. Grunge and I are South Park fans, and we decided these amalgamated beasts were akin to Al Gore's famous ManBearPig—half man, half bear, half pig. We did Al Gore impressions.

The trail is a breeze through here for rock-hard folk such as we. I feel as strong as I have ever been in my life. All of us, even the mighty Captain, are at our peak.

Sky and I stopped by the Front Royal Visitor's Center yesterday, and being overtly musical, we were drawn to a display about Bing Crosby, a town hero. We hummed "Swinging on a Star." Sky's uncanny memory served well as we hiked today, and she recalled lyrics about mules and pigs and carrying moonbeams home in a jar. By the time we set up camp this afternoon, I had it down pat on Twangin' Perry. We sang it over and over with great empathy for the mule, seeing as how we lead a pack-mule life ourselves.

Grunge and I told the ManBearPig story, and Momma Llama scolded us: "Give Al Gore a break. I went door-to-door for him in 2000."

Doug told a good Shenandoah story. He was hiking alone and came to a parking area on one of the many Skyline Drive crossings. There was a view, and he sat on a stone wall to rehydrate and gaze out over the hazy Shenandoah Valley. Predictably, one of the jillions of minivans pulled up, and out popped four stair-step kids, a frantic mom and a frazzled dad. Pandemonium erupted when one of the kids snatched another's handheld electronic game. As the mom waded in to restore order, the dad walked over to Doug.

"Looks like you're out for a while," he observed.

Doug explained that he was a Georgia-to-Maine A.T. hiker, and the dad looked at him with awe and envy. "I wish I could have an adventure like this."

Doug suggested that when his kids grew up, perhaps the fellow could plan his own adventure—A.T. or otherwise. The man smiled back at Doug. "You're too young to get it, but once you reach a certain age, you just can't do something like what you're doing. You just can't."

Silence intervened as the two took in the countryside. "I wish I was you," the man said ruefully. "You don't know how lucky you are."

"That's about the saddest comment I've ever heard," Doug told us.

June 2, Journal entry of Ultragrunge at Bear's Den Hostel

Edged up in the high 80s today, hottest we've seen. Not good, seeing as how we hit the infamous Roller Coaster. Due to a narrow corridor, the trail has few switchbacks and runs drastically up and down for a dozen miles. Wowie zowie—what a drag.

After 19 miles, it was nice to pull up to Bears Den Rocks, a placid view to the west. I bummed a smoke from Captain Stupid for a nicotine buzz while I took in the vista. He handed me a pack with five fags left and informed me that he has not had a cig in more than a week. "I was down to two or three a day, and I'm past the worst of the withdrawal," he said. He looked over at me and smiled. "Sky's after me to stop." Captain Stupid a health nut, what next?

Bears Den Hostel was off-trail, half a click away. We did laundry and showered, and everyone is downright mellow. In the bunk room the inevitable came up. Is anyone going to take a stab at the Four State Challenge?

It goes like this: You start north in the wee hours of the morning at Loudon Heights, which is the last spot on the trail bordering Virginia and West Virginia. So the first state is Virginia. Then you step into West Virginia, hike down to the Shenandoah, through Harpers Ferry, and over the Potomac. That's West Virginia, state number two.

Next: Maryland. Hike along the C&O Canal towpath, up Weverton Cliffs and then for about 35 miles along the mostly level ridge of South Mountain all the way to Pen-Mar Park and a tad beyond, to Pennsylvania. Step past the MD/PA border and you've been in four states. Do all of this before midnight and you join the elite class of thru-hikers who have hiked in four states in less than 24 hours. Momma Llama laughed out loud at the concept, saying her trick foot rules her out. Pollyanna says the idea doesn't make her socks roll up and down, and Sky Writer thinks it's a macho thing—notches in the belt. But Blue Devil, Bone, Doug, and even Captain Stupid are interested, as am I. Blue Devil called Indu, and she'll help. The plot is afoot. Tomorrow, as Momma, Polly and Sky head to Harpers Ferry, the rest of us will hike 18 miles and camp at Loudon Heights, the northernmost spot on the trail in Virginia.

According to the *Data Book*, we have 43.1 miles to cover. If we hike 24 hours, we need to cover 1.8 miles per hour. Judging from the profile map, there are some climbs—all less than 1,000 feet—and flat ridge-walking. With Indu's support, we will be free of packs and get hydrated at road crossings. Is this the fun I think it'll be or a forced march with bone grinding on bone and feet forced to a tipping point of pain and exhaustion?

My best experience in life has been accompanied by excruciating pain rolled up in hunger and thirst and folded within overwhelming exhaustion and unendurable tedium. The four-state challenge should be a full-force blast! Wooohooo!

SUBJECT: **Almost halfway!!!!**
DATE: **June 3, 7:50 p.m.**
FROM: **Sky Writer** < singinghiker@yahoo.com >
TO: **M. J. Spangler** < mjspangler@transpolymerintl.com >

Dad, Mom sent your new company email address. So, you're Vice President of Supply Chain Management at Transpolymer International. Very impressive! You'll be out of the country forever. No big difference, I guess, since I haven't seen you in 11 months.

I mean it when I say I miss you and want to see you. If you get vacation, come and see me out here. I noted your emails expressing ongoing concern about the craziness in Tennessee. I still have bad dreams, but my friends were my sanctuary.

We are in Harpers Ferry tonight. I talked to Mom, and she said to charge lodging for all of us tonight to her credit card. So I set us up in a B&B near the Appalachian Trail Conservancy Headquarters. We hiked 20 miles to get here and reunited with Brave Phillie, the man who hurt himself weeks ago and rehabbed.

The ATC took Polaroids of us for the thru-hiker book, and I got to meet Laurie Potteiger (trail name Mountain Laurel) who thru-hiked in 1987. I asked her questions via email before the trip, and she remembered me! She had heard all about us and seemed delighted to accept our invitation to eat dinner tonight at the Anvil, which cost Mom a bundle. But man, was it good. Laurie told us to get all the joy out of the trail we possibly can, but she also asked us to figure out a way to give back. This trail is a miracle. We have to keep it alive, so I'll do my part.

Dad, I guess you and Mom are barely in touch, and I'm okay with that. If it doesn't work, it doesn't work. But reach out more to me. Answer this email. I need you both, even if you're not together.

June 4, Transcript of Captain Stupid recorded during the four-state challenge

Yesterday was logistical preparation for today. From Bears Den Hostel, we went about seven miles to Blackburn Trail Center, where you can supposedly see all the way to D.C. and the Washington Monument. Too much haze. We hiked to a road crossing at Keys Gap. The five of us planning to do the Four State Challenge met Indu, again in her borrowed minivan, and she took us for a run into Harpers Ferry to hit the P.O. and make the obligatory stop at the Appalachian Trail Conservancy HQ to get our photos in the thru-hiker book.

Indu took us back to Keys Gap and we hiked to Loudon Heights, setting up camp by 5 p.m. I sawed redwoods while the others fidgeted. At 11:30 p.m., I'm ready. I'm recording this at midnight. Everyone has on headlamps and full packs. We're off.

We've covered less than a mile to the first road crossing, and Indu takes our packs. We carry nothing. Indu will meet us with water and food at road crossings, so all we need are headlamps. Now, we motor in earnest. Without packs and with moderate terrain, plus a cloudy day with temperatures predicted in the mid-80s, conditions aren't bad. The tortoise was right: "Slow and steady wins the race."

A pitch-black night. We crossed a carless highway bridge over the Shenandoah and climbed back into the woods, where the trail gained high ground, passing Jefferson Rock, a promontory overlooking the Shenandoah as it is about to merge with the Potomac—a place once visited and commented upon by Thomas Jefferson. We dropped to the lowest point in Harpers Ferry, near the arsenal commandeered by John Brown, and crossed the Potomac on a pedestrian walkway affixed on the railroad bridge. Now, three miles of crushed-stone towpath next to the historic C&O Canal—paper flat.

A while back, still dark, we left the towpath, went under a highway overpass and up 1,000 feet of switchbacks to the Weverton Cliffs side trail. It's inky black out, so we missed the view—one of the best on the A.T.—and rolled along a level ridge to this place, Crampton Gap, where there's a big stone monument to war correspondents.

Indu is here to mark our first 12 miles. We've walked nonstop, so Indu insists we take 20 minutes to rest and drink. It's about 4:30 a.m.

Ultragrunge is pacing. A minute ago she said, "Those miles won't hike themselves." The girl is amped.

How energized and serene I feel! This is working. Just finished another seven miles to Turners Gap. We had to climb and descend. Trail was mostly old timber road—perfect treadway. Dawn broke. Indu brings Little Debbie cakes and Gatorade. We rest. Grunge just piped up, "Man up! It's nearly nine o'clock."

Doug's the voice of reason, saying, "Grunge, my love, we've made about 20 miles. 23 to go. Let's pace ourselves. This next couple of hours put us over the halfway hump, and after that, it'll start telling on us." Grunge glared.

We town trotted out of Turner Gap, but cruise control kicked in. When we came to Maryland's ridgetop Washington Monument, I refused a short side trail for the view. No side trips for the self-proclaimed "laziest hiker on the A.T.."

Now, a couple of miles later, sweet Indu, our raven-haired guardian angel, appears at State Route 40. More fluid, less snacks. I'm still "on mission" and motivated. Blue Devil and Bone are bitching. Doug has a studied placidity. Ultragrunge—the female standard-bearer—shows no weakness.

About 27 miles under our trail runners now. About 16 to go. We pass Annapolis Rocks and surge to the next Indu rendezvous. The trail remains lovely ridge-walking. Minimal elevation change. Spectacularly nondescript. Blue Devil and Bone are dragging. Doug and Grunge are competing. He is good-natured. She has fire in her flat belly, which I suddenly notice is no longer pierced. Hmmm!

Finally at Wolfsville Road, and if the *Data Book* is right, we've gone about 33.5 miles, way more than we've done before. It's 2:30, which means our pace has dropped off, but we're still on track to make the border easily, unless the wheels come off the buggy in the next 9.5 miles. Loading up on water and food. Doug's insouciant smile is pasted on. Ultragrunge is pissy. Blue Devil and Bone have fallen behind, and Indu says she may not be at the next crossing when we get there. She'll wait for Blue Devil and Bone. "No frrickin' surprise," Grunge mutters, and Doug gives me a conspiratorial smirk. I stick a liter bottle in the back waistband of my shorts just in case. Grunge and Doug do not.

————

Another road crossing. No Indu. We share my water. One-third liter is not enough. Next highway, a few miles on.

————

Sprawling in a gravel parking area near the road crossing at Raven Rock Road. Here is my re-creation of the conversation:

Grunge: "You'd think she'd go back and forth to supply us if they can't keep up."

Doug: "Oh, sure! Stupid, inconsiderate Indu. It must be something cultural."

Grunge: "Cut the sarcasm. Less than six miles to go, and I'm parched."

5:30 p.m., and Indu comes roaring up. "Oh, please. Oh, please. I am so sorry. I need to give you water and food and then go back to help Rafer and Bone." She leaves water and goodies and vanishes down the wooded highway whence she came.

"Rafer!" Grunge squeals. "His name is Rafer, and now we know. Woohooo!" Doug is in stitches: "His old man must have been a Rafer Johnson fan." I know about Rafer Johnson and his storied athletic career, which included a Gold Medal at the 1960 Olympics, and so does Doug. We inform Ultragrunge on the powerful heritage of Blue Devil's name.

"Let's finish for Rafer!" she screams.

————

And so it was that we force-marched the final six miles through more lovely forest and past some pretty views we didn't bother to look at and pulled in to Pen Mar Park a little while ago, at about 9 p.m. We did our duty and walked past the park to the authentic state line. We stepped a few feet past to make sure and then ambled like octogenarians to a huge picnic pavilion overlooking twinkling Waynesboro to the west. "I feel like dog offal. I wish I had never done this," Doug blurted. Grunge agreed.

I now proudly record this statement: Aside from massive chaffing and throbbing feet, this was nowhere near as bad as I figured. I proclaim myself a hiking god.

YAAAAAY!

_____

Grunge's ringtone is a snatch of "Don't Cry for Me Argentina." Blue Devil reports that his feet and Bone's ankles—along with assorted other physical and emotional complaints—force a decision to throw in the towel seven miles short of Pen Mar. Grunge has a shameful smirk on her face, but shows remarkable restraint in saying, "Don't sweat it guys. You put in a great day." The decision is for all of us to meet in two nights at Quarry Gap Shelter, 20 miles north of here.

_____

The park is officially closed, but no one has chased us off. We'll risk arrest and sleep on picnic tables. "Blue Devil and Bone were the smart ones," Doug muttered. "If I ever suggest something like this again, shoot me."

"Yeah," Grunge cooed. "I'll remember that. But at least we know about Rafer."

June 5, Journal entry of Pollyanna at Pen Mar Park

Not much doubt who had fun over the past two days. Sky, Momma and I have had a grand time getting reacquainted with Brave Phillie, who is ecstatic that he's done two 20-plus days in a row with minimal pain in his injured foot and ankle. "I'm so strong I might just pick you babes up and carry you all to Katahdin," he boasted.

Surely we had more fun than the other five out there ahead of us somewhere. We'll catch them tomorrow, as they follow up their "challenge" with recuperation days. What macho dolts! I would have expected more from Grunge than to try to prove something.

I'm noticing more and more of the rocks we've been warned about, the ones deposited when the glaciers decided to peter out and dump their load. Maryland, they say, is not that bad for rocks. The big problems begin in Pennsylvania. Nonetheless, there have been spots where we boulder-hop for a hundred yards or so and other places where rocks clog the trail. My trusty Raichles will get me to Duncannon, where I plan to pick up Salomon trail runners—a switch from boots to shoes.

I'm easing into this Pollyanna thing. Brave Phillie says it's my own fault. I should have picked a trail handle for myself to preempt the inevitability of having one picked for me. But I must admit, I am a Pollyanna. I refuse to look for the sour side of any person or situation. I believe most people are decent and willing to be nice when given the opportunity. We saw an instance earlier in this trip when that assuredly was not the case, but I'm talking about the preponderance of human beings I've known. If my companions want to make fun of me for enjoying hiking in the rain, so be it.

A note awaited us at a big picnic pavilion at Pen Mar. Our chums spent last night here—illegally—and it appears we may, too. We Yogied a family picnic when we got here this afternoon, and I'm tempted to stretch out on a picnic table and sleep tonight. The view west is too pretty to walk away from.

8

Lost Love, Lost Weight and Them Pennsylvania Rock Blues

GIMME SHELTER

Whether they are called lean-tos (in Maine), huts in (New Hampshire) or shelters (everywhere else), you miss a good bet if you don't frequent these trailside havens while on a thru-hike. Shelters are a legacy of Mac-Kaye's vision, a place for the trail tribe to gather and add to the lore of the A.T. Nation. Thousands upon thousands of deep thoughts and pithy comments have sprung from fireside shelter chats going back decades. The mice, the hilarious entries in trail registers, the chance to intermingle with strangers—all this is a part of the aggregate A.T. experience.

Shelter etiquette is probably in black and white somewhere, but the true definition of good manners at shelters is based on common courtesy. If you are out for a couple of days, hang loose before settling in. It is customary to yield to long-distance hikers if they arrive later, assuming they want the space. Groups should be small, and if they use a shelter area to camp for the night, they should not sleep in the shelter. If you arrive by headlamp and the people in the shelter are asleep, go about your business quietly. If you get up extremely early and others want to sleep in, same rule. When you encounter fellow travelers at a shelter, don't assume they want to watch you get drunk. If you carry marijuana, keep it stowed. If you have a tendency to make bigoted remarks or act like a jackass, only stay at shelters when nobody else is there. Otherwise, grace the premises with your absence.

Which is the best shelter? That is as subjective as any A.T. topic. Blood Mtn. in Georgia has a great view, but no water and an overabundance of skunks. Overmountain in Tennessee is a converted barn with perhaps the most beautiful view of them all. Partnership in Virginia has a shower and nearby pay phone to order pizza. Quarry Gap in Pennsylvania is an architectural masterpiece. Eckville, also in Pennsylvania, features running water, a solar shower and a flush toilet. West Mountain in New York is way off the A.T. and has no water, but on a clear night, Manhattan twinkles in the distance. RPH in New York has a nifty water pump and pizza delivery. Limestone Spring in Connecticut may be the only shelter supplied by a spring emanating from a limestone cave. Mt. Wilcox South in Massachusetts— similar to Blood Mtn.—has been there since it all began. Happy Hill in Vermont has the best name. In Maine, perhaps Rainbow Stream is the winner, because it is right on the stream and one of the last places you'll stay on a NOBO thru-hike.

A tent is an insular cocoon providing privacy unknown in a shelter. A tarp is lighter, but offers less protection from rain, mosquitoes, snakes and voyeurs. The best nights, the funniest moments and the most engaging conversations generally happen in shelters. ■

June 6, Journal entry of Doug Gottlieb at Quarry Gap Shelters

The Bly Gap Gang is reunited this evening, and we picked the classiest shelter yet for the occasion. We're currently in a thin spot in the NOBO pipeline, and because of the "challenge" a couple of days ago, followed by two easy days, five of us got to Quarry Gap early and set up shop in one of the two "condos." Blue Devil and Bone straggled in looking sheepish, but Grunge graciously admitted they were wise to stop early during the "challenge." "No way I'd do it again!" she proclaimed.

Some of the group took longer to arrive than others. The swimming pool at Caledonia State Park provided suburban-style pleasure they chose not to resist.

It feels good to see the Bly Gap Gang intact near the halfway point. Not one of us has made a big deal about staying together the whole way, but there is a real feeling of family that I am reluctant to lose.

Quarry Gap is two log structures, with a covered eating and cooking area in between, and a roof running across the front of the entire shelter. Tonight it is ours. Brave Phillie commandeered a couple of stoves and pots, and he's fixing a tasty noodle dish with chicken, mushrooms, onion, red pepper, pimento and some kind of canned soup. On the side, he brought in artichoke hearts and black beans mixed together and blended with creamy Italian dressing. How he got all that in a teeny Vapor Trail pack, I don't know, but nine thru-hikers were barely able to consume it all.

The aftermath of the "challenge" is unpleasant. My knee is barking. Ultragrunge's feet are in flames. Blue Devil complains of swelling in his Achilles tendons. He soaked his feet in the stream near the shelter. Bone whines a lot.

Who is the hero? Captain Stupid! He suffered few ill effects and is happy as ever. He found a floppy hillbilly hat and an orphan plaid blanket left behind in the shelter. He donned the hat and wrapped the blanket kilt-style around his bountiful waist and broke into a hillbilly buck dance, singing and laughing and embodying all that is fun, free and nonsensical about a group of people who have chosen to walk for half a year. Bone chimed in on his banjo, and Sky and Pollyanna joined the dance. Soon we were clapping, singing—contributing to the lunacy, with Captain Stupid at dead center.

Three backpackers came from the north, watched us wordlessly and thought better of even stopping. "Don't leave," Sky Writer yelled. "Come join!" They eyed us suspiciously and hoofed it down the trail, adding hilarity to the proceedings. Grunge, aching dogs and all, grabbed the Captain and spun him around, a compact Ginger Rogers maneuvering a plus-sized Fred Astaire. How can this not be fun? No excuses.

June 7, Journal entry of Blue Devil at Pine Grove Furnace State Park

I left this morning well aware that my aching tootsies and my sore back—rewards of my failed try at the Four State Challenge—would slow me to a crawl, so I figured I'd set a slow pace and ease the pressure. The morning was clear and, for June, pretty cool, and I had a long stretch of mountain laurel in late-stage bloom all to myself. All through the hike, we've seen laurel and rhododendron and a panoply of wild flowers (my favorites are May apples), but late laurel in the solitude of the morning was the balm I needed to ignore my pain and concentrate on what's so right about a hike that takes you past so much gorgeous wild biota.

Rocks have not really been so bad, but I am told they get worse farther north, so I'll lay off the self-pity and take rocks as they come, seeing as how I'm sure everyone heard enough of my bellyaching last night about my tortured feet. I'm hurtin' in the heart too, with Indu not likely to show up soon.

Indu's family story plays itself out all over America. After moving the Patel family (mom, dad, Indu and a younger brother who has taken the name Mike) to Connecticut three years ago, her dad established himself with a big company, and they're working hard to become citizens. Indu is a computer-science genius, as is her dad, and getting an academic scholarship to UV was no big problem. She broke away early before starting classes and moved to Virginia to establish independence from her controlling, but loving, parents. She says if they discovered she has fallen for an African-American, she would enter a disaster zone.

My family is so mongrelized I have trouble wearing the African-American mantle, but I have little choice. My skin and hair and facial features point in several directions, but my friends think of me as black, so there it is. Neither of my parents would be upset if I brought Indu home, but my smiling countenance would create a firestorm for Indu's family. For now, I'm fortunate to have Katahdin ahead—a serious preoccupation—and since we've hit the midpoint, I realize that the "endless trail" is finite.

Easy hiking today, and despite unpleasant rocky spots, no worse than I recall in Maryland. I pulled into Pine Grove Furnace, a state park with the remains of an iron forge, ahead of my posse. After being in nothing but national forests and national parks all the way to Front Royal, we now meander through state lands. I found a pleasant spot and waited until the whole crowd arrived to make our way to the nearby general store for a thru-hiker tradition—the famous half-gallon ice cream challenge. Everyone except Brave Phillie and Pollyanna decided to do it. BP did it last time he came through, and it left him queasy. Today BP was timekeeper.

Some starving NOBO set a new time record a week or so ago—just over 2.5 minutes—earning a new trail name, Cherry Vanilla. We coaxed Captain Stupid to go first, assuming that if he was born to compete in something, this had to be it. He dove right in. His failure was astonishing—halfway through, he got a brain freeze and ducked over to some bushes to completely offload not only the ice cream but everything he'd eaten since breakfast. "Glorioski!" Bone hooted. "He sounds like Doug at Apple House." This sent everyone, even the Captain, into spasms of laughter.

On it went. Momma Llama got about halfway into her plain vanilla and said she just didn't want any more. Grunge, the most competitive of the Bly Gap Gang, worked her way through her fudge ripple, but she had little to say about it and was pretty green around the gills for an hour or two. Bone Festival ate his chocolate like a little girl—not even getting halfway. What wimps!

Then, my turn: cherry vanilla, just like the champion. I ate steadily, determined not to get a brain freeze. The first quart was easy—like a couple of the pints we knock off so easily—but the second quart worked on me. I felt bloated polishing off the final spoonful, and I have never been so glad to be finished eating anything edible. My time was the best yet, 12 minutes, though not championship territory.

With his vanilla, Doug was Little Miss Muffet trifling with his curds and whey, taking tiny bites and long pauses as if he were afraid to charge for glory. We taunted him, cajoled him, excoriated him, insulted him, and nothing worked. He finished in the ignominious time of 22 minutes. Sky Writer was pathetic. She ate less than half and walked off somewhere. Pollyanna went last with an awful concoction called birthday cake—gaudy colors and gooey frosting. I was sick just looking at it, but she craved gooey sweets. Five minutes and 54 seconds—done, with no ill effects. You never know.

We're in the Ironmasters Mansion hostel, once a stop on the Underground Railroad. Now a black dude can openly walk through here with impunity. True progress.

June 7, Journal entry of Brave Phillie at the Appalachian Trail Museum

I stole away from the Bly Gappers after the ice cream craziness for a solitary stroll around the Appalachian Trail Museum. Trail folk created this place in an old stone grist mill, a labor of love for people who revere the endless trail, a resting place for a thousand odds and ends recalling many, many decades of A.T. memories and the people and places of the trail.

I wandered from one display to another, recalling bigger-than-life personalities such as Gene Espy, Grandma Gatewood and Ed Garvey. I first started doing trail work before I was in the service. Over the years—aside from hiking—I've swung pulaskis, cut blowdowns with crosscut saws, dug out waterbars, and worked on countless reroutes, never regretting a bit of it. This place is a sanctuary for all of us who love the miracle of it all.

I came across an old Mt. Katahdin summit sign, the one telling mileages to places near and far—including impossibly distant Springer

Mountain. My God, what memories that sign triggered! Like a movie montage racing through my mind, I summoned mental pictures of all the characters and gorgeous locations between Springer and Katahdin. I stood there and wept for so much—Marina, my sweet unappreciated wife, gone forever. Earl Shaffer. My new friends, who I try to deserve. The half of the trail unhiked on this trip with a new Katahdin summit sign waiting at the end. How can such a self-absorbed soul as myself sustain all the good this long footpath has showered on me?

I walked out of the place feeling that good kind of exhaustion a man feels at the end of a hot day's hike. Ready for water and food and sleep. Ready to gear up for the second half of the last great American adventure.

June 8, Letter from Momma Llama

Ms. Jackie Christie
3318 Killdeer Court
Glen Ellyn, Ill. 60137

Dear Jackie Girl!

This is one of only three letters I've written this entire trip. Mainly, I phone and email. Consider yourself special! How many times have I wished that you were still with me? So much of what I see, feel, hear, taste and even smell I want to share—everything except BP. He's mine, girlfriend!

Nineteen rocky miles today, with a few annoying ups and downs, to arrive at a campsite near Boiling Springs, a spot where copious quantities of spring water feed an idyllic lake surrounded by parks, trees and waterfowl. We hiked into town for water, beer and pizza and idled for a while, soaking our feet and wondering what it would be like to live here, work at some stressless job, reside in a floral bungalow, grow orchids, take a walk each day, listen to classical music at night, wear clean clothes and take showers whenever you want—the stuff thru-hiker dreams are made of. Still, I imagine people here have the same concerns we Chicagoland types must bear.

We passed Center Point Knob today, the psychological midpoint. Nothing dramatic, just a wood sign. However, with every step north from there, I was on the downside. This really will end.

I used to think about returning home after this is over and settling into retirement. I figured that would involve fun with you and the rest of my chums. Now I just can't imagine what will happen. Will I figure out some Boiling Springs ideal that includes this man I only know as Brave Phillie? We never discuss specifics, other than adventures we hope to have together. But where will we end up—that place where we eat breakfast, clean bathtubs and invite our friends? What will it be like when I know his real name, and he knows mine?

Here's the good news: I'm not worried. We'll work out an arrangement to serve us both. I walk each day wondering if my injury will stay in check and if the Bly Gap Gang will put up with my mother-henning and where we will stop for lunch so I can retape, and where will we lay our heads at night?

I see from your letter that you and Jack are clicking. Jump into the deep end of the pool! Give this guy every chance! For now, I'll curl up in a little ball with my hands around my pizza-distended belly and be happy. Georgia to Maine or bust!

So much love to you!

June 9, Journal entry of Brave Phillie at Cove Mountain Shelter

Today we lit out over the Cumberland Valley for more than 20 miles to this shelter chock-full of friendly NOBOs. This stretch was once on paved roads before trail people acquired land to put a footpath along this long, flat farm valley. It got up in the high 80s, and my bad foot was feeling rough. I started from Boiling Springs with plenty of water and set a snappy pace all morning to get through the better part of the mileage.

It was the last hot mile that got to me. So often, as I stumble into the day's final mile, I fantasize about the scruffy shelter at the end. I build this humble shack into a castle, a Ritz-Carlton of pleasure, knowing full well it may smell like a wilderness locker room, a mouse privy and a mold culture all rolled together. All the while, on a day when miles disappeared like a bag of M&Ms, I suddenly have feet of lead. The more I ignore the distance, the more the final-mile distortion zone wraps me in its tendrils. This zone is as real as a stream to be forded, a mountain to be climbed, a storm to be braved. Somehow, that frickin' last mile knows you're almost done and the *final-mile distortion zone* imposes itself on my hike like a fart in a phone booth. It happens in almost every last mile, even at the end of a short, otherwise effortless, day. I always give in and realize that what should seem like minutes will feel like eons.

After I set up, I made the downhill scamper to the spring. So often shelters and camp sites are up high. It is, after all, a ridge trail. When water is available, it is often necessary to pick your way down a steep pitch on the mountainside to get to it and then labor back up like a pack mule with full bottles—the final insult of the day, particularly bad if the weather is real hot, real cold or real wet. But hey, you have to drink! I remember an old sergeant who used to get in our faces and bellow, "You drinkin' enough?" He knew then what I've learned over a lifetime. Every situation is better if you're hydrated, and everything turns sour when you're not.

Momma Llama and I hiked together all day. As we got a few miles into the valley, we met a day hiker jotting notes in a spiral notebook. He was a college professor and trail enthusiast involved in the Appalachian Trail Mega-Transect. He described the concept of using the long, thin line of the A.T. as a static measuring point for environmental data, a way to take the environmental temperature of the Eastern Seaboard. This professor was one of many citizen scientists enlisted to work on this effort.

Momma Llama and I got into a back-and-forth about the Mega-Transect and decided to learn more about it after this adventure. The more I talk to her, the more I crave her company. We discussed the taboo about discovering the other's off-trail name. We can dispense with that when the trip ends and decompress back into the rat race. She has a different take. She worries that there is a dreamlike quality to the trail, what she calls "a fantasy lens we use to relate to each other." I see no harm in it.

I reminded her of the day we took our spill north of Pearisburg. I told her my true feelings that day, and she came right back at me with hers. I asked if anything had changed since we cleared the air that day, and she said, "Yes. I love you even more now." We were standing next to a hedgerow, a private place out of the worst of the broiling sun, and she put her arms around my neck and her head on my sweaty shoulder. We stood like that for a long time, and I asked if she might want to live in Georgia with me someday. "Sure," she told me. "Or maybe Chicago or Colorado or Florida or Costa Rica or Hawaii."

THE MEGA-TRANSECT

ccasionally you hear about an idea whose elegance and simplicity make you wonder why you didn't think of it first. The Appalachian Trail Mega-Transect is one of those. You have a 270,000-acre trail corridor with a network of thousands of dedicated volunteers attached. Why not use it for something other than hiking?

The A.T. could not be better situated to measure Eastern U.S. air quality. It can also serve as a measuring platform for soil and water quality, as well as the spread of pests, pathogens and invasive species headed both north and south. By observing flora and fauna, volunteer citizen scientists can make species-specific observations and develop data links regarding the impact of climate change.

This dovetails with the evolving trail project. Volunteerism has always been at the core of the A.T. Why not engage existing volunteers to work toward keeping the air, water, soil, flora, fauna and beautiful views forever intact on and around the A.T.?

Purists may quibble with anything that brings more people to the trail, especially if not for the sole purpose of hiking. The quibblers have a point. A hiker once argued with a friend about the importance of reducing traffic on the trail to preserve the "trail experience." He pulled out a variation of an old preservationist chestnut: "I think the A.T. should only be open to you and me—and I'm not so sure about you."

If the effort is not geared toward maintaining a healthy trail environment for the long run, then its short-sighted approach will contribute to its eventual demise. If the trail can be a living lab to learn about what it takes to keep it healthy, then go for it! ■

June 10, Journal entry of Ultragrunge at the Doyle Hotel in Duncannon, Pa.

A quick hop this morning to Duncannon, an iconic trail town and sentimental center point of the A.T. I'm tired of the so-called midpoints, but when we cross the river, we'll dispense with that crap.

Bone and I stopped at a rocky promontory called Hawk Rock that looks out over Duncannon and the Susquehanna Valley. Over decades, a parade of local yahoos have decorated the rocks with spray paint declaring love for their babes, allegiance to their teams or a variety of expletives. Dogooders have painted over the damage, but perpetrators return to perpetuate the tradition.

I was hotter than a two-dollar pistol, so I stripped off my tee shirt and caught a breeze in my sports bra. Bone was admiring me. After 1,100 miles, I don't mind boasting that my body is worthy of admiration. If Bone would quit mooning over Sky Writer, he might discover there are other catfish in the sea, some of whom look pretty foxy in hiking shorts and a navy-blue sports bra.

I thought of Bruce Springsteen's fading blue-collar rust belt as we ambled down to the Susquehanna. A freight train lumbered way down below issuing an occasional long blast. I felt so sad and utterly detached from the life I'm living up here. The commercial and industrial world drones on. The information age buzzes. Some live high. Others suffer on starvation wages. As thru-hikers, we're disengaged. Is this trek a self-indulgent escape from convention? Are we temporary refugees from quiet desperation?

I asked Bone, "Should I have joined the Peace Corp, instead of doing this?"

"That's the jackpot question for thru-hikers," he responded. "Look at Doug. He fights an existential black hole every day, wondering if he's wasting his youth on adventure when little brown babies are starving in Africa. Here's my take: I need time away from career decisions, my meddling family, college—whatever else. When I hit Katahdin, I'll shift gears. For now, I have a rare gift—time for clarity of thought. I won't squander it with misplaced guilt."

We walked in silence down to the road and followed white-blazed utility poles to the main drag of Duncannon. Bless trail planners who dispensed with wilderness obsession and occasionally routed the trail through towns such as Hot Springs and Damascus, where natives are friendly to scruffy, bearded men and stubbly-legged women who stroll in from a hippy time warp. Any other town would have a flurry of 911 calls. Duncannon sees us as the next wave of NOBOs, a source of a few honest bucks, a chance to offer somebody's kid a shower and a decent meal. Thus, we repay Springsteen's rust belt.

We arrived at the glorious Doyle—a century old, with a corner turret topped with a rusting cupola. It's a four-story brick edifice with an ornate second-story wrap-around porch five decades past its glory. The gal who checks us in and says our room will be available in a couple of hours agrees there is not much at the Doyle that hasn't seen better times. It's a cheap town night. Who cares about the rumors of a hiker finding a dead guy in his room? Who cares if you have trouble getting the window up to let in a little air and then, when it starts to rain, you can't get it back down? This is, after all, the Doyle. Respect for tradition is in order.

After Bone and I had pizza, we dashed through a thunderstorm to claim our room. Without discussion, we roomed together. Since the bathroom down the hall was vacant, we conserved water by showering together—a couple of kids having a good time. Is this young buck over Sky Writer? I've got patience.

June 11, Journal entry of Bone Festival at Peters Mtn. Shelter

A late start this morning and a long stop at the All-American Truck Stop. We celebrated the folly of thinking that profit is possible by offering AYCE to thru-hikers. My memories of hiking out of trail towns will be of trucking out with the burden of a massive breakfast. I'm used to grits in the South, but I have serious trouble with scrapple—a creation of Pennsylvania Dutch folk made from unspecified pork pieces blended with cornmeal. We speculated that the pieces include eyelids, stomach, bladder, etc. Sky turned green and left the table. These pork parts form a malleable blob molded into a loaf, cooked and sliced. Brave Phillie lives for the stuff, saying it fulfills a pent-up need for fat and protein. As I waddled over the Susquehanna bridge and up a thousand feet, my guts protested. I sweated pork grease and emitted flatulent sound and fury.

One bad piece of news regarding eating establishments is that free refills end at the Mason-Dixon Line. It is customary in the South to keep refilling glasses with cola and iced tea. Not so in the North. I regard rehydration religiously, so it's a letdown to have this privilege deleted due to a regional custom.

Everyone was mellow last night as we dined at the Doyle. We're drained from the segue into hot weather, and the short day was a blessing. We hiked a mere 10 miles today, to provide more recuperation. Since the water was down scores of rock steps placed by muscled volunteers, we played rock-paper-scissors to pick the water toters.

We've hiked for a couple of days with Amazing Larry and his black mixed breed Amazing Rover. Rover, like other dogs we've seen, carries his food in a custom-fitted doggie pack. He stays right by Amazing Larry's side, and when they stop, he collapses and snoozes. Larry says he plans to put in a huge day tomorrow, so we probably won't see him for a while, if at all.

Amazing Larry has a solar-powered recharger for his smart phone, from which he blogs about his thru-hike, a fund raiser for an animal shelter in his hometown of Boise. He's raised nearly $2,000 so far. Amazing Rover seems unaffected by this heroism on behalf of his fellow canines.

Doug's ailing knee has benefited from short days, and today's terrain—flat and not as rocky as advertised—was a godsend. We both regret the Four State Challenge. "I could have trashed my trip there," he said.

Doug and I solved all the world's problems and a few of our own. He's serene with his decision to become a high school teacher, probably in English Lit, although he might eventually get into counseling. He also wants to be a volunteer church youth leader. "You can't imagine how good it feels that I'm not fighting this anymore, and I have to thank Pollyanna for forcing the issue."

I kidded him that he better get used to Pollyanna, because we all think they're an item. He snapped back that despite the friendship, there has been no move to cross the line into romance. My suspicion—although I'm no Dr. Phil—is that the two of them see that there might be very serious stuff on the horizon, and they are nervous about first steps: *Fear of commitment.*

As for my own struggle, I made additional progress yesterday on accepting a life not centered around Sky Writer. Grunge and I showered together and shared a room—more innocent than it sounds, but I am suddenly aware of the spunky Texan.

Ultragrunge began this trek with spiky red hair, piercings galore and (we all thought) no tattoos. I found out yesterday that she has a blue butterfly on her left butt cheek—our little secret. What fascinates me as weeks drift by is how her hair has grown out—full and fiery—drastically softening her fair features and hazel eyes. She has slowly removed studs and rings from her nose, eyebrows, navel, tongue and ears. All that remains is a little gold globe on her right ear lobe. Her phenomenally athletic physique is decidedly feminine. The shower was a feast for the eyes. At one point she laughed and suggested that I take a picture to make it last longer. Sadly, I don't shower with my camera. I bet Earl Shaffer didn't have days like this.

EARL

If one was asked to narrow down the pantheon of Appalachian Trail icons to a triumvirate, the first two would be easy. Benton MacKaye was the visionary who created the dream, and Myron Avery was the logistical wunderkind who organized the nuts and bolts of making it all happen. The third person might be up for debate, but for many it would be the trailblazer of thru-hikers, Earl Shaffer.

He may well have had the first trail name, Crazy or Crazy One. His equipment list for the 1948 hike seemed gleaned from an army surplus shop and a hardware store. Here was a man so eccentric that he often hiked sockless and poured sand in his boots to toughen his feet. After being in harm's way as a radar technician in the South Pacific during WWII, Earl returned

home with what might be referred to today as post-traumatic stress disorder,
partially resulting from the death of his best friend at Iwo Jima. When he
was discouraged by experts from attempting to hike the trail in the Spring of
1948, Earl ignored them. Who cared if we had just been through an eco-
nomic depression and a massive world war? Who cared if people were pick-
ing up the pieces of their lives in postwar America with no time to get the
trail in hiking-shape for the first time in years? Earl was ready to hike, and
off he went. When he crested Katahdin four months later, Earl's story went
out over the AP wire and was picked up internationally by radio and news-
papers. He was the first A.T. thru-hiker, something no other soul could ever
claim.

For the rest of his unconventional life, Earl was a solitary figure. He sup-
ported himself. He worked for the trail. And he hiked. In 1965, he took a
SOBO thru-hike. In 1998, the 78-year-old donned his pith helmet, flannel
shirt, antique-style backpack and struck out from Springer. That fall, he
commemorated the golden anniversary of his 1948 trek by becoming the old-
est thru-hiker on record.

Earl is gone now, but in a spiritual sense, his presence is anywhere on the
trail you look for it. Every thru-hiker should observe a moment of respect for
Earl, the man who did it first before there were hostels, free refills, Gore-
Tex, trail towns, shuttle services or all the other things that make the trail
easier in our modern era. ◼

June 12, Transcript of Captain Stupid recorded at Rausch Gap Shelter

Less than 18 miles today to Rausch Gap Shelter. A wall with a
spring coming out, meaning no downhill trek for water. This makes the
laziest thru-hiker very happy. As Pennsylvania hiking days go, this was
the paradigm. Follow a rocky flat ridge. Dip down off of Peters Mtn.
about 800 feet and back up over 1,000 feet to regain the pancake-flat
ridge of Sharp Mtn. Along the way, investigate what little is left of old
mining settlements that have deteriorated to virtually nothing, leaving
hardwoods, ferns and flowering wild strawberry in their wake.

Today was the A.T. as Green Tunnel. You hear that about the entire
trail, because little of it is actually bald, as in the south, or above timberline, as in the north. Most of the path is wooded trail. You may be
thousands of feet above the surrounding countryside without knowing it. You're in a Green Tunnel. Which is not all bad, mind you. You

rarely need sunscreen unless you go to sleep in the occasional open meadow.

Today was the perfect example. A couple of pretty views, but mostly walking a ridge so broad and with so little topographic relief that you might as well have been on a tree-covered plain. It was cloudy and breezy, even a little cool for a change. I chose to walk alone with my thoughts, a devoted Green Tunnel denizen.

Yay!

Sky Writer is nearby, blowing celebratory bubbles. The wind catches them and sends them in colorful cascades up, around and out of the shelter. What are we celebrating? Back in Duncannon, I wandered by the fire station and asked a fireman if they had scales. He invited me in. I sucked up my moment of truth, removed everything but my hiking shorts, stepped on, and gasped! I pondered the number over the last couple of days and announced the amazing truth a few minutes ago. I am down to 248 pounds. Assuming I started at about 345, I am one small canned ham short of having knocked off the century mark, 100 big ones, the grail of all weight-loss enchiladas. When I figure how much water I swig down, how many calories I burn in a typical day and the fact that I have not regained my enormous appetite since I lit out on the approach trail, I guess I should have expected this miracle.

Sometimes I'll click in behind a hotshot NOBO and follow him uphill to see if I can keep pace. Usually I can stay in sight as long as I want. I have the legs, the lungs and the heart. I remember when the cab driver charged extra to run me to the top of Amicalola Falls on my first day. I called it the 700-foot salvation and wondered deep in my heart how many times I would gladly pay cash to avoid 700 feet. There were a thousand times in the first six weeks of this hike when I would have shelled out the pesos. *Now I don't even think about it!* I could never match Grunge, Doug or Blue Devil. I'm close to Bone and Pollyanna though. And it gets better every day.

Yay!

June 13, Journal entry of Sky Writer at 501 Shelter

Easy five miles down to Swatara Creek this morning. We exploited the serendipity of a broad shallow river combined with a scorching day. I claimed a flat rock under the pedestrian bridge and snoozed like an alley cat until Blue Devil found a bucket and mercilessly doused me. Everyone laughed so hard I had to join in.

Captain Stupid splashed around in no shirt. The flab dissolves from his body hourly, and the activity is tightening up what's left. He'll never be Brad Pitt, but at least now he no longer looks like he needs a Size 62 DDD Maidenform. I look forward to seeing the normal-looking guy he should be by the time we get to Katahdin.

Up to now, we have not been all that put off by the rocks, but SOBOs say they pick up soon after crossing Swatara Creek. We climbed a thousand feet out of the valley on a shady series of gentle switchbacks and followed a ridge to William Penn Shelter. Sure enough, we hit serious rocks.

My take: They slow you down. They're no fun. They make us cradle our sticks in one hand and scramble up and down with the other. But the terrain is so level in Pennsy that you still make great mileage with minimal effort. My main concern is for those of us wearing shoes rather than boots. I fret about turning my ankle.

William Penn is a cantilevered chalet-style shelter swarming with carpenter bees burrowing pencil-sized holes into logs and crossbeams. Sharing the shelter with them was the famous Darby O'Gill, a diminutive NOBO (5'2" in his boots) who left Springer on New Year's Day. We've followed his odd narrative in trail registers since we began, and here he is dressed in thrift-store attire, with a time-worn frame pack weighing in at nearly 70 pounds and a matted mop of bright red hair and a beard. "I like my creature comforts," he said.

His accoutrements are spread throughout the shelter, where he has holed up for two days to relieve his arthritic back. He asks if there is anything we don't need, and we assemble a pile containing a butane lighter, spare boot laces, Linda's tattered Buckeye bandana, Doug's short gaiters which he stopped wearing after "the challenge," a Power Bar, a half-used tube of Ultrabrite and one of the Captain's dreaded packets of pasta primavera. Darby scooped his arms around the swag and raked it toward him like a stack of poker chips, the fire of greed in his eyes. He's an odd amalgam of native wisdom, streetwise cynicism and survivalist paranoia. He claims to be on his fourth thru-hike. "Sometimes I take close to 10 months which is why I start early," he confided.

He told us that many trail types poke fun at him behind his back. "You all are different—friendly folk." Pollyanna patted his dusty old shoulder. "We love you," she whispered. We got ready to move on, but not before I saw Brave Phillie place some green in Darby's hand. The hard-shell jarhead has a big heart.

June 14, Journal entry of Doug Gottlieb at Eagles Nest Shelter

Pulling into 501 Shelter last night was a different ball game. It's a four-walled building with a polygonal plexiglass skylight for daytime and electric lights at night. There is running water and a solar shower. I got in line for the shower and afterwards changed into a tee shirt I'd rinsed out back at Swatara Creek. I felt almost human.

Frick and Frack, an eccentric married couple, are among our fellow tenants. Frick, the husband, got buy-in on a feast. Since we're close to Highway 501, he coaxed a guy with a car to shuttle him to a grocery store and go whole-hog for dinner. All the rest of us agreed to split the grocery bill and provide the wherewithal for a big cooking fire. This is food we're discussing here! The game was on.

By the time the food arrived, Brave Phillie and Blue Devil had scrounged enough fire-wood to torch a small castle, and the fire settled into marvelous coals. BP and Frick—Control Freaks of the Universe—made personnel decisions about who'd do steaks, salads, beans, etc. It came together with military precision.

Steak so tender, I could cut it with a plastic knife. Beans cooked in titanium pots with fatback, onions and peppers. Baked potatoes jacketed in foil with salt, butter and sour cream. Leafy green salad with mushrooms and onion slices. Apple pie and coconut cake! Plenty of cold soft drinks. Even though there is a "no alcohol" rule at the shelter, there are a couple of beers for each of us. Linda gave me one of hers, and I nodded off in a hoggish haze, my head on her shoulder.

Naturally, we slept well, and I was off early with Bone and Grunge this morning. The first five miles were slow-going due to rocks, and when we got to Shuberts Gap, we decided to ease off the dam into a little lake fed by cool spring-fed creeks. Bone and I stripped to the waist and slipped in. Then, here came Grunge, also stripped to the waist and demonstrating all that is aesthetically pleasing about the well-conditioned female form. Bone and I gave each other approving grins, swam around in the frigid water, and got out to air-dry. By the time the others arrived, we were reclad. "We will not speak of this," said Grunge with a wry smile.

I stopped alone later at a power-line cut and gazed south toward I-78. Someone once noted that America's Interstate Highway System has made it possible to travel from coast to coast without seeing anything. Frantic Americans in trucks and cars careening along an infinity of trajectories toward countless destinations. Am I any less intent on foot travel than they on their motorized transport? When I go back to living as they do, will I take something from this place to make the world more useful in my eyes and in God's? I met a chipper day hiker the other day, a 1985 thru-hiker, who said not one day has passed since he left the trail when he did not stop at some point to wistfully recall his trip. "It's a daily reaffirmation of my hike and of my life," he said. "God's gift! Don't waste it."

June 15, Journal entry of Pollyanna at Port Clinton, Pa.

A huge family reunion gathered last night at Eagles Nest, commandeering the entire shelter and much of the available tent space. We found spots for our tarps and tents, but the situation got intolerable as the drinking picked up, dogs got in our gear and kids ran amok. When a couple of tipsy teenagers cut down a sapling, Brave Phillie went in search of the resident patriarch and found an aging red-nosed man in a folding chair, a glass of bourbon in his tremor-afflicted hand.

"You people are clueless!" Brave Phillie said. "You need to sober up and get your brats and dogs under control."

The old man's tremor consumed his entire body. He wagged a finger at BP screaming, "You go to hell!"

BP shook his head. "Let's pack up," he said. "The only way to put a stop to all this is to nuke this bunch." We transplanted to a quiet spot off the side trail to the shelter and had a pleasant evening. Thru-hiking is a moveable feast.

I started first this morning, walking alone through the mist, intent on getting to Port Clinton early to clean up and relax. Though I was on a ridge, it did not seem that way. The topography was gentle, and a forest of mature trees with a uniform tapestry of the richest green ferns blended into a seemingly endless silent, swirling vapor—my favorite place in Pennsylvania.

I heard gentle footsteps and turned to see Momma Llama. "Isn't this wonderful?" she whispered, not expecting an answer. We hiked in silence, hoping this magic would last, which, of course, it did not. Breezes cleared the sky and cooled the air, and the final five miles were a snap, even the severe 800 feet down to the Schuykill River Valley. We triumphantly made our way into Port Clinton, yet another trail town battling age and decay and opening its arms up to us and our limited wealth. We walked into the P.O. at 9:30, and found mail drops and letters.

We gathered it all and schlepped like bag ladies to a quiet spot on the sidewalk where we sat sorting and reading. I looked at Momma, the button-down attorney, and laughed. "I could never imagine myself unbathed, no makeup, skulking into a weird little town nowhere near anyplace and plopping down on the sidewalk to handle my affairs."

Momma agreed. "Pollyanna girl, let's dance at each other's weddings." I put my money on dancing at hers first. We went to the Port Clinton Hotel for a room. The lady who managed the hotel was just opening the bar and set us up. "This is an old place, you understand? The bathroom's down the hall, and we got laundry and TV," she said.

We crossed the street to the Port Clinton Peanut Shop, where a delightful woman sold us caramel corn. We finished showering and were well into watching *The Scarlet Pimpernel* on a fuzzy channel when Sky showed up. She said some of the group was going to a free camping pavilion and some to the hotel. The plan was to converge later on the downstairs restaurant where the hamburgers are an art form and the french fries come in barge-size portions.

"It's just 3:30," said Momma Llama. "Nothin' to do but watch TV, eat caramel corn, drink Cokes, read books and scratch our hind ends for two and a half hours. Then we just go downstairs to the restaurant. Can you give me any reason why Port Clinton isn't the greatest place we've ever been in our lives?"

SUBJECT: **Where has love gone?**
DATE: **June 16, 9:30 a.m.**
FROM: **< bluedevilonat@yahoo.com >**
TO: **< Inpat63@aol.com >**

I have so little time to compose this, brief moments to collect my thoughts to reply to a message that just reached out of the computer screen, grabbed my throat and yanked me out of a mood of elation and expectation and hurled me into a dark depression in the twinkling of an eye. Indu, what can I say? I was so sure there would be another of those messages where you tell me you think of me all the time, can't wait to see my smiling face, long to hear me on the phone—and what I get goes against anything I could have conceived of in my bleakest moments.

You say your parents have come down hard, that you attempted to tell them about it and they cut you off at the knees, that the prospect of our ever seeing each other again is not only impossible, but it is unthinkable in a cultural sense? Indu, I was raised in an atmosphere steeped in diversity (I'm a living symbol of it) and religious, cultural and racial tolerance. Not everyone has this advantage, but so help me, I can't see how your parents can order you not to see me again or how you can go along with it.

Here's where I stand: I love you still. I respect your pain, but I will not abide this forced breakup. I'll hike out of this little town in a few minutes and have you on my mind all day, all night and on and on to Katahdin. Promise me you'll answer when I try to call later on by cell. Don't let them tear us apart. We're not the freakin' Montagues and Capulets here. This is the 21st century. We can call our own shots, can't we??

June 16, Journal entry of Brave Phillie at Eckville Hiker's Center

This is a little Eden on a lightly traveled road next to a white-frame house where the caretaker resides. It's enclosed with bunks for six, and since there were NOBOs here before us, the Bly Gap crew is tenting. We have a solar shower and water from a tap at the house. I just cooked at the picnic table and now I'm in the shade with Momma Llama on the lawn watching the caretaker on his riding mower. This is another of those places where the carpenter bees have taken up residence in the woodwork. We've been dive-bombed consistently, just like at William Penn. I watch bluebirds tending to their parental duties—so beautiful in the bright sunlight.

After crashing at the pavilion in Port Clinton last night, I shoved off in great weather this morning for the climb back up to the ridge of Blue Mtn. The trail followed the ridge and eventually dipped down to Eckville Shelter. Great views from Pulpit Rock and the Pinnacle, where we saw a patchwork of farmland disappearing into the haze from the Blue Mtn. bowl toward the horizon. If someone takes a photo to capture the A.T. in the Keystone State, it's usually from the Pinnacle. It previews a ridge route to Lehigh Gap, the eco-disaster I've told the Bly Gap Gang about.

We've had time to shower, cook, and catch up on naps. Perfect, right? Well, no. Blue Devil sweet-talked his way into the home of a friendly family this morning to get to his email. He found a message from his Waynesboro squeeze, Indu, who told him that she spilled the beans to her parents. Her father lowered the boom and told her that she was forbidden to see, phone, or email him ever again. She sent one last email to say it was all over. He, predictably, went ballistic.

The good thing was that in typical Blue Devil fashion, he was (as Momma Llama calls it) verbalizing. She and I were *in loco parentis* (another of Momma's terms) for the poor kid. We hiked together, battling rocks, relaxing at vistas, and letting him talk. At one point, he buried his face in his hands and boohooed. Momma leaned against him on one side, and I, old buzzard that I am, leaned against the other. I've seen grown men cry, mostly in combat. I've shed tears myself, losing friends in battle and having a wife slip away. That explains my sympathy.

"I can't let her go," he sputtered. "This can't happen to me."

Momma smiled in that wise way of hers. She told him he was one of the privileged folk of the world. "You are accustomed to having things go right. You're gifted with brilliance, beauty, strength, and intellect. You even sing well," she said. "Now, you've had one of life's most precious possessions snatched away—your first love. Let's face it, if you go grab her and run off to have the happiness that's rightfully yours and hers, it won't work. She'll be estranged from her parents. They'll be miserable, and if they are, you will be too. Face the facts."

Blue Devil gazed beyond Blue Mtn. and into the afternoon haze. I saw the first flicker of realization that he was powerless.

June 17, Journal entry of Momma Llama at the Borough Hall, Palmerton, Pa.

We haven't done a real humdinger of a day for a while, so we all decided to put in nearly 25 miles to Lehigh Gap. The profile map showed a thousand-foot gain to start followed by a long, level stretch before 1,200 feet of easy downhill into the gap. The Eckville caretaker said thru-hikers do it often. The only problem is the rocks. "That'll slow you down, so get an early start," he warned.

Well, we're close to the longest sunlight day of the year, so we assured ourselves of tons of daylight by starting in the murk of predawn. We watched the deep forest go from gray to green as we scaled the ridge. There was stark mystery you only get in the early morning, as we stood on the rocks at Dan's Pulpit and studied the ridge we'd hiked on yesterday. Somewhere in the farm valley below, someone was driving metal against metal about every 30 seconds. A pile driver maybe. For miles it continued, unceasing. I braced for its every impact. The rocks were not constant, but God, were they frequent. My feet and ankles felt every step.

Around a spot called the Knife Edge and another called Bear Rocks, I climbed up, over or around big boulders. Somewhere in the rocks just after Bake Oven Knob, Blue Devil and I lost the trail and wasted 15 minutes looking for the next blaze. A SOBO walked up and pointed to a perfect blaze that even BD's young eyes never saw. How does that happen, to have the trail right in front of you and not be able to see it?

An ecstatic Grunge finally checked the "bear box" in hilarious fashion. She was in the vanguard and came across a boorish day hiker casually having a bowel movement about three feet off the trail. "You nitwit," she said, "This isn't a privy!" He hitched up his pants, left his pile behind and walked on. Yechh!

Soon, Grunge saw something from the corner of her eye, a great big bear, hunched on his hindquarters, letting fly with a pile of scat before ambling silently into scrubby hardwoods. "It must have been my day for seeing fat animals relieve themselves," she observed. Then, not five minutes later, a yearling bear ran across the trail in front of Grunge, little more than a black blur. And with that, all of us have seen a bear. I, of course, remain the bear-spotting champ.

Blue Devil and I stuck together and spoke only occasionally of his broken heart. He seems melancholy but not disconsolate. There's no triumphing over heartbreak, I've learned, you just need to wait it out. We pounded downhill into Lehigh Gap, tired and parched. At the west end of the river bridge, the old Blue Devil luck struck. A couple of gorgeous girls who'd just finished their shift picked us up and whisked us through rush hour to the Palmerton Borough Hall, just in time to sign in for a stay in the basement. There were bunks, showers and places to hang our dripping clothes. This is known as the Palmerton Jail, but it's really a community-hall basement set aside to serve thru-hikers. The stay is free. We just had to show I.D. at the police station. After the whole crew arrived, we rested our tired dogs. "I told you guys the rocks were neither as bad nor as easy as you might expect," Brave Phillie pontificated. "They are what they are. Some nights your feet are hamburger."

We splurged at Bert's Steakhouse, a retro rock-and-roll diner. I had meatloaf, lima beans, coleslaw, a Coca-Cola and a chocolate shake—all guilt-free.

A BUNCH OF CRAP

here is no "polite company" among thru-hikers, at least insofar as topics considered taboo in conventional society. Take, for example, the subject of evacuating human waste, an obsessive preoccupation for many.

Most take great pride in their regularity. Typically, after months on the trail, one will rise, eat breakfast, pack up, start hiking and within 20 minutes, it's time for download. The discharger retreats to a spot away from the trail or any water source and tends to business. Some carry a trowel. Most use the old Boy Scout cathole method. Clear away leaves and duff, clump out some dirt with the heel of your boot, make your deposit, use t.p., find a stick to corral the herd into the hole, replace dirt, tamp down and point yourself back toward Katahdin while eager microorganisms dutifully decompose your waste and return it to the natural world from whence it sprang.

That's best-case scenario and does not encompass other possibilities, which include:

- Diarrhea: *Only those with iron constitutions do not at some point eat too much Thai, barbecue or Dutch scrapple at some stopover, causing disastrous on-trail travails. Pity the solitary spirit who gallops into the trees three or four times a day. Few carry enough t.p., leaving many to sacrifice a favorite bandana.*
- Privycentrism: *This fixation is common to those who feel their need after dinner or breakfast necessitating the use of a shelter privy. Some thru-hikers develop total comfort with privies bordering on perverse affection, while others simply tolerate them. Regardless, those using a privy day by day must adjust to the knowledge that he or she is regularly placing his or her hindquarters on a constantly shared surface that is rarely cleaned.*
- Constipation: *The thru-hiker who hits this bump in the road must take medicine or pray that the inexorable continental drift does not take place during boulder hopping.*
- Creativity: *Some hikers are a couple cards short of a full deck and take odd pleasure in their functions. Messages have been left in the snow by mercurial urinators. Many hikers enjoy figuring out the most comfortable way to affect Number Two. Case in point: The rappel method. A SOBO back in 1973 came up with this concept during Maine blackfly season as a way to comfortably move heaven and earth with alacrity and comfort. The idea is to disappear to a quiet*

spot, select a stout sapling, grab it with one hand as if rappelling and lean back to allow gravity to do its work. Soon, your bare backside is clothed again, and hungry blackflies must look elsewhere for exposed flesh.

- Expediency: *Sometimes, a tortured trekker faces adversity under the most dire circumstances. One felt ill while hiking along a cliffside in Tennessee's Laurel Fork Gorge. There was no time to waste, so he grabbed a tree, hung his skinny hindquarters out over the gorge and dropped the proverbial deuce 80 feet to rejoin nature. A hiker in Maine, again cliffside, produced a snake-like coil on a granite surface near the trail. Thinking fast, he found a flat stick, picked up the object as if with a spatula and flipped it into the abyss. Peering over the edge, he noted that his gift had landed sunny-side-up on a sheered-off pine mast. For months, it served as a mute sentry protecting the sincere efforts of all hikers who try to do the right thing to protect the fragile environment of "Spaceship Earth." Sail on, grand ordure of Maine!* ■

June 18, Journal entry of Ultragrunge at Leroy Smith Shelter

Don't let any flatland poseur ever say I'm not good. I'm sexy; I'm ripped; I'm the buffest NOBO out here, and I've now seen bears. After being the only one not to see a bear, I have now seen two, good for second place in the Bly Gap Gang bear-watchers sweepstakes, right behind cocky Momma Llama, who will be going down soon.

Today we had a sweat-inducing climb out of Lehigh Gap. A couple of hot chicks that were diggin' on Blue Devil yesterday met him and me after breakfast and whisked us from Palmerton right back to the trail. We climbed out of the valley in the cool of the morning, a steep rocky pitch. This is a Superfund site thanks to zinc smelting in the past century. The EPA shut the operation down in 1980 and has been trying to rescue the ravaged landscape ever since. The whole top of Blue Mtn. is scoured down to rock and sterile soil, and revegetation is taking decades.

A front came through on the exposed slope, and though it wasn't cold, it was a mother to keep my balance coping with wind and wobbly rocks. A gust tipped Blue Devil over, and he landed turtle-like, with his arms and legs waving. We hiked through treeless desolation. A rattlesnake slithered across the road, just like Death Valley. All we needed was a couple of cow skulls and a few circling buzzards. A single-engine plane dropped seeds into a combination of sludge, ash and lime scattered on the slopes in an attempt to grow vegetation. Good luck! The place looks like the moon.

After all this depressing terrain, we hiked back into the woods and down into Little Gap before climbing back to the ridge on a tumble of blazed boulders. Then 10 miles to this shelter, old and full of NOBOs and short-term section hikers. We were bone-dry, and the water source is a trickle. When I filled up, I drank a liter. Then I filled up both bottles and my entire cook pot to save a trip. After all our bellyaching about rain, we whine about drought. Every pleasure has its price.

June 19, Journal entry of Bone Festival at Delaware Water Gap, Pa.

The Water Gap! Like Damascus, Harpers Ferry and Hanover, this is a landmark you hear about time after time, and finally, you're there! I knocked off all 20 miles by 3 p.m., picked up my mail drop, checked into the hostel, showered and now I'm kickin' back as my cronies trickle in.

I'm bunkmates with Beethoven's Curse, a NOBO Music undergrad from Princeton. He's a really smart musician who decided he needed this in the middle of his college career. He has been behind us for months and was delighted to meet us today after reading and hearing about our adventures. He's a clarinetist who plays classical and jazz, and he's working on jazz compositions. When he passed Sky Writer earlier, she promised that she and I would do a little set for him tonight.

May God bestow richest blessings on the Presbyterian Church of the Mountain for this little hostel right near where the trail passes through the gap. I'm not made of money, and this helps. If I make it big in business, I hope I never get so rich that I don't appreciate simple luxuries such as zero days. I haven't had a day off in so long that tomorrow seems more like a pleasant theory, a hallucinogenic concept, rather than a reality. A day where I do not have to walk anywhere at all—how can I contain myself?

Today was our last battle with the Pennsy rocks, pretty bad until we got to Wolf Rocks, the approximate southern extent of glaciation on the A.T. Once I plowed through that boulder farm and peered into the haze from the lookout point there, I agreed with Brave Phillie. Rocks are what they are. We've seen their worst, and we're still standing.

When I got to Kirkridge Shelter, I made a run to a nearby spigot and loaded up. Headachy due to dehydration, I perched on a rocky ridge, a sentry post towering over the patterned farm properties below—green and brown in the summery haze, which were crisscrossed by country lanes, county blacktops and highways with solitary vehicles moving soundlessly in the distance. The Water Gap's siren call pulled me off my back and northbound.

I came to a pipeline cut where men in coveralls were operating ear-splitting heavy machinery. A guy in tattered jeans and hardhat, carrying a snake pole, was making notations in a notebook. He had been hired by the pipeline company to catalog endangered eastern diamondback rattlers, making sure they were not disturbed. I asked if there were many rattlers in the area, having not seen one myself. He looked past me, and with the careless grace of an expert, he stepped a dozen feet away and pulled up a writhing four-foot rattler. He gently affixed his fingers behind the big guy's business end and held him out for my inspection.

"How many have I walked right past without knowing?" I asked as I stepped back.

"Plenty," he responded. "These babies like rocky ridges."

Hiking down to the Water Gap, I stopped at rocky overlooks and peered at the river a thousand feet below. Traffic zoomed frantically over the I-80 bridge, and the bellow of tractor trailers echoed off the cliffs of Mount Tammany across the river in New Jersey. I strummed "Twangin' Perry," feeling as young and free as a man can feel. Now I'll stroll to Doughboy's Pizza for the best stromboli east of the Mississippi.

SUBJECT: **Feelin' no pain**
DATE: **June 20, 2:07 p.m.**
FROM: **Sky Writer** < singinghiker@yahoo.com >
TO: **Clara Spangler** < claraathome@att.net >

Mom, you can't grasp the joy of a zero day. I got my chores done yesterday, and today I just walk around this trail town, eat what looks good and sing with Bone and Beethoven's Curse, a NOBO who caught us here yesterday. I ate at Trail's End Café, a little spot right off the white dots. I love talking to Beethoven's Curse and hearing his take on the trail talk about us. He said all four females are more beautiful than he imagined, but that's just the pink blazes talking. You know the old saying, "They're all beautiful at closing time?" For guys on the A.T., it's the same thing. When guys get distracted by women, we say the pink blazes are confusing him.

Captain has lost more than 100 pounds. His face has character now that the jowls are going away. He got a ride to Stroudsburg and bought two T-shirts, a new pair of shorts, new socks and a new hat. I didn't recognize him. He's beautiful!

Something weird at the P.O.—a fat envelope from Dad with a copy of *Pride and Prejudice* and an AmEx cash card for $1,000. Before I read the letter, I was angry. It just isn't right to not communicate with your kid while she's out on the adventure of her life and try to make up for it with cash. But the letter was disarming. He's ashamed for not being in touch for so long. He said you all are communicating about me with civil tongues and that he sometimes wishes we could reassemble the broken parts and make it like it was. We know that will never happen. Forgive me for saying I blubbered when I thought about it. I even prayed—not for things to be put back—but for anger and ill will to dissipate so that we can get on with our lives. Tomorrow a wuss day, ending up at another hostel, with time to loll around like anachronistic hippies at a place called Sunfish Pond. They say there are gazillions of bears in NJ and NY, so I'll have my eyes open.

9

Bears, Delis, Clean Breaks and a Peek at the Emerald City

THE PURITY OF THRU-HIKING

What officially constitutes a thru-hike? Some say it must be finished in one fell swoop of hiking, with allowance for a liberal sprinkling of zero days. Others say that if you complete the entire A.T. in a 12-month period you get credit for a thru-hike. Others say this is plain nonsense. If you do the whole trail in a reasonable period, it's a thru-hike. Otherwise, it will be defined as a section hike, and who really cares—you did the whole trail, didn't you? Actually, some people care a lot, and plenty of heated discussions have echoed around shelters about how the terms are defined.

For instance, some people attest that you must walk past every white blaze on the trail to say you've done a thru-hike. Others say it is okay to leave the trail on a side path to a shelter and then return to the trail the next morning on another side path from the same shelter, missing a few hundred yards of the official A.T., and still say you've done the whole trail. Purists claim you must backtrack to the original spot on the A.T. you left the night before. Whatever!

If you come to a highway and hitch into a town, what should you do when you hitch back? Some say you should cross back over the road and make sure your path intersects with the exact spot you left off the day before, so as to form an unbroken line from Springer to Katahdin. Others say that is laughable. Then there is the belief that slackpacking (depending upon your definition) is cheating. You should go full pack the whole way, or your trip is tainted. If so, the majority of thru-hikes are impure.

Most of the above is honest quibbling, but there are interpretations with fudge factors built in. For instance, some say if you hike 2,000 miles or more, you're a 2,000 miler. This sounds the same as being a thru-hiker, but if you just hike 2,000 miles, you can skip 180 miles or so. If mosquitos get over-whelming in New York, skip ahead to New Jersey or Connecticut. If the 100-Mile Wilderness in Maine is too much unbroken trekking for your taste, hitch a ride out on Jo-Mary Road and avoid about half of the 100 miles. It is disingenuous to fudge this way. People who affect the thru-hiker pose but are not really hiking the entire trail are known pejoratively as tour hikers. Then, there are people such as Bill Bryson, whose book, A Walk in the Woods, *is among the funniest and most readable accounts ever written on long-distance hiking. He never claimed to be a thru-hiker. His quirky achievement stands on its own merits.*

Odd behaviors crop up among hikers. Yellow blazers are those who use their thumb to hitchhike on a yellow-lined highway past a stretch of trail they wish to avoid. Later, they conveniently ignore that they skipped a sec-tion and still claim to be thru-hikers. This breed is not to be confused with pink blazers. A pink blazer is a lonely male who hikes faster in an effort to catch up with female hikers or slows down to allow them to catch up. A pink blazer might even reverse trajectory and double back on previously hiked trail to reunite with females he left behind.

Another obscure term is aqua blazing, which means to eschew foot travel in favor of self-powered water travel such as a canoe. When the A.T. paral-lels the Shenandoah Valley, a hiker looking for variety can hike into the val-ley and paddle over to Harpers Ferry to reconnect with the A.T. Only the most liberal interpretation would allow this to be part of a true thru-hike.

It is not necessary to hike from one terminus of the trail to another to achieve thru-hike status. Those wishing to avoid crowds at Springer and early-season bugs at Katahdin may attempt a wraparound. This means you start somewhere near the middle and hike south or north. When you reach the end, you go back to the middle and hike in the opposite direction to the other end. Another variation is the yo-yo, in which you hike from one end of the trail to the other and then turn around and start back from whence you came. This is covered by medical plans under "psychiatric."

One much-maligned group of hikers are those who never worked a day in their lives and whose trips are financed by doting parents looking to keep their pampered darlings occupied and out of sight. The assumption is that these folks live high on trust funds. Hence, the label Trustafarians. Most hik-

ers who meet trusties discover they are a pleasant breed possessing a love of discovery and a sense of humor. Why shouldn't they be happy? They are young, wealthy and footloose. ■

June 21, Transcript of Captain Stupid recorded at the Mohican Outdoor Center

I had a long talk with Brave Phillie last night. He's made good taking the computer knowledge he picked up in the service and using it to build a business. He has stashed several million dollars away by providing what customers want cheaply and efficiently—an inventory-control system for large independent retailers that continues to make money. BP doesn't want to work much anymore. He needs someone to run the show under his supervision, with the eventual aim of handing the whole thing over to the new guy. I guess it's clear where this is headed. He says he went from thinking I was a flaky slob of a pretender of a phony of a sham to marveling at how I plod along and make everyone—including me—believe.

After a trail town mega-breakfast this morning, we traipsed across the Delaware River into New Jersey. We hiked through dew-dappled forest to Sunfish Pond, the southernmost glacial pond on the A.T., a beauty spot bathed in the glow of a perfect noon.

It was the first day of summer, informally recognized as International Hike Naked Day. As we reached a grassy area on the southern shore of Sunfish Pond, we met a group of 20 naked pedestrians, ranging from comely teenaged girls to strapping college-aged guys to middle-aged men and women on the negative side of the watchability index to a few spry elderly types with a cavalier attitude toward the inevitable impact of gravity on those parts of their bodies prone to sagging. Leading the way was a zaftig woman who proudly displayed her robust physique and expertly tooted a piccolo. She wore a sparse ensemble—Tevas and flowers in her hair. The mob filed behind her, singing, laughing and having more fun than anyone we've seen since Springer.

After delighting in this parade of nudity, Brave Phillie, Momma Llama, Sky Writer and I relaxed on the lakeshore, munching nuts and raisins. Brave Phillie reminded me of the night we hunkered down in a blizzard at Spence Field and how he compared me to a bumblebee, an aerodynamic paradox.

"I never dreamed you'd get to Neels Gap," BP drawled. "Now you can outhike me. You could give Grunge and Blue Devil a run for their money. I've talked to you enough to know you have a working knowledge of IT. Why don't you come down to Georgia after we finish and take over my business?"

The question hung in the air. Momma and Sky scoured me with their eyes. Hey, this was a big deal. I looked at Brave Phillie, this tough SOB with one of the kindest hearts I've ever known, and replied, "I'll tell you what. While you and Momma go back and finish up your missed stretch of trail in Virginia, I'll tie up loose ends back in Ohio and make sure Mom is okay. Then I'll come to Georgia and see if we can make it work."

Then I dropped the 200-megaton bomb: "But only if Sky will join me."

Again, a long pause and probing eyes, this time in Sky Writer's direction. "I'll think about it," she said. And for the first time ever, Sky and I acknowledged that we're thinking about a future together. My heart pounded like a steam locomotive. Sky's pale face was as red as a wild strawberry. Momma Llama was beaming, and BP was tilted back in the grass—his hands behind his head—staring skyward with his characteristic vacant smile, chewing on a stalk of grass. It was a watershed in the life of my spirit, a flashpoint we all will remember and discuss fondly for years to come—I hope.

Later, we made our way a couple more miles to regain the Kittatinny Ridge and found a grassy spot with a view over a complex of forest, meadows and mountains. My heart was calm. I sat quietly with Sky Writer, surveying a world that suddenly belonged to us. I didn't need to know her real name or if she will really go with me or even if there will someday be a Captain Stupid, Jr.

Yay!

Now, we sit at the Mohican Outdoor Center. Fewer than 11 miles to get here today, and for a few bucks we get bunks, shower, kitchen privileges, soft drinks—all a man whose prospects just went into orbit could possibly want.

June 22, Brink Road Shelter register entry from Doug Gottlieb

Be not forgetful to entertain strangers: For thereby some have entertained angels unawares.

—Hebrews 13:2

Welcome to the continuing adventures of the Bly Gap Gang, a close-knit group of NOBOs on an inexorable track to Katahdin. The lovely ladies are Momma Llama, Pollyanna, Ultragrunge and Sky Writer. The pathetic lugs with them are Brave Phillie, Bone Festival, Captain Stupid, Blue Devil and yours truly—I'm Doug Gottlieb, the one with no trail name.

For you SOBOs, here's the word on the rocks you're already seeing here in New Jersey: Yes, they get worse in Pennsylvania. No, they won't ruin your life. In fact, if you ignore the whining from other NOBOs, you'll find the rocks in Pennsy are countered by level ridges, which allow you to make great time. It's alright, Okay? Plus, when you get to the Water Gap, you'll get the best pizza and stromboli we've eaten, at Doughboy's. The hostel in the Gap is wonderful. Contribute generously.

If you're southbound, you can make it to Mohican Outdoor Center in an easy day's hike from here. Everything you need, including showers.

Now, for the excitement. Two bears—a momma and her adorable cub—wandered around the perimeter of this shelter around dusk looking for handouts. As darkness closed in, we still heard them out there and captured their eyes in our headlamps.

Seeing these bruins capped off a superior day. Fine ridge-walking along abandoned roads on the Kittatinny Ridge—a stretch for praying, meditating or just zoning out. This trip is tantamount to Christ's 40 days in the wilderness, although he surely had a much rougher time of it. Aside from having all the equipment, food and clothing we need, we also have companions to nurture our spirits. Plus, we don't have Satan tempting us with all manner of easy ways to go wrong. Or maybe we do. There is temptation out here to resist doing small tasks to support others in need, to make unkind remarks no matter how small or subtle, to allow fatigue to get in the way when you have a chance to give useful trail intelligence to an inquiring SOBO, and to just generally go clueless when you have a chance to improve a fellow traveler's trek. Heat, dehydration, hunger and general trail fatigue obstruct my natural inclination to serve strangers. I pledge to do better. If you remember having seen me north of this place, let's hope I behaved accordingly.

Tibetan monks traveling on foot across Himalayan escarpments sometimes launch slender strips of paper into mountain-wind currents to descend to pilgrims on paths far below—tiny epistles offering prayers for good health and safety to others as they ascend on their separate journeys of trial and purification. A struggling Christian pilgrim, I leave this register entry as my shred of prayer paper. The A.T. is a river of hope. Hope to observe the clouds, the stars, the beasts and the flowers, and to keep them in our hearts. Hope to see who or what is around the next crook in the trail. Hope to isolate within our souls the peace to accept and embrace wherever we'll go after we share Katahdin's summit. My hope is that my aspirations will come into clearer focus, and God willing, may yours be similarly beneficial to you and your companions. May your boulders be widely spaced, your storms brief, and your springs free-flowing.

June 23, Journal entry of Pollyanna at High Point Shelter

Doug, Bone and I took off in the cool of the morning. We came to a grassy crest liberally sprinkled with rocks and took off our shoes and socks for what Bone calls a "groove-in." He broke out his banjo and went into his own melancholy world before stopping and opening up his heart.

He said that as he went through the Water Gap he was on an emotional high, but for reasons he can't fathom he's in a nosedive. "Every time I come to a road," he said, "I think about sticking out my thumb. I can be back in Colorado in a few days."

Each time he thinks he's adjusted to the fact that Sky Writer will never love him, he goes back into a funk. Now that she and the Captain are solid, he can't take the constant reminder. "It's a manic-depressive meat grinder," he lamented. "Hike ahead," Doug suggested. "Hook up with other NOBOs. Change the scenery." Bone looked at us with a dour smile. "It wouldn't matter. She's still back there. I got a letter back at the Gap from Molly McMahon. I might go home and get a big dose of her."

Doug and I hiked on, and I finally saw a venomous snake. Doug was 30 feet ahead, and suddenly, he stopped short and went to one knee using a twig to prod what looked like a reddish worm. "I think we're looking at a baby copperhead," Doug said. "I wonder how potent this little guy's bite is." We were never to find out, because it vanished beneath trailside ferns. Bone caught up and watched the tiny critter disappear. "I missed my chance to end it all, Cleopatra-style," he lamented.

Moods brightened as we pulled up to a sandwich place at U.S. 206, a deli with beverages, assorted subs, heroes and breakfast sandwiches. I had a bagel with cheese, egg, bacon, mayonnaise and ketchup and washed it down with a giant Pepsi. I sprawled on a bench outside, a bloated human blimp. Despite the temporary discomfort of food binges, we recover quickly. Our bodies route the massive influx of nutrition into our systems. At the half-gallon challenge, I felt a little queasy, but only for 30 minutes.

We tracked rocky trail and watched with displeasure as the sky darkened to the west and produced mist. When we reached a big picnic pavilion on Sunrise Mtn., we were soaked through. The sky looked like tarnished pewter, and the wind whipping over the ridge made me feel hypothermic. Doug noted my chattering teeth and insisted that I get out of my wet clothes and into my sleeping bag. Always the gentleman, he turned his back while I stripped and shimmied into my bag.

All I remember of the afternoon was more shivering. High Point Monument loomed above in the fog, but since it required a side trip, I kept going. High Point Shelter was mobbed with short-termers and NOBOs, so I planted my Zoid on a flat spot. Doug put his tarp right next to me, and I talk to him through the nylon wall as I snuggle in the paradise of my bag. I know I'm good when I get to the end of a miserable day and get comfortable. I know I'm good, and so does Doug. And so is he.

June 24, Journal entry of Blue Devil at Pochuck Mtn. Shelter

I never got comfortable last night, and when I nodded off, I rolled off my ground cloth, partly out from under my tarp, so that half of my down bag was exposed to a relentless rainstorm, and if you know anything about down, you understand that rules one through 10 are *never get a down bag wet*. My summer bag is ethereally light and rated to 45 degrees—well and good under dry conditions—but get it wet, and it's a noisome, soggy wad of dead weight. I mean, just damn! I grew up in Florida. When I woke up in the rain before dawn, I put on my headlamp and and whispered to Doug that I was going to hike to the secret shelter to hole up and wait. I covered five miles quickly and got to the worst-kept secret on the A.T.

A compassionate thru-hiker named Jim Murray has built a cabin in a gorgeous field for the pleasure of thru-hikers. I met a couple of NOBOs there who've been ahead of us the whole trip—a freshly retired California couple who decided to discover America by hiking the A.T. They're in their mid-fifties, and their trail names are Jo and Bev—Joanne being the woman and Beverly, the man. They suggested I hike into Unionville to drown my sorrows in the soda shop.

It got warmer as morning went on, so I napped as I waited for my compadres, who all took the side trip to the "secret shelter." "Not much of a secret if it's mentioned in guidebooks," Brave Phillie opined. Just before heading back into the rain, we heard a fearsome racket from the pasture. We peered into the fog and saw a male donkey attempting to mount his female love interest, and she was having no part of it. Each time he got himself all comfy, she gave him a quick swivel-hipped motion, which sent him toppling from his dominant perch.

"You show him, girl!" Grunge hollered. "Show that pig who's boss!" "Don't give up big boy," I shouted. "You know she wants it!" Momma Llama asked me if the lady donkey told me that. I had no reply.

A little later I got the big blockbuster from Bone. He and I hightailed it down a little country road to get to Unionville for mail drops. We hit the P.O. and headed to the heralded soda shop, where we inhaled sandwiches and milkshakes. Bone asked if I needed extra food, and I said, "Sure, but why are you giving it away?"

"It ends here for me," he said. "My banjo is wet and and sounds like crap anymore, and that's pretty much the state of my attitude. You know what's eating at me, and so does everyone else. I'm making a clean break."

I've come to know this little guy well over the last couple of months. He's been a big brother prodding me toward a less cocky attitude. He's quick with an encouraging comment, regardless of lousy weather or rocky trail. I said, "I know what's gnawing at you, but you're resilient dog. Man, we're way past halfway, and the best part is ahead."

He leaned back in his chair, linked his fingers over his belly, smiled and sighed. "I look out the window and see that street, and I know it's my ticket away from pain," he said. "The sooner I get on a new track, the quicker I can look forward to the next morning. Lately, when I wake up, I can't keep from crying. I can't change what's causing it. I need new surroundings.

"So go forward without me, my young apprentice. Nurture what I have taught you deep within your breast and conquer Mahoosuc Notch and Mount Katahdin. Stand strong and pure as I have instructed. Be a servant to your friends. Refuse to antagonize your enemies. Remember my music. Etch my manly countenance into your memory. Emblazon my teachings into your very moral fabric, and you will never stray from this great, serpentine footpath we call the A.T. And when you stand atop the Big K, whisper my name, and your quiet voice will carry across the continent to my expectant ears."

Everyone in the shop had stopped what they were doing—eating, fixing sandwiches, reading the newspaper—and stared silently at Bone, amused but also aware that something major was happening in this young man's life.

A customer was headed to Pittsburgh and offered Bone a ride. Bone had apparently said quiet goodbyes to all the others, leaving me for last. He walked out leaving me in rueful contemplation before Sky and Captain strolled in 10 minutes later. Sky seemed unsurprised, but she still leaned against the Captain's shoulder and cried. "I can't stand not having his music," she said. "I may never have it again."

I returned to the trail and followed an old railbed, wandered through meadow and field, and road-walked a while before walking around the perimeter of a federal wetland with a massive flock of Canada geese. The weather was raw and misty, making my soggy tee shirt inadequate. I reached Pochuck Mountain Shelter and sat at the picnic table, thinking of Bone as NOBOs gathered. The cohesiveness of the Bly Gap Gang—something we had taken for granted—has unraveled a bit. Now my gnome-faced brother with the slightly obscene trail name heads west, not north.

CALLING IT QUITS

It is no shock when an aspiring end-to-ender calls a hike short within the first 100 miles, but once a NOBO gets past Damascus, much less Duncannon, the decision to quit begs investigation. How could someone get that far, invest that much time and emotional currency, and decide to hang it up? Often, the reason is clear. A nagging injury, despite a regimen of pills and rest, deteriorates into intolerable pain. The decision makes itself. But what about a trekker who seemed happy and healthy just days before and suddenly, inexplicably, calls it quits?

Sometimes it has to do with an inability to connect with members of the group or with clashes of personality that become insufferable. For the lone hiker, it may be that solitude erodes one's peace of mind. Facing another day without companionship becomes unthinkable, and for whatever reason, willing companions do not materialize.

For others, it is the ennui of the Green Tunnel's repetitive miles. How many million steps can one person stand during the monotony of the mid-A.T. states? Day after day of redundancy chafes at some people's sanity, while others see differences in texture, hue, sight and sound hour by hour. The languor of one more day of slogging through heat, rain or drought is unendurable. The thought of returning to a life with the freedom of an automobile, the luxury of a shower, fast food no more than five minutes away, cable television, shopping malls, thermostats, washing machines and all the other things one sought to escape becomes obsessive. The traveler grows weary of waking at 3 a.m. with a gypsy moth caterpillar crawling on his cheek, filtering water from a suspect source, eating packaged glop for days on end, feeling excruciating pain on his swollen left big toe with every step, or hearing a singularly dull story from a hiking companion for the 58th time. The trekker wants the easy life back.

The A.T. is for everybody, but the huge dose of a thru-hike is not. A variety of personality types can handle long-distance, but only one in four will complete the challenge. Everyone starting out knows this. When someone stops before finishing, the decision is honorable and should be respected by all trail lovers. Maybe someday this dejected spirit will return to the exact spot and resume. Maybe not. ■

June 25, Journal entry of Brave Phillie at Breezy Point Lodge, Greenwood Lake, NY

We left this morning in the first decent weather in a while, feeling lower than a snake's belly in a wagon rut. Bone Festival was the most cheerful character in the group, other than Pollyanna. To have him abruptly leave is bitter. I knew he was feeling rough about things between him and Sky, but I never realized he was serious about heading back to Colorado until he told me privately a couple of days ago.

I had this on my mind as I wandered through the woods to the boardwalk over the marshes of Pochuck Creek. When development started closing in on the trail corridor, a decision was made to put a boardwalk over a marshy floodplain. This resulted in a unique configuration of boardwalk and bridge over a topography that will likely never be developed, seeing as how much of it is already wetland. I strolled across the swamp with Momma Llama before going off-trail a few hundred yards at New Jersey 94 to a gardening store that attracts the hiking trade with ice cream.

Then we climbed up Wawayanda Mtn. to Pinwheel Vista and looked across Vernon Valley and the wetlands, over to Pochuck Mtn. I pulled out a cigar and lived the lush life for a little while, but then it was back to business. I promised everyone if we could make it to Greenwood Lake, I'd spring for rooms at Breezy Point Inn and have a zero day tomorrow. This meant 22 miles, not an overwhelming chore, but around the NJ/NY border the rocks make for slow-going.

At one point, a grouse exploded onto the trail in a cloud of dust and feathers not 10 feet from Pollyanna, performing the old routine of flitting about in the underbrush and trailing her wing as if injured and vulnerable to attack. I've seen this any number of times, but Pollyanna was taken by surprise, not realizing that the momma was just trying to distract our attention from her young'uns. She let out a movie-worthy scream, and Blue Devil came running back to rescue her. He let out a belly laugh when he heard what had happened, and Pollyanna—always a good sport—chuckled too.

We meandered along easy trail until not long before the state line. Serious rocks began along the ridge of Bellvale Mtn. Ultragrunge said it was like hiking across whalebacks, one after the other. Finally we hit easy trail over to NY 17A, and got a quick hitch into Greenwood Lake. The normal drill is to hitch two at a time, one girl and one guy. No surprise that the girls—with rare exceptions—get rides quickly. The girls are the bait. The guys provide security. Momma and I went last and got the sixteenth car. A blue-collar type headed home told us as much of the story of his life as he could on the way to the P.O. I picked up a mail drop, and when I walked outside, a man was eying a Marine patch on my pack. The old leatherneck gave us a ride to the Greenwood Inn and sprung for a couple of beers in the bar. I don't know what I like better, a free ride or a free beer. Yeah, I guess I really do know.

Greenwood Inn is right on the lake, with a better-than-decent restaurant. I showered and shaved before joining Momma Llama for dinner. I chose a steak, and she picked chicken cordon bleu. Not bad for a couple of scruffy trail rats.

This evening we sat out on a deck looking over the marina, the lake and mountains beyond, a living wake for old Bone. All the stories we remembered were funny. Captain remembered early days of the hike, when each day was a new disaster. "Bone took time to stay back and cheer me up," the Captain recalled. Guess he just lost what Momma calls "the passion."

SUBJECT: Happy Birthday to . . .Me!
DATE: June 26, 8:34 p.m.
FROM: < ATMommaLlama@charter.net >
TO: < JackieChristie@aol.com >

Got your email birthday card. Sounds like your love life is good as mine. Brave Phillie tells me I'm not smart to be hiking with the castoff wooden hiking stick I picked up on Blood Mountain, so he took delivery of a new pair of hiking poles for my birthday. I wondered why he was creating so many enticements to get us all here yesterday before the P.O. closed. I unceremoniously tossed my old stick in a trashcan, but I confess I'm not altogether sure about these newfangled sticks. Some purists say they leave unsightly scratch marks on trail rocks and do damage to moss and plants alongside the trail. Still, I'll leapfrog out of the stone age.

The Bly Gap Gang got an ice cream cake with 60-year candles to celebrate the horror of admitting to being 60. After I blew out the candles, I apologized for my constant fear of damaging my injury-prone feet, which results in my mother-hen obsession with "Where are we stopping for lunch?" or "Where are we staying tonight?" This particularly irritates Ultragrunge, and we've had words about it. But everyone told me to relax—we'll make it. We've been without Bone Festival for a few days now, and none of us seems able to give him up. Sky, despite her devotion to Captain Stupid, is despondent.

Greenwood Lake probably gets slammed by winter, but what a summer spot! Boats cruise quietly up and down its length. The mountains hover above, green and silent, perhaps a little resentful that people have settled here and stolen the solitude. A great place for a zero day! Knock on wood, no pain for quite some time. Yesterday, with all the rocks toward the end, was a good test, and I feel great. As for the future, Brave Phillie and I enjoy each day, loving each other, staying on trail-name-only basis.

June 27, Journal entry of Ultragrunge at Fingerboard Shelter

We're totally in New York. After zeroing at Greenwood Lake, we felt like we'd OD'd on Red Bull this morning. Pollyanna, Doug and I lit out early. I do better if I minimize hiking with Momma Llama, with her anal-retentive efforts to control our daily schedule.

We got a quick ride back to the trail from a 16-year-old girl headed to her summer job, and she obviously had major hots for Doug. This was the first time we females couldn't brag about attracting the quick ride, and Doug actually blushed when we gigged him about it later. That chick was smitten!

Easy-going for the first few miles, with the exception of Cat Rocks and the Eastern Pinnacles, big outcroppings on the Bellvale Mtn. Ridge. After that, we spent time at Fitzgerald Falls, really charged up with all the recent rain. Pollyanna and Doug took off their shoes and soaked in the cool water. I hiked on alone.

At Mombasha High Point, I was eager for the promised glimpse of Manhattan, but the summer smog precluded any hope of snatching a peek at the Empire State Building. Or so I thought. As I squinted in the appropriate direction, I kept trying to imagine I could see the skyline. Suddenly I went into that zone we entered on the peak of Big Bald when we encountered the humming bird. The sun went behind a cloud, and the light and shadow in the miles between Mombasha and New York City were altered by some power of optics, physics, meteorology, aero- and hydrodynamics. For a scant 30 seconds, Manhattan made itself manifest. I was Dorothy—minus Toto and the Scarecrow—gazing open-jawed at the Emerald City. By the time I picked out the Empire State and Chrysler buildings, the view was again obscured by summer haze. I wanted it all back, this time with the World Trade Center towers back where they belong. Wowie zowie!

I hiked six miles of roller coaster before a precipitous descent down a rocky pitch known as Agony Grind, slow-going but no great challenge on a dry day. It was just past noon, and Fingerboard Shelter was only five miles away, so I waited at NY 17 for Doug and Pollyanna. They arrived five minutes before a cheap public bus pulled up to take us into Southfields, where we lunched at an old-fashioned diner, the Red Apple Restaurant. A giant Coke and a greasy burger with lettuce, tomato, cheese, onions and pickle along with fries and coleslaw. Health food!

We hitched back and worked uphill to the Lemon Squeezer, a massive rock formation with a narrow cleft necessitating pack removal. We had to climb out of it—no big deal, since we were able to hand the packs up to Pollyanna, who went first. These obstacles are a breeze for young punks, but when I think of people in their seventies doing the trail, I admire them for maneuvering their old bones around some of these roadblocks.

According to the map, we were in Harriman State Park. Back in the 1920s, this was where the first sections of the A.T. were designated—hallowed hiking territory. Fingerboard is a granddaddy shelter dating back to 1928. The stone relic was packed with girls from a church group. When Doug walked up shirtless, there was a collective sigh from the chorus of 14-year-old gigglers and a bristling, protective attitude from the adults. Doug seemed clueless about his masculine appeal. Oh, he knows, but he plays it cool. We set up nearby and pooled ramen noodles with odds and ends in our food pokes. Black flies abated, and the temp was cool, time to spread out on a grassy spot and read some trashy sci-fi I cadged off Blue Devil. I dug out two Snickers I'd scored in

Southfields. We discussed favorites, and the top three were Snickers, Baby Ruth and Reese's. Power Bars are unpalatable. Traditional candy bars rule!

Captain Stupid's secret weapon is those nasty gel packs that come in chocolate, banana, strawberry and other puke-inducing flavors. Before he heads uphill, he rips one open, squeezes out a mouthful and chases it with a slug of water. It has the consistency of baby poop, but he claims it's like pudding. His salvation is his insistence on hydration. Despite his reputation for laziness, he carries plenty of water and makes spring detours to keep his super-sized physique saturated. He sweats like a plow mule.

The last vestiges of a brilliant sunset have dissipated through the hardwoods. I'm on my flat belly writing by headlamp, melancholy about Bone's absence. After he knew Sky Writer was lost to him, we noticed each other—Duncannon comes to mind. But with Sky around, he would never enjoy even a Grade-A, super-sexy babe like me. Maybe I'll take a look at Blue Devil.

June 28, Ledger entry from Sky Writer at the Graymoor Friary ballfield pavilion

I've encountered fellow travelers calling New York and New Jersey the dregs, but the Bly Gap Gang digs this corridor. Today was among the top five since Springer, starting with one of those misty mornings when the sun conjures up apparitions from vapor and shadow. Deer materialized before the mist enveloped them again. I passed William Brien Shelter which is built into a cliff wall like a hobbit hole.

Then came an enchanting section along a flat ridge, bracketed by mature hardwoods and a forest floor carpeted with lush blueberry bushes bearing little green berries. The bears will go nuts over this place when the berries plump up, juicy and sweet.

As I crossed Palisades Parkway, I witnessed the oddest spectacle. I stood in the wooded median dividing two-lane portions of the freeway and took in the chaotic blend of sound, fumes and speeding vehicles. Then a red-tailed hawk exploded from the forest depths, struggling to stay airborne with the burden of a writhing eastern diamondback. The laboring raptor flapped furiously up the road before losing its sinuous load.

What a sight! The rattler dropped 20 feet onto the sun-baked blacktop and slithered for the woods and possible safety. A car swerved to avoid it, almost causing a collision with a truck, resulting in a mad blast of horns and screeching tires. Inevitably, the snake was run over across the back half of its body. Still, it struggled heroically to escape the pavement and reached the shoulder. The hawk circled back, zeroed in and struck again, snatching its prey in a quick touch and go, darting straight back into the woods. Blue Devil came along, and I had a bear of a time convincing him of what had happened.

We wandered through soggy Beechy Bottom before climbing to the crest of West Mountain, where we looked down at the freeway knifing through wilderness. Later, from the same ridge, we got a view of Bear Mtn. and its big tower. We looked over the Hudson Valley, the land of Washington Irving, with barges floating downstream and tiny trains tracking the river's edge, hooting doleful strains.

Pollyanna and Doug were atop Bear Mountain, guzzling power drinks yogied from tourists who had driven up for a look downstream. A front was clearing the air, and sure enough, Manhattan lifted her hazy skirt. It was tempting to find a train and go there for a few days. Instead, we descended a thousand feet to a picnic area next to Hessian Lake and dined on hot dogs and ice cream from pushcarts before following white blazes through Bear Mtn. Zoo, the lowest spot on the A.T. at about 124 feet above sea level. The only bears some thru-hikers see are in this zoo. Pity! I posed at the Walt Whitman statue and coaxed Doug into taking my picture with the Captain.

We traversed the Hudson on the Bear Mtn. Bridge, with wind whipping out of the northwest. We climbed out of the valley and rolled along an old coach road with views of the Hudson, before settling into a determined pace, bent on reaching Graymoor Monastery. By 4 p.m. we set up shop at this pavilion next to a soccer field with a couple of section hikers bound for the Water Gap. The breeze gave us respite from bugs, and we put our sleeping pads on benches like hobos.

A man from the monastery stopped by. He prayed for our safety, for us to be illuminated spiritually by our time in the woods, for God to bring us peace during difficult conditions and fulfillment during agreeable ones. We called a pizza place. Soon hot pizza and cold soft drinks were under siege. The Captain took a cold shower in his hiking clothes. Now he's taking a soggy nap and looking pretty silly.

June 29, Transcript of Captain Stupid recorded at RPH Shelter

Yesterday seemed rough, 20 miles of ups and downs. So what did we do today? Another 20 miles, a little easier, with smaller elevation variations. Here's what's great: You know you're never all that far from civilization as you walk through New York, but you get a pretty good wilderness feel. We saw creeks, wetlands, great views and little encroachment by summer homes, industry and whatever else.

It drizzled at mid-morning. I hit a road crossing with a water spigot and hydrated. Then I plodded ahead alone, an automaton spiritlessly placing one foot ahead of the other. Oddly, it was not wholly unpleasant. I had no desire to talk, to take in the essence of the wilderness or to think deep thoughts.

This region is crisscrossed with roads used for troop movement during the Revolutionary War. Now it's only a whisper of a wilderness covered with third growth hardwoods. Given time, will this protected passageway become a mature forest such as we saw south of Bear Mtn.? Is this the legacy of a protected hiking corridor?

The trail meandered past Canopus Lake, where I spooked wild turkey. At a cliff on the far end, I spied on canoeists. Their voices carried to my perch with supernatural clarity, combining with the distant roar of the Taconic State Parkway arcing over a nearby ridge. The next five miles to RPH Shelter were effortless, and when I got here a grazing buck looked miffed that the Law of the Woods essentially demanded that he leave.

I worked the handle on a water pump right next to the shelter, and in seconds my shaggy head was awash and cool. I am clean, hydrated and satisfied to put my mini-recorder away and recline on a bunk with a blank mind. Some past traveler left a copy of *People Magazine,* a decadent pleasure. No bugs or stifling heat. Somewhere back there, Sky narrows the distance between wherever she is and me.

Yay!

June 30, Journal entry of Doug Gottlieb at Morgan Stewart Shelter

A kind soul wandered in to RPH Shelter last night and said he had a car nearby. Would we like a ride this morning for breakfast goodies? Well, duh, of course. Pollyanna and I returned with pancake mix, milk, eggs, bacon, sausage links, butter, syrup, O.J. and gourmet coffee. Love those trail angels! Momma Llama has the flair of a short-order cook. She created crepe-like pancakes. We daubed them with butter and wrapped them around sausages. I OD'd on O.J. There is never too much town food.

I stole silently away, crossed under the Taconic Parkway and climbed up to Hosner Mountain's long, easy ridge. For several miles, I paralleled the parkway, watching miniature cars streaming in both directions 700 feet below, an area where farms and forest struggle against the inexorable encroachment of mini-mansions. It all played out quietly around a huge cloverleaf intersecting with I-84.

As I neared the interstate, I followed a residential street to the tune of chained and fenced-in dogs who barked with such fury that I had to wonder if hikers had abused them in the past. I crossed I-84 and climbed a few hundred feet over a few miles toward the crest of Mt. Egbert and nearby Morgan Stewart Shelter. My thoughts ran deep, and I was startled to look ahead and see an assemblage of a dozen women in some sort of odd garb. Squinting intently, I realized they were nuns, a chanting group of God's servants clad in traditional habits and sensible shoes. The eldest of the procession was in the lead, intoning a litany and waiting as the rest of the group responded.

When I got to within 20 feet, I reacted passively—stepping off-trail, removing my bandana, folding my hands at my waist and deferentially bowing my head. They filed past, never missing a beat, a multi-aged assortment with serene countenances going about their woodland business. The last nun, young and pretty, smiled and whispered, "Thank you." I instinctively replied, "God bless you." As I watched them disappear down the trail, I wondered if it was appropriate for a humble Presbyterian to speak up and say what I said. I answered my own question. Of course it was.

I was disappointed to see Morgan Stewart Shelter swarming with boys from a church group. I yielded to the clueless bunch and found a spot for my tarp. Checking the shelter log, I discovered my Catholic friends had signed in. One of them—I assume the young nun bringing up the rear—had thru-hiked several years ago before taking her vows. She wrote that this hiking foray was becoming a tradition in her order. "A way to get closer to God by seeking Him in natural surroundings. It's transcendent to be with God in nature," she wrote. "This is not automatically true for all of us. I encourage these hikes to help my sisters find a broader dimension of our Lord." My kind of nun.

As my pals arrived, they grumbled when they saw the wild group of 12-year-olds. When an adult leader came over to talk, Brave Phillie told him that we did not mind tenting but that it is not appropriate for youth groups to take over shelters. The man was contrite. He said they were out for one night and were unsure about where they were. With a world-weary look of disdain, BP pulled out a map and showed him.

Meanwhile, the brats ran rampant—screaming, fighting and doing nothing to endear themselves to us. As is invariably the case, one was a loud, chubby kid desperate for attention. He fell off a rock and stood up sobbing and looking our way for sympathy. Before any of the resident bleeding hearts could offer kind words, BP hollered out, "Oh too bad! The little fat kid hurt himself." Pollyanna and Sky, though horrified at his insensitivity, could not keep from laughing as the kid ran back to the shelter.

Oblivious to common sense, the kids built a smoky fire that smoldered into the darkness. As we settled in for shuteye, we heard a grisly scream. One of the leaders ran to our camp and asked us to check out a kid who had fallen into the fire. Brave Phillie and I trotted over and saw that the kid had serious burns on his upper thighs. He was in pain and headed for shock. Our guidebook said it was 1.1 miles to Depot Hill Road, a dirt side road. We called 911 on a cellphone, and gave a location description to the dispatcher. "They'll catch hell getting here in the dark," Brave Phillie said. "Let's get two people carrying the kid and a load of flashlights to find our way to the road."

The kid put his arms around our shoulders and held on through his tears while Blue Devil and I interlocked our hands and wrists under his butt. Then with BP, Sky, Grunge, the Captain and one of the church leaders carrying flashlights, we made steady progress along easy trail. Switching carriers frequently, we kept a snappy pace only thru-hikers could manage. As we neared the road, we saw flashing lights. EMTs had gone back and forth in the dark searching for the crossing. Our lights were their beacon.

A couple of competent EMTs took the kid from our arms and got him situated in their vehicle to check his vitals and get him ready for transport. "Those are serious burns," one of them said. "The quicker we treat, the better. You guys did nice work." I looked in on the kid. "Thanks, Mister," he blubbered. "I'm sorry I screwed up." The adult leader asked us to tell his partner he was going with the kid and to mind the others overnight until he could get back. Then we walked back to the comfort of our sleeping bags. "Just when you think you hate the little turds, something happens that makes you feel sorry for 'em," Brave Phillie mused.

July 1, Journal entry of Pollyanna at Wiley Shelter

I contemplate July. Now well into the fourth month, I am into the rhythm of the trail. This is no glorified camping trip. It's a way of life I have come to love with all its rain, heat, drought, tedium and chronic pain. I have been waiting for this all my life. What causes me trouble is the anxiety of considering that it will all end. I will not choose to walk all my life. I need to achieve something beyond this. But since I don't know what that is, fear of the unknown eats away at the serenity.

I can live with that; I'm a big girl now. I confess that there are times when I think living like this forever would not be altogether disagreeable. I roll out of my bag at dawn, stuff the bag, deflate my sleeping pad, contemplate the day as I eat, brush my teeth, adjust my pack and head out. Some are as automatic about this routine as I, and others take longer, but we have all come to terms with the mundane aspects of trail life—food, equipment, the minor anxieties common to life in the wilds—and have time to contemplate uncomplicated pleasures and cope with minor miseries.

Last night's rescue mission showed what thru-hiking can do for you. We reacted quickly. No fuss. Just calm decisions unimpeded by fear of walking off into a dark, sinister forest. So accustomed are we to this life that we automatically know what to do.

I hiked with Blue Devil most of the day. His brooding spells have tapered off. Like all of us, he has learned that a broken heart heals. He is certain that when he finishes the A.T. he wants to head for an even bigger adventure—maybe the Pacific Crest Trail. "I was thinking I might go to Austin with Grunge after we hit Katahdin," he mused. "I could work this winter and head for the PCT next spring. Whaddaya think?"

I asked if Grunge was aware of his plan, and he said that she wants to do the PCT someday. He's not sure when. She also thinks he should go with his dad's advice and go to Duke. I agreed. "There is so much at Duke for you," I said. "Soak it up. The PCT will be waiting. College is too much fun. Believe me."

We walked past Nuclear Lake, a spot where there was a nuke lab of some kind decades ago. "I don't care what anybody says," BD remarked. "I won't drink water from that puddle." He stayed quiet as we made our way through the Green Tunnel to West Dover Road, famous for the Dover Oak, reportedly the biggest oak tree on the A.T.

We took a long break as the others caught up. Beethoven's Curse, AWOL since the Water Gap, strolled up with Sasquatch, a long-legged blond who captured the eye of every male in the crowd. Sasquatch was keeping a 20-mile-per-day average, and Beethoven's Curse decided to hook up with her for a while to see how long he could last. Sasquatch eyed the females in our group with a smug smile and said, "Sometimes men can keep up. Sometimes they can't." She turned on her heel and walked off with stork-like strides and dutiful BC in her wake.

An ancient pickup pulled up, and a shirtless, hairy-chested man with a prodigious beer gut and a giant gray beard stepped out. "You guys thru-hikers?" he growled. We nodded affirmatively. "Well, I'm Zeke Skinner. I have a cooler of beer in the back. Take all you want." Within seconds, twist caps bit the dust, and we set in to swig beer and rip open bags of chips supplied by this Jerry Garcia lookalike. "Drink it all," he said. "I love thru-hikers. Makes me remember when I wasn't the only hippie around."

So began Dionysian revelry, jokes and tall tales. No one left there sober. With eight miles of rolling trail ahead, it's nothing short of miraculous that someone wasn't injured. The only casualty was Doug's pride. He was a happy drunk. He walked ahead, singing and laughing, even occasionally skipping before disappearing altogether. When we gathered at Wiley Shelter, Doug was not to be found. In his semi-stupor, he had walked past the shelter site all the way to the NY/CT border before realizing his three-mile-round-trip error. When he returned, his high spirits had given way to a splitting headache.

In the shade with Grunge and the Captain, I drifted into a reverie induced by fatigue and alcohol. Suddenly Grunge screamed, "Look at the size of that bad boy!" Buzzing and dodging erratically around the shelter was the largest bee-type insect on planet earth. It seemed bent on exploring every square inch of the shelter. "It's big as a tennis ball!" Captain bellowed as he lumbered to his feet, a book in his hand ready to swat. The yellow intruder hovered near him and with an A-Rod swing, he connected book with bee and sent the humming monster sailing into the sunlight. Unfazed, the kamikaze insect returned and buzzed around every crevice and cranny with renewed vengeance, finally forcing mass retreat. Satisfied that he had bested us, he vacated the shelter and disappeared into the trees at top speed, leaving us laughing like the exhausted sots we were.

SETTLING IN

At times, as happened with Bone Festival, a thru-hiker endures an existential crisis, a moment of profound dejection, loneliness or conflict that precipitates that most difficult of decisions—calling it quits. If walking for days, weeks and months has taken an irreversible emotional and spiritual toll, calling the trek off is a wise decision, if not an agonizing one.

Fortunately, there is a positive flip-side. The successful thru-hiker discovers that trail life works. Like the fabled postman making his appointed *rounds regardless of crappy weather, the thru-hiker comes to accept cheerfully the inevitability of lousy weather, the monotony of the Green Tunnel, irritation and conflict with other human beings, loneliness for far-away loved ones, chronic pain, and a need for the comforts of normal life.*

What keeps one going despite all these inescapable reminders of pain and suffering is knowing that patience is the panacea to secure the traveler on an even keel. Three days of rain hold the promise of a fourth day dawning bright and cheerful. If the fourth day brings five inches of rain running down the back of your neck, there's always the fifth day. When the trail becomes monotonous beyond comprehension, a trail town will appear, or you will walk around a bend in the path and come eyeball-to-eyeball with a big sow bear and a couple of cubs looking back at you as if to ask, "Did you ever doubt that we'd eventually show up?" Or the companion who was a perfect pill in the morning will offer that afternoon to hike downhill a hundred vertical feet to get water for you—a peace offering to your aching knees. Or a text from home will let you know that you are loved, missed and welcome to return in due time to the cozy comforts you so desperately crave.

Forbearance and perseverance are the most valuable virtues for a thru-hiker. These qualities are what get 25 percent to the far terminus. There are a few out there who have such a sunny world-view that they wonder why patience matters. To them, it's all wonderful! But these folk are rare, and though the rest of us love them, it is only because we can forgive their disgustingly rosy dispositions. ▦

10

Dunroven in Connecticut, Meeting Prime Meridian and Porkies in Massachusetts

July 2, Letter to home from Blue Devil

Dear Mom and Dad,

While you two sit in air-conditioned comfort at home and at work, dine daily on tasty victuals easily prepared or cooked to-order for you in any number of delightful local multicultural restaurants, sleep each night on clean sheets and high-tech mattresses, work at interesting jobs that pay well and offer you any number of fascinating people to work with, and pursue myriad leisure activities that are educational and fulfilling . . . I, your long-suffering son, continue on this mad pilgrimage I have chosen and that you—for the most part—are financing as a reward for my academic, social and extracurricular success, despite the fact that both of you thought I was nuts to pick this adventure over an infinite number of others from which I had to choose.

I sit here in Kent, Connecticut, contemplating the wisdom of the last few months and taking stock of how I feel about my decision to become one of the few dark-skinned faithful to tread within what is predominately a Caucasian domain. The good news is that only on the rarest of occasions has race been a factor. I am too busy putting in daily miles, thinking about logistics of travel and supply, making sure I am eating adequately nutritious food, drinking pure water, and attempting to stay on good terms with my friends and the new travelers I meet each day bound north and south.

The state of my sanity and physical health is remarkably good. Never mind that I have a little poison ivy rash on my right shin and calf, a scrape on my left elbow and right hand from a fall I took the other day, grotesquely disfigured toenails on each of my little toes, and black-fly and mosquito bites all over. Despite these petty discomforts, I am at peace. As I checked out of school and into this trip, I suffered the same old adolescent anxieties I've grappled with since I crept past puberty, my own little personal purgatory of angst and internal stress wrapped around fears that I could never live up to the ideals I've set for myself and you have established for me as well.

For whatever period of time it takes me to get to Katahdin, I will meditate on my future from whichever mountaintop, shelter or trail town I happen to be on or in at the time. My friends—and oh, what a brilliant and intellectually diverse bunch they are—are always available to hear me out when I go through Hamlet-like discourses on where I should head and what I should do. All of them are like, "Go to Duke, knock the ball out of the park and then worry about more adventures." So you'll be glad to know that I will not be joining the Merchant Marine, hiking the Pacific Crest Trail, running off to the circus or marrying a beautiful East Indian Princess. I will do what the plan was all along. And guess what? I am at peace with that.

As for now, I sit outside the IGA after hitting the P.O., sorting out all my new supplies and neatly repacking. Kent is almost too picturesque to be true. Brave Phillie has an old Marine buddy who has a farm near here with a big rec room and lots of space. He and his wife will cook and slack us for the next couple of days.

Today's hike was full of heat and bugs. Blessedly, black flies go away at dusk. But mosquitoes take that as their cue to rev up their worst. It's a constant battle with infernal winged demons from hell.

You are the greatest parents ever. The more I'm out here, the more I realize that you two have infinite patience to put up with a precocious, preening punk like me. If your patience holds out, I'll make you proud of me. Mom, forgive my run-on sentences. I know you hate them, but I like to exercise this rare freedom anyway I can.

Love,
Rafer

July 3, Journal entry of Brave Phillie at Dunroven Farm

Last time I hiked through this neck of the woods, I was on my own. Since then, my buddy Al Chandler moved nearby. When I told him months ago I was going hiking again, he said he'd kick my wiry old butt if I didn't let him know when I came through. When Al was in my unit, neither of us technically saved the other's life. But we saw our share of suffering and tragedy. In the process of helping each other, we formed a lifelong friendship.

A couple of years ago, Al and his wife, Pam, cashed in their chips and moved to a little farm bequeathed by Pam's parents—20 acres between Kent and Sharon with views of the Berkshires, and a few horses and sheep. Fortunately, they made enough money in their working lives that they really don't have to do much more than piddle with this property and invite their grandkids over to play with the horses and chickens. I kid Al that the sheep are around to keep him occupied in his lonelier moments. He leers, and asks, "So what's your point?"

As we gathered behind their big frame farmhouse last night—after running through maybe 10,000 gallons of hot water for showers and laundry—the Chandlers grilled burgers and brats and put out a spread of potato salad, baked beans, green beans and watermelon, followed by two batches of hand-cranked ice cream. Blue Devil told me if I made one remark about the watermelon, he would not be pleased. That kid keeps anticipating what isn't going to happen. Al picked up on Blue Devil's knack for busting my chops, and for the rest of the evening the two of them gave me no peace. I prefer to be ignored.

Momma Llama was mellow today after Al dropped us off from his rusty club-cab Ford. For the first several miles, there were ups and downs, but free of packs and fortified by good food and a great night's rest, it came easily. The view over the Housatonic River Valley matched up with the perfect weather. Here it is almost the Fourth of July, and it's kind of dry today with sunshine and temperatures no worse than low-80s.

As we picked our way carefully down St. John's Ledges to the river, I remembered hiking through here years ago in a frog strangler, just marking time until the end of the day. Today I feel rested and strong. I have so much love for this trail and so much love for this woman. I've lost love and friendship on way too many occasions in my life, and I told Momma Llama that I felt so good today that it's frightening.

We came off the ledges and walked along the level River Road we would follow for five miles. "It's tougher for us than for these kids," she told me. "Doug and Blue Devil struggle with their own destinies, but all of them are still too young to know what loss and failure can do to you. You and I both have experience with that. That's what'll make things work for us."

She took her eyes off the flat road ahead and gave me a sweet smile—pure bliss for an old knuckle-dragger who thought his main pleasure in life would be solitary hiking trips and fishing with Monopod. We hiked among the sycamores, maples and elms, with the Housatonic to keep us company. The last nine miles was a collection of PUDs, so we were bagged when we hit Sharon Mtn. Road, a gravel state forest road Pam had located where the A.T. crossed. Everyone waited for us in high spirits.

Al smoked a turkey and Momma and Pam cooked dressing, vegetables from the garden, rolls and strawberry shortcake. "When you guys come to dinner, there're no worries about leftovers," Pam said. "I love cookin' for hungry people."

Momma and I sat in the backyard with fireflies and shooting stars to keep us company. Everyone else watched a *Simpsons* marathon on a satellite channel. They didn't know what they were missing.

July 4, Journal entry of Ultragrunge at Dunroven Farm

I thought the Chandlers had a dream life here at this mystical spot in the Berkshires. But I talked girl-to-girl with Pam last night and realized that this idyllic life has only been going on for a couple of years since they were able to make Dunroven Farm their home. Before that, they each had another marriage, and kids to boot. Add in stress of military life and all kinds of moves during Al's post-military career, and things had not been so dream-like. "Now that we've got all this, we know how to love it," she said.

She said Al idolizes Brave Phillie, who is known among his old friends for helping in times of trouble. When Al's son was seriously injured in a bicycle accident 20 years ago, BP stepped up to pay rehab costs not covered by insurance. When Al tried to pay him back later, BP told him to help someone else someday. "You wouldn't believe how that changed our lives," Pam said. "It's why we love having you here."

Today was dry and clear. We hiked 16 miles, most of it easy ridge trail, plus a few flat road miles through the Housatonic Valley before bending away and ascending back to the ridge. At a spot called Rand's View, we saw 50 miles to Mt. Greylock—spitting distance from Vermont.

Al and Pam picked us up in the afternoon and took us for pizza followed by fireworks. We watched with a jovial crowd from a grassy expanse next to a lake. I leaned against Blue Devil and nodded off. "Girl, now I know you have ice water in your veins," he told me as he jostled me awake. "Who else sleeps during fireworks?"

I looked at the rest of the gang as they reclined on old blankets—the quintessence of Americana. Hiking the world's greatest footpath together, enjoying fireworks on the Fourth of July and lazing in the grass on a perfect summer night. Al shepherded us back to his pickup, and we returned over serpentine roads to the tiny paradise of Dunroven Farm. Tomorrow, full packs and a prediction of rain. But for now, life is good.

July 5, Journal entry of Momma Llama at Maria McCabe's, Salisbury, Ct.

Al fixed pre-sunrise breakfast and dropped us off where the trail crosses a highway near Salisbury. Steady rain fell in cool, annoying drops. A lousy day for hiking, but that's what we do. We had six mostly uphill miles to the peak of Bear Mtn., where the view amounted to fog and rain. Then we descended steeply into Sages Ravine, a highlight of the A.T. in Massachusetts, but on this day a wet, slippery, miserable obstacle. Admittedly the forest and the streams were gorgeous, but the trail required us to pick each step carefully. Pollyanna took an awful fall that left her on her side with her pack half off and tears mingling with rain streaming down from her hair. It's the only time I remember seeing this tough cookie cry.

I watched helplessly as she slid and tumbled and couldn't help but recall the nightmare near Pearisburg. An unfamiliar character stepped politely around me and went quickly to her. He was blond, tall and—hey I may be in AARP, but I'm still a girl—studly. He knelt down, gently placing his hand on her shoulder, and said, "Stay put." He removed her pack as gently as a pickpocket and straightened her legs while she stared blankly at him. She had a massive bruise on the back of her right leg, along with cuts and scrapes on her hand, arms and elbows. No apparent breaks, pulls or tears.

After helping her regain her footing, the demigod pulled out a tarp and strung it between two trees on the slope right over a log where Pollyanna could sit out of the rain. He whipped out a first-aid pouch and worked on her cuts and scrapes with the precision of a paramedic—cleaning and bandaging. "There," he finally said. "No permanent damage, but it's always a good idea to attend to cuts out here in the boonies."

Captain Stupid and Sky Writer appeared, with Doug right on their heels. "I'm Wonder Boy," the young man told us. "You gotta be the Bly Gap Gang. I started two weeks behind you, and I've loved following you in the shelter logs. You made a name for yourselves after that dustup in Tennessee.

"So, you're Pollyanna," he said, giving her another quick once over. "That's what I figured. Didn't want to seem presumptuous. Maybe I'll see you up the trail." And then, with a snowblinding grin, he was gone, with all of us staring in appropriate wonder at his departing figure. Displaying a keen grasp of the obvious, Sky squealed: "He's gorgeous." About that time, Ultragrunge reached us and trilled, "That blond guy was a total fox." All of us guffawed, with the notable exception of Doug. Gee, I wonder why?

We plodded for miles, missing great views due to relentless rain and fog as we slithered down the crags to Jug End. We dropped into flat woods and reached Massachusetts Highway 41. Brave Phillie looked at me pointedly and gave me a number to call—Maria McCabe in Salisbury. It took a while to thumb rides, but soon we were making our way in several thumbed carloads down Connecticut 41 to Maria's cozy farmhouse-style home on the main drag in Salisbury. As we cruised the dreary two-lane, the driver of the minivan who picked me up noted points of interest, including Meryl Streep's lakeside mansion.

Pollyanna wasn't complaining. Just the same, she's never been the querulous type, and it was clear to BP that Maria's place was the perfect spot for a banged up hiker. Maria, a dynamo in her eighties, settled us into various bedrooms and carefully delineated her house rules. She and Captain Stupid have become wise cracking chums. She helped us get laundry, pizza and other creature comforts that comprise paradise to a hiker.

Where's Wonder Boy? Out in rain and misery? Based on starry-eyed comments from Grunge, and Pollyanna, as well as Doug's brooding, he's not forgotten.

HITCHHIKING

*P*arents, spouses and other loved ones who watch their darlings disappear for months into the A.T. wilderness are often not informed until later that their kids often stuck out their thumbs and depended on the kindness of strangers to get from places where the trail crosses roads into nearby towns. Without the support of motorized trail angels, long-distance hikers would have no practical way to get to post offices, grocery stores, hotels, outfitters, restaurants and other places providing necessities and luxuries they crave. If *the trail goes directly through a town, which it rarely does, or if it is less than a mile's stroll, then walking works. Normally, however, towns are miles away, and adding hundreds of miles of walking on highways to a thru-hike is an unpleasant prospect, certainly more dangerous than walking on a normal trail.*

When parents and loved ones become aware of this practice, it is often viewed with alarm. As if being in the wilderness for months on end isn't perilous enough, the adventurers put themselves at risk by hopping into vehicles with perfect strangers. Fortunately, the truth is counterintuitive.

According to The Thru-Hikers' Companion *published annually by the Appalachian Trail Conservancy and the Appalachian Long Distance Hikers Association, hitchhiking is generally okay. According to this guide, people who live near the trail "are aware that a person with a full pack, 'athletic' aroma, and thumb out is probably not a vagrant." Rarely have there been bad experiences. There is no denying that you are always at risk of being one of the unlucky people who gets picked up by a loser. So it makes sense to hitchhike in pairs and for women to pair up with guys. This is no insult to the capabilities and hard-earned independence of women. It's just that someone with bad intentions is less inclined to cause trouble if he has to fight his way through another guy.*

Most of those supplying rides are affable and interested in hearing about your adventure. It isn't unusual for them to take you to multiple stops and wait for you to pick up mail drops and groceries before offering to drive you back to the trail. The rule is to thank trail angels at least three times. Also, dropping them a line at the end of the trek is a way of paying them back in full.

Hitching is illegal on interstates, the Blue Ridge Parkway, Skyline Drive and other places, including all of New Jersey. This writer was attempting many years ago to get a ride on an interstate entrance ramp when a state patrol car drove up. "I'll be back in 30 minutes," the deadpan officer remarked. "Don't be here!" I assumed this meant I could keep thumbing, and I got a ride before the cop returned. I still appreciate his willingness to bend the rules for a scruffy wayfarer. ▪

July 6, Journal entry of Sky Writer at Mt. Wilcox North Lean-to

I suffered from tunnelitis today. You hear people squawk about the misery of the middle states, the minimal views, the smallish mountains, the lack of wilderness. I suppose all that is true. But what a luxury to have frequent access to nearby towns, trailside delis, convenience stores—even a friary where you can attend morning mass. It was so wild and remote in the South, and as we head farther into New England, the goodies are an increasing rarity. Almost every day of hiking in these middle states from Harpers Ferry to most of the way through Massachusetts has worked for me. I loved the frequent places to sleep in a real bed and do laundry. Lighter packs! And when weather has been hot, dry or wet, at least the terrain has been less demanding than in the southern states. Today, though, I gave into the lumpy ups and downs. The woods were pretty, but the sky was gray and low. The crests were enveloped in swirling, view-killing mist. I couldn't even be coaxed to sing.

Maria took some of us back to the trail, and the rest hitched a ride from a house painter in a minivan. The consensus is that we will stay on trail for a while, having spoiled ourselves lately. Early on, we came to the Shay's Rebellion Monument. Renaissance man Blue Devil filled us in on its historical significance. "Is all that crap really true," Brave Phillie asked, "or are you just a major league B.S. artist?"

"Yeah, it's true," Blue Devil retorted. "And when the man who thinks the South should have won the Civil War calls me full of B.S., the planets are way out of line." I'm glad they smile when they talk this way.

The shelter is full of section hikers tonight. The sun came streaming through about an hour before it set, and we should have pleasant weather tomorrow. I will recover from tunnelitis and set my sights on Vermont.

July 7, Transcript of Captain Stupid recorded atop Beckett Mtn.

This is a rare time we're resorting to a bootleg site. We listened to Doodad, the Springer caretaker, and have stayed serious about the "leave no trace" ethic, which requires using authorized campsites and shelter areas. But sometimes there is nowhere else to crash.

Sporks are poking and gouging at all available cook pots, and I'm discovering stimulating new combinations of old ingredients. Sky convinced me to transition away from freeze-dried, saying it destroys brain cells.

Yay!

My pot contains ramen noodles—I know, I know, the most unoriginal of hiking foods—but I'm combining sage, the last of my cheese with the mold scraped off, an itty-bitty can of white chicken meat and cream gravy I cadged from Momma Llama, who for whatever weird reason had it in her pack. I've come up with a brimming pot of what I call Beckett Mtn. casserole. Blue Devil stuck his polycarbonate spoon into my pot and pulled out a wad with big strings of cheese hanging from it. He contemplated it suspiciously as it cooled and then popped it in his mouth and chewed soulfully.

"This is fine, dog," he said. "The sage put it over." He reciprocated with mac and cheese blended with sardines in hot sauce. Major seal of approval.

Brave Phillie cooked up his second batch of red beans and rice with Cajun seasoning. He calls it Coonass Hobo Stew. And now for cream gravy, tuna and noodles from Momma Llama. What have I done to deserve the bliss of eating all I want while still losing weight? Sweet Grunge is making one batch after another of a cheesecake-flavored pudding with raspberry sauce and crumbled graham crackers. She didn't cook tonight, cleverly trading dessert for a sampling of entrees.

We booked 17 miles today over rolling but never particularly difficult terrain. A typical day in Massachusetts, but hotter than an equatorial tin roof. I found a tick on my leg, grasped him between thumb and forefinger and plucked him off. I've heard from locals that some summers they're all over. Yuck!

This morning, I met the most obese human I've seen since Springer (other than the old me). He was in his mid-thirties and topped 300 pounds. He was out for a day hike and crossing the bridge over the Massachusetts Turnpike, sweating like a hog in heat and glad to have an excuse to talk.

"I've never done this. I'm not cut out for it," he lamented. I explained that I was heavier than he is when I started. He was incredulous, but Sky backed me up. "Maybe I can do it too," he said. I encouraged him but provided the admonition that wanting it and sticking with it are concepts miles apart.

"Whatever," he said. "But I salute you." He unceremoniously dropped his pants and mooned interstate traffic streaming below the pedestrian bridge. Sky gasped and rummaged for her camera, while I— no longer ashamed of my body—dropped trou and joined my chubby colleague in insulting the traffic, and saluting my own success.

Yay!

July 8, Journal entry of Pollyanna at Thomas's place in Dalton, Mass.

I say it too often, but this seriously was one of the primo days of this trip, if not my life. I had rare energy and set off like lightning. Doug was feeling similarly. He had a little smile on his face, daring me to get on the trail ahead of him. I hiked hard—just under a jog—for nearly half an hour before he could catch me. Even then, he was trotting to close the gap.

I was just getting ready to walk on some stepping stones under a few of inches of water lapping up from Finerty Pond when he caught me. The recent rain, combined with beaver activity, caused the overflow, and the only reason Doug caught me was that I stopped to put on my red Waldies to keep my shoes dry.

Doug hollered, "Caught 'cha!"

"Yeah, but at least my socks are dry," I countered.

He waited like a little gentleman after we crossed the wet spot, and I switched out of my Waldies. We continued along the pond bank and stopped to watch a momma wood duck and her tiny charges splashing and quacking around. Suddenly—and boy am I glad Doug was there to verify this—a leviathan bullfrog leapt toward the fuzzy ducklings, took one in his mouth and disappeared below the surface with only a ripple to show he had ever been there. The mother was freaked for maybe 30 seconds, and then she gave up and ushered her brood to a safer part of the pond. We stood gaping at the vacated spot before noticing daddy frog emerge onto the bank among some reeds. A tiny webbed foot protruded from his mouth for a few seconds, and then, after a big gulp, the foot was gone, leaving the king of the pond sitting placidly.

In just over an hour, we were at October Mtn. Shelter for a mid-morning break. I munched teriyaki beef jerky and drank a liter of fruit punch. Doug ate his customary beer nuts, and I told him it's a sin to put sugar on perfectly good peanuts. "Be careful or you'll end up with Beer Nuts as your trail name," I cautioned.

It was less than a dozen miles to Dalton over one of the loveliest, flattest ridges we've seen since Pennsylvania. We pulled into High Street by 2 p.m. Such an easy day! I felt up to another 10 miles. But when the trail dips out of the hills and into a town, it's special. A guy named Tom lets thru-hikers put tents in his yard. We walked to his place first, intent on sharing Doug's tarp. What a cozy prospect!

We sat with Tom on his front porch, and he gave us ice cream. As we savored each bite, we kept thanking him. He smiled and observed that he doesn't always receive such enthusiastic gratitude for his trail magic. We laughed and said that our unwritten rule is that you always say thanks at least three times to a trail angel. "I've heard about your adventures through the grapevine," he said. "The trail is better for having you on it." That was the nicest thing anyone has said since Springer.

Then, out of the blue, Doug asked me for a date. Weird. He wanted to take me for a beer and then to Angelina's Subs for the sandwich of my choice. First we took a romantic stroll to the coin laundry, where we washed up in the restroom, changed into rain gear and washed every stitch we had in one big load. In no time, we were 90 percent clean and clad in fresh duds. Doug sighed, "I could wash this shirt 10 times, and it would still have thru-hiker perfume."

"You picked the right date," I cooed. "Matching B.O."

We sat in the pleasant confines of the Shamrock Inn and Pub drinking black and tans drawn by a hiker-friendly barman. The rest of the group—ready for a little alcohol to temper their afternoon—wandered in. We were mellow and well-behaved except for when BP and the Captain got into a belching contest. Momma Llama put a stop to it by letting out the loudest belch of all. A truck driver would have been cowed.

We gathered in Angelina's for dinner. Captain Stupid—the king of popular culture—began crooning an old Louis Prima song about Angelina, "the waitress at the pizzeria." His hoarse baritone resonated to the sidewalk, and all within earshot smiled. We were welcome here. We had no idea what kind of rain, pain, hunger, gloom or joy lay in the miles ahead. It was still too far to worry about it having an end. We would enjoy a night here without concerns about deadlines, boyfriends, insurance payments, programming smart phones or whatever else we used to worry about. A perfect night in northwestern Massachusetts.

ENTITLEMENT

The word comes up more than it should in relation to the A.T.: entitlement. The feeling some long-distance hikers have that all the angels, the magic, the hostels and the other amenities of trail life are part of what they are "entitled" to simply because they have the wherewithal to spend months on the trail. Decades ago, thru-hikers were a rare breed. Special services for hikers made little sense. These days, a cottage industry has built up around the thru-hiker culture, allowing hikers to indulge in luxuries unimaginable years ago. Much of what hikers receive is a product of people with big hearts, and the sad thing is that hikers sometimes take what is available and show minimal, if any, heartfelt appreciation for this largesse. A few are downright rude. A self-serving attitude emerges, in which the traveler thinks he or she is a troubadour, a person who deserves to be treated specially simply because he or she is on an adventure. The solution? Always thank a trail angel at least three times. 🔳

July 9, Journal entry of Doug Gottlieb at Mark Noepel Lean-to

Blue Devil and I started early, wandering residential streets of Dalton before tackling an easy thousand-foot climb over several miles up North Mountain. Pollyanna and Grunge zipped past, promising to meet us at the Cobbles, big chunks of marble looking over Cheshire, a wee trail town nestled in the Hoosic Valley. We passed mountain bogs, and had the weather not been dry in recent days, we probably would have gotten wet feet. It's weird to see swamps on ridgetops.

Later, as we sprawled on the rocks and spied on Cheshire, Grunge told us that she talked last night to one of her old professors in Austin. He's starting a publishing business on the side and he wants Grunge to help him run it. "He's 20 years older than I am and has always been a little busy with his hands," she said. "But I can handle him. Publishing is one box I want to check, and he knows it. I'll go slay that dragon when I finish this. No job search, no fear of the unknown. I gotta love that. He said I can take as much time as I want when I finish the hike and then head down to Austin. I can wrap up my degree while I'm working."

As the midday sun radiated, the cobbles got steamy. Down below, as they have in so many other little mountain towns since Georgia, the conscious beings went about their appointed tasks, oblivious to latter-day hippies looking down from on high. We're anachronisms in an age when twenty-somethings are expected to be ambitious, self-centered and industrious. We are self-centered, I suppose. Who do we serve beyond our selves? But ambitious and industrious? Hardly! We're glorified hobos.

We descended into Cheshire, with the looming prospect of Mt. Greylock to the north, and stopped for an ice cream soda. We all knew that we would soon pass out of the middle states and the proximity to decadence they provide.

Feeling wistful, we left Cheshire and took on four miles and 2,000 feet uphill to Mark Noepel Lean-to. I fell into a cadence, remembering

Sunday hymns in the pew next to Mom. Rock and roll, jazz and classical are fine, but hymns have lyrical inspiration and a driving tempo to
get me uphill with wings on my shoes. I knocked off the climb with
gusto and cooked rice, dehydrated beef, and soup mix.

Pollyanna arrived as I cleaned up, and magic happened. We met our
first SOBOs from Kathadin. They were hiking together: Double Dog, a
crusty veteran in his late fifties, and a pal he met in Maine, Prime
Meridian. PM was a recent graduate of the University of Georgia who
sported a curly black beard, the only thing keeping him from looking
like a fresh-faced kid. He was juiced to meet us, because he had heard
other NOBOs talking about our fracas in Tennessee. He cheerfully
shared a half-hour's worth of valuable trail intelligence.

"Maine and New Hampshire tighten you up like a sphincter on a
roller coaster. Climbs that are literal scrambles straight up mountain-
sides, bogs where mud and water soak your feet, and bog logs that tilt
and toss you into the muck—all of this fused into stresses and strains on
your body and spirit," he warned, but always with a smile of wonder on
his face and laser-intensity in his eyes.

"For NOBOs, it really starts at Glencliff in New Hampshire. All the
way through Vermont, you'll see great mountains. But once you get to
Hanover and hike to Glencliff, that's when it really begins. That's
where you start up Moosilauke and begin about 400 miles of butt
kickin'. But here's the beauty of it: From there to Katahdin will be the
greatest hiking you will ever do for the rest of your life, and you guys
will have had 1,700 miles to toughen up for it. Plus, the worst of the
bugs will have passed. And Katahdin, you have to climb it yourself to
see. Best mountain on the A.T.!"

Pollyanna and I were disarmed by this guy's love for hiking, an
energy and reverence for the trail we had never seen. I filled him in on
a few "can't miss" spots south of us, but I realized that he had already
been getting the scoop from NOBOs ahead of us. We couldn't bring the
same thrill that he delivered so naturally to us. There was an aura of
wholeness to this meeting with Prime Meridian, a shared completion of
the trail as we clasped hands. Never have I seen a thru-hiker so totally
absorbed in the experience. As a token of respect, I offered Slim Jims to
PM and Double Dog. Double Dog ate his on the spot, intoning in a classic bass, "Doug, this is the best Slim Jim I ever ate." They zoomed to the
top of my list of favorite hikers.

Tomorrow we make our way to the peak of Mt. Greylock and then
down and up into Vermont. Pollyanna and I have been talking about the

thrill of heading into the final big three: Vermont, New Hampshire and Maine. Is this dream world finite after all?

July 10, Journal entry of Brave Phillie at Seth Warner Shelter

The lean-to was jammed last night, so Momma and I slept under the trees. It was a night filled with incidents. At 2 a.m., Captain Stupid went berserk when he woke up to find porcupines munching on his trademark black boots. Footgear gets soaked in sweat, and salty residue is left behind. Porkies chew to get at it.

Captain was in his skivvies, caterwauling and waving his sticks. When the porkies started for the woods, each with a boot in its mouth, the Captain attacked. One dropped its load and skittered away, but CS whacked the head of the other and killed it stone dead. Then he got mad, something I've never seen with him. He was angry for killing the porcupine and madder, still, that the porkies damaged his shoes. He got the shredded uppers and laces configured to where he thinks he can get to the next highway and go for new ones. But man, this guy was hopping mad!

Later, after Sky Writer cried over the death of the innocent porcupine and everyone else laughed themselves back to sleep, we got more commotion from the SOBO kid we met yesterday, Prime Meridian. After eating too much back in North Adams, he woke up about 4 a.m. with a gastrointestinal storm in his innards. The moon was down, so he donned his headlamp and headed into total darkness for the privy. He found it under siege by prowling porcupines. Not wanting to get involved in another porkie war, he wandered into the woods to take care of urgent business. If this wasn't enough, his headlamp failed. There he crouched in the inky abyss, clueless about the way back to the shelter. He said he heard "something big"—likely another huge porcupine scratching in the underbrush nearby. "I figured I'd lean against a tree and wait for daybreak," he said. Fortunately, someone else took a trip to the privy, and he followed their light through trees and briars to safety.

This morning, Momma Llama and I got up real early and walked to the peak of Mt. Greylock, the tallest since Virginia. Like last time I was here, I got emotional looking at the memorial tower, a tendency I share with other combat veterans. The air was cool, and the view was clear for summer. The peak was deserted. They say Melville was inspired by the whale-like shape of Greylock as he looked out his window while writing *Moby-Dick*. Odd that it was written in the New England mountains.

It was nearly a 3,000-foot drop down to North Adams, the last town in the Berkshires. Momma Llama and I were the only Bly Gappers who didn't need to hit the P.O., so we just kept going. The forecast was for hot and hazy, so we sat in some shade before the long climb out of the Hoosic River Valley—the last we'd see of that river, or of Massachusetts and its pretty state forests.

We labored in afternoon heat to gain the ridge for a last close-up view of Massachusetts. Then we were in the Green Mountains of Vermont. We had easy trail to Seth Warner Shelter, where I stayed last time I came through. The only difference is this time it's full, so we're tenting. The heat must be getting to Momma Llama. She told me she might as well be hiking with a cigar store Indian. I stay quiet at times, but I thought that was healthy behavior out here in the woods.

11

The Green Mountains, Skyhawk's Redemption and White River Immersion

July 11, Journal entry of Momma Llama at Melville Nauheim Shelter

Trouble in paradise. I accept that being in close quarters with other people under physically exhausting circumstances, temperature extremes, lots of rain—all the unavoidable components of long-distance hiking—can cause friction. I accept it, but I don't have to like it.

Brave Phillie has difficulty understanding that simple speech is part of relating to people. He will go for hours during which the extent of his commentary amounts to grunts, belches and grudging nods. A few times a day, he emerges from his trance, but a more consistent flow of information is useful when you travel along a footpath with constant visual and aural revelations.

The sexy retired Marine and I are alone here tonight. I can't remember a totally empty shelter in a long time, and I am savoring solitude. No other Bly Gap Gangers are here, as they all hitched into Bennington to split the cost of a motel room. Pollyanna promised to bring alcohol for my stove, so I didn't go with them.

For the past couple of days, as I hike with or without BP, a mixture of anger and anxiety sweeps over me. Why can't he get it that I need him to come out of this shell and participate in being together? I mentioned it yesterday, but he reacted as if it's my problem, not his. "You gotta dance with who brung ya" was how he characterized it.

We came out on this adventure with a need for solitude. Ironically, we are crammed together at night under tiny tarps or in shelters, sometimes next to our friends, other times randomly juxtaposed with a total stranger.

Brave Phillie lives for peace and quiet. He sits placidly, tending to his journal, studying a map or reading a book. I love quiet time alone with him, wordlessly delighting in his presence while I tend to my personal business. I thrive on peace and quiet as much as the next woman. But Brave Phillie should understand that I need to talk. I will not let this rest.

On another subject, Captain Stupid found new trail shoes at an outfitter yesterday and was thrilled with how light and comfortable they are. I love to see an experienced hiker ponder an equipment change over a long period and finally take the plunge. The Captain has long been considering a change to trail runners. The porcupines left him with no choice. He was like a kid on Christmas morning sporting his new Salomons.

The hike today began with a climb up to a powerline right of way where we spotted the biggest bear yet. Open power-line cuts allow berries to thrive, so it's no shock to see a foraging bear. We enjoyed him at length before he ambled off in search of richer pickings. We looked down into Bennington, and despite its hiker-friendly reputation, we stayed on the trail. Aside from the steep climb from Highway 9 to the shelter, this was an easy day with my best friend. I just need to figure out a way to open him up.

GEARHEADS

Every long-distance trekker takes equipment seriously. You can't climb a wilderness peak and have your pack disintegrate, nor can you discover during a blinding rainstorm that your "waterproof" pack cover is porous as cheesecloth.

Some settle for low-tech stuff, moderate in price and a little on the heavy side. As long as the gear works and doesn't fall apart, they are satisfied. Others select equipment that is light and reasonably durable. These folks enjoy the advantages of equipment technology but remain complacent about its endlessly boring list of specifications.

Then there are the gearheads. Their waking hours before, during and after a hiking trip are caught up in researching, shopping, comparing, weigh-

ing, packing and repacking. Their love for stuff is at times an impediment to deriving pleasure from the more aesthetically pleasing aspects of their activity.

Gearheads are useful to other hikers who simply want to buy their equipment and then forget about it. A gearhead can provide a fellow hiker with a list of necessities in which each item is weighed to the ounce. All his labor allows the less-obsessive outdoorsperson to just buy the stuff and get on with life.

Let's face it, when the experts narrow the very best trail shoes down to an elite few, why quibble? Just buy what's pretty. If you pick between two or three brands of light-weight packs or sleeping bags with superior ratings from Backpacker Magazine, *you can't go too far wrong. And if you are choosing between Campbell's or Lipton, Starkist or Chicken of the Sea, is it really all that important?*

Tyros can rest easy knowing that it is never necessary to worry about equipment decisions. Eager gearheads will gladly take care of that. ▪

July 12, Journal entry of Ultragrunge at Caughnawaga Shelter

Fourteen miles from Hwy. 9. I am freakin' hungover from Mexican beer I drank last night to chase down the tamales and tacos we got at the Mexican place in Bennington. Bennington is so great. Why did I spoil it by going on a beer toot? Sky, Polly and I shared a king-size bed at the hotel, and all I remember is waking up feeling like a sack of porcupine crap. Sky said it took some effort to keep me from getting us all in trouble. I ended up soaking in the tub and crying to Polly and Sky about my troubled past.

In my early high school years in Houston, I went to Sunday School. I was a Girl Scout. In my junior year, I rebelled and turned into a chunky neogoth. I dabbled in booze and drugs before my parents got me in a program. A good high school counselor convinced me to put my energy into physical activities, and when I graduated from high school, I was a hard-driving punkster bent on skating, climbing, running and backpacking. I stayed on that track more or less in Austin at UT.

On this trip, I've softened up. I looked at how natural Sky and Pollyanna are and began subtracting studs and rings and growing my hair back out. I've held myself to two beers and stayed away from any other substance—until last night.

When we got back to the trail, the 1,500-foot climb to start the day seemed like El Capitan. Old-fashioned detox, sweat reeking of alcohol, and every breath falling short leaving me dizzy and nauseated. Blue Devil hung back and made sure I drank plenty of water and told me to go slow. "I've been there," he said. "You sweat out the poison over a couple of days." High up on the ridges, we walked through beautiful spruce forest, but every step was a tiny apocalypse. I would have been happy to stop at any point, but I would have been miserable if I had just been lying there—a no-win situation.

Ten miles—a lookout tower on Glastenbury Mtn. Blue Devil insisted we climb up, and I reluctantly complied. Wowie zowie! What a great look at the Greens, as well as big Greylock way back behind us. "See, I told you," BD gloated.

Now we are in this old Caughnawaga Shelter, my favorite name for a shelter since Wawayanda back in New Jersey. A couple of NOBOs who have been following us for months caught us here today—total strangers to us—but we are old friends as far as they're concerned after having read our register entries. Tinkerbell and Skookums. There's a SOBO from Katahdin too—Sweet Tooth. Blue Devil plied him with questions, and I sprawled on my pad like a slug. Maybe tomorrow I'll be okay. Maybe tomorrow.

July 13, Journal entry of Sky Writer at Stratton Pond

I was blue this morning. I miss Mom and Dad. The funk wasn't helped by gray skies and drizzle. Five miles in, we worked through sloshy areas caused by beavers. I know beavers have a perfect right to perform their natural duties, but my mud-covered shoes were not appreciative.

At Deerfield River, a cute little man had set up a big tarp. I was hiking with Grunge, and we sat under the tarp eating hot dogs and potato chips—plus all the Pepsi we wanted. What a sweet man! We played the "cute" card and put him on a high for the next week. We crossed roads, photographed day lilies and tackled 1,800 feet up Stratton Peak. The Green Mountain Club caretakers on the summit—volunteers for decades—showed us a one-room, solar-powered hut on the mountain top. Later, atop the rickety firetower, we pondered how Benton MacKaye supposedly had his original inspiration for the A.T. while looking at the Green Mountains from the top of Stratton. Since there was no tower, he made do by climbing a tree.

We pulled into the Stratton Pond area too late to get space in the shelter. What a shame! This was an adorable shelter with a covered area out front and a great picnic table. We'll use tent platforms. Whatever blew away the rain brought in cool air. Here it is, mid-July, and it's chilly tonight. I miss my cool-weather bag. I'm going to shut down my headlamp and hunker down to generate heat.

July 14, Transcript of Captain Stupid recorded at Griffith Lake Campsite

It wasn't that long ago that I traded for a much lighter bag—not a bad idea on nights where you sweat rather then shiver. But, oh man! Last night got frigid. I never got warm. Dammit!

I started early to work up heat, and as the morning went along, the air warmed up enough to go back to a tee shirt. It was 10 miles of easy hiking, some of which followed a neat little river, to a road that led to Manchester Center. The plan was to pretend we were fudgies and do the touristy thing. Momma Llama has a stomach ailment, so she and Brave Phillie retreated to a hotel. The rest us of decided to to hunt for freebies. When we got to the road, there were trail angels offering free root beer. Sky, the root beer queen, was ecstatic. Then, a man and woman gave us homemade brownies.

Yay!

After stuffing ourselves, all six of us started hitching, and things were looking bad. Finally, a huge van went by with two guys really checking out the female scenery—*if you know what I mean, and I think you know what I mean!* Sky cried out, "Oh, they'll totally be back to pick us up!" Sure enough, they dutifully roared back to the tune of our appreciative cheers and whistles and took on the whole crew. All the trail angels applauded as we piled gear and bodies into the van. The two guys were headed to a job and in a hurry, so they dropped us off at a corner and drove away with wistful smiles on their faces. We got dessert at Ben & Jerry's Scoop Shop. We did the P.O., laundromat and resupply routine, reassembled and decided to stay overnight on the cheap. But hotels were pricey, so we called a cab to get back to the trail. A woman soon appeared in an unmarked minivan—not a cab—and when asked about any place we could crash, she called the cops for suggestions. The invisible voice from the phone said, "Take 'em to the skate park." We crammed packs and people into the creaky Caravan and wound up at a deserted skate park, with giant mats for sleeping under the stars and the rusty moon.

Sky giggled, and said, "I hope Brave Phillie and Momma Llama are comfortable and that Momma is getting over her"—at this point she made the universal sign of quotation marks—"stomach ailment." Clever girl, that Sky!

July 15, Journal entry of Doug Gottlieb at Big Branch Shelter

We got undiscombobulated and reassembled on the A.T. north of Vermont 11 and 30 after a lousy night's sleep at the Manchester Center skate park. We woke up soaked in dew. The lady cabdriver from last night came by early and whisked us back to the trail, where we found Momma Llama and Brave Phillie. Momma is feeling better, she says, although the consensus is that her "feeling better" has nothing to do with getting over her "stomach problems." Town time is great, but it puts a hitch in my step the day after. Nonetheless, we had some good laughs yesterday.

We motored hard on a long ascent up Bromley Mountain. Clouds had moved in, and mist was falling. No view. I was dehydrated, so when I came to the hand pump in Mad Tom Notch, I was ready to rehydrate. No luck: The pump was not working. So I continued on over socked-in Styles and Peru Peaks and descended to Griffith Lake for much-needed water. I mixed powdered stuff in my water bottle and grooved on sugar.

Six gloomy miles to Big Branch Shelter. Man, I was draggin'. I found a spot in the shelter as the sun started to emerge. The mosquitos were insane! I slathered DEET all over. Then I looked out into Big Branch and saw Starvin' Marvin, a NOBO I last saw somewhere in Virginia.

"That you, Doug?" he called out. I waded into the stream. We found a shallow spot and sat, two terrapins cooling our jets and dodging skeeters. Marvin told me he took a week off to go to his uncle's funeral, and that's why we caught him. He wondered if the Bly Gap Gang was still intact, and I said that only Bone Festival had dropped out.

He leered at me. "Does that mean his blonde girlfriend is available?"

When I explained that Sky had taken up with Captain Stupid, Marvin's jaw dropped. "You mean the big Orca dude?" I told him yes, and then he asked about the availability of Pollyanna or Ultragrunge (he called her the red-haired chick). I said he'd have to find out for himself. Then I got to wondering about Pollyanna. Sometimes I think I need to hike alone and then come back and talk things over with her.

When our skin began to prune, we headed to the shelter. The Bly Gap crew was straggling in and discovering that shelter space was a lost cause. So everyone set up their own shelter and swatted mosquitos. Later, as we began cooking, Starvin' Marvin moved in for the kill on Pollyanna and Ultragrunge. They treated him like an old pal, but nothing else. Marvin got the vibe and drifted off to his own space.

Tonight, a choice: sweat in your sleeping bag or stay exposed and swat those god-awful humming machines.

July 16, Journal entry of Pollyanna at Clarendon Shelter

Clarendon Shelter needs cleaning. There's a torn-up down bag in here and lots of garbage to sweep. Captain Stupid scrounged fire wood, and we're burning feathers—bummer! Still, it's one of the few shelters with a little meadow out front.

I have a lengthy missive to write, because today was among the most remarkable of our trip. Oddly, when we started from Big Branch this morning, our day promised to be unremarkable. We moved out fast, and at 1 p.m. we descended to the Mill River suspension footbridge, where we found the river well charged. Sky Writer and I crossed and found two middle-aged tourist types sitting pensively on a rock. "Cheer up!" I called out. "No mosquitos, and the sun's out. What more could you want?"

The man was a bald, chunky fellow with a trace of a Southern accent. He smiled and said, "Forgive us. We're sorta paying tribute."

He gestured to a plaque mounted above the entrance to the bridge that read:

BOB BRUGMANN
Feb. 18, 1956—July 4, 1973
Lost at this site while
hiking the trail he loved
Clarendon Gorge Bridge
Replacement
Supported in his honor
by family and friends

This was hallowed ground dedicated to the memory of a 17-year-old thru-hiker who drowned at this spot on July 4, 1973. It turned out that the man we were talking to was a 1973 thru-hiker, Skyhawk, who had hiked with Bob for a few weeks in Maine and New Hampshire before Bob hiked on alone. "I've always wanted to see this place," he said. "After Bob died here, I continued on to Springer feeling that I was hiking for two people. I always felt guilty that I got to stand on Springer and Bob didn't." Sky and I are touchy-feely types, and without thinking, we hugged Skyhawk and Lynn, his wife. He explained that during the early summer of 1973, this part of New England received the worst rain since 1927. The footbridge washed away, and Bob fell in while attempting to use a fallen tree to get over the river.

The rest of our group strolled up and heard the story. It was a tender moment—contemporary thru-hikers doing what they could to comfort an old-timer. Skyhawk said Bob was a brilliant kid and likely would have been a high-achieving adult. "His brother was a thru-hiker too, and he's gone on to become a world-renowned environmentalist."

Skyhawk described the many differences between hiking the modern A.T. and hiking in 1973. Equipment, food, amenities—the whole culture surrounding the trail—were different in those days. He gave me his email address and insisted I keep him informed of our progress. He then led us upstream to a great swimming hole and bid us farewell.

It was a perfect day for swimming. The river was flowing briskly from the recent rain and goose-bump cold. A few adults and kids running around and having a great time—all was right with the world! Except for one thing. We heard screaming and noticed a little girl—maybe 10 years old—caught in the flow and stuck in a spot where water was rushing through a wide gap between two big rocks. Her leg was caught in a crevice, with current pushing so hard she was unable to get free. Her dad was fighting from downstream to reach her, and she was having trouble keeping her head above water.

Doug and Grunge rushed over, but were reluctant to float downriver, because they feared crashing into her and forcing her head underwater. They splashed to a spot where they could work upriver. I sprawled on the rock ledge above and reached down. The girl was utterly freaked and flailed around trying to grab my hand. Blue Devil grabbed my ankles and lowered me closer. I grabbed her wrists and she clasped mine! I pulled with all I had, and she worked her leg loose from the crevice and floated down to Doug and Grunge. They twisted and lifted her out of the current and over to the riverbank, where her mom and dad hysterically threw their arms around her.

I stood watching and shivering, despite the mid-80s temperature, and suddenly a jacket was around my shoulders. "That kid wasn't gonna last much longer," Brave Phillie whispered. "If you hadn't pulled her loose, she was a goner."

Doug folded me in his arms. Her name was Melinda, and I joined her parents in crying—all weak and warm in the jacket and suddenly aware of how much I love being held by Doug. After Melinda and her parents calmed down, I jokingly said that my Girl Scout Gold Award training prepared me to do the right thing, and Ultragrunge looked at me in astonishment. "I'm Gold Award too," she said. "I can't believe we've hiked this long and never told each other that." This former neogoth was a dedicated Girl Scout? How did that happen?

Later at the shelter, Doug and I strolled to the stream and sat quietly as darkness approached. He sensed I needed company but not talk. I'm honestly not interested in romance while I'm hiking, but sometimes this guy makes it tough.

July 17, Journal entry of Blue Devil at The Inn at the Long Trail

Everything happened so fast yesterday. Loafing in the sun next to the Mill River, I suddenly heard voices with that edge of panic you only hear when a bus is hurtling over a cliff. I saw Pollyanna on her belly, reaching for all she was worth. I used her as a human lifeline, and she pulled little Melinda out of the crevice.

It worked! The kid twisted free and floated right to Doug and Grunge. By the time we gathered with the kid and her family on the riverbank, there was a wild mélange of tears, laughter and gratitude spewing from all of us. Doug and Ultragrunge could never have gotten to her in time. The dad told Pollyanna she saved him from watching his child drown before his eyes. Between what happened in Tennessee and this, enough drama!

I thought about that as I hiked today, about how once people reach middle-age they rant about how young people are convinced they're bulletproof, no chinks in their armor. I plead guilty, and what happened today won't change me, but twice now I've seen people's lives in the balance, and whether it was Ultragrunge pointing a handgun like a pro or Sky whacking a cracker punk in the head with a shovel or Pollyanna stretching like a rubber band to save a kid—it's clear that death is just around the corner. You might dodge it, but it's still there. After all this heavy thinking, I enjoyed a couple thousand feet up to Killington Peak. The climb through an evergreen forest soothed our souls after the emotional buzz from yesterday.

We knocked off the miles to the highway near the famous Sherburne Pass where the A.T. intersects with the Long Trail. We had been hiking the Long Trail and the A.T. simultaneously since we crossed into Vermont. At Sherburne Pass, the Long Trail diverges and heads 170 miles to the Canadian border, a spot for a thru-hiker to gaze northward and think, "Maybe someday."

We hit the inn, where some of us shared rooms and others tented across the highway. Then we all headed to the Irish Pub for dinner. Since my driver's license doesn't lie, I sneaked sips of beer from mugs floating around our table—a great night with less of the usual sarcasm. I sat between Brave Phillie and Sky Writer, and at one point we sang "Show Me the Way to Go Home." Sky topped us by getting out a piece of paper with "Amicalola lyrics." Everyone listened with the faraway look people get when they hear Sky singing.

"If Skyhawk hadn't shown us that swimming hole, Melinda woulda gone toes up," Brave Phillie muttered later. "Now she can grow up and and amount to something. Maybe when he finds that out it'll give him some comfort."

I can't stop thinking. We started at Springer months ago, headed straight for the Mill River so that Pollyanna could work her magic—a predetermined sequence. None of us denies it. The way Skyhawk played a part in the scenario is kismet.

July 18, Journal entry of Brave Phillie at Wintturi Shelter

Today was tough, owing to last night's demon alcohol consumption. I used the grit earned from my years in the Marine Corps and a few thousand trail miles to push myself at a steady clip. We pulled into this shelter by late afternoon—17 miles that seemed like 30. Cloudy and viewless, a day to be alone with your thoughts. We saw a few SOBOs, but for the most part, we had the path to ourselves as we rolled over hardwood ridges. If you were of a mind to, you could imagine it was a couple of hundred years ago. It was that peaceful.

I hiked part of the day with Momma Llama and made an effort to engage her in conversation. She seems to think I don't do enough of that, and for whatever reason it made her happy. She laughed at me a lot, sometimes when I was not trying to be funny. I wonder what the hell she's gathering from my comments. I can't figure her out, but I always feel extra spring in my step when she comes around a bend in the trail.

Despite our overindulgence last night, things came together late in the day. First, the shelter was empty. Blue Devil grabbed a broom and swept it out nice and neat and acted like we should kiss his butt. Then everyone cooked quickly, as if we were in a race to get to sleep early after last night's honkytonking.

Here's where the good luck came in. Just as we were finishing cleanup, the bottom fell out—one of the most impressive gully washers we've seen—and here we sit, high and dry. Captain Stupid had gone to the privy and got stuck there before deciding that the rain wasn't stopping any time soon and making a mad dash back to the shelter. With all his blustering and shaking around, it was like a soggy grizzly had burst into our midst. You have to love this guy, but he takes maintenance.

Today is Monopod's birthday, so I borrowed Momma Llama's cell phone and gave the old fart a call. We sang him "Happy Birthday," a pleasant way to end a lackluster day. By tomorrow, I'll be 95 percent recovered.

July 19, Journal entry of Momma Llama at Happy Hill Shelter

There's an unspoken undercurrent of enthusiasm as Hanover looms closer. Everyone put in 20 miles today to Happy Hill Shelter, which leaves about five miles to Hanover—a short day followed up with a zero day. We'll need it. The 20-miler was loaded with MUDS. It was in the middle-80s with humidity. Captain Stupid careened flat on his back in several inches of mud and slime. For the rest of the day, he had mud encrusted on his arms, legs and pack.

Today was Vermont at its finest. Mountains and fields—my favorite trail combination. I love to follow a ridge of oaks and maples and then break into open field to look over distant ranges, which stood as silent sentinels well before any human memory. It's as if I awakened from a centuries-long dream. How these big hills got here, apparently the result of a massive buckling and upheaval caused by a collision of long-separated continents, is inconsequential. I'm just pleased to hike across these open spots to observe what has ultimately happened, the result of nature and man. I passed birch groves and forests of maple above fern carpets. There was a crazy quilt of wildflowers in the meadows, and the bees and butterflies were active as ants. I stopped at times alongside the fields just to hear the hum . . . and nothing else. Aristotle said, "Nature does nothing uselessly." I now comprehend his wisdom.

Oddly, the others had trouble grokking my enthusiasm. They were hot, pissed-off and hell-bent for Hanover. There have been other days when I was preoccupied by my own petty discomforts and wondered what other people were happy about. Maybe it's my turn for a stretch of harmonic biorhythms.

After 16 miles, we arrived at White River Bridge, a prime spot for a swim. The river was charged and flowing hard, and we took turns plunging in and swimming. Captain jumped from the rocks, grabbed his legs and executed a human cannonball for the ages, a big fleshy projectile creating a splash that may have slightly altered the earth's orbit. When he emerged on the rocky riverbank, he admitted the impact hurt like hell, but he still managed the self-deprecating grin we've learned to love. We dried in the sun and located sandwiches and Orange Crush at a hiker-friendly store near the river. We had an easy climb over four miles to this shelter, a charmer built of native rock.

Brave Phillie and I decided at Sherburne Pass to share my tiny Sierra Designs Flashlight. Even though our companions razz us about erotic encounters, a tiny tent is no place for amorous endeavors. Despite the close quarters which might seem like a perfect inducement for romance, two aging lovers would need to be contortionists to enjoy whoopee in these contraptions. Tonight I'm just happy for mosquito netting.

Brave Phillie is cracking me up. A few days back, my trail vibe was polar opposite from the wonderful one today, and I was on his case about his taciturn personality. He was clueless, but eager to please. Now he makes forced small talk. Today we were perched on a dead log, quietly enjoying a snack. He seemed concerned that we weren't talking, so he commented, "Man, the bark on this log sure has a pretty pattern." Then he just looked at me as if to ask, "What do I say next?" I burst out laughing, and he looked even more confused and exasperated. "Do you know what you need to change about yourself?" I asked. He stared back. I answered my own question, "Nothing, not a single little thing." He smiled his distant smile and walked on.

SUBJECT: **Hanover at last!**
DATE: July 20, 6:26 p.m.
FROM: **Sky Writer** < singinghiker@yahoo.com >
TO: Clara Spangler < claraathome@att.net >

I remember the awesome feeling of walking into Damascus and thinking, "We've come so far, but just think how it must feel for a

SOBO to be here." Now I know how it feels to be a SOBO in Damascus—identical to being a NOBO in Hanover. We are 440 miles from the end, and although we are all aware of how drastically difficult this stretch will be, we see it as a reward for having come this far.

I woke early. Blue Devil and I slept in the cutest little stone shelter called Happy Hill. The mosquitos were on a rampage, and BD let me get real close to share his mosquito tent. For whatever reason, the skeeters died down this morning. I skipped breakfast and sped over ridges and meadows that had not shaken off a low-lying mist. I came to blacktop that led through a pretty old suburban area into Norwich, Vt. I went under Interstate 91, across the Connecticut River and uphill into Hanover, the home of Dartmouth College.

Hanover is not hiker-friendly in terms of lodging. I'm online at the Dartmouth Outing Club, and they told me that rowdy hikers in past years had poisoned the well for adorable, well-behaved hiking sweeties like, for instance, *me*! The greeks have pretty much shut hikers out, although I have to believe that Grunge, Linda and I could coax our way into any frat house in anyone's universe.

As the Bly Gap Gang began showing up, we gathered over coffee at a café and decided to pool resources for two nights at the Sunset Motor Inn. It's two miles from downtown Hanover, accessible by a free public bus—cool! Two rooms split eight ways: El cheapo!

We cleaned up and headed to town to take care of P.O. business, food purchases, snacking, browsing in shops, eating ice cream, buying *Villa Incognito* by Tom Robbins, snacking and, of course, snacking. Dad sent a guilt-induced letter with a Visa cash card. Plus, I got the money you sent. Wow, if I keep the parental remorse meter turned up, this trip will cost half of what I budgeted.

I need to tell you something I've been holding in my heart. Captain Stupid and I will end up in Gainesville, Ga., after this trip. You probably suspect that I've fallen in love. The Captain started fat as a whale. The first time I saw him on Frosty Mtn., he was a caricature, so fat that he seemed more comic figure than real person. Aside from giving him sympathy, I couldn't take him seriously. Since then, he has lost so much weight that he just looks like a big stocky guy. And he still has 400 miles to go!

Another thing, I looked in the mirror after showering, and for once I felt good about what I saw. I love the condition of my body. My skin looks great. Even though my hair has taken a beating after being pulled back in a tight ponytail day after day, it looked passable after a shampoo and rinse. Long-distance hiking and being in love may be the best two things a woman can do for herself.

Tomorrow, a zero day. No chores. Sleep late, watch cable, stroll through this elitist college town and enjoy the Captain's company. I can't wait for you to meet him.

12

Hanover!, Glencliff—Prelude to the Whites, the Joys of Hut Food, the Agony of Descent

July 21, Journal entry of Ultragrunge in Hanover, New Hampshire

The flowers bloom, the songbirds sing,
And, though it sun or rain,
I walk the mountain tops with Spring
From Georgia north to Maine.

—Earl Shaffer

After a short hop in from Happy Hill yesterday and a lot of sleep last night, I walked around downtown Hanover today feeling like a gunslinger—lean, mean and comfortable in my battered trail runners, shorts and tee shirt. No makeup. No jewelry. Just my red mop of hair and my fine-tuned physique. The guys love it.

I wandered onto campus and mixed it up with a few Ivy League preppie lads playing Frisbee. I effortlessly took them to Frisbee school. What I like about the A.T. me is that I'm less confrontational and more good-natured. I didn't have to butch it up to keep those guys at bay. I acted naturally, liking the way they responded. I can't wait to try this out in the real world.

A lanky blond fellow coaxed me into a coffee shop. He was friendly enough, but I knew he saw me as the perfect conquest. A quickie this afternoon, and the hiker babe is out of his life tomorrow—very convenient. I finished my coffee, gave him a peck on the cheek and headed back to my friends. I'm beginning to appreciate adulthood.

Pleasurable as this zero day is, I'm antsy. I remember Prime Meridian, the NOBO back in Massachusetts who told us that for a NOBO the best part of the adventure begins in Glencliff, three days from here. He said the White Mountains and beyond to Katahdin are what the A.T. is all about. Since then, I've been impatient to cover the ground to Glencliff. Today, I almost feel I'm wasting time.

But another part of me says slow down. Wowie zowie! Less than 450 miles to go. It's like reading a great book, and when you see only a hundred pages left, you dread coming to the end. A zero day is the closest any of us may ever get to heaven.

I just finished reading a dog-eared copy of Earl Shaffer's *Walking With Spring* we've been passing around. I understand how wonderful it was for Earl to make this walk from Springer, watching the flowers time their blooms on into the summer, hearing the birds bracketing the ridges with their tireless warbling, and realizing that spring lasts well beyond June for a NOBO. It's part of us forever.

My back is against an ancient oak, part of this Ivy League bastion. I'll take Austin anytime; it fits my pistol. But I give Dartmouth its due. College towns come no prettier than Hanover.

July 22, Transcript of Captain Stupid recorded at Trapper John Shelter

A few years ago, long before the thought of hiking this behemoth was even a twinkle in my eye, I saw a print ad for a luxury car. A smug, aspiring CEO-type was on a splendid country road in a European or Japanese automobile—one that would probably cost four times my highest-ever annual income. He was contemplating his goals and saying something like, "I will achieve the vice presidency of my corporation. I will own a (fill in the make and model of the car, which I honestly can't recall). I will hike the Appalachian Trail." These goals had boxes next to them, and the car box was checked.

As I recall my mindset before the A.T. and compare what my preconception of hiking it was compared to actually, by God, doing it, there is a massive gap. When I consider that some Madison Avenue type tossed a thru-hike up on the wall as a box that this squash-playing overachiever would knock off, it annoys me. I did some thinking on the zero day yesterday and concluded that the very concept of this endless trail is sacred territory never intended for insertion into a bucket list.

I think about Benton MacKaye. What was it like for him, if the story is true, to climb a tree on the peak of Stratton Mtn., take in the Green Mountains to the north and south and suddenly have an epiphany that ultimately led to the seed of an idea? Fertilized by human imagination, the seed took root in an article in a professional journal suggesting a path transecting the crests of the Appalachian range. What would MacKaye have thought of this man driving in climate-controlled comfort who casually determined that the trail would one day be his?

I can only guess. But I do know this: The longer I'm out here, the better I know myself, the stronger I feel, the more I want to make sure I take in all of what nature has to offer while also loving and being loved by the people sharing this with me. In terms of weight loss, I have left a small man behind on this trail. I have burned him up as calories. I have crapped, urinated, spat and sweated his venomous influence out of me. I have circulated untold gallons of pure spring water through my system and made the fruits of the Appalachian watershed part of my fiber. I have shared this trail with a woman who saw past the toxic evil twin who has left me. She loves the man who emerged from this 1,700-mile process of change. So my suggestion to the man who thought up the advertisement: Do your penance to Benton and take your schtick elsewhere.

I walked with Sky Writer a lot today, and she was in a lyrical mood—singing and jabbering on and on—totally jazzed about getting into New Hampshire. As I talk to people who have hiked the whole trail, the consensus is that New Hampshire and Maine are the most exciting states. Some pick one or the other, and some pick both. Vermont was terrific, but Sky and I sense that it's about to get even better.

Yay!

Today was Vermont-style hiking. Enough climbing to keep you engaged and on your game, but easy enough to make the miles roll by pretty quickly. It was hot again as we ascended 1,200 feet to Holts Ledge near the Dartmouth Skiway. The steep descent to the little shelter had my knees yipping. Trapper John Shelter was occupied by a combination of section hikers and a couple of NOBO thru-hikers we hadn't seen since they passed us in Virginia—Kamikaze and Thoroughbred. They were thrilled to see Sky, less so to see me. These two are in their mid-thirties, pretty clearly gay and clad in kilts. Their enthusiasm for Sky was not due to her considerable feminine charms but for her music. She sang quietly for them. A good evening for conversation and company. Not many bugs. One day closer to Glencliff, the gateway to the White Mountains we've been glimpsing for days.

BENTON

*H*e's been gone so long his memory has passed into myth. Photographs of Benton MacKaye reveal the craggy profile of a New England elder states-man befitting a personality responsible for a vision of such gravitas. Is it true that it hit him like a lightning bolt when he climbed a tree on the peak of Stratton Mtn. to capture a better look at the Green Mountains? Although versions of the story vary, many believe that as he looked up and down the range that day, he formulated the initial concept of a footpath running the length of the Appalachians, from New England, probably Mt. Washington in the White Mountains, to the Southern Highlands, possibly Mt. Mitchell in North Carolina.*

His 1921 essay titled "An Appalachian Trail: A Project in Regional Plan-ning" was the first formal proposal. His dream had as much to do with a comprehensive view of how a trail would benefit the working class as it did with developing a lengthy place to take a walk. Ever the socialist, he was a champion of those who toiled at the lower reaches of the industrial world. He loved the idea of a trail accessible by train from the developing eastern megalopolis. Workers could escape annually from urban drudgery for a cou-ple of weeks of communion with nature. His concept was more complex than just building a trail. It related to how a trail could restore a common man's self-esteem and the way he coexisted with a complicated world.

As the trail took form with amazing alacrity, MacKaye was testy at times with those making it happen. As a visionary, he was at loggerheads with the pragmatists who loved the trail and delighted in the nuts and bolts of plan-ning it and building it. In his later years, he was able to appreciate the suc-cess of the project and to enjoy accepting some credit for it. Late in life he wrote, "I am the man who, more by luck than anything else, happened to pro-pose the project. Then others went and did it."

This Harvard-educated guru's stamp will always be on the A.T. His men-tal blueprint—once thought to be evanescent—will take on even more sub-stance as the decades slip by. Thru-hikers who don't bother to learn about him miss a chance to have a fuller appreciation for the endless trail. Without knowing Benton, they will never fully understand why it is so important for the trail to thrive for centuries to come. ▪

July 23, A letter from Doug Gottlieb to his mother

Dear Mom:

I know you worry excessively, but I take comfort in knowing you're passionate about life, enjoying your work and loving your friends. I hope that means you don't have much time to waste worrying about me.

I received the cash card you sent to Hanover and was on the verge of sending it back. I talked to Pollyanna, pouring my heart out as I'm prone to do. She set me straight with a little practical compassion. She said there is great pleasure for you in imagining my enjoyment of those dollars. By returning the card, she said, I risked hurting your feelings and robbing you of that pleasure. She said you are an immeasurably sweet and patient woman to put up with me. So, here's the deal: I'll use the money to treat my friends and myself to a special extravagance we might not otherwise enjoy—dinner, lodging and breakfast at Pinkham Notch. I hope that sounds good to you, sweetest of all moms.

You understand, of course, why I must pay for this trip myself. I am at the point in life where I should pay for my own diversions. Pollyanna and Blue Devil are getting most of their trip paid for by their parents as a graduation gift—a fitting tribute for high academic achievement. Brave Phillie and Momma Llama are both wealthy after toiling hard and investing wisely during their working lives. Captain Stupid had his modest assets restored after his mother and aunt tracked down his Cousin Guilford and twisted his tail (you remember that story). Sky Writer's trip is funded by herself and the collective guilt of her parents. And Ultragrunge, close to graduation at the University of Texas, piled up dollars during her college years applying nervous energy to part-time jobs. We're a diverse lot, but two things we have in common are generosity to one another and an overarching love for the trail.

So what is your boy excited about these days? For starters, I'm edging closer to the majestic land of the high New Hampshire peaks—timberline vistas I've missed so much from the Northwest. I run into one SOBO after another lamenting that they have left the high adventure of Maine and New Hampshire to hike in the more mundane central states of the A.T. They have the slightly wild-eyed look of mythical characters emerging from a sere wilderness after months of fending off fierce beasts and subsisting on locusts and honey. The Bly Gap Gang, on the other hand, has the seasoned look of hard-hiking types who tempered their experience with the amenities of hostels and trail-side delis.

In your letter, you exercised your parental prerogative to stick your nose in my personal affairs and ask, again, if I have romantic interest in Pollyanna or she for me. How can you sense from thousands of miles away that there is a spark there? Pollyanna and I do a formal minuet in which we reveal friendliness, affection, and even romance from time to time. But the sticking point for thru-hikers is that we are out here for the freedom and independence of trail life. Each time it seems natural to say or show something that would suggest taking another step forward in our relationship, one or the other of us backs off.

Today was killer. We put in just short of 20 miles and went up and down Smarts and Cube mountains, a lot of ascending and descending. We wound up at spiffy little Ore Hill Shelter, which we shared with a group of four SOBO men in their sixties who started at Katahdin and are looking forward to easier trail.

Great privies here. Twins with drawbridge doors controlled by a weight-and-pulley system. Privies are gross, but "leave no trace" philosophy dictates using them. Captain Stupid and I wound up there together and discussed affairs of the heart. He is farther along in his than I am in mine.

I still have not picked a trail name and feel pressure from Brave Phillie, who constantly tosses out possibilities. He calls me Preacher, because he sees me reading my Bible. Ultragrunge calls me The Man With No Name. Whoever I am, please remember in gloomy moments that there is a young fellow in the wilderness who loves you.

Love,

Doug

July 24, Journal entry of Pollyanna at Hikers Welcome Hostel in Glencliff, NH

Just emerged from my last shower for 80 miles, assuming I get one at Pinkham Notch. I sit at a picnic table outside the Hikers Welcome Hostel gazing ruefully at the pattern of mosquito bites on my freshly shaved legs. Females in the Bly Gap Gang avoid the European look by occasionally shaving. We delight in washing our hair. Sky and I—with our longish locks—find that the sweat, bug bodies, and dirt particles make for gross hair texture and appearance. We wear ponytails to keep it out of our eyes, but by the time we get a chance for serious showering—the kind where you stand there in amazement for 10 minutes before even beginning to wash off—our hair is abysmal.

Doug must have had the urge to score points this morning. After I had just remarked about my overall appearance having cratered, he looked at me with a little grin and asked, "You really don't get it do you?"

"Get what?"

"You look good under any and all circumstances," he replied. "You are incapable of unattractiveness. Even Sky sometimes looks faded. But you—never!" I was on a high for the next few miles.

We had over seven miles today. Doug, Captain Stupid and I left before the others, as we were anxious to get to the hostel and get something akin to a zero day. We hiked through a swampy area with bog logs. The air was filled with the characteristic call of the white-throated sparrow that we've heard off and on for weeks. Some think they're saying "O Sweet Canada Canada Canada," but I prefer "Old Sam Peabody Peabody Peabody." It varies in tempo and cadence as we travel north.

Captain Stupid is a whistling savant who mimics any bird we come across. He nailed the white-throated sparrow, and as we walked through the swampy area, he had them going crazy. They thought the Captain was an interloper. "Little do they know I am anatomically incapable of breeding with their little girlfriends," he wryly observed before tweeting out another salvo.

Hikers Welcome is a no-frills place, but the management is wonderful, especially Fat Chap. I tossed a couple of things in my bounce box to forward ahead to the P.O. in Gorham on the other side of the Whites. I'm lightening up through this next stretch, because SOBOs have me scared about the big climbs. Brave Phillie tells me to cool it and remember that I have nearly 1,800 trail miles to my credit. I think of all the steps I've taken, pounding on the feet, stress on cartilage, bruises on my waist from the belt, and chronic soreness. I stretch and bend to ease the discomfort. How can any trail intimidate me now? I am Pollyanna, Sovereign Queen of Trails!

Rain clouds roll in, and I soon will abandon this pleasant spot to run for cover. The guys are inside watching *Blade Runner*, except for Doug, who sits nearby catching up on his journal while he and I wordlessly take pleasure in each other's company. I occasionally catch him stealing a glance at me, and he does the same with me. After all this time together, we enjoy each other on simple terms. We realize that reaching Katahdin will either force us to talk things over or just walk blindly away. That is the point where we vacate this parallel universe we've occupied so contentedly for these past months and wrap ourselves in whatever reality we select. I almost wish we could do a yoyo and turn around at Katahdin, head back south and be right back here in a couple of months—converted from NOBOs to SOBOs.

Damn! I just swatted a bloated mosquito feasting on my knee and splattered blood on my nice, clean skin. And darn! Rain is splashing on my writing pad. Tomorrow, good weather is expected, and I will scale Mt. Moosilauke, the first natural above-timberline peak we've seen! On to the Whites!

ON TO THE WHITES!

The young SOBO, Prime Meridian, had it right when he sang the praises of the White Mountains. When the A.T. crosses the highway at the tiny settlement of Glencliff, the fun begins for the NOBO, and the hardest work of the trip ends for the exhausted SOBO. From New Hampshire Highway 25, a NOBO encounters an ascent of nearly 3,700 feet, one of the biggest continuous climbs on the A.T. If you choose to ascend Mt. Lafayette the next day, you will have a 3,800-foot ascent. What must be factored in to these colossal climbs is that there are other serious ascents in between them. For every mammoth climb, there is an equally laborious descent guaranteed to leave your knees feeling like handfuls of sawdust blended with squishy gelatin.

Given the scope of this challenge, why is it that NOBOs begin and sustain their trip through the Whites with wonder and elation, the sort of emotion that rides easily in your heart and gives you a full, ecstatic glow from within your chest? It's because you finally get above it all. You hit terrain so dramatically different that you feel a rebirth in your hiking spirit. Though you continue to hike through forest—mostly spruce at the high elevations and lush hardwoods down below—you also experience miles of walking above timberline.

In the Whites, you see imposing rock formations, stunted conifers, moss and lichen. The continued trill of the white-throated sparrow and the polite chirp of the dark-eyed junco take on a new dimension, because they are in a magic zone where you walk among and above the clouds, where rain gets colder and wind penetrates your skimpy parka, where people succumb to lethal July weather and experienced hikers get in trouble due to exposure. Often the trail in the Whites and beyond into Maine is exceptionally steep and rocky, requiring hand-over-hand climbing, a particular challenge in wet weather.

It is also here that you sometimes have no appropriate place to camp, because camping in the krummholz zone above timberline is considered an affront to delicate soil and plants. Since there is a stretch in the Whites of *more than 80 miles without convenient access to a shelter and not very many campsites, thru-hikers find that they must either pay a significant amount of money to stay in huts managed by the Appalachian Mountain Club (AMC) or appeal to the kindness of the staff at the huts to "work for stay." Working for stay means performing chores the "croo" members assign you. You are allowed to sleep on the floor and enjoy dinner and breakfast once the paying guests are assured of having all they want. The AMC hut system is ideal for well-to-do hikers out for a few days who enjoy having good food and cozy bunks provided for them. Thru-hikers typically don't see themselves as the touring types, and many are curmudgeonly about having to pay or work when they would just as soon camp. Unfortunately, due to concerns about impact on the areas around the A.T., campsites are not always available. The AMC is the A.T.-maintenance group in the Whites, and it is charged with protecting the trail, as well as making it hikeable. When campsites are provided, they are managed by AMC caretakers, who sometimes collect a fee and make sure you use platforms and apply "leave no trace" methods. By and large, croo members and caretakers will work with you to assure your safety and relative comfort. They also represent a system some hikers resent.*

There has been controversy over the years generated by hikers who think the relatively posh (if you can call a place with community bunkrooms and no showers "posh") environs of the AMC huts cater to the upper-class and relegate the humble thru-hiker to a subservient role. The AMC argues in return that it is trying to work out the best system to preserve the delicate environment above timberline for the large number of people who wish to enjoy it. The argument will continue between the purists and elitists, and no matter how the AMC and the Forest Service choose to administer their policies, there will never be a total truce. Smart thru-hikers do what they have done since Springer or Katahdin—figure out the lay of the land and put the system to work for themselves. As the Bly Gap Gang trudges up Moosilauke, they enter a zone of difficulty that will not ease until they reach the crest of Mt. Bigelow 220 miles away. During that period, they will see some of the wildest country in the eastern U.S. and do a tremendous amount of ascending and descending on some singularly remarkable mountains. ■

July 25, Journal entry of Blue Devil at Eliza Brook Shelter

Ease and difficulty are as much a state of mind as anything, so when I say that today's 17 miles was the hardest day of the trip for me, I posit that this is a purely subjective point of view, although I have plenty of objective data to support my claim, starting with nearly 4,000 feet of climbing to start off the day, followed by a drop-off-the-table 3,000-foot descent that left my ankles and knees in dire need of a break. Then it was major ups and downs for the rest of the day all the way to this place, Eliza Brook Shelter.

When I came dragging up Moosilauke this morning, Doug, Grunge and Pollyanna were waiting at the top and raving about how much easier the climb was than they expected. There we were at more than 4,800 feet, looking ahead to the first spectacular view of the Whites. "We better drink this all in while we can," said Ultragrunge as she scoped out the Lafayette Ridge and beyond to Mt. Washington. "Who knows how much of this will be in rain, fog or whatever over the next few days?"

The Moose is a revelation after months of tree-covered ridges. The summit is a big meadow scattered with rocks from a glacial epoch. I sheltered from wind behind a boulder wall, drained my water, munched on Doug's beer nuts and took in my first sweeping view of the best part of the A.T. I was having a bad day. How else can I explain why I was pissy while the others lounged around saying the long climb was a girly walk?

Three girls approached—Privy Prisoner, Finnlander and Treadmill— possibly the jolliest bunch we've encountered since Springer. Privy Prisoner refused to reveal the derivation of her name, and her friends said she already had too much information about them to allow them to spill the beans. So they stayed cheerfully mum on the topic. Finnlander, although a native-born Finn, is thoroughly Americanized, seeing as how she moved to Connecticut at age four. Treadmill was a trim, dark-haired girl from Georgia with a knack for staying on an even keel.

The three met at Katahdin Stream Campground and have been inseparable ever since. They started in mid-June, and despite the bugs and the bogs of the 100-Mile Wilderness and the rugged peaks after that, they hit Moosilauke in good spirits. "It is soooooo hard north of here and soooooo much fun," Finn told us. "I feel sorry for you and envy you at the same time."

Hiking as a trio of good-looking girls had provided this group with royal treatment at the huts, lots of trail magic in Maine and plenty of male companionship—not all of it desirable, but nothing they couldn't handle. "We hiked from Lonesome Lake Hut to Beaver Brook yesterday so that we'd have a short hike to the hostel at Glencliff," Treadmill said. "We figured the climb today would be tough, but it was soooooo easy!

And the weather is soooooo perfect, and we're taking a zero day tomorrow! What could be better?"

Everything was "soooooo wonderful" to this bunch, and although I'm usually cynical about people soooooo thrilled with life, I never doubted their sincerity. Behind them somewhere was another companion, Balladeer, famous for her proclivity for matching a song with every situation or topic. They told us she was having knee trouble and was moving slowly. Finnlander warned, "She may not be as perky as we are."

But she was. I encountered her on the long climb down the backside of Moosilauke, and when I asked if her name was Balladeer, she beamed and burst into song, the freakin' "Bear went over the Mountain." "They're already over the other side, and here I am with another thousand feet to the top. But I guess all that they can see is the other side of the mountain, so it's no big deal." Joining her in her labors was Sprout Eater, a Cornell grad and expert naturalist cheerfully bound for Georgia.

Moosilauke is worse going down than up. The trail is paralleled in places by cascading Beaver Brook and has rebar where the trail gets steep and rocky. Captain Stupid and Sky met me at the highway crossing at Kinsman Notch, and we started a long uphill to the east peak of Mt. Wolf. By the time we got there, I was thoroughly bagged.

By the time we got to Eliza Brook Shelter, I was dehydrated, hungry, headachy and generally pissed off. The place was packed with NOBOs, including Kamikaze and Thoroughbred, resplendent in their kilts and insistent that Sky should sing for them. "Give her a break, dammit!" I barked. "Can't you see she's exhausted?" Everyone looked shocked at my outburst, but I didn't care. Sky, Captain and I are on a tent platform tonight under one tarp. Tomorrow, we hoof it to Mt. Lafayette and then one more mile down to Greenleaf Hut.

July 26, Journal entry of Brave Phillie at Greenleaf Hut

Using Momma's smartphone at Glencliff, I checked on space at Greenleaf Hut. Bingo! They were slammed until a big group canceled out a couple of hours before I called. I reserved space for all of us on my AmEx. Only Momma Llama knows about it, so it was up to me to make sure everyone was committed to following up the long hike over Moosilauke yesterday with another ball-buster today to Greenleaf.

Normally Blue Devil is one of the strongest, but when he got up this morning, he made noises about trying to get work for stay at the Lonesome Lake Hut, only about six-miles from Eliza Brook. I hated to do it, but I said, "What's the matter Blue Devil? You turning into a wuss?"

He was in a crappy mood yesterday, and he was keeping it up today. He gave me an ugly glare and started out alone. I heard him mumble, "I don't have to take crap from that old fart." It made me wonder if I should tell him why I was pushing everyone to Greenleaf, but I decided to hold off. Momma disagreed, and she loped ahead to let him know there was a kind intent behind my surly remarks.

We had a 2,000-foot cliff-like climb up Kinsman Mtn. followed by a 3,000-foot drop down to Franconia Notch. We were looking at nearly 4,000 feet to get up Mt. Lafayette, and I had some selling to do to get everyone off the idea of hitching over to North Woodstock. They'd been talking to other hikers and were attracted to restaurants and hotels, but they hated the thought of spending money. When they saw Blue Devil start out—despite his sullen disposition—they commenced one of the longest climbs on the entire A.T.

Man, was it a bear to have such a big climb for the second day in a row. Momma and I brought up the rear and went into cruise control. Relentless step after uphill step. Halfway up, clouds gathered, and we were socked in with mist and wind that got worse the higher we climbed. When we reached timberline, the wind seemed like 70 miles per hour, so I guess it was really about 50—raining by now, and cold enough that we put on layers and covered up in our thin rain parkas. We rolled along the ridge and finally neared the peak of Lafayette, famous for one of the best views on the A.T. Today, it was wet, viewless, windy and cold—the nastiest July weather imaginable.

Lightning moved in from the west—worst case to be on a peak during an electrical storm. We caught Pollyanna and Grunge, who were considering heading off the trail and descending cross-country. I shouted over the wind and thunder, "We're almost to the Greenleaf Hut trail. Get there fast and go downhill to the hut. It's dangerous to try cross-country." They nodded and took off with young people's speed neither Momma Llama nor I could muster.

When the trail to Greenleaf Hut branched to the left, we were at the fag end of our energy. The big climb took all we had, and there was little left for the tedious descent to the hut fighting wind and boulders— just over a mile, more like a marathon. We passed a little pond and fought a headwind as we approached the hut. As we walked inside, cold and dripping, the Bly Gap Gang greeted us with cheers. "Now we know why you were driving us along like an old drill sergeant," Doug said. "Too stubborn to say you were treating tonight."

Blue Devil hugged me and looked me in the eye with a big grin. "You always get the last laugh, you old mountain goat," he whispered in my ear. "You know I love you, dog."

"I ain't nobody's dog," I growled back.

"Oh yes you are," Momma said. Her voice throaty from the cold air, and her hair plastered against her forehead. "You're my goat and my dog."

We got into dry clothes and shivered at the dining room tables. The croo members said they'd been hearing about the Bly Gap Gang from NOBOs who passed on our tale, like the old round robin game we played in grade school. The more it gets passed along, the more it changes. Nobody believes the standoff ended with no shots fired and with Sky Writer hammering a punk with a shovel. Regardless, whatever version he heard must have sounded good to the hut manager who promised to pass the word about our approach to the huts we'd see in the next few days.

Then in came Kamikaze and Thoroughbred, drowned muskrats with their beards, hair and kilts dripping rain on the hut floor, asking "You guys got work for stay?" The manager looked them over and smiled. "We'll see what we can do," he promised. "But don't drip all over the place if you can keep from it."

I went to a bunk and napped in my sleeping bag. Hypothermia left my bones, and I was ready for salad, fresh bread, soup, roast beef, peas, corn, strawberry shortcake—food is everything after a day like this. I drank glass after glass of water, and felt 20 years younger. "You're in luck," one of the cooks said. "The weather is clearing. You'll walk through a nice window on the way to Zealand Falls." Sky Writer sang "Blue Skies," my favorite. I'll remind her to sing it again somewhere up the trail.

July 27, Journal entry of Momma Llama at Zealand Falls Hut

Oh brother, was today a reward for living right, or what? We had a wonderful breakfast. Why not? We were bona fide customers thanks to Brave Phillie. He told me he spends so little money on backpacking that it's silly not to splurge. Doug told us this morning we'll all stay at Joe Dodge Lodge at Pinkham Notch compliments of a cash card his mother sent. He's a good son and a good friend.

Today broke clear and cool. We labored back up Mt. Lafayette and looked out over the sprawling mountains and up the range to the tiny buildings and tower arrays on Mt. Washington. Why are terrible days so often followed by breathtaking ones? BP, Ultragrunge, Pollyanna and I looked out over the Pemigewasset Wilderness like beer-gut tourists, except without minivans and Hawaiian shirts.

Vultures drifted on thermals a thousand feet below. Thick white clouds filled in the lower elevations, providing the sensation that for a brief time we were cloud-walking deities, masters of a rolling domain. Grunge piped up, "Is that a falcon?"

My eye followed the implied sightline of her finger, and I spotted a peregrine falcon, little more than a flashing dot arcing gracefully into its blazing stoop pursuing unsuspecting prey below. For several moments—before it disappeared behind a ridge—we witnessed the fastest creature on earth. "There's not treasure enough to replace this," Pollyanna whispered. Another of those ephemeral humming-bird moments.

We pulled into Galehead Hut before noon and attacked modestly priced bread and mushroom soup. No matter how dazzlingly beautiful a day may be, how engaging the company or how thrilling the wildlife sightings, food remains the core of our motivation. I rarely have erotic dreams while backpacking. Instead, I dream of chocolate, pasta, vegetables and fresh fruit. Last night I dreamt of sitting in a bakery waiting for hot cherry pie. We burn literally thousands upon thousands of calories each day beating our feet on rocks, roots and dirt. Our taxed bodies evolve into vessels of hunger, veritable temples of desire for whatever sustenance we can gather. Something as simple as a break for soup and bread becomes a coveted event in the midst of any day—no matter how otherwise exhilarating the day may be. I'll never forget the time we were in a trail town relaxing in a pizza parlor. Captain Stupid took a swig of beer followed by a gulp of pizza loaded with double cheese, pepperoni, green peppers, onions, black olives and mushrooms—I remember every detail with graphic clarity—and bellowed out, "Aaaahh, pizza! Food of kings!"

Climbing out of Galehead was steep before we topped out on South Twin Mtn. and began a six-mile drop to Zealand Falls Hut. As we pulled in, one of the croo told us that if we would help move some shingles and boards under a tarp behind the hut and sweep out the bunk rooms, we'd be good to go on work for stay.

Within an hour, our duties were complete. We gathered on the rocks at Whitewall Brook, which flows in front of the hut near the top of the falls. We soaked and wrung out our clothes, using sunshine to dry the sogginess from the day before. Sky plucked a dazzling ivory pebble from the stream and recited a fresh haiku:

> White stone tumbles
> In rushing Whitewall current—
> Which one is sweeter?

Flat on my back on the rocky stream bank. Quiet voices intermingled with the rushing stream lulled me into perfect repose. A gentle nudge from Brave Phillie alerted me to dinner. He smiled apologetically, and I told him I had what I wanted.

Zealand Falls Hut is packed. We are cheerfully relegated to the breezeway between the main building and the restrooms to snooze on our pads. I write by headlamp as Brave Phillie creates weird buzzsaw music.

Sky and I whisper in the dark, attempting to determine what the snoring sounds like. Sky nails it. A bear has been pursued for hours by a pack of hunting hounds. After outdistancing them and shaking them off his trail, he rambles at top speed. Suddenly he is entangled in ancient barbed wire affixed permanently to hardwood trees growing over and around the wire, making it impossible to tear loose. The exhausted ursine twists and struggles, thoroughly entangled. Escape is a lost cause—hanging sideways, torn and bloody, a hopeless victim of despair. He falls asleep and sucks in gales of night air, producing a deep guttural rhythm. That is Brave Phillie's snore.

A guest stumbled over my feet as he searched in dim light for the restroom. The sound of the brook replaces the darkness that settled over the valley we will wander through tomorrow morning. It's like something out of Tolkien's Middle Earth.

July 28, Hut register entry from Ultragrunge at Mizpah Spring Hut

Ooohh, these hut breakfasts! Sky, Pollyanna and I are shameless. We flirt with the croo guys and get extra coffee, bacon and pancakes. Doug sweet-talks female croo members, so we're working both teams. Of course, this costs them nothing, so perhaps they think they're giving us a workover. Hey, I'm down with that.

We followed the A.T. paralleling Whitewall Brook along the same valley we surveyed from the hut last night. The trail followed an old railbed running a level course along the shoulder of Whitewall Mountain. We meandered along and over Whitewall Brook, staying on a flat or gradual downhill course all the way to Crawford Notch, the least-taxing stretch of the A.T. in the Whites and a relief for our aching knees.

When we bottomed out at the notch, we rested next to the bridge at Crawford Brook to filter water and soak our dogs before bracing ourselves to tackle nearly 3,000 feet of climbing over the next six miles to Mizpah Spring Hut. Brave Phillie noted that they call the low spots in the ridges "gaps" in the south and "notches" in most of New England. Out West, they call them "passes." Regardless, it's murder on feet and knees walking down into them, and demanding on the heart and lungs walking up out of them.

For a while, the climb was on graded trail, an unaccustomed pleasure in New Hampshire. Then the going got rough with steep pitches and rocky spots where we had to scramble. When we got to the cliffs of Webster Mountain, we could see Route 302 far below and beyond that to the ridge we had hiked along earlier in the day. Another sunny day with low humidity and cool air. We climbed ever higher. Here the trail was friendly, gentle undulations with occasional vertical spots to scale up or down, and a few boggy places. It's a good day in the Whites when you just have one big climb. The sky was utterly cloudless, and we were up high enough that the temperature was just about perfect. About a mile from Mizpah Spring Hut, we met a married couple, SOBOs from Arkansas known as Lone Wolf and Wolf Bitch. "I call myself 'Wolfette' when I write to my mom," Wolf Bitch told us. "She'd never go for the 'bitch' part."

Lone Wolf grinned and said, "There're days you live up to the 'bitch' part."

Wolf Bitch had an REI utltra-light pack like mine. It was holding up well, but it bore scars from blowdowns she scraped past in Maine. "By the time y'all get there, they'll be cleared out. There's tough country between here and Katahdin," she said. Then came the obligatory add-on phrase we always get from SOBOs, "But you're gonna love it."

Mizpah Spring Hut was jampacked, and we decided to use the nearby tent site rather than work for stay. Pollyanna and I set up and wandered to the hut to sweet talk the croo guys. We settled in to play a board game.

By the time everyone else came rolling in, we were freaked to hear that Captain Stupid had slipped and tumbled on one of the steep climbs, receiving cuts and bruises along with a badly twisted knee. He kept his good humor while limping to the hut, but he was exhausted and in pain. Commandeering the hut first-aid kit, Sky cleaned the cut areas and put disinfectant on them. Then she fed him warm soup before taking him to a tent platform to settle him into his sleeping bag with a triple dose of Vitamin I.

A croo member told us to come back later and he'd give us leftovers. "The word is to treat you guys good," he told us. "You're icons!"

Pollyanna told him how much it means to get trail magic. I love that girl. She can feed people a line of bullshit and believe it herself, and the guys eat it up. Between her and Sky and sometimes me, we can maneuver in or out of any situation. My hard edge has softened, while Sky and Pollyanna are tougher and more assertive.

I spent the early part of the evening comparing notes with a young French couple hiking from the Androscoggin River to Hanover. They're in America for a few months and plan other hikes in Wyoming and Washington. As I was talking to them, a brawny SOBO trail-named Loggerhead sat next to me and barged into the conversation. Two things about him annoyed me. First, he was coming on to me big-time. I hate it when some self-impressed lug attempts to put the snake on me knowing full well we're headed in different directions—a good time he can walk away from the next morning. The other thing that annoyed me was that he totally ignored my French friends.

Later, after he knew he was being rebuffed, he wandered over to Sky Writer to get another—albeit friendlier—dismissal. My new friends commented that when he discovered they were French he acted downright rude to them, refusing to acknowledge them if they made a comment or asked a question. Jeez, I'm leery of people who turn their nose up before they even know you. It's a form of intolerance I can't tolerate.

Wowie zowie! I love evenings in the huts. I love the still darkness of shelters and tent-sites, with all their quirky night sights and sounds, but I also like the break of electric lights—thanks to the AMC's solar panels and wind generators—providing a bright place to commune with fellow travelers.

Tomorrow we gird our loins for Mt. Washington. The forecast is primo. Clear and cool, zero probability of rain. We can layer up and hope for a view of the ocean from the crest of the biggest mountain we've seen since the Smokies back in April.

July 29, Journal entry of Sky Writer at Madison Hut

I was brimming with emotion this morning. Of course, those who know me well would ask, "And this is unusual because. . .?" I hate it, though, when I keep fighting back tears and making everyone wonder, "What's wrong with her now?"

After the Captain took his fall yesterday, he tried to laugh it off—his big area of expertise—but it was clear he was in severe pain from the twisted knee. He was climbing down a steep spot, and his foot got stuck in a root. As he tried to yank his foot away, he toppled backwards and found himself hanging upside down with his knee and ankle all twisted around. It took all I had to push him up enough to get the pressure off his joints. Even when he struggled with all his might, he couldn't free himself.

It was absurd. We were laughing and crying, terrified that he was seriously injured, and unable to get him loose. When Blue Devil and Brave Phillie arrived, BD and I got under the Captain's torso and pushed up while BP extended a hiking stick from above and pulled. Soon Captain got upright after working his aching foot loose. We helped him to the bottom of the mini-cliff to sprawl next to the trail. "We're a mile and a half from Mizpah," Brave Phillie said. "Can you walk?"

The Captain got upright and took a few ginger steps. "It'd take a friggin' Huey to carry me," he groaned. "I can do it."

Do it he did. Every step was agony, but I also know his ability to keep moving under the most unbearable circumstances is—and I use this word rarely—incredible. As we labored, he said he was determined to keep pace no matter what.

As we packed this morning, he tested his knee. For the first 25 or 30 steps, the situation appeared hopeless, but as he got his blood pumping, he was ready to take a shot at a little less than 12 miles to Madison Hut, although he had to go up and over Mt. Washington. "Uphills may be easier than downhills," he predicted. I could tell he would go to any lengths to stay with the group—and me.

As we ascended steeply out of Mizpah Spring, I thought about the other part of the day that would seem weird. About 12 years ago, when I was 11, my parents decided to take a road trip in New England. It was in August, right before I went to school. We flew into Boston and followed the coast to Salem, Freeport, Acadia National Park and then to the White Mountains. I had a great time, clueless to the sorry fact that this was the last time we would travel as a family. Before the next summer, my parents had separated, and less than a year later, they were divorced.

For me, the highlight was the Cog Railway to the peak of Mt. Washington. I have vivid memories of the sooty smoke, the shrill whistle's blast echoing over distant peaks and the slow progress as the train inched upward, forcing me to lean forward and smack my sneakers against the floor impatiently. The peak was a wonderland with rock-strewn mountains in all directions. I couldn't sit still for lunch in the snack bar and walked outside with a soft drink and a hot dog (this was long before my efforts to go vegetarian).

I remember Mom and Dad laughing at me. I wore a windbreaker and a toboggan even though it was late summer, and I cried when we had to go back down. I wanted desperately to spend the night at Lakes of the Clouds Hut, an easy downhill hike from the summit, but that was not to be. I don't recall any outstanding family memories after that trip—an indication that my world was crumbling around me while I remained oblivious.

After an easy uphill stroll this morning, I finally got my wish to visit Lakes of the Clouds, with the massive peak of Mt. Washington growing ever larger as we approached. The northwestern wind shoved the clouds out toward the Atlantic, and we were left with high sky and long views. As we approached the hut, the wind generator roared and the surface of the nearby water was white capping. A few minutes out of the wind to freshen up in the restroom was perfect. The Captain was jolly, but his knee was aflame.

We labored to the summit of Mt. Washington with high winds growing ever fiercer, at times powerful enough to knock us sideways. I zipped the legs onto my shorts and put on both my tee shirts and my polypro long-sleeves beneath my parka. It was still cold.

Finally, I had returned to Mt. Washington from a different direction, under wildly variant circumstances and using a dissimilar mode of transportation—my feet, as opposed to a stinky old cog railway. The Captain knew I carried an emotional burden, and after reaching the peak and exploring as long as the wind would allow, we went inside where he treated me to corn chips, all-American health food.

I spotted a family—a mom, a dad and a gangly 11-year-old with blond pigtails and glasses. The parents watched in amusement as their coltish daughter roamed around the building talking to anyone who would listen, asking questions and dying to be noticed. This was just too much, and it intensified when she walked over to us.

"How long have you been hiking?" she asked. Her eyes were dancing, mirrors of myself a dozen years old.

Captain saw that I was smiling and crying simultaneously, so he took charge. "Are you familiar with the Appalachian Trail?" She nodded affirmatively.

"Well," he said in a pompous tone, "we started hiking at Springer Mtn. in Georgia five years ago and finally made it to this place. We hope to finish at Mt. Katahdin in Maine three years from now."

She bought the humor and brushed off the nonsense. "When did you start, really?"

"Late March," I told her. "We've hiked more than 1,800 miles."

Her dad walked up. "I see you've met Laura," he said. "She's determined to hike on the A.T., but we don't have time for backpacking on this trip. Can you hold up under her questioning?" We spent half an hour with Laura and explained why she should pursue the dream and why the grisly sight of the Captain's red, throbbing knee should not deter her. I gave her an Appalachian Trail pin I had bought on a whim in Hanover, and her eyes widened as she looked at her mom and dad to see if it was okay to accept. It was, and she affixed it to her Acadia National Park ball cap. I jotted down her email address and promised to make her a cyberpal.

Walking outside, we took a final look toward the coast, hoping for a glimpse of the ocean, but even with the cleansing wind, we had no luck. As we descended, the wind tapered off. We listened to the deafening whistle of the Cog Railway, as Laura and her parents headed back down. We negotiated the next six miles wondering if we should have taken the railway down to save the Captain's knee. He whined good-naturedly, and we pulled into Madison Hut late in the afternoon. A few SOBOs had commandeered work for stay, and we wondered what the hut manager would do with us.

"We met your friends earlier," he said. "They hiked down a few miles to the Osgood Tent Site. They told us you two were the big heroes in that fracas down in Tennessee."

"She's the hero," Captain responded. "I was just happy to come out of it with my head still attached."

"Whatever," the manager said. "We'll find you a spot to crash." So detached from our friends, we're surrounded by merry guests with a rowdy streak. They enjoyed my singing, and now I'm ready to sleep after a day that was physically, spiritually and emotionally draining. Laura Lawrence came through when I needed a lift.

July 30, Transcript of Captain Stupid recorded at Joe Dodge Lodge at Pinkham Notch

I went heavy on Vitamin I again last night. It worked. I slept like a chubby baby. I may have also been helped by two slugs of Jack Daniel's one of the croo stealthily provided before lights out. Apparently they had recently had an AMC staff party called MadFest, an annual blowout for croo members who take the time and energy to get here. I was a lucky recipient of leftover liquor.

It had been an emotional day for Sky. She scooted her sleeping pad next to mine and put her arms around me seeking comfort. Thanks to my lovable teddy-bear body, I have never been what you would call a chick magnet. You are correct in the assumption I know you're making that I have never even laid down a bunt with a woman, much less made it to first base. While I'm on the baseball analogy, let me just say I've been riding the bench, man! Sky Writer is the only woman who has cared to enter my life.

I am in love. Love builds apprehension and self-doubt. I did what was necessary to make Sky happy. Seeing as how we were in a public place, that didn't go far, but it was the first time these two lovers have done much more than exchange a couple of nervous kisses, a critical stage in this relationship.

"If you don't want me to leave you, I'll stay forever," I whispered. I remember every exact word I spoke. I needed a response.

"I know," she said. Hmmmm. "I know." That is acknowledgement but not agreement, right? I woke up needing clarification.

Breakfast was flavorless thanks to my state of anxiety. My fear of rejection would eclipse Mt. Washington in scope. It's easier to not know. Also it is easier to not ask than it is to ask and not get the answer you're looking for. That's what preoccupied my thoughts, wrenched my guts and twisted my heart as we walked into the still, bright morning and labored up Mt. Madison. We were alone with a marvelous view of Mt. Washington watching distant automobiles toiling to the peak. The mountain was stark, sculpted by some giant unseen hand, with its profile etched against a bright morning sky. A clear view over the Great Gulf. Time to get things straight.

"Sky, my love, we are about to drop off the edge of the earth over the next few miles, picking our way through rocks down to Pinkham Notch," I said. "How would you like to make this horrible next few hours a whole lot better for my poor knee?"

She giggled. "What have you got in mind, Captain?"

"Tell me if you want me around. And I don't just mean this after-noon, or until we get to Maine or even all the way to Katahdin. I wanna know if you could imagine a lifetime with me. Marriage, children, a minivan. Or will you be a torch singer, some mysterious, massively tal-ented woman who never commits—just goes with the flow of life?"

"Gee," she said. "If I wade through what you just said, I'm picking a marriage proposal out of the verbiage. Stop me quick if I'm wrong."

"No. You're not wrong. You don't have to say yes or no, but at least let me know if it's something you would consider over the next few weeks."

"I've thought it through already," she said. Her voice was husky, and tears were springing out of the corners of her eyes. "Do you want the answer?"

"I'm terrified to hear it." My voice broke, and tears streamed into my beard. "Don't you understand that last March I would never have imagined this? I was looking at living with my mom, slogging away at a hopeless job, terrified of women, because I knew they had no place for me. But this A.T. has changed me so drastically. I left another person back there as I lost all this weight. A little man with all the fears and weaknesses and self-doubts I've battled all my life. It's more than trans-formational; it's transfigurative. This trail, and the Bly Gap Gang and you—more than anything, you—have converged on this mountaintop and given me courage to change. So, yes, I want the answer."

My speech, clumsy and heartfelt, gave her time to get a grip. The tears stopped, and she laughed. There was a look on her face I couldn't pin down. "Captain, you really don't know what I'm going to say, do you?"

"Oh, no," I answered. "I really don't."

She put her clenched fists on her hips. Gentle wind blew in her hair, and I would challenge anyone to name any woman on earth more beau-tiful than she was at that moment. "Mr. Captain, I will commit myself to a lifetime with you. I will marry you. I will have your babies. I will drive your minivan. I will be Mrs. Stupid. And you know what?"

I must have looked like a child who stumbled into the living room on Christmas Eve, and—good grief!—Santa Claus really was there. "What?" I gasped.

"I mean it. I really will."

Yay!

Hours later, we arrived at Pinkham Notch. Along the way, emotional floodgates burst. We opened our hearts as we picked our way down the rocky scree of Mt. Madison and down the steep trail, through the conifer forest, and later among hardwoods as we rested next to the suspension bridge swaying over roaring Peabody River. Gravity pulled us through the afternoon as we embraced the certainty of a future together.

It was early when we got to Joe Dodge Lodge on the highway in Pinkham Notch. At check-in we learned we were all in one eight-bunk room—not ideal for a pair who just pledged their lives to each other.

As we gathered for dinner, Blue Devil said the remaining distance to Katahdin was just 319 miles. "We need to pay attention," he warned. "We need to make sure this doesn't end too soon." The Bly Gap family nodded. Sky squeezed my hand. "Isn't it great that we don't want it to end?" she whispered.

A discordant note came at the end of the meal. An AMC staffer gestured to our group: "This is the Bly Gap Gang. You may have heard about some of the problems they had in Tennessee. We're glad they're safe here with us tonight." There was polite applause.

As our spokesman and surrogate father figure, Brave Phillie stood up and said, "We appreciate y'all being so accommodating."

Six California men in their thirties were at the next table. They had indulged heavily on brown-bag wine, and one of them stood and raised a glass. "I detect a Southern accent there fella. You must be from where they filmed *Deliverance*." He looked around with the transparently stupid smile of a drunk whose sense-of-humor filter is clouded. Affecting an atrocious Southern accent, he said, "I hope you boys ain't gonna be squealin' like piggies and keepin' the rest of us awake tonight."

A groan went through the room, and BP gave the guy a squint, "You little fellas from the land of fruits and nuts are the big experts in that area, aren't you?"

Oh boy. Doug stood up and in a couple of graceful strides, he was between the combatants. "Everyone in this room understands that both of you would be just as happy if that little exchange had never taken place, am I right?"

Doug looked hard at Brave Phillie, who grudgingly said, "Yeah, I agree."

One of the California guys showed some gumption: "Our friend here feels the same. Don't you Billy?"

Billy looked trapped and angry, but he came around. "Yeah, sorry."

Blue Devil muttered, "What was that cracker thinkin'?"

After dinner, I stole away to this quiet spot to record this. Tomorrow, a big up and down to Carter Notch Hut. I'm signing off to return to the lodge and find . . . oh, you know who I'm looking for. Question is: Will she *really* drive any man's minivan?

July 31, Journal entry of Doug Gottlieb at Carter Notch Hut

A short day, but I've done 20-milers with less effort. We are at the last AMC hut. We did work for stay and delighted in flaky wedges of apple pie for dessert. The first mile was easy, paralleling Ellis River before bending around Lost Pond. When I caught Pollyanna at the pond, she didn't see me coming. In her hand was a box turtle, which she treated as a rare and irreplaceable treasure. Her face reflected transcendent joy, as if she had traveled all these months to experience this single moment. I was an interloper unable to resist intruding on her privacy. She looked up at me and beamed, then put the turtle off-trail and watched him creep away. Neither of us spoke, another of those moments the trail provides, sometimes after hours of monotony and dull pain. We began a four-mile ascent over the multiple peaks of Wildcat Mtn. and past the ridge-top ski-lift. I thought of how much easier it would be to cheat and use them to scale peaks. Treasonous thoughts.

Foot for foot, this was one of the most demanding climbs of the trip, a rocky uphill treadmill. Pollyanna observed that perhaps the only thing worse than climbing it would be descending it. It was just plain hard work. When we finally reached Peak A of Wildcat Mtn., it was time to drop more than 1,000 feet to the hut in Carter Notch. The murky clouds eliminated what must have been eye-popping views.

Last night I borrowed Blue Devil's cell phone and found a private spot to call Mom to thank her for funding the night in Pinkham Notch. She told me that this adventure of mine is hers as well. She has a strip map of the A.T. hanging on the refrigerator and another at work, which she updates with yellow highlighter every time she hears from me. "I'm hiking with you vicariously," she said.

I laughed. "You're lucky it was vicarious today. The climb was awful."

She told me I'm a minor celebrity among her friends and in the community. She was interviewed for a feature in the weekly paper. "I was nervous about this at first," she said. "Now I'm part of it."

Mom sprung a surprise. She has a boyfriend. "You know him, Jack Marshall. He was an old fishing buddy of your dad's. His wife died a few years ago, and we kept running into each other around town. Then he started coming to our church, and now we're, gosh, I guess you'd call it dating. I feel like a teenager." I remembered Jack. Any time I tagged along to fish or hike, Jack made me feel important, not some fifth-wheel brat. "Mom!" I shouted. "That's great! I hope you all have a blast together."

"You know what's funny," Mom said. "One of my friends said Jack started coming to church just to have an excuse to see me."

"Do you think it was divine intervention?" I asked.

I think about how important it was for Mom to hear my voice and get my approval. Insulated as we are from the conventional world, we still play a part in the lives of our family and friends, even if only with phone calls or emails. I think of trail journals and letters getting passed around. I recall what I thought it would be like out here before the trip and how different it has turned out to be. I imagine them stopping in the midst of their busy days and contemplating my adventure, thinking of gorgeous mountaintop views, wild-animal sightings, cozy campfires—all the niceties of trail life. I imagine they don't consider climbs like the one this morning or rain, mud, mosquitos, and other nagging realities of life in the woods.

That's much of the point of the A.T. experience. It is not an unproblematic stroll through the mountains. It is a life fraught with logistical brainteasers and joys. You take it on with the confidence of an achiever. I know I will finish, and what I learn about myself and from my friends along the way will pay off somehow down the road.

August 1, Journal entry of Pollyanna at Hiker's Paradise Hostel, Gorham, NH

Another backbreaking climb this morning. It was only 1,500 feet, so I got it out of the way quickly. There were a few smaller climbs today, but mostly I hiked rugged level and downhill trail. I was in cruise control, alone with my thoughts for hours. My goal was to reach Hiker's Paradise Hostel early this afternoon and take a zero day tomorrow, the first since Hanover. I started early, leading the pack all day.

My last day in the Whites was a winner. Who knows if I'll hike here again? Every mile is a gift. I know the word is trivialized, but the views down into the Androscoggin Valley were *awesome*. I was up so high that the early August air was crisp and pleasant despite the sun streaming down, unfiltered by cloud cover. I remember how on July 1, just south of the Connecticut border, I felt thoroughly inured to the daily demands of the A.T. Now, my body, mind and spirit have dovetailed into a hiking machine.

After a really long descent, part of it paralleling the Rattle River, I reached U.S. 2, a few miles from Gorham, and went against my personal rule against hitchhiking alone. A teenaged boy in a pickup truck came along and knew exactly where the Hiker's Paradise was. He pointed out beautiful birch trees and told me I should come back in the fall when the birch leaves turned to flaming colors.

When I checked in at the Paradise, I learned that Momma Llama had prepaid a unit for both nights! There are conventional hotel rooms here, but also sectioned bunk rooms. I showered and changed to town togs before venturing outside feeling inhumanly fresh.

"Well, for somebody who tried to commit suicide back at Sages Ravine, you don't look any worse for wear," said a voice behind me. I turned around, and there was Wonder Boy, barely recognizable with a fresh shave.

"I took a week off for my brother's wedding. I hoped I'd run into you again," he said. This guy has so much self-confidence that a girl almost wants to throw herself on him and surrender to the inevitable. Blond hair, trim waist, broad shoulders, ripped muscles (no wonder he walks around shirtless), a snowblinding smile and a truly endearing manner. He asked if I'd like to amble over to the P.O. As we strolled along, I tried to convey my appreciation for his kindness during my mishap in Massachusetts. He brushed the comments aside: "Like you wouldn't have done the same for me."

Wonder Boy is from Boston (obviously well fixed), and his thru-hike is part of a year of adventure after graduating from Princeton. "My dad wanted me to go to Harvard—just as he and his dad and my brother did," he said. "I refused, but stayed Ivy League." He was a business major. Law school's next. Is this guy on a fast-track, or what?

At the P.O. I picked up a major drop and letters from family and friends. I sorted through the food packets and shifted a few things into my bounce box. "This is great!" I said. "I don't need anything else. I won't need to resupply for another week or so." Wonder Boy grabbed the entire food box, balancing it on his noggin like a circus virtuoso, and walked along with me. He has an effortless knack for being simultaneously indispensable and desirable.

Back at the Paradise, the Bly Gappers were still nowhere to be seen. My early start put me well ahead of them. We shared a washer and did our stuff in one load. He invited me to his room for Cosmic Brownies, and when we walked outside later, Blue Devil, Doug and Grunge were unfolding their stiff bodies from the bed of the same pickup truck I'd hitched with earlier. The kid gave a friendly wave and drove off as Doug stared blankly toward Wonder Boy and me. He didn't seem too pleased. I felt a smidgen of satisfaction to be the object of a little healthy jealousy. Wonder Boy walked over to the three of them and, with his effortless charm, helped with their gear. Grunge gave Wonder Boy the google eye for my benefit.

My friends went into town to check off items on their to-do lists. The afternoon before a zero day is utter bliss. Burning feet, swollen ankles and throbbing knees are released from their frenzied agony with a little Ibuprofen. I slipped into a dreamless nap. Later, we wandered to a Chinese buffet. How can a restaurant profit from AYCE when a group like ours swarms in? We remorselessly pillaged egg rolls, Chinese dumplings, and sweet and sour goodies. With all the soy sauce and hot mustard, we risk lower-gastrointestinal disaster, but you only live once.

Wonder Boy coaxed me into a walk. I told him about my college days at Ohio State, my Psych major and my dread of finishing the trail and having to figure out a career direction. I went on and on about how trail life was perfect for me, a relief considering that months ago I wondered what I was getting myself into. Wonder Boy. Wonder Boy. Oh, that Wonder Boy!

August 2, Journal entry of Blue Devil at Hiker's Paradise Hostel

I called my parents last night and had one of the best conversations I can recall with them. No suggestions, admonishments, call-downs or remonstrations. Two parents talked to their adult son and enjoyed hearing about his latest adventures, and I guess I'm still enough of a kid at age 18 to enjoy the feeling of incipient adulthood. Mom asked for the thousandth time how I felt about them coming up and visiting, and I said they'd see me soon enough, without all that trouble.

Dad was impressed by the way the others have stepped up and treated the group during the trip, so he told me that as a reward for my spending less on the journey than he had calculated, I could use the credit card to pick up the tab for an off-trail overnighter somewhere in Maine, and my response was, "Hey Pop, you don't have to offer twice."

The weather today was horrible, lots of wind and rain, and even though it's early August, it was cool. I can imagine what it must have been like at over 5,000 feet on the big peaks. I got diligent yesterday and got my logistics squared away so that I could spend today doing just what I've been doing: lounging, talking (one of my specialties) and reading. Somehow, I made it to 18 without reading *The Catcher in the Rye*. I read a stray copy I found at the hostel. Doug said J.D. Salinger was a recluse in Lebanon, N.H., very close to Hanover, before his death a few years back. My God, what a book!

I can't express the utter euphoria, ecstasy and sheer pleasure of a zero day after laboring all the way up here zero-free from Hanover. I suggested we take more of these on the way to Katahdin, and everyone agreed, even fidgety old Brave Phillie, who is less crusty and much more—there's no other word for it—lovable which I attribute to Momma Llama. She's tamed this old savage. We sit and talk like old buddies which I love considering what divergent character types we are.

Ultragrunge and Sky Writer stopped at a drugstore and stocked up on nail polish. I got my toenails done in fluorescent orange and a blond A.T. symbol bleached into the back of my hair. Grunge learned to mess with hair color in her neogoth days, when she went purple for a while. She streaked Doug's hair, and he was displeased enough that he coaxed Sky to borrow scissors and shorten his locks. Captain Stupid allowed his toenails to be painted. Brave Phillie blew us all away by letting Grunge paint his toes, the highlight of a great zero day—a jarhead with orange toenails.

We all went out for pizza, except Wonder Boy and Pollyanna, who went someplace alone. Doug was disconsolate in the midst of our revelry. Captain Stupid sang again about Angelina, and we all remembered enough of the words to join in.

I hate watching Doug in a funk over the reemergence of Wonder Boy. Pollyanna enjoys his company, and the two of them have disappeared together a few times, *and* Wonder Boy has his own room. Doug hasn't said so, but it is practically written in giant block stencil on his forehead that he is green-eyed jealous of this guy, with all his suave urbanity, his erudition and his sex appeal. Now, when it comes to the looks department, Doug and I can top just about anybody's list, but this Wonder Boy is a major player. I'm tempted to tell Doug to quit waffling and make his play, but who am I to dispense advice? I lost my love, and I won't pretend to be an expert in the ways of woo.

August 3, Journal entry of Brave Phillie at Gentian Pond Campsite

There was talk of two zero days. But when we got up this morning, the weather was clear as a shot glass of grain. Instead of wasting blue skies, we decided on short days through the Mahoosucs. I'm the only one in the group who's done Mahoosuc Notch, which is reputed to be the toughest mile on the A.T. I get a kick out of how these well-conditioned kids are listening to horror tales from SOBOs about how rough the notch is. Sure, it's tough, and so is the overall Mahoosuc Range, but after nearly 2,000 miles, you can fall back on your confidence.

Momma and I led all day, starting with a climb out of the Androscoggin Valley and then following a roller coaster to end our at 12-mile day at this place. We paid the price you often pay in the Mahoosucs after lots of rain. The trail was boggy and slippery, and a few of the bog logs were wobbly. I managed to slip on one, twist my bad foot, and get my clean zero-day body all wet and muddy. We saw a few deer, along with a fair number of bear and moose tracks. This country isn't as popular as the Whites, not as crowded. Nonetheless, by the time we reached the shelter—a really nice one—it was packed with some of the usual NOBO suspects.

I compared notes with a Harpers Ferry-bound SOBO named Kennebec Ken, and we agreed that we are in the most challenging stretch on the A.T.—all the peaks between Bigelow and Moosilauke. "I'm not saying it gets easy after Bigelow," Ken told me. "I'm just saying you won't see as many uphill and downhill grinds." I assured him the same would be true after he spends the night in Glencliff.

Wonder Boy politely inquired if he could set up next to Momma Llama and me. Since mosquitoes don't appear to be a problem, Pollyanna decided to accept his offer to sleep under his tarp rather than set up her tent. "Oh, brother," Momma muttered. "This kid's the real deal. If he hangs around and keeps PA under his spell, Doug may take a header off lover's leap." Typically for me, I hadn't noticed a problem, but I guess she's right now that I think about it. Doug has been glum.

After dinner, Momma Llama and I took in the moon and the stars. I told her I had trouble understanding what a woman as attractive, intelligent and educated as she is could see in an old jarhead. She told me, "You're selfless and kind without realizing it. It's your way. You're a controlling old fart, but you don't mind being ignored when you're that way. Just leave it at that." I guess that was enough.

As I write by headlamp, the porcupines are getting frisky. I suggested to Captain Stupid that he may want to kill a few and put some more notches in his belt. He told me to cut the chatter, because he'll never live down the porky encounter back in Massachusetts. Sky Writer tried to scowl at me, but that is not a face made for scowling. She told me I wasn't funny. Hell, I think I was downright hilarious!

13

The Notch, High Peaks into Infinity and a Bit of Betrayal

THE MAHOOSUCS

Nowhere else on the A.T. is there a stretch to match the White Mountains for sheer preponderance of peaks above timberline and huge climbs and descents, one after the other. An exhausting hike by any but Himalayan standards, it is also enormously rewarding. As a NOBO leaves the Whites, hits the Androscoggin Valley and takes a well-deserved break in Gorham, he is wise to lay off high-living and try to recharge his energy. The Mahoosuc Range is little relief from the Whites.

Years ago, a fun-loving SOBO emerged from the Mahoosucs and celebrated reaching Gorham by spending his evening sipping suds. Even after a zero, he was not himself when he headed south into the Whites. He was known thereafter as Red Dog, after the beer he guzzled to excess. The same mistake has been made by NOBOs over the decades of Gorham's existence as a trail town. The only difference is that they carry their hangovers into the Mahoosucs.

Although not as lofty as the Whites, the Mahoosucs embody the same gritty feel. Then there is Mahoosuc Notch, surely the toughest mile on the trail. A canyon filled with boulders bigger than vacation cottages, it takes an interminable spell to traverse and results in tumbles, scrapes and bruises.

Mahoosuc Range is blessed with the most beautiful high ponds and lakes anywhere. Dream Lake, Moss Pond, Gentian Pond and Speck Pond inspire a

sense of peace only high-altitude bodies of water can provide. Speck Pond—
deep, timeless and mysterious—is where every NOBO remembers what a
thru-hike is all about.

What NOBOs sense as they get deep into the Mahoosucs is a wildness
they will feel from the Maine border and beyond to Katahdin. The detached
quality of wilderness is enhanced and the experience deepens. The spell of
the Mahoosucs settles over you. ▪

August 4, Journal entry of Momma Llama at Full Goose Shelter

We're doing this right. Just nine miles today, a chance to relish the
Mahoosucs and reconcile ourselves to the importance of savoring every
step of Maine. We hit the state line this morning after hiking over bogs
and up hand-over-hand climbs. We gathered at the border to pay tribute
to our passage into the great state of Maine.

When all had assembled, Sky decided we needed a ceremonial inter-
pretive dance to celebrate our arrival into the last of the 14 states on
the A.T. She did what she called the swan. Gently flapping her arms,
twirling and shuffling, she glided past the state line sign graceful as a
skimming dragonfly.

Then Blue Devil. Hands on hips, he vamped a funky, strutting dance,
imitating Wilson Pickett singing "In the Midnight Hour." He jumps from
urban schtick to erudite suburban preppy to a variety of other poses,
none of which seem to be the real him.

Brave Phillie and I waltzed back and forth over the border as I sang
"Tennessee Waltz," popular on my old AM transistor back in the day.
BP picked up some steps somewhere in his murky past, including a big
finish with a skillful dip. Wonder Boy picked up Pollyanna and spun
her around on his shoulder like a helicopter rotor until they toppled
and collapsed into Maine, each thankfully in one giggling piece.

The Captain wisely calculated that Doug wasn't in the mood for all
this. So, he grabbed Doug's hand and Ultragrunge's and began skipping
around singing "Here we go, gathering nuts in Maine!" It was just plain
stupid and got even more hilarious as the Captain broke away and did
the Curly routine from the Three Stooges. He headed backwards, keeping one foot in place and kicking himself along with the other to move
himself over the Maine border and out of New Hampshire for good.

We merged in a big group hug, and Brave Phillie removed his
ancient Phillies cap, encrusted in dirt and salty sweat, and placed it
over his heart. "Lord," he said, "we've all whined and complained about

the weather and the bugs and the climbs for months now, but look where we are. We hope wherever old Bone is you're watching his back, and we ask you to do the same for us all the way to Katahdin. Amen." Our first invocation from the least-likely source.

Maine starts out tough. Muddy, rocky, and steep, engineered to get up and down peaks quickly, with little regard for grade. At times hiking sticks are lifesavers, while at others you toss them below while you negotiate down a tiny cliff or try to figure out a way to get them out of your way as you climb up a rock pile.

It's important to be careful on the bog logs. Some shift slowly as you negotiate them, taking your feet below muck level. If you slip, you usually can balance yourself like a circus acrobat astride a Lipizzaner. Or you may end up taking a misstep into the ooze or even worse, falling headlong and hoping for the best. If you are being followed by a heavier companion—Captain Stupid, for example—you pray you have stepped off the bog log before he steps on. Otherwise, you can be catapulted upward and sideways, a human projectile destined for a muddy plunge. That very circumstance occurred this afternoon, with poor Pollyanna taking a partial mud bath.

So it was with mud on our feet and legs that we pulled into Full Goose Shelter. There was room for all of us for a change and a nice spring out back to facilitate canteen showers. We are quiet tonight. I just looked at the wall of the shelter and saw where someone has carved the following inscription, "Jerry Flankersheet sucks goobies." An insightful comment on a deserving young man.

August 5, Journal entry of Ultragrunge at Speck Pond Campsite

It seems the more energy you waste anticipating things, the more they turn out not to live up to expectations. Mahoosuc Notch was really cool, but all the buildup from the SOBOs was misplaced. Still, the place took a chunk out of me.

Here's how it played out: We were only planning to cover the five miles over to the Speck Pond Shelter today. I was annoyed about this, but one thing I've learned is that if you want the advantages of traveling with people you love, you sometimes bite your tongue and go with the flow. At the beginning of this trip, I did not consider myself to be a "group ethos" type. But there were a lot of things about me at the beginning of this trip that have changed. A glance in the mirror tells that tale.

I could justify this truncated day by remembering that this stretch is reputed to be the toughest on the trail. Still, it is just five miles for cripes sakes! I figured to hit it quick and have time to swim or read or (if he/she is hot) schmooze with the caretaker.

Going up and over Goose Eye Mtn. was great yesterday. I got the sense of being in the wildest country since Springer. This morning, it was up and over Fulling Mill Mtn. in bright sunshine and a gale of wind before a deep descent into the "dreaded" Mahoosuc Notch. Blue Devil was with me, and the two of us were determined to prove how easy it all was, swaggering twits that we both are.

It rained last night, and despite having the wind die down as we headed into the notch, the rocks were dripping and slippery. Mahoosuc Notch is a deep canyon between Fulling Mill Mtn. and Mahoosuc Arm. It is as if a giant took a mallet and hammered a wedge between the mountains to assure a deep cleft. After the giant left, dislodged boulders tumbled to the bottom, leaving hikers no choice but to weave through them.

Blue Devil likened it to a gargantuan 3-D maze, following blazes up, around, under and over boulders. The farther we went, the tougher it got, at times leading through dank boulder caves smelling of moss and mold. Deep in the canyon, the place was sunless and forbidding—great fun! I stepped up the pace to challenge Blue Devil.

Then, oops! I squeezed through a fissure between a couple of boulders, and in an effort to take a shortcut, I came to a spot where I had to descend a 12-foot drop-off. I worked along a horizontal crevice and came to a place where my left foot needed to cross my right. I leaned backward with the tilt of the rock to disentangle myself. I really needed one of my sticks, but I had shortened them and lashed them to my pack. So I decided to do a spin maneuver, from facing toward the rock to facing away. My planted foot slipped on the wet granite, and down I slid, so fast I could only brace myself and hope for the best. I landed with a jarring collision that twisted my left ankle, banged up my right knee and jolted my spine as my tush crashed flat on the rock. I must have banged my head on a boulder, because I'm sure I was only semi-conscious for a little while, if not completely zonked. It was only when I heard Blue Devil. urgency in his voice, calling my name that I looked up and saw that handsome brown face peering from above with panic and concern. "You okay, Calves?" he asked.

"I don't know. I just got here," I muttered.

He had trouble actually getting to where I was, because he was trying to keep from stepping on me. I moved my parts and decided nothing was numb, nothing was broken and everything was miserable. Blue Devil gingerly inspected my new collection of cuts and bruises. "I'll wait to clean off all this blood," I said. "Let's just get through here and count ourselves lucky."

Even with my little emergency, we completed the traverse of the mighty notch in about 70 minutes. I cleaned up my bloody arms and legs in a stream, and we started up Mahoosuc Arm, a 1,600-foot ascent that's as demanding foot-for-foot as anything on the A.T. I grabbed trees to pull myself over or around rocks and often my hand came away with either a slug or disgusting slug slime. I held one up to show Blue Devil, and he called me a wimp. I threw the slimeball at him, plastering gooey revenge on his T-shirt.

Dripping rocks made this climb far from routine, but we finally descended to Speck Pond campsite. The caretaker *was* hot, a girl who was apologetic about charging a fee and fun to flirt around with. "If I get up early enough tomorrow morning, I'll fry up Canadian bacon," she promised. I stripped off everything down at the pond—to hell with what Blue Devil could see—and stepped in. God, it was cold! I stayed in long enough to rinse off the blood and slime. Then, naked in the high mountain air, I rinsed out my clothes.

Blue Devil skinny-dipped as well, and there were no wisecracks between us. We lay on a flat rock beside the little miracle of Speck Pond, trying to figure out if it was the prettiest spot on the entire A.T. "I'll bet it's a mile deep," Blue Devil said.

"Be careful, Calves," he said, looking at me with a guileless smile I'd never seen from him before. "You might just fall in love with me." He calls me Calves, because he claims I have the best set of female calves on the A.T. He's right.

August 6, Journal entry of Sky Writer at Frye Notch Lean-to

If you know something you're not supposed to know, does that disallow you to discuss it with affected parties, even if you think they should know?

Last night I found a quiet spot next to Speck Pond and sat watching how moonlight and clouds alternated between shadow and light on the peaks and the opalescent surface of the pond. I was minding my business when I heard someone approach, a lone male intent on achieving my same state of silent contemplation. I chose not to make my presence known, and a few minutes passed. Then someone else materialized out of the darkness, and I heard the following conversation:

"Been nice knowing you Doug. It's doubtful we'll see each other after tonight." It was Wonder Boy.

"Why's that?" Doug asked in a neutral tone.

"Well, once you've filled your cup, you move on, if you take my meaning. I've had enough of the Bly Gap Gang, and you guys have had enough of me."

"Sorry you feel that way," Doug mumbled.

"You should be happy. I had my little tumble with Pollyanna. Now you can have her back. She's nice, but not my type. I'll slip away by headlamp in the morning, and you can get back to normal."

There was a long pause, and I was rooting for Doug not to let this pass. "Wonder Boy," he said, "I don't know how you define a 'tumble,' but I know Pollyanna well enough to be sure that whatever casual fun you two had, she still has a sparkling reputation. So can the crap. It's not the right way to talk about people."

Wonder Boy chuckled. It sounded so ugly. "Think what you want, Doug, old buddy. I know what I know. I'll move out of your way." With that, he vanished in the darkness.

Doug stood in perfect silence for a while, sighed tragically and walked away into the dark. How could anyone say that about Pollyanna? I know Wonder Boy is being cruel, but why? My blood boils to hear Pollyanna shown such disrespect behind her back.

This morning there was no trace of the self-impressed Adonis. I considered it good riddance, but when others commented on his absence, I saw that Pollyanna was puzzled and hurt. Now I stand silently by, watching her and Doug suffer.

The caretaker brought fresh-fried Canadian bacon. "I smelled it cookin', and I was prayin' I'd get some," Brave Phillie said. It disappeared in two minutes, and the thank-a-trail-angel-at-least-three-times rule was implemented in spades. Sweet little vegetarian that I am, I stuck with my customary breakfast bars. Then we were off for a rigorous 10 miles to Frye Notch. We started by finishing the climb up Old Speck. The peak was cloaked, so we dispensed with a visit to the observation tower and started a 2,700-foot descent to the road at Grafton Notch. Light rain and high-altitude wind didn't help.

Of course, when we hit the notch, we soon started right back up with a ponderous, wet climb up Baldpate Mtn. On a clear day, we would have had great views from the exposed rock faces, but on this day, we could see maybe 50 feet ahead, and the rocks seemed icy slick.

Dropping off into murky fog, we descended steeply again before getting to the shelter at Frye Brook, our fingers and faces numb. Just our luck, three NOBOs who passed us in Virginia and left a pretty negative impression have claimed space in the shelter along with some short-termers who had broken out a stash of pot. The NOBOs—Jerkoff, Sir Jerksalot and Jerkhead—are trying to see how high they can get, and it's enhancing their obnoxious personalities. You can just look at the trail names and get some idea of how excited I am about seeing them again.

"I remember you," one of them said. "We saw you like down near Shenandoah or someplace. Why don't you come out of the rain and sample a little of this primo devil weed?" My theory on pot smoking on the A.T. is that people should not do it in shelters. If the hypothetical forest ranger appears in his Smokey Bear hat, everyone is implicated. If people want recreational substances—I admit I've had a toke or two—they should keep the party private. Maine has decriminalized, but it's still problematic to get caught with weed, even in small quantities.

I went in search of a place to set up. When I found a suitable spot, Pollyanna appeared and set up next to me. As I nestled under my tarp and Pollyanna got cozy in her Zoid, we discussed the disappearance of Wonder Boy. "He seemed like a nice guy," she said. "I was having fun with him, although I would never see him as my type long-term. Do you think it was something I did to make him just disappear like that?"

I felt I couldn't betray what I heard last night, so I just said, "Hey, girl. If he left without saying anything, that tells you all you need to know. He may be rich, witty and all that, but he's also a superficial, self-obsessed twit. Consider yourself lucky that you still have a decent guy like Doug around." She was silent behind the opaque wall of her tent, possibly considering that her flirtation with Wonder Boy may have done more to hurt Doug's feelings than she would have wanted. Now she had her own feelings hurt. Soul-searching going on in the Zoid tonight.

August 7, Transcript of Captain Stupid recorded at Hall Mtn. Lean-to

No matter how I sugarcoat it, I'll never grow accustomed to forcing myself out of a warm sleeping bag on a rainy, cold morning and putting on a wet rain jacket, packing up sodden gear and hoisting a dripping pack to move out into an August day that somewhere other than here dawned warm and dry.

Yay!

We started with a short, steep climb up Surplus Mtn. and then another of those steep drops over rocks and roots with cascades of rainwater sweeping along the trail in a devious assault on our shoes. Oh, how I hate days like this! Climbing out of Dunn Notch, I was scared out of my wits when a massive bull moose—his rack bobbing majestically—crashed out of the conifers and stopped on the trail 30 feet from Sky and me. He looked up and down the trail and seemed less than pleased that the two of us were blocking the direction he apparently had in mind.

"We're staying right here, big guy," I hollered. "It's too wet to hang around waiting for you to decide."

His expression changed. I'm serious. He sneered and snorted at us as if to say, "I could kill your puny butts, but I'll be nice and get out of your way." And he did. He started off on the trail away from us, with his big haunches flexing and disappeared in the swirling rain and fog we've battled for two days. "I think I just wet my pants," Sky told me. "But it's raining so hard it won't matter." Something always happens to make an otherwise dismal day downright memorable.

I'm sure the climb up Wyman Mtn. has much to be said for it on one of those days when Bambi is strolling around, when bluebirds are whistling along to "Zip-A-Dee-Doo-Dah," when the bears are having a dancing jubilee, when SOBOs make room in the shelter and serve lady fingers, when the sun is high, when the air is cool and dry and scented with jasmine and when all is right with the world as in Browning's *Pippa Passes.*

This was not one of those days. The Frye Notch potheads likely never left their moldy bags this morning. Little's the pity. But an equally squalid assemblage was crammed into the Hall Mtn. Lean-to, passing bottles of cheap wine and urinating right out of the shelter into the rain to avoid getting wet. Sky and I witnessed this delightful sight for as long as it took a few more rain drops to run off our noses. We found a well-drained spot and set the tarp up nice and high so that we could move around comfortably on the ground cloth. The only reason I don't miss my Hubba these days is that no matter how lousy the weather, it's always a delight to wake at two in the morning and hear delicate Sky snoring like an apnea-afflicted sumo wrestler.

By 6 p.m., the storm wrung itself out, and a steady breeze revealed blue sky. Sky got a pot boiling and produced a frothy mess of red beans and rice, with the Cajun sauce we stole from Brave Phillie. Grunge had a Ziploc of broken cookies sent by her mom that have somehow gone uneaten since Gorham. Blue Devil kicked in his dad's homemade teriyaki jerky. We strung a clothesline, and the dry breeze restored a mild sense of conviction that our future holds something other than ooze, slugs and rain.

Doug and Pollyanna talked under Doug's tarp, looking serious as a quadruple bypass. "What's with them?" I asked Sky. "Are they hashing out Wonder Boy?"

Sky confided that Wonder Boy, despite all outward appearances, was an unmitigated creep. Somehow, Doug knows this, but is not inclined to talk people down. Doug and Pollyanna's intense discussion is their own business. I would like to see them ease into the sort of bliss that Sky Writer and I enjoy, but it seems hard for them.

Sky and I talked this afternoon about that distant day in March when we first met. I waddled up to Sky and Bone on the flank of Frosty Mtn., wheezing, gasping and straining like a flogged slave for every foot of elevation gain. My heart and lungs suffered the wages of inactivity, smoking and gluttony. Was it Sky alone who inspired me to stick with it? Was it the entire Bly Gap Gang? Love of the trail? I now know joy and adventure are always ahead. I have the confidence to make it happen.

For now, I can't wait until tomorrow. When I get to the next town, I'll hit the scales for the second time. I saw my reflection in Speck Pond the other day and thought it was someone else. I told Sky that when I finish, I will walk at least five miles per day. I will figure a regimen of caloric intake and stick with it. I can do it. I paraphrase Scarlett O'Hara, "With God as my witness, I will never be a lard-butt again."

Still, something troubles me. When Sky Writer indulges in idle girl talk with Pollyanna and Ultragrunge, she always drifts in the same direction, sunny recollections of her childhood. She talks of outings with her parents, toys she played with, television shows she watched, and bubblegum music she listened to. The others go along with it, but don't share her obsessive inclination to keep circling back to the same topics.

I suspect Sky can't accept the trauma of her parent's divorce, and she tries to erase it by recreating those years, minus the angst. I am her security blanket, a comfortable port in a storm of bad memories. I fear that once she works through all this, she may not need me. I prepare for rejection that I doubt she has even considered. I know she doesn't want to hurt me, but I can't avoid a sense of foreboding.

August 8, Journal entry of Doug Gottlieb at Bemis Mtn. Lean-to

Back in that parallel dimension we call the real world, where you often work, sleep, exercise and do most everything else indoors, weather is an annoyance or a minor pleasure. Out here, weather is at the core of your day and is often the foremost influence on your state of mind. The past few days over this rugged terrain were made far more difficult by rain, wind and cold. Everyone took spills and got soaked to the skin, with mud caked on clothes and exposed flesh. Even though it's August, I found myself shivering. Nothing is more of a drag than getting out of the bag into a bleak, wet morning and forcing yourself to don a clammy shirt, frigid pants and a dripping rain parka—all of which reek with the mildewy aroma of wet dog. The lesson I've learned is that if you soldier on, good weather always returns. Everything was soggy this morning, but as the day progressed, solar power went to work. Dry patches appeared on my trail runners. As the sun got higher, the morass transformed into paradise. Except for permanent bogs, the A.T. became dry and pleasant again.

We put in about 13 miles to cover a little more ground now that the weather is cooperating. We had a long downhill into Sawyer Notch, a long uphill up little Moody Mtn., another long downhill to Black Brook Notch, and then a rocky ascent to Old Blue Mtn., the first peak on the Bemis Range. Ever since Glencliff, it's just as Prime Meridian and all the other SOBOs described it—hardly an easy mile in sight and just plain glorious.

Sky joined me as we hiked the last six miles of the day along the ridge of the Bemis Range, which included Elephant Mtn., a favorite mountain name, right up there with Standing Indian. Sky knows her trees, and she made sure I noticed the stands of black and red spruce. She stuck her nose into the topic of Wonder Boy, informing me that she had been a fly on the wall when he confronted me at Speck Pond. She felt she'd heard a conversation she had no right to hear. I told her she'd done nothing wrong and that she could speak freely.

She said she was suspicious from the beginning about Wonder Boy. "He seemed a little too perfect," she said. "I sensed something rotten. It was the way he looked at people. He always had this smirking attitude that he could peer into your deepest thoughts, while revealing nothing of himself. Then I heard the way he toyed with Pollyanna's reputation just to get at you. It was meanness."

I agreed, but I told her I was in no position to repeat that trash. "I don't think you should either," I told her. "It's one thing for Pollyanna to think he just walked away. It's worse for her to hear that he gratuitously badmouthed her."

Sky agreed and told me that Pollyanna enjoyed the attention from Wonder Boy. "What girl wouldn't?" she asked. She assured me Pollyanna had indicated to her that there was no substance to the flirtation. "Since I'm just coming right out and saying things, I'll tell you Pollyanna is crazy about you," Sky confided. "She had a little fun yanking your chain styling around with Wonder Boy. It was petty, but that's something women do to men sometimes."

I told Sky I appreciated her for seeking me out today. I told her of my long talk with Pollyanna last night, and how she made a big deal out of how rude it was for Wonder Boy to walk away from the Bly Gap Gang without a word of farewell. But my sense was that she was hurt more on a personal level, not just for the group. Whatever. For the first time since I met her in Hot Springs, I felt uncomfortable talking to her.

Sky and I followed the ridge over bog logs, across rock, overlooking bright vistas of big mountains in our future. Sky stopped and spread her arms out as if to embrace the ocean of peaks and burst into her "Amicalola" tune:

> Past the Mahoosucs
> down through the notch
> Up past the shoulder
> We'll make it, just watch
>
> Mighty Katahdin
> Craggy and freeeeee
> We will embrace you
> our destineeeee!

Finally we pulled up to this shelter—full of NOBOs, some of whom we recognized from months ago. It's great to rediscover Amazing Larry and Amazing Rover, who we last saw north of Duncannon. In typical A.T. fashion, they reenter our lives. Rover struggles with rough trailway, which accounts for why we overtook them. "I practically had to carry him through Mahoosuc Notch," Amazing Larry griped. Amazing

Rover, oblivious to the criticism, calmly chewed a stick. Larry is still working the fund-raiser on his blog and is over $4,000 now.

I found a secluded spot for my tarp. I ate mac and cheese with tuna—always a winner when in doubt. Sky helped walk me through some anxiety. Does Captain Stupid know how lucky he is? Maybe the big guy is not so stupid after all.

August 9, Journal entry of Pollyanna at Gull Pond Lodge in Rangeley, Me.

I revel in a zero day. The grueling grind since Gorham has left me dog-tired. I have a surpassing feeling of pleasure following good food and beer. What better place than the bunk room at the Gull Pond Lodge here in Rangeley, a little town spanning a narrow spot in Rangeley Lakes.

We've not been making the mileage we expected, which strained our supplies. We had a meeting of the minds at Bemis Mtn. Lean-to last night and decided to get out today. We trucked more than 17 miles to State Route 4 and hitched into Rangeley. We picked a good day for it. The first five miles were a long, steep descent followed by a long climb. Then the terrain rolled along the rest of the day with none of the dizzying elevation changes we've seen since Glencliff.

We stopped at Sabbath Day Pond Lean-to, where Grunge and I soaked our feet in the pond watching a wading fisherman artfully work the bank. Grunge yanked her feet out of the water and examined her right big toe. "Good God!" she hissed. "It's a leech!" I was grossed out, but Grunge was fascinated. She detached it and whistled to the fisherman. "Do me a favor. Use this bloodsucker for bait. Send him to his doom."

Obligingly, the angler sloshed over and adroitly affixed the leech to a hook. Within minutes, he pulled in a quarter-pound fish. He held it up for us to see, and said it was a chub—junk fish. "I'll feed him to the eagle," he hollered. With a mighty heave, he tossed the writhing fish on the bank, and from the top bow of a nearby spruce soared the first bald eagle I'd ever seen in my life. It snatched the doomed chub and disappeared over the tree line. We clapped and whistled like middle-school cheerleaders, and the old fisherman nearly split his waders from all the female attention.

Later we wandered over ridges and bogs in bright sunshine. I marvel at the swamps and mud on ridge tops. You would think this mushy topography would settle exclusively in the lowlands, but no such luck.

It dropped into the low 60s today, and with the wind I was glad to have on long-sleeved polypro. My clothes have rips along the seams and holes where the fabric wears. My lightweight parka leaks at the seams—breathable and waterproof no more. About all it does is protect me from wind and help seal in body heat. When we reached the highway, I hitched with Doug. "I'm feeling cute," I told him. "Fourth car." It was the third, a pickup with two fishermen headed straight to Rangeley.

"I'm cuter than I thought," I crowed as we jogged to the waiting SUV.

Doug smiled. "A regular Kim Kardashian."

Rangely has it all. Gull Pond Lodge has the requisite shower and bunks. It also has a P.O., an IGA, a pharmacy, an outfitter, a laundromat—what we crave in our darkest trail hours. Good restaurants and pubs, too.

Amazing Larry and Amazing Rover are with us tonight, although Rover has to sleep outside. This may be the last we see of them, because Larry wants to make sure his canine pal gets two full days to allow paw damage to heal.

Doug asked me to save dinner for him tomorrow night, and I said fine, but only if I get to treat. He looked at me with some of the spark I haven't seen lately. "I can be bought," he said. "And on a zero day, my price is reasonable."

I'm delaying my chores until tomorrow and using tonight to read, write, eat pizza and overindulge in Chunky Monkey. One nice note: Blue Devil was in an almighty hurry this morning, bent on being first into Rangeley. Turns out his dad is treating us to a couple of town nights, so the Gull Pond stay is on the gentleman from Jacksonville. Blue Devil double-timed to get it all handled before we arrived.

Doug is on the bunk above mine, muttering about an article he's reading in *Backpacker Magazine* about the High Cascades. "You have to come hike with me," he said. "The Appalachians have plenty to recommend them, but you haven't hiked until you hike out there." I took a solemn vow I would.

Doug and I are making eye contact again. Whew!

August 10, Journal entry of Blue Devil at Gull Pond Lodge in Rangeley, Me.

Good old Dad! What a great guy to spot us two nights in this jewel of a place, where the citizens adore thru-hikers, the pizza is unmatched in the free world, the beer is free-flowing, the women go easy on the makeup, the hunting dogs actually capture and barbecue the game, the fish jump into boats voluntarily and the surface of Rangeley Lake is an array of diamonds in the mid-August sun!

After the merciless trekking of recent weeks, this place is a balm for trail wounds. I checked myself out in a mirror, and not only am I rail-thin, I am also an anatomy lesson in cuts, gashes, scrapes, abrasions, superficial bruises and a few deep-tissue contusions. A thru-hiker's body is a leg support system. I have Olympian tone and musculature below the waist. And even though the sticks work a little on my arms, my chest, shoulders and trunk are stick-like. I'm a lean, mean, string-bean of a hiking machine.

After some logistics this morning, I goofed off until dinner with Sky, Captain Stupid, Momma Llama and Brave Phillie. Grunge is sleeping in, and Doug and Pollyanna are planning a soiree together, and the girls are oooohhhin' and aaaahhhin' about how sweet it is to see them paying attention to each other again after all that Wonder Boy nonsense.

I kept a promise to the Captain today. We shook Sky at the Laundro-mat and walked to the pharmacy. They had scales, and Captain was ready to weigh—first time since the fire station in Duncannon. He took off his shoes and socks, handed me his wallet, removed cap and tee shirt, stepped on and reached up to nudge the counterweight—so focused on the moment that he didn't notice a slender apparition putting one foot behind him and pressing down real hard. "Oh my God!" he moaned. "I'm ten pounds heavier than I was in Duncannon!"

I split my guts laughing and stepped back, hoping the Captain wouldn't lay a haymaker on me for such cruelty, but in typical style, he roared right along with me, as did some of the other customers. Then he stepped on again, for real, and I nudged the counterweights to 200. It needed more, so I tapped upwards to 205, 206, 207 and then at 208, it balanced. "My Lord, Captain!" I shouted. "You're at 208!"

Back on the street, Captain predicted sub-200 when we crest Katahdin. "I'm just not hungry very often," he told me. "Last night, I drank a couple of beers and ate a big salad. No pizza. Something wonderful has happened." I put my arm around his shoulder as we walked. The change is profound beyond imagination, and it transcends the dramatic physical reduction in his size—no longer is he the simpering, self-despising slob we met at Springer. Even though he'll never be sculpted, his confidence has skyrocketed, and Sky Writer is his girl. I am proud to call this guy my friend. We padded down the sidewalk, a pair of feral tomcats, comfortable in our skin, not afraid to sleep in a different place every night, travelin' light.

Although my feet ache, I am otherwise free of pain as I write tonight. I plan to get a great night's sleep, a big breakfast and an early start tomorrow cuz I want those big mountains up ahead. Maine is the best. Sky is bluer here; clouds are puffier; forests expel a clearer form of air, and when I inhale, it sweeps me back to a simpler era, decades before my birth, when America still had some innocence.

SUBJECT: **Be careful what you wish for!**
DATE: **August 11, 7:20 a.m.**
FROM: < ATMommaLlama@charter.net >
TO: < jackiechristieqt@aol.com >

Sorry to hear your love life is not all it should be. Live vicariously through me until something better comes along. I am about to haul out of Rangeley, a little north woods tourist mecca. Rangeley Lake is shimmering turqoise in the morning sun. Before I leave, I will eat bacon, butter, flapjacks, syrup and juice. Then, serious ups and downs. Judging from the maps, we have four great big mountains ahead of us over the next few days. After the fourth one—the Bigelow massif—we descend into a different world of forests and lakes, the north woods at last.

As for Brave Phillie and me, ooh là là! He gives me a level of respect I have craved all my life. But he's not one to get walked on. He isn't afraid to speak his piece, but he's fair-minded most of the time. One fear remains: Will we discover we're not simpatico off-trail? It's a fear I can't wait to explore. We are deep in the tunnel. The light at the other end beckons. See ya soon babe!

August 11, Journal entry of Brave Phillie at Poplar Ridge Lean-to

Years ago, when I hiked this stretch of Maine the first time, Saddle-back Range made a big impression. I climbed it about this time of year, but the circumstances were different. Due to bad water, I went through a bout of diarrhea and vomiting. I set up my tarp in a secluded spot, and for about 12 hours I was right miserable. The only thing worse was the time I took shrapnel and sat in a mud puddle in the rain waiting for relief.

Anyway, by the time I got strong enough, I climbed Saddleback. Once I got to within 500 feet of timberline, the weather deteriorated into wind squalls, black clouds, hail and thunder—the quickest developing weather system I had ever seen. Foolishly, I kept climbing, hoping to get over the crest and down to the lean-to. I battled wind that pushed me off the trail time after time. Hail peppered me like BBs. It rained and got cold. I doubted I could get to the lean-to, but I could never set up a tarp in that wind. Thank God I got to the shelter and met a couple of fit-looking middle-aged women amazed I had come over the top in those conditions. They saw I was hypothermic and helped me get out of my clothes and into my sleeping bag, where I generated heat from my body core and drank the hot tea they provided.

After dark, when I had gotten to a point where I was just barely the right side of warm in my soggy bag, one of the women quietly nestled beside me and whispered, "Are you warm enough, honey?"

I told her I was just about okay, but not quite. She unzipped my bag and said, "I'll make love to you. Otherwise you might not make it through the night."

I chuckled and told her not to feel beholden. Honest to God, I thought she was kidding. "This could be life or death, sweetheart," she told me. "I won't take no for an answer."

She didn't, and somehow my willing spirit generated the wherewithal within my exhausted body to follow her lead. I still think about that a lot and realize that in no way did she save my life, and I'm not ashamed that I didn't put up a fight. I told the story to Momma Llama, but kept out the part about the lady jumpin' my bones. Somehow she suspected something went on though, and she said as much. "No Momma, that just wouldn't have worked," I told her. "I was too beat."

She looked at me and laughed. "One thing I love about you is I can tell when you're lying," she said. "You're fibbing like crazy on this one. I hope she was fun." The funny thing is that I'm pretty sure the other woman slept through the whole thing, which was just as well, because I sure wasn't up for a twofer.

Unlike then, today's weather was postcard perfect. After we shuttled to the trail, we started a long, long climb heading up through a stand of maples. We passed a few alpine ponds and labored up a thousand more vertical feet. Sky hiked with me for a while and pointed out a grove of Eastern Larch as we broke above timber line. That's when I always feel the climb has ended. Once I can see in all directions, I don't notice the effort anymore. I feel that when I'm above the trees I've "come home." Momma Llama experiences the same thing on mountains out West. Maybe we're closer to heaven.

Near the top of Saddleback, Sky showed me something I'd never seen, a little white-flowered growth the guidebook calls diapensia, the kind of thing Sky loves. Then we hit the crest. I found a rock and sat. Sun high in a cloudless sky, no puff of wind. Birds chirping down the slopes. I'm a man of simple intellect. I know when I've found balance, and today I found it with my friends up on Saddleback.

We had five miles more to the lean-to, much above timber line. Momma and I savored it, feeling strong after the zero day. "Let's take another at the Kennebec River," she said. "We need to make this last." I agreed. I'll sleep like a drunk baby tonight.

August 12, Journal entry of Ultragrunge at Crocker Cirque Campground

Wowie zowie, I'm a climbing animal. My body is at its peak. My cardiovascular system is ideal for load carrying. If I can't brag to my trail journal, where can I?

We dropped steeply to Orbeton Stream and then ascended 2,500 feet over six miles to the peak of Spalding Mtn. I led and felt like a big dray horse working and working, never feeling a need to stop. I waited on the peak, soaking up the glory, and Blue Devil caught me. "Let's take the side trail to Sugarloaf," I begged. He agreed, and we practically scampered to the top and saw why the A.T. was rerouted off this peak. It's a ski mecca. But it was worth the extra effort for another clear-skied view.

Before descending, I whipped out my cell phone and called Mom, who whooped in delight, spooking her coworkers. "Less than 200 miles to go," I told her. After talking to Mom, I confided to Blue Devil. "It's odd about my folks. They're glad to hear from me, but they don't take much interest in this hike. Once they got me out of rehab and on a successful college track, they decided I was mission accomplished and moved on. That hurts. Your parents aren't that way, are they?"

Blue Devil grinned. "My parents will jump all over me if I give them an opening. They have interesting lives in their own right, and they're plenty smart, but they're completely interested in everything about me. Sometimes it's annoying, but overall, I appreciate it. It kills them that I asked them not to visit me out here, but I needed a buffer from their hovering before heading off to college."

"Yeah, get that degree at Duke," I replied. "Then you can support me in the upscale manner I demand."

"Oh yeah, dog!" Blue Devil muttered. "Hollow words from a chick who spends her nights under a tarp."

We started back down to the A.T. "Hey, Calves!" Blue Devil squawked. "Do you need to be in such a freakin' hurry? You're gonna wear me down to nothing."

I paced myself, descending to the south branch of the Carrabassett River. Then one more climb up to the campsite. I set up my tarp and curled up with a copy of *Ecology of a Cracker Childhood* by Janisse Ray. Blue Devil lay next to me and settled into *Angle of Repose* by Wallace Stegner. It was all very domestic, like old married farts.

I contemplated the near future. I have an amazing opportunity in Austin. I can finish my degree and make decent money in the new job. But I wonder, how many times will I contemplate being on the trail as opposed to mundane professional tasks day after day? Is this the ultimate curse of the A.T.?

I spoke to a hiker named Rubber Knees the other day. He was only out for a few days, but had thru-hiked back in 1992. He said he pondered his thru-hike every day. "You live with the fact that once the adventure is over, you must return to reality," he said. "That doesn't mean you won't get out and have more fun in the future. But face it, most of us can't spend every day hiking or canoeing or sky diving. You gotta work, unless your rich uncle conveniently croaks." How long in the real world before I get trail antsy?

August 13, *Journal entry of Sky Writer at Horns Pond Lean-tos*

I'm worn threadbare tonight. Nearly three weeks since Glencliff, and every day we've been scaling huge ascents and lumbering down incalculably long descents. I'll work my way down a rocky slope—one minute on my rear end, scraping over a long step down, the next tossing my poles to a spot down below so I can climb down hand-over-hand—and ask myself if I'll ever hit bottom?

Oh, my aching knees!

This morning, I got up early to take care of a certain necessity, and on the way to the privy, I saw the biggest bull moose in the world—just standing there as outhouse sentry. In the half-light, he seemed bigger than a real world moose. He was a King Kong moose, a CGI moose. When I caught him in my headlamp, he snorted like air brakes. He awkwardly rotated on the narrow trail and ambled toward the woods. When I got back to the campsite, everyone asked why I screamed. I notice no one cared enough to leave their sleeping bag and attempt a rescue, not even the Captain.

We started with an incredible climb over the south and north Crocker peaks. Then a 3,000-foot plummet—a knee-masher—down the other side of Crocker to State Route 27. Captain and I saw another moose, a little cow who scooted away before we got close. "See," said the Captain. "There's no big deal about a moose."

I gave him a dismissive glare. "You didn't see the last one!"

Our goal is to zero at Caratunk, but the temptation at the highway was to hitch to Stratton for another day off. We kept going. Even the self-proclaimed laziest thru-hiker said we need self-discipline. I heard that! But what about my aching tootsies?

We made a steep climb of about 2,000 feet up to the Horns Pond Lean-tos, and I'm so glad we pushed on. The Bly Gap Gang attacked the climb together, one of the last big ones for a while. Blue Devil pretended we were climbing Everest and kept shouting out landmarks like "Camp Four" and "Camp Six." Ultragrunge said there is a cure for cancer at the lean-to. The sooner we get there, the quicker we save the world. This is the sort of absurdity that draws on adrenaline and makes miles stream by.

Here at Horns Pond, we are less than 1,000 feet below the highest crest of Bigelow Mtn., perched beneath a couple of little spur peaks known as the Horns. The pair of lean-tos is nestled in a little declivity surrounded by cedars, with a perfect alpine pond where I spent much of my afternoon.

Tomorrow morning brings a glimmer of hope. We ascend this massive mountain, and then we return to normal. Massive peaks taper off pretty much until Katahdin. There will be robust climbs, but rarely will we see the backbreaking climbs and descents we've battled since not far into New Hampshire. The magnificent exception will be Katahdin, the biggest single ascent of the trip. I yearn for the North Woods, seeing big lakes and listening to loons.

Horns Pond has a caretaker, so again we pay to play. This one is a cute guy, and Grunge is making sure he sees her as she does her breathing and stretching exercises. She has such an amazing physique—compact, muscular and enticingly ample in her tight sports bra. She loves being ogled. The caretaker plans to bake apple cornbread tonight—his first attempt to cook in a dutch oven, so he refuses to guarantee results. Plus he's tripping over his tongue gaping at Grunge. But heck, if it's cornmeal and apples, and it's hot, what's to mess up?

Captain is cooking for both of us tonight, and he says he'll clean up too. He knows I had a down day. That final climb up from the valley sapped me, and when I pulled in, I just wanted to collapse and recharge. Momma Llama tells me that the beauty of youth is that a good night's sleep erases the travails of the day before. After 50, she says, the damage of a hard day takes longer to recover from. As Brave Phillie says, "You need to stay within your limitations."

A group of SOBO section hikers is using the other lean-to tonight. They told us the climb up over Little Bigelow and Bigelow were killers from their direction, but as NOBOs, we have most of the battle of Bigelow won. They raved about the views at various spots along the summit ridge. We're in a slow spot in the NOBO pipeline, our northbound friends scattered ahead and behind. Tomorrow, we may get a peek at Katahdin from Avery Peak on Bigelow. After all these months!

August 14, Transcript of Captain Stupid recorded at West Carry Pond Lean-to

I record atop the world here on Bigelow's Avery Peak, named after one of the giants in A.T. history—part of his legacy. Thank you Mr. Avery, wherever you are—hikers' heaven I guess. Now that I've seen your peak and plaque, I promise to learn more.

Brave Phillie got here first, and we've gathered to follow the direction of his finger and squint northeast into a cloud-free morning sky with uncharacteristically clear August air. There's Katahdin! A sneak peek of Katahdin from here in August is rare, so I feel blessed. Way below is big Flagstaff Lake, its surface a multifaceted shimmer. My arm encircles a smiling Sky Writer. Listen as she hums a Creedence tune as we ponder our feat. We have run a gauntlet of peaks.

Yay!

Between us and the Big K loom rocks, bogs, roots, lung-ripping ascents, knee-pulverizing descents, all mixed in with the various curve balls the weather will fling our way. But we are past the glorious daily grind of the Whites, the Mahoosucs and the long chain of mountains we traversed over the past few days. I will miss these big hills, but I'm glad this part is over. More later.

––––––––

We're through for the day, after more than 17 miles, much of it a long downhill taking us past what seemed like a million cairns, down from Avery Peak and then up again over Little Bigelow. Around there somewhere we hit 2,000 miles. We are all 2,000-milers, but none of us are yet thru-hikers.

Now we adjust to new terrain, the North Woods. We went up and over a couple of glorified hills, but for the most part, we hike with much less altitude variation. We hiked through hardwoods and pines, as I conversed with white-throated sparrows.

West Carry Pond Lean-to is filled with NOBOs and section hikers. We've finally caught a couple named Junco Lung and Mickey Mantle. I've been noticing their clever observations in shelter logs for months. Mickey Mantle tells me he picked that name because if he gets to be whoever he wants, it's for sure going to be his favorite person of all time. Junco and Mickey are in their late forties, and have been making great time until the past couple of weeks. The rugged stretch of mountains has wrought havoc on Mickey's knees, sadly the same fate that befell the real Mickey Mantle. They have been doing short days with a liberal sprinkling of zero days. Another of the NOBOs is Nobomad, a scrofulous, middle-aged schmo with a toxic personality. From what we heard and read in shelter logs, he's known for bragging that he has never washed his clothes since Springer. He subsists on M&Ms and peanut butter, and his face and hands are as grimy as his clothes. His trademark is that when he gets up at night to pee, he takes about three steps out in front of the shelter and lets fly. If anyone complains, he gets violently angry. He also leers at all the women he sees, which makes the Bly Gap Gang prime territory for him.

We are next to a pond and hearing our first loons. It starts as a comical chortle that works into a wild frenzy—hence the name "loon." I see them diving out in the lake, bobbing complacently one moment, then gracefully disappearing below the surface before reappearing nearby after what seems an impossible interval. Sky and I quietly watched a dreamlike sunset as loons serenaded us.

Tomorrow: a huge landmark, the Kennebec River. All the exotic-sounding venues that once seemed so far ahead that we almost thought they were fictitious are now showing up in our radar, then gliding past and giving way to more. Oddly, none of us have Katahdin fever. However, when I consider taking those last steps and then walking back down Katahdin and into the parallel universe apart from the A.T., I experience a melancholy that settles into a dark spot in my heart and jostles for space with the joy I feel tonight. I choose not to fight it.

MYRON

Back in the mid-1920s, the chairman of what was then called the Appalachian Trail Conference was Judge Arthur Perkins, a true gentleman and a capable organizer. His contributions to the ATC were considerable, but none of his decisions was more important than the one to enlist the able support of fellow attorney Myron H. Avery.

When Benton MacKaye wrote that he proposed the A.T. project but "others went and did it," no single person is more worthy of credit for "doing it" than Avery. From the outset, he was involved in recruiting, training, scouting trail routes, managing trail construction, and writing and editing guidebooks. A taskmaster who did not suffer fools easily, he was exceptionally loyal and supportive to those willing to roll up their sleeves and make a commitment along with him. He was known to spend 50 weekends a year on the trail, to survive on five hours of sleep per night and to equally commit himself to his career and his family. He was a genius, a workaholic and a martinet. Generous to a fault, he paid many costs out of his own pocket. Incidentally, he was the first to hike the entire trail, a task he accomplished in 1936 after hiking in sections over many years. Not surprisingly, these were working trips to measure the trail route and evaluate its condition.

Although Avery—more than any other soul—executed the MacKaye vision, the two of them were not on good terms. Much of their discord arose from a conflicting view of how to deal with federal plans to build the Skyline Drive through Shenandoah. A committed idealist, MacKaye fought the idea of a roadway on an unspoiled ridge. Avery, an indefatigable pragmatist, decided to work with the road-building contingent and even managed to get federal assistance and support for the trail project. It's strictly a matter of opinion as to which of the two was correct. Regardless, they had a falling out that was never fully repaired. Although they made an effort to speak kind words to each other late in Avery's life, they were never allies. The philosophical tension that inevitably led to an irreparable schism reveals the diversity of talent, vision and philosophy that has been an integral component for the A.T. Vision and pragmatism do not always see eye-to-eye, but no great project is possible without both.

A Type A dynamo, Avery maintained an unsustainable standard and flared out like a supernova at age 53 from a heart attack. It is impossible to imagine that his spirit, drive and energy died with him in 1952. In an existential sense, it lives on with volunteers who have carried the A.T. torch for well over half a century since his passing. It is easy to imagine that his spirit *visits Avery Peak, standing hands on hips, dreaming up projects for a work crew. Then he takes a few moments to look below over Flagstaff Lake and northeast toward Katahdin.* ■

August 15, Journal entry of Doug Gottlieb at Rivers and Trails Hostel, Caratunk, Me.

We struck camp quickly this morning hell bent on getting across the Kennebec and beyond to the pleasures of a full-service hostel. Total mileage was around 14, and it seemed so easy. These are the North Woods I've longed to hike in.

At one road crossing, a fellow was parked in a pickup with a cooler of beer, soft drinks and chocolate milk. He also had salty snacks, donuts, and bagels with flavored cream cheeses. His trail name is Pompatus of Love, and he hiked from Harpers Ferry to Katahdin two years ago. He treats hikers a couple of times a season. He gestured at his frisky rottweiler: "He's coming when I do the southern half next year. His name's Steve Miller, but I just call him Steve."

Blue Devil and I surged ahead, anxious to clean up and resupply for two days to Monson. We pulled up to the Kennebec at mid-afternoon and waited for the ferry guy. There it was, the broadest unbridged river on the A.T., the only part of the trail we would not actually walk. When a woman drowned there in 1985, the decision was made to provide a canoe ferry and discourage crossing the old-fashioned way, fording it on your own two feet.

"Man, this is a wuss river," Blue Devil complained. "Let's ford it like real men."

I told him you never know when they might open the gates upstream and suggested we just play by the rules. He ignored me, switching into his Crocs and tying his trail runners around his neck. He steadily worked his way across, balancing with his sticks. The water lapped around the bottom of his shorts but never threatened his pack. Soon, he was on the far bank, beaming at me.

My decision to wait was fortuitous. Pollyanna appeared and was uncharacteristically angry. "There's a reason they have a rule here," she said. "Why did he risk his life just to get across ahead of everybody else?"

I nodded with all the sincerity I could display, delighted that I had not yielded to an urge that would have had Pollyanna on my case big-time. We enjoyed each other's company as the rest of the Bly Gap Gang came strolling up. Blue Devil was sprawled out asleep across the way, and he got blasted by the rest of the gang, with the exception of Ultra-grunge and Brave Phillie. "Hell, if you guys weren't here to holler at me, I'd do it myself. I forded last time," BP drawled.

Before long, a nice fellow paddled a red canoe over and ferried us two at a time. He works at the Rivers and Trails Hostel, and we went there after we got across. We went through our typical flurry—resupplying, showering and writing in journals. There was one Cherry Garcia left, so I snatched it quick.

A little while ago, I sat with Pollyanna under a starless sky mulling what we would do with tomorrow's zero day, the next-to-last on the trip. I said I was going to read *Cold Mountain*. She had read it earlier and thought it was great. "Do you like love stories?" she asked. I had trouble making out her face in the darkness.

"I guess so," I answered. "I think I'm ready to live one. I'm weary of being a hobo, just traveling and studying. Ready to stop being a loner." She sat quietly and then reached over and took my hand. "Let's climb Katahdin together," she said.

My voice broke, but I managed to say that was fine with me. Inexplicably, I thought of my dad. I remembered the pain of losing him and my inability, even as an adult, to come to grips with making commitments with the knowledge of how painful loss can be. I had a revelation that the prospect of loss should never prevent the joy of commitment. I squeezed Pollyanna's hand. It was too dark for her to see my tears.

August 16, Journal entry of Pollyanna at Rivers and Trails Hostel, Caratunk, Me.

Grunge, Sky, Momma Llama and I spent this morning primping like a giggling gaggle of 14-year-olds. Momma's friend, Jackie, sent a box of nail polish, razors, shaving gel, sample bottles of skincare products, emery boards, combs, a hairbrush, scented shampoo and rinse, facial mask, face lotion, peach-scented hand cream, vanilla-scented foot lotion, chocolate-scented candles, and cheap bracelets and neck-laces—all to share and enjoy for one day. We got our legs in the best shape in months. Even with cuts, bruises and insect bites, our legs look astonishing.

I spent way too much time in the shower washing and rinsing my hair. We finagled a hair drier, and we all look like models. Ultragrunge is spectacular. I can hardly remember the spiked 'do she sported on Springer. Bless Jackie's heart!

To top it all off, a goofy girlfriend of mine sent a red sundress. There was no way I could carry it with me, but before I stuck it in a big envelope to mail back, we took turns wearing it. Sky looked like a runway model, and I felt pretty glamorous myself. Grunge was a little stocky and short for it, but she put her feminine attributes to their best advantage as she prissed around. Momma Llama looked like she was on the red carpet at the Oscars, one of those aging but spectacularly preserved megastars. The short haircut Momma started with is longer, but I always see her in a pony tail. With it down, she looked awesome. Brave Phillie grinned like an idiot. Captain Stupid has an identical expression for Sky. And Doug is delighted to see me looking like a real girl.

Rock and roll was playing on the radio, so we danced outside, frequently changing partners. Grunge and Blue Devil should enter a competition. They're killers on a dance floor. Captain is maladroit, but Sky is a swan. Doug and I were two kids at a sock hop. BP and Momma Llama need to go out for dinner and dancing in their post-trail life. We pampered ourselves, danced, sang and read. Doug will finish *Cold Mountain* tonight. He's inhaling it, while I'm mesmerized by *Unbroken*.

Oh, how I'll miss this trail and the surprises it delivers day after day! But one thing I look forward to when this is over is the girly stuff I've been dying for—particularly bubble baths. I feel so clean, and my hair feels so silky—just like in a commercial. My arms, legs and face feel smooth. I smell yummy, and the clean sundress makes me feel beautiful. A woman in shorts, tee shirt, battered trail runners and a ponytail is lovely to behold. But sometimes I want to get prissy like an uptown babe. In no time tomorrow, I will have sweated away the fresh dew on this zero day pumpkin.

After all the dancing, Doug took me for a walk. He wanted to get at something, but my mood was so bubbly, I think he thought better of it. There was a time on this trip when this might have put him into one of his brooding moods, but now he's managing his concerns without letting them eat away at him. Our conversation ran to what's left on the trail and not knowing what comes afterward. The closer we get to the end, the less I worry. If I can hike more than 2,000 miles, I can figure it out.

As I was writing this, Grunge plopped down on the bunk next to mine and fell into a deep sleep. She's childlike in repose, her mouth open and her face relaxed and innocent—no hint of her customary bravado. How can I live without her and the rest of the Bly Gap Gang to share all the fun?

I need quality sleep. We hit Monson in two fairly long days so that we won't feel so guilty about taking another zero day. If rule number one is, "Never turn down food," rule number two should be, "Never feel guilty about a zero day."

August 17, Journal entry of Blue Devil on Moxie Bald

We chose to do this, so we have nobody to blame but ourselves. It's about 20 miles to Moxie Bald Lean-to, a long walk that includes somewhere around 3,500 cumulative feet of climbing. The gradual climb from the Kennebec to the peak of Pleasant Pond Mtn. (except for one drastic uphill stretch) was pretty easy. Then we strolled to Bald Mtn. Brook Lean-to, where I cooked my main meal, but then it got gritty with a long climb up Moxie Bald, whose peak I'm enjoying now, a pretty spot despite a bit more rain and cold than I prefer. I chose to stop here for an extended break to write in my journal. To avoid discomfort, I've layered-up to fend off the wind and hold in heat, an odd thing to worry about in August, particularly for a kid like me from Florida who thinks staying warm in the summer is normally not a concern.

Yesterday's zero re-charged my batteries. A NOBO named Skookums stopped to talk this morning before blasting ahead at a near trot. He started six weeks after we did and has been hiking hard, because, according to him, if you hike alone you might as well hike hard and fast to kill what he called the "overbearing monotony of this infernal trail." He was a nice enough guy, but he says he can't wait to finish because he really hasn't been happy with trail life since he began. "For two cents, I would have chucked this back in North Carolina," he told me. "But once you start and your friends are following the trip, it becomes a point of pride." He is a volunteer fireman in his Kansas town who convinced some businesses to pledge money to benefit the fire department. "Can you imagine if I had bailed out on all the people who committed to help? I'd have felt lower than a nanny-goat udder." Poor guy! All this time out here and not having fun.

Oh well! At least I am, despite the many nagging annoyances of trail life, some of which we explored yesterday as the girls were pampering their feet and trying to get me to undergo another toe-painting session. I have sworn off painted toes, because this trip has instilled a desire to travel light with a no-frills attitude—no tattoos, jewelry, outrageous hairstyle, funky clothes, etc.—just the bare necessities to take on the elements of life that transcend all things superficial, including nail polish on my toes.

Grunge shares Burt's Bees Peppermint Foot Lotion. We're freaked because she ran out and won't get more until Monson. The peppermint, after a long day on the A.T., draws pain out of your dogs—or at least desensitizes you to the discomfort. We compared toes. Grunge lost the nails on her little toes early and has odd little spikes attempting to grow back out. Others of us have had random lost toenails, including me—the middle nails on both feet—and we also have damaged toes where the skin underneath the nail has become dark and bruised. Will our feet ever be the same?

I'm glad I cooked early. I covered 15 miles to Bald Mtn. Brook by 1:30 and was hungrier than usual. I cooked ramen and herring in hot mustard sauce to satisfy a peculiar craving. I also had black olives straight from the container. Still not enough. I had six Snickers bars, so I ate the first and second and waited to see if they would satisfy. No luck. I ate two more and waited again. Still ravenous. After numbers five and number six, I experienced profound satiation. Satisfied by sugar, chocolate, noodles and fish, I began a drastic two-mile ascent up Moxie Bald, feeling like a woman in labor dashing up 20 flights of stairs to the delivery room. It took nearly 90 minutes, tortoise-like for me, one of those rare times I paid for eating too much, and I mean rare, because it is hard to carry enough to overeat when you burn the calories we do.

Now I need to pack up and head into more than two more miles of "edge of the world" downhill to Moxie Bald Lean-to. I should be rested after napping on the zero back at the Kennebec, but I just can't wait to settle into my bag and hibernate tonight.

August 18, Journal entry of Brave Phillie at Shaw's in Monson, Me.

Monson is the first trail town for SOBOs. Sadly, the last for us. We're on the eve of our last zero day, and for the first time I detect Katahdin fever, particularly in Blue Devil. He's feeling put-upon by the girls, except for Grunge. They got down on him for fording the Kennebec and poking fun at Doug about the scar on his face—as if Doug really cared. So he's got the fever, and he's stoked to move beyond these hostilities. We haven't had much friction on this trip, and he's having trouble with it. I told him my experience with women is that when possible, let time pass. A woman's sweeter nature lets you get back in her good graces.

A warm, muggy day—walking in and out of showers with thunder mumbling behind the hills. Only a couple of minor climbs, some ponds and a few streams to ford. Momma Llama and I were with Ultragrunge, clipping along right smart and knocking off the first 10 miles before lunch, when we pulled up to the Piscatquis River. Mosquitoes were feisty at the river bank, so when we stopped to change into Crocs, we hurried. I noticed that out in the middle of the river, slightly downstream, was Nobomad. He's a bad dude. He was stark naked and seemed to enjoy showing off his unimpressive endowment.

"He's a total creep," Grunge muttered. "Pretty weak in the junk department, too."

We ignored him and started the ford. We unhooked waist belts, tied our footwear around our necks and picked our way across using our sticks like extra legs. "Hey, buddy," I hollered to Nobomad, "make it a point not to see us again." He leered at Grunge and Momma while making a sort of hula motion with his hips. Grunge bent forward at the waist with her pack riding up above her head and mooned the jerk. I was impressed by two things. First, she sports a nice sternside. Second, she has a fine tattoo of a butterfly back there.

"See ya, shorty!" she hollered as she pulled her shorts back up. We slogged six miles to State Route 16, an easy stroll with a few rain drops to dodge before we pulled up to the last paved road we'd see for 100 miles.

Time to hitch into Monson. "Tenth car," said Grunge. Twelve vehicles came and went before number 13, an old-fashioned VW Microbus, locked up its one good brake and pulled over. Our benefactor was a guitar player headed for a gig at a store in Monson—a long-distance hiker who picks up trail rats.

"I bought this buggy used in Orono, back in 1970 when I was a long-haired hippie," he recalled. "I'm still a hippie, even though the only hair I grow is on the sides, but I remain an advocate of peace, international understanding and universal free love." I didn't tell him I'm an ex-Marine, maybe a little martial for his taste, but I guess I agree with him. I suppose "universal free love" might be a little far out, but anyone who has been in combat won't argue with peace.

I'm writing this at Spring Creek Barbecue. Surprisingly, these down-easters have a knack for the stuff. Monson makes me nostalgic for my childhood. Later, as I looked out over Lake Hebron, all blue and smooth under the clearing sky, and almost asked Momma Llama to chuck the rest of the trip and settle down here with me forever. But, what the hell! Less than 120 miles to go. ZERO DAY TOMORROW!

August 18, Shelter register note left by an anonymous traveler

Back in a musty age when Old-World monkeys were still a common sight and just before flying pigs emerged from the land of the trembling conifers, I took up my burden of a simple bedroll, tin-plated cooking utensils, a few strips of beef jerky, some crumbs of hardtack and an assortment of varicolored bandanas, and tightened my tumpline to strike out into the fogenshrouded peaks of Cetacea in search of the rare and wondrous howling mountain whale-monkey.

Oddly, it was on the wild and arcane approach journey that my real adventure occurred. It transpired as I ascended the secret maze of trails up the escarpment of the Charteussian Cliffs—upwards, ever ascending, laboring, gasping, sobbing—until, with thrilling finality, I collapsed—heaving—at the plateau rim.

There, I was confronted by Zeegor, the miniature ogre, who posed me no threat as I had once caught him swimming naked, the supreme embarrassment to smaller ogres and an assurance of eternal safe passage for the one who has witnessed the little monster's shame. He snarled at me and made a grudging gesture granting me narrow ingress to the scree-strewn tableland before me.

As I blithely accepted his offer and walked briskly past, I paused and considered whether I should attempt to gain more from the little beast than a mere free pass. In that moment of avarice, I cemented a fate that in future years I would often regret and occasionally treasure. No life would ever bear comparison to mine. I would never pass an hour without considering the weighty kismet of this moment, never again. And it all led back to a second's simple whim, a wisp of greed to which I chose to yield.

I will never speak of this again.

14

Monson,
the 100-mile Cooldown
and Katahdin's Kiss

August 19, Journal entry of Momma Llama at Monson, Me.

I think of Garrison Keillor's Lake Wobegon as I walk these Monson streets and contemplate Lake Hebron. Churches, stores, houses—all a bit timeworn. A seagull or two patrol the lakeshore, and an intermittent stream of vehicles cruise the main drag, making for a somnolent afternoon.

I quit trying to pick my favorite trail town. They all have their charms. My perception of them is based on how far I've gone when I reach them. At Hot Springs, my confidence was tentative. By Damascus, I was hitting my stride. In Harpers Ferry, this was no longer an adventure so much as a way of life. Later, as we hit Duncannon, Port Clinton and all the other embracing towns leading to Hanover, each became its own trinket on the trail-town charm bracelet.

Now, Monson. Sleepy, friendly to hikers, oblivious to our odors and idiosyncrasies and, as always, happy to take our money. Dawn and Sue run Shaw's Lodge, a rambling hostel with bunkrooms, showers, laundry and a breakfast to die for. It was once the domain of jolly Keith Shaw, a rotund bundle of energy, who died a few years back. Now you still can enjoy the casual hospitality desperately sought by jaded NOBOs ready for the last stretch and eager SOBOs thrilled to hit their first trail town or ready to head for home and escape this insane pursuit.

I hit the general store and made my final P.O. pickup earlier today. My pack is loaded for 100 miles—all the way to Abol Bridge. At this point, I know necessities down to a knife edge and have dispensed with items I don't care to bear. When I left the firm a few weeks before I began hiking, I thought I was one hell of a lawyer. Now I know I'm an even better thru-hiker. I was born for this. Thank God I didn't neglect the impulse.

Pollyanna and I took a walk last night and wound up at a concert at the general store. Our VW hippie from yesterday was with a few locals playing guitar, banjo and mandolin. No shock that Sky Writer had joined in. They were mesmerized by her voice, her long locks, her spectacular legs and the immeasureable sweetness of her voice. She was singing "Amicalola," and the local patrons watched with dreamy smiles.

> Now we're in Monson
> close to the end,
> Lake Hebron's waters
> helping us mend.
>
> Katahdin is calling
> 100 miles,
> reluctant to end this
> unreconciled.
>
> Amicalola,
> we'll never forget
> you're where we started
> where all of us met.

I no longer worry about the pain in my heel. It flares up from time to time like a call from a nagging aunt, but it has brought me more than 2,000 miles. It will bear up for 117 more. The 100 miles is really no big deal. You just carry a lot.

LOGISTICS

A NOBO *enters the 100-mile Wilderness having long since perfected the logistics of trail life. No two thru-hikers use an identical system, but there are several approaches to resupplying, which can be mixed and matched accordingly. Some buy the bulk of their food ahead of time, box it, address it, apply postage and have it sent to them by a loyal relative or friend at appropriate times. For these obsessive-compulsive types, there is little left to the imagination. If they decide they hate mac and cheese or ramen a few weeks into the trip, their anal-retentive goose is pretty well cooked. Others buy what they need as they travel. They learn that some towns have ill-stocked grocery stores without items they desperately crave. The most successful systems mix the above two methods and make use of the "bounce box," a carton of goods addressed to one's self and sent ahead for pickup at a distant P.O.*

It's Murphy's Law that you typically reach the P.O. at two minutes after noon on Saturday, which means that your precious package may not be available until Monday morning. This is fine if you are just as happy to take a zero day, but it can be one of the few scheduling problems on a trip uncluttered with calendar demands.

Whichever approach is preferred, by trail's end, it works. This logistical fine-tuning will carry on with a thru-hiker in a permanent fashion making him or her an expert in traveling light in future peregrinations. ▪

August 20, Journal entry of Ultragrunge at Long Pond Stream Lean-to

There is a deli-gas station in Monson where they serve half-decent pizza. I went there for lunch yesterday with Brave Phillie and Sky Writer, and we ate at a picnic table, basking in bug-free sunlight. BP eyed me with his Ed Harris squint, "Grunge. If I hear you say 'Wowie zowie" one more time, I'm gonna pop a vein."

I took a swig of beer and replied, "I've grown my hair out and ditched the studs and rings. I guess the only remnant of the old me is 'Wowie zowie.' When we hit Katahdin, I'll drop that too. It's getting pretty stale."

The new me. The spunky chick walking into a wilderness with her newfound friends to take on the big adventure of her life. The streamlined female who has rejected the trappings of whatever protective enclosure she clung to in high school and college and is ready to emerge from the chrysalis—an unknown quantity. I'll head back to Austin, but who will I be?

Today was easy: an undulating stroll leading past lakes, Little Wilson Falls and lots of streams. The weather was sunny and pre-autumn cool, what we live for. At Big Wilson Stream, I saw the biggest bull moose ever. I had stopped for pistachio nuts and to gaze through the canopy, past the ether into the cosmos. There he was, calmly taking in a spaced-out human disinclined to make room on the trail. His head tilted a little, and he made his way off the trail, through reeds, trees and mud, before heading with graceless splashes into the stream. He sashayed across as casually as you or I would go to the kitchen for a beer and stepped out on the other side to regain right of way.

Long Pond Stream Lean-to was half occupied when I arrived, and I claimed a spot. Ten minutes later, along came Nobomad, and the human chunk of dog excrement threw his gear next to mine. I picked up my stuff and moved out. "Remember?" I asked. "We told you not to show up again." I set up my tarp before walking back to the lean-to. A middle-aged woman named Tweety Bird, hiking from Monson to Kathadin, smiled and said, "You convinced him. He said he was pushing on to Cloud Pond. He made me uneasy."

"People know when they're not liked," I told her.

Later, Brave Phillie and Momma Llama plopped their stuff in the shelter. I told them about Nobomad. "What do you bet we see him again?" asked Momma. I won't take that bet. That jerk is so totally gone.

August 21, Transcript of Captain Stupid recorded at Chairback Gap Lean-to

I was headachy and out of sorts this morning. So of course, there was a steep, slippery climb up Barren Mtn. in cold and rain. I lapsed into mind-control, concentrating on whipping wind, grinding headache and rocky ascent—daring every particle of misery to defy my ability to climb past the summit. At the top, my head cleared. I stood with rain pelting my bare skull, the man who hits himself on the head with a hammer because it feels so good when it stops hurting.

Sky and Pollyanna appeared like two gorgeous, wet rats. They wondered why I was standing there, and I told them that I had conquered misery and wretchedness by facing it head-on. They rolled their eyes and continued on. I allowed the glamorous rodents to pass so that I could hike alone. Rain continued unabated, as did the frigid gale. My glasses became so fogged that I put them in my shorts pocket, even though I'm nearly legally blind without them. Then, slightly to the right of the trail, I saw a huge dark object. Bear, moose, Al Gore, ManBearPig, Tyrannosaurus Rex? What was this?

I decided to keep walking while keeping a laser focus on the looming imminence that may possibly have been threatening fauna. As I got within 30 feet, it moved away, keeping parallel to the trail. I froze, snatched my glasses and squinted at whatever it was.

It was moose, a big daddy bull, and when I began walking again, so did he, zigging onto the trail and keeping a brisker pace than mine. The muscles tensed spectacularly in his big glutes as he went up and over a rise and vanished.

One night over a dream-inducing campfire, we discussed evolution, intelligent design, a personal god, an agnostic's god, no god at all and the various permutations of such talk that dwindle into the ashes of the wee hours. My thinking is that it doesn't matter how it all got here, as far as religion or science go. You either think it happened randomly or somehow with the hand of a supreme being. To me it's all anecdotal, and my collection of anecdotes are piled on top of each other. Today's moose, a bald eagle, a wild azalea, a woman who sings like an angel—the more I am out in these woods and mountains, the more I struggle with the concept of randomness. How could so much patterned perfection in all its random magnificence just happen? Sometimes I believe that a lyrical or spiritual personality has a better answer than a scientist. But who am I? Just an incredible shrinking man hiking in frigid weather in shorts and tee shirt who can't explain his own place in the universe, much less anything else.

Burdened by deep thoughts, I continued along gloomy ridges before coming to a conundrum a mile or so from Chairback Gap Lean-to. The ridgecrest through here is covered with slabs of gray slate. At times the path goes over a flat slate surface with a slippery texture that's exacerbated by the driving rain. My obstacle was at a 35-degree angle—wet, glistening and slippery as snot on a brass doorknob. There was no going around it thanks to undergrowth and blowdowns.

I pondered. I would lumber to a running start and use momentum to defy the slope and run up and over the top of the 30-foot hurdle. I walked back a ways to provide room to create a head of steam and broke into a gallop that carried me 10, 15, and finally, 25 feet toward the top. I came up short. Momentum decayed into inertia. My feet froze. I had only a few feet left, but I was terrified to move or dig in my sticks for fear that I would slip and crash down. I began a backward slide on the mirror surface of the slate. There was no controlling this, and by the time I neared the bottom, my feet zipped out from under me. My right knee and the unyielding slate crashed together in a collision for the ages. I sprawled in a puddle experiencing pain so intense I felt simultaneously nauseated and faint.

Wondering if I had come this far to be incapacitated, I let 60 seconds pass. The pain, nausea and faintness dissipated. Although my knee was cut, scraped and bleeding abundantly, the joint's basic machinery was intact, albeit grossly offended. I washed blood away with handfuls of rain and climbed up the rock on hands and knees, reaching the top utterly spent.

Yay!

Chairback Gap Lean-to was mobbed with NOBOs, including a couple of the typical young, skinny, bearded white guys who make up so much of the NOBO tribe—Solemate and Whinin' Wolf. I told them that I'd been chuckling at their register entries for months, and it was a pleasure to finally meet them. "We've slowed way down," said Solemate. "Can't stand the thought of finishing." Whinin' Wolf agreed, although he added that it wouldn't be bad to land on a couch watching trashy movies and drinking beer.

The water situation at this place is wild. You climb down a veritable cliff in front of the shelter to a spring and then juggle your water containers as you climb right back up. I am under Sky Writer's tarp. Listen to her hum. Candy bars and beef jerky for dinner. I won't even think about cooking.

August 22, Lean-to Register entry from Sky Writer at Logan Brook Lean-to

We got soaked last night from blowing rain. Then we woke up to colder and wetter weather this morning, one of those when nothing was spared. Sleeping bag, clothes and gear were soggy with rain that found its way into every nook. The Captain smiled and asked what was worse—staying in soggy bags or emerging like glistening larvae to pull on clammy shorts and rain jackets. Another choice for me is whether to put my face in my hands and cry (what Captain calls a Self-Pitying Heap) or to laugh at Captain's antics as he ignores his own misery and attempts to cheer me up.

After getting our sodden possessions assembled in the lashing wind, we ran to the crowded shelter. Kamikaze and Thoroughbred were among the crowd and told us that all the mess blowing through is the final remnants of Hurricane Elvis who stayed politely out in the

Atlantic and lost steam before dodging west to regurgitate his weakened remains. Thoroughbred's smartphone weather app predicted clear, cool weather by midday—a wonderful prospect.

We plunged into fading Elvis and made our way across the rest of the Chairback Range. On a clear day, all the crags and cliffs would have made for great vistas. This morning it was a series of rock scrambles, ankle-deep water and more rough weather. We worked our way down to the West Branch of the Pleasant River. Whatever force of nature blowing the mini-hurricane through from the east just kept on pushing once the clouds and rain were gone, leaving a cloudless sky in its wake to dry things fast.

I reached the river with the Captain, and it looked to be a challenging ford. I switched to Crocs and entered water that was muddy, chilly and fast. Solemate and Whinin' Wolf started ahead of me, and Solemate went down. He and his pack were nearly submerged for a few seconds and he permanently lost one of his sticks. Moving without panic, he regained his footing and got his sodden equipment to the north bank.

With water above my knees, I hoped to do better. We took underwater baby steps and crossed without soaking our packs. Solemate grinned ruefully as he wrung out his clothes—poor guy.

We began the big ascent up Whitecap Mtn., the final climb of substance before Katahdin. The climb from the river to the peak is about 3,000 feet. When you add ups and downs of peaks along the ridge leading to Whitecap itself, the cumulative ascent is killer. It took hours. It didn't quite qualify as being above timberline, because there were stunted cedars scattered around, but there were plenty of bare, rocky spots. We spread out gear to sun dry. Katahdin resembled a gaudy postcard, its granite top and scarred flanks on display—an irresistible siren enticing us northward. Everyone mimicked our drying process, and Whitecap looked like a yard sale, with shirts, pants, sleeping bags, tarps and socks—not to mention shriveled hikers—scattered randomly among sun-dappled rocks. Juncos flitted madly, resentful of our intrusion into their domain.

Now I sit beneath my tarp, 1,250 feet below Whitecap's summit, visions of Katahdin interrupting any attempt at clear thought. I'm so ready, so excited to finish this and head for the next adventure. Captain is cooking spaghetti. He carried a jar of sauce these many miles along with canned mushrooms and fresh red pepper. He just asked if I thought we could eat it all. For such a bright guy he asks dumb questions.

August 23, Journal entry of Doug Gottlieb from White House Landing

Pollyanna and I vaulted ahead of our friends this morning. We've been hearing from SOBOs about the one-pound hamburger at White House Landing. Since none of our chums is interested in making the side trip to the landing this afternoon, we lit out early to knock off more than 20 miles to get here.

We hustled down a long descent to the East Branch of the Pleasant River and then up Boardman Mtn. The next 14 miles were the easiest we've seen in a long time. Before noon, we reached Cooper Brook Falls Lean-to. We couldn't remember if there was another shelter on the trail with a view of a waterfall. A man offered me a Mars Bar, and I hesitated. "You've gone over 2,100 miles," he said. "Take this." I split it with Pollyanna, and we thanked him the requisite three times.

We motored to Antlers Camp and checked out Ft. Relief, the best privy on the trail. It has windows with curtains, a vanity and a wash basin. However, it is, after all, a privy and stinks like most others, and that's why I rarely use them. Since Boy Scouts, I've been a cat-hole man. Why not contribute back to nature?

Later we hit a side trail to White House Landing and plodded to a rickety dock on Pemadumcook Lake looking across to the little fish camp. At the end of the dock was an air horn and instructions to blow it once and wait patiently. We did, and nothing happened. Finally, a guy named Bill emerged from one of the buildings and strode purposefully down to a big aluminum boat and breezed across the lake to get us.

We were way early for dinner—time to go to the bunkhouse, shower and put on clean shorts and tee shirts for the famous one-pounder. A squall blew through south of us, and an astonishing double rainbow appeared with one end diving right into the lake a half mile away. What treasure lay submerged there?

A few other hikers lounged in the dining room, none we had met before. Among them was a NOBO we had been hearing and reading about, Smilin' Quincy. Turns out his middle name really is Quincy, and he has a reputation for being a grump. When he started the trip, he added "Smilin'" to his name vowing to change his sullen ways.

He had cigars, and he offered a few to Linda and me. "I haven't smoked anything since I tried a cigarette in junior high and got sick as a dog," Linda said.

"You don't inhale cigars," I told her. "Puff and savor the aroma." She lit up. After a few puffs, she stared dreamily across the lake. "I might

smoke one of these every year or so," she said. "It's very relaxing."
Smilin' Quincy smiled.

After the one-pound burgers and before heading to the bunkhouse,
we settled into Adirondack chairs, watched the sky turn purplish-
orange in the west and shivered as we waited for the first evening stars
to materialize from a darkening sky. I asked Pollyanna if she minded if
I became a part of her life after the trail came to an end in a few days.
"Really?" she queried. "Are you that dense? I've told you all along that I
plan to be independent while I'm thru-hiking. But after that, sure." I
didn't know exactly how to take that, but I did like the tone. "I'm glad
we're climbing Katahdin together," I said. She smiled. I feel no anxiety
about finishing. Nope, none at all.

THE 100-MILE WILDERNESS

It is a 100-mile hike, but it's a stretch to call it a wilderness. Nonetheless, there are few places east of the Mississippi wilder than the trek
from Monson to Abol Bridge. Still there are dirt roads to cross and a couple
of fish camps available for overnight stays for those willing to take side
trips.

Wilderness is a state of mind. For a NOBO, the view of Katahdin from
Whitecap is as close to an expansive wilderness view as a thru-hiker will see.
You may see vapor trails in the sky and a column or two of industrial smoke
in the distance, but roads, structures and other signs of human impact are
hard to pick out. It is a fitting finish, a cooldown at the end of a long work-
out, a century of miles to wind down the greatest adventure a person will
likely ever have.

For the SOBO, the 100 miles is an amazing beginning. After a one-day
emotional tornado at Katahdin, the first long stretch of trail is an old Disney
nature flick in gaudy color, with blue lakes, azure sky and accommodating
wildlife.

Some accounts portray the 100 miles as remote, intimidating and so
dangerous it can't be finished by normal mortals—a canard disproven
regularly by thousands of ordinary hikers. It has its challenges, but it is not
overwhelming.

The reward of finishing for a NOBO is the view of Katahdin from Whitecap and later, just after emerging from the wilderness, the closer view from
Abol Bridge. ■

August 24, Journal entry of Pollyanna at Wadleigh Stream Lean-to

Breakfast this morning, though not up to gourmet standards, was substantial. Hey, if someone sets up shop this far away from everything, I'll eat what they put in front of me—no complaints. Bill gave us a boat ride to the far end of Pemadumcook this morning to save a mile of hiking on the side trail. I smiled at Doug as we zipped through the stillness, disturbing every living creature with the roaring outboard. We were back on the A.T. within a few minutes of hitting shore.

Except for going up and down Pataywadjo Ridge, we had remarkably easy hiking. After two exhausting days, this flat 12 miles was the Garden of Eden with weather on order from Adam and Eve. I loved hiking with Doug alongside lakes and streams, across bog logs and past the birches and conifers. After all the punishing weather, maybe we finish lucky.

We met a pair of spry ladies out for a few days who were in the mood to talk, and on this day we were in the mood to accommodate. They were up from Boston for adventure in the North Woods. When I told them I was a Gold Award Girl Scout, they whooped with elation. They had been Girl Scouts and were still adult volunteers. Doug and I heard thousands of interminable tidbits about their thrilling Girl Scout adventures, and we were polite enough to act interested.

Later, Doug affected a little-old-lady voice: "We worked as a team to sell Girl Scout cookies in Boston when we were 11 years old. What if I were to tell you that we sold more cookies than any girls in Boston that year? Four kinds, not the variety they have now—just four. My Goodness, what a boring, tedious old biddy I am. If you don't walk away soon, I'll just go on talking past sundown."

"That's so mean!" I protested. "They were sweet."

"Sweet, yes," Doug replied. "Interesting? No, no. no."

We lazed on the sandy shore of Nahmakanta Lake before wading in and swimming. Warm, dry afternoon air was an antidote to the chilly water. We hiked on to Wadleigh Stream Lean-to, a perfect spot to read, relax and cook an early dinner from our dwindling food supply. Doug started ramen, throwing in odds and ends of tuna and spices. I shared blueberry crunch upside-down cake—a cheesecake pudding packet with a pouch of blueberries and another of graham cracker crumbs. Such slop!

Doug produced a cigar, a parting gift from Smilin' Quincy. We shared it, and he chided me for breaking my "one cigar per year rule" after just one day. "This is only half a cigar," I explained. "Technically, I'm on the wagon."

Soon the fool's parade trickled in, including all the Bly Gap folks except Ultragrunge and Blue Devil. Doug noted their absence and smiled lasciviously, speculating that maybe they were making up for lost time before this trip slams shut. He was indelicately stating what we all were thinking.

A full camp tonight. While others cooked and did chores, Doug and I walked to the stream and lazed on a flat rock. "I'll go back to Columbus after all this," I told him. "I need to get my stuff squared away and think about what's next."

Doug looked at me with a sort of smile I haven't seen before. "I'll head to Seattle," he said. "I need to see Mom. After that, I know what I want to do. I just don't know where." He looked like a little boy who had moments ago planted a flower seed and was intently watching the dirt to see what would happen next. I gazed back and smiled. As I write this—all snuggled in my bag, next to Doug in his—I'm still smiling.

August 25, Journal entry of Blue Devil at Hurd Brook Lean-to

I hiked with Grunge yesterday in perfect weather, and we talked a lot and shared deep secrets, as Grunge once again proved that there is unseen feminine compassion under that crusty facade. During these five months, she has learned a few specifics about the uncertainties and empathetic nature beneath my cocky demeanor. With a lengthy lead-in statement about the inevitability of it all, seeing as how we've spent five months together experiencing bliss and duress, I told her I had fallen for her.

"I love you too," she replied. I almost expected her to add a big "duh!" Instead, she gave me a ghost of a smile. "You need to come out to see me in Austin before you start Duke. Someday, we'll hike together again, and it's okay for us to love each other." Then, she kissed me, my first since I last saw Indu all those weeks ago.

We bootlegged near a beach on Nahmakanta Lake, not far from Wadleigh Stream Lean-to, because we wanted to be alone. We shared my fraying tarp. I'm not all that experienced in the art of romance. Hey, give me a break, I'm only 18. But I am an apt pupil and well-prepared, while Ms. Grunge most definitely is a willing instructor who provided a tutorial that left me a changed man. This morning we skinny-dipped and got back on the trail for an easy 20 miles to Hurd Brook Lean-to.

We stopped late in the morning at Rainbow Stream Lean-to—surely one of the loveliest shelter spots on the entire A.T.—and munched our remaining candy bars. Grunge made two points: (1) We will not to speak of last night to anyone, as it is our special secret. Ok, fine. (2) She is five years older than I am, and although she recognizes we are in some level of love, she also knows that based on our adventurous natures we will lead full, aggressive lives during the years I finish my education. She thinks it is likely we will grow apart and that I should be prepared for that.

"Just damn, Calves!" I said. "I get through telling you how I feel and hearing how you feel, and now you're telling me not to expect too much."

She chewed on a blade of grass and looked out at the stream. Her pale skin, her red hair, her spectacular physique, her freshly emerged affectionate nature and her truly brilliant mind are so amazing. How could I have not gone crazy for her from the start?

She gave me a lazy glance and neatly summed up the situation: "You're just a kid, and I'm not much more than one, so here's the lesson you need to take away when we split in a couple of days. Thank your luckiest star that we're turning each other loose to live these lives of ours. I've had guys get infatuated with me a time or two, and I've learned to let things cool for a while to make sure the infatuation doesn't evaporate when they spot a hot piece of tail during their travels. You got that?"

I told her I understood, but I didn't like it. She kissed me gently and hoisted her pack. "Let's get going. I've got Katahdin fever so bad I'm about to pop."

The next eight miles were easy, paralleling the shore of Rainbow Lake. We took a side trip to the dam to see Katahdin again. It's far too massive to care about us, assuming it's capable of conscious thought concerning which I have major doubts, but seeing it getting closer hour by hour, I share Grunge's growing desire to attack the slopes.

A climb up Rainbow Ledges provided yet another view of Kathdin. I photographed Grunge facing the Big K with her arms outstretched. When I look at this picture in 30 years, will I see a life partner or the sweet object of a long-extinguished passion?

As we reached Hurd Brook and filled our bottles, we noticed a frog, still as a rock and undisturbed by our movements. "Fascinating amphibian fact of the day," Grunge said. "Frogs drink through their butts." Maybe. All I know is Grunge and I have one more night under my tarp. I think of tomorrow as a festival, a pilgrimage to Katahdin Stream. This is true adventure. Can I ever match it again?

August 27, Journal entry of Sky Writer at Birches Campsite, Baxter State Park

A couple of years ago, I came to grips with my emotions. Through high school and into college, I was a crybaby. I couldn't stop the waterworks. I finally got a grip. I don't regret learning to control my overt displays, because although I became calmer and shrewder, I was no less engaged.

Today I gave myself back to my feelings. There's a whirlwind of events, stimulation and too great a sense of impending closure for me to remain aloof. I shed a thousand tears in a mixture of supreme happiness, finishing anxiety, thrilled anticipation and profound loss. At times like these, emotions rule.

This morning started conventionally. We reached the highway near Abol Bridge, the end of the 100 Miles, where a sign provided a dire warning to SOBOs about the need to be prepared for wilderness risks. We chuckled at the breathless caveat, but in truth, a rookie could get in big trouble out there. To us, it was just a long stretch between resupply.

We walked down blacktop and over Abol Bridge, gawking at Katahdin in its tourist leaflet glory, a flat-topped eminence clad in a skirt of conifers and topped with a huge rocky crown streaked with glaciated gashes.

Tractor-trailers rumbled by, laden with trees stripped of their limbs, ready for sacrifice at the altar of sawmills and pulp plants—a screaming reintroduction to civilization. We swarmed the little store. I bought breakfast bars, almonds and candy bars to energize my ascent. Thoroughbred bought me bubblegum. I grabbed a couple of one-liter Cokes and gave him one to split with Kamikaze. Why this craving for Coke after days and days away from it?

Captain bought Little Debbie oatmeal cakes, and I handed one to Pollyanna, suddenly realizing we would soon part ways. I sobbed and we got wrapped up in a tangle of arms patting and caressing. Brave Phillie kissed my cheek and wiped a muddy tear from my face.

We plunged back into the woods paralleling the Penobscot and heard timber trucks across the river. Five miles in, the trail branched away from the big river to track the Nesowadnehunk River and pass into Baxter State Park. This was a North Woods Eden—a spotless stream, a couple of waterfalls (Big and Little Niagara) and finally, Daicey Pond. We took a side jog to the pond, and there it was again, Big K, so close you could pat it. If I broke my leg, I'd crawl on hands and knees to Baxter Peak.

> Daicy Pond waters
> North Woods terrain
> 2,000 milers
> no step in vain!

> Amicaloooola
> vision so pure
> Leading us northward
> Katahdin's lure

We took a sentimental stroll around lakes and over bog logs, all the while serenaded by the musical motif of our trek, the five-bar call of the ubiquitous white-throated sparrow. I felt full, ecstatic, deeply regretful. Tears couldn't cry themselves out.

Then we were at that place called Katahdin Stream Campground, which five months ago seemed as remote as the moon. We watched a cow moose and her calf wading in the stream. We walked past tiny lean-tos and over a footbridge to the ranger station, where we learned there was room at the Birches, a campsite for thru-hikers. A ranger asked if there was a hiker known as Sky Writer among us, because a man was looking for her.

What man? I spotted Dad—natty as an L.L. Bean model—crossing the bridge over Katahdin Stream, beaming like a school boy caught snatching cookies in the cafeteria. The old resentment evaporated as I sprinted to him and felt myself wrapped up in those familiar arms, and again, out came the tears. He cried too, and we stood there hugging, snorting, laughing, sobbing—the things we do when people we care about suddenly reappear after a painful absence.

"How did you know?" I said sputtering through tears and snorts. "How could you ever have known when we'd get here?"

"Your mom talked to Linda's mom. We calculated a window around yesterday, today or tomorrow," he told me. "I flew from Berlin to New York to Bangor and hoped for the best." He paused to dab tears. "I rented a van like the Bennetts suggested, the 'Bly Gap Express' and got here yesterday. My gosh, you're beautiful Doodlebug—skinny as a rail." He looked around at my grinning tribe. "I know you," he said. "You're Brave Phillie and Momma Llama. You're Blue Devil."

"I'm easy," Blue Devil said, and we all laughed.

"And you're Pollyanna, and you're Ultragrunge. I can't forget the Captain, and the tall fellow there has to be Doug, right?"

I hugged Dad and told him he scored a hundred. "Now, all I have to do is click my heels together, and I'll be back in Colorado, right?"

Dad had a portable grill, hamburgers (grain patties for me), beans, potatoes, coleslaw, cookies, even a cake from a Bangor bakery with a "2,000-Mile" inscription. We feasted, and Dad did all the work. After gorging, we hoisted packs to head to the Birches. Dad asked if I wanted to go with him to a cabin outside the park, but I told him I need to stick with my posse.

"Can I climb to the top with you tomorrow?" he asked.

I told him no. "As happy as I am to see you, Dad, you haven't exactly earned that right. I want to share this exclusively with the Captain and the others. Please understand."

"I haven't exactly earned much of anything," he said. "I was afraid you might be angry at me for even showing up."

I was fresh out of anger. Five months in the woods have put my animosity to rest. "I long since came to the realization that you and Mom were finished. When I climbed Mt. Washington and remembered that vacation all those years ago, I decided to remember the happiness we knew back then. So, if you want back in, there's room. Just bear with me if I occasionally get pissed off."

It was not unwelcome to have Dad in this hodgepodge of goings on. We strolled to the Birches, and I made sure Dad and the Captain hung out. Then Dad was on his way back outside the park, armed with phone numbers to inform our fans—unreachable by cell—about what was happening. He promised to meet us tomorrow afternoon. This was so great! Dad with his big van solved all the minor concerns about how we would transport ourselves back to wherever we needed to go as we returned to . . . what?

August 28, Katahdin's Kiss

Doodad was invited to join a trail crew upgrading waterbars and eroded spots north of Caratunk. After a few days of hard labor, he gratefully took his leave and headed for Baxter State Park, reasoning that if he was in Maine, he should make a summit run up Katahdin. He began under the stars—first climber of the day—with a light load plus his customary camera gear. He headed up the Knife Edge, a challenging route that leaves climbers with their hearts next to their Adam's apples. His pace was leisurely and he stopped often to tinker with his camera gear.

Soon after he started, Pollyanna and Doug clicked on their headlamps on the other side of the mountain and passed through Katahdin Stream Camp-ground to tree-lined Hunt Spur Trail. They greeted the first gray vestiges of dawn in the spray of Katahdin Stream Falls. From there, the trail grew steeper, rougher. Still, they moved quickly as trees became smaller and more widely separated. They carried daypacks borrowed from the ranger station at Katahdin Stream, laden with water, snacks and rain gear for a climb of well over 4,000 feet to the crest of the 5,267-foot peak, the longest ascent on the A.T.

They broke out of the trees and looked back to see the onset of their final trail day spreading its glow over woods, lakes and streams. Fresh rays converted myriad lakes and rivers into a scattering of glistening bright spots— seemingly the remains of a colossal mirror broken and scattered eons ago.

Pushing hard, they exploited the luxury of physical conditioning honed daily for months and followed blazes and cairns upward to steep stretches of scrambling and bouldering, occasionally assisted by iron handholds driven deeply into the granite. The higher they climbed, the harder the wind blew, at times briskly enough to make them stagger.

"I love this," said Pollyanna. "It reminds me of Mahoosuc Notch—so much fun you don't notice how hard it is."

Their upward crawl continued as they worked steadily along the narrow rocks of Hunt Spur, until at last they scampered up and over the edge to the Tableland. Here they saw a little subarctic-alpine wonderland running level and uphill toward their ultimate goal—Baxter Peak. They stopped at Thoreau Spring, not so much for rest but to make the experience last longer.

"The guide book says Katahdin is an Indian word for 'Greatest Mountain,'" Doug said. "Why not something powerful and mysterious like 'Mountain of Doom?'"

"You've been playing too many video games," Pollyanna groaned.

On they went. The sky was cloudless, the wind fresh and vital. The early start provided them sole possession of the summit. They moved rapidly, their goal clearly in sight, both of them hoping secretly that the finish would not be anticlimactic. Skipping from boulder to boulder, they came within 100 yards of the fabled summit sign.

"Wait," said Doug. "We have a piece of unfinished business. Don't I have a promise to keep?"

"You're kidding!" Pollyanna squealed. "Don't tell me you have a trail name?"

"Correctamundo," he answered. *"But you have to guess it."*

"Oh, that's totally unfair. I can never guess it. Give me a hint."

Doug smiled, his eyes glistening with tears blown across his cheeks by the wind. *"It is what we almost are."*

Linda's eyes shimmered as well. *"It is what we are,"* she whispered. *"We're finished. We're done. Oh, we're through! Thru, your trail name is Thru!"*

Doug put his arms around her, and for the last time, they were frozen in the parallel universe of their thru-hike, as wind whipped their clothes and stung their cheeks. *"I always sensed you wanted to hit the top before I kissed you,"* he whispered. *"But I don't care. I'm gonna cheat."*

"Me neither," Linda said between sobbing and smiling. The first kiss was clumsy, knocking Linda's sunglasses half off. She snatched them and stuck them in her pocket. The second effort went more smoothly, as did the third, fourth and others beyond.

"Promise me we'll figure out a way to be together," Doug said. *"I can't leave here without knowing that."*

"We'll see," she said. *"C'mon, let's get this done."* She turned on her heel and moved purposefully toward the rock pile of the summit. Thru hung back to watch her walk to the sign, as thousands had before her, and place her hands gently on the surface. Mounted on an easel of weathered planks, the sign read: *"Katahdin, Northern Terminus of the Appalachian Trail, a Mountain Footpath Extending Over 2,000 Miles to Springer Mtn. Georgia."* Below are a number of destinations, including Springer, and the distances to them.

She turned to Thru, and he knew it was his turn. He pulled a pebble from his pocket that he had picked up on Springer and placed it on the summit cairn. Then he knelt, placed his forehead on the sign and prayed out loud: *"I give thanks that I was able to stay well and uninjured to the end, and for Pollyanna, the best part of my hike. I'll get back to you later, when I can think more clearly."*

"That goes double for me," Pollyanna said, her head tilted skyward and her eyes closed. *"Just insert 'Thru' for 'Pollyanna.'"*

Coming up from a place called the Chimneys on the other side of Katahdin was a sixtyish couple moving confidently and quickly for their age. *"You beat us,"* the woman said. *"We thought we'd be first this morning."* She smiled at her husband. *"These two could be us 40 years ago."*

Cleaning his glasses with a wool muffler, the man nodded. *"We climbed this big rock on our honeymoon exactly four decades ago,"* he recalled. *"This is the first time we've been back, and she badgered me every step of the way."*

Looking out over the Tableland, Thru saw hikers spilling over the edge of the mountain's flat top about a mile and a half away. He pointed and cried, "Look, isn't that Brave Phillie with Momma Llama? And there come Sky and Captain Stupid."

Pollyanna squinted. "Look, Kamikaze and Thoroughbred are crawling over the edge. Wow, the wind's blowing their kilts like crazy. This might get X-rated."

"That guy in the red toboggan has to be Smilin' Quincy," Thru yelled. "Oh boy, there come Grunge and Blue Devil right behind. Woohoo! They came up en masse."

Pollyanna and Thru hunkered down and huddled close to watch the traveling circus make its last lap.

August 28, Transcript of Captain Stupid recorded at Katahdin Stream

We're packed and ready to pull out. Sky's dad (he insists I call him Mark) has a cavernous van to hold us and our gear. Looks like Smilin' Quincy, Kamikaze and Thoroughbred are hitching with us down to Bangor. The more the merrier. The Bly Gap Express will be busting at the seams.

I've found a few minutes to chatter into this minirecorder for the last time. I want to talk about the summit this morning while it's still fresh. I remember the first day when I paid extra to be driven to the top of Amicalola Falls to save myself from a climb. The ascent up Katahdin is about six times higher, and I had not one-millionth the trepidation about Katahdin that I did for Amicalola.

I spoke to Ultragrunge as we packed up for the trip out of our alternate dimension. Normally she's a hard-boiled realist unwilling to give credence to half-baked notions bordering on spiritual or mystical realms. But she was uncharacteristically moved by her experience today. "When it was all over, I stayed behind for a few minutes as the rest of you started back down from Baxter Peak," she confided. "I closed my eyes to breathe in that rarefied air. Then I went out of body, as if I were ascending toward space, looking down at myself standing there alone and the rest of you working your way across the Tableland—Google Earth in reverse. My astral body rising steadily upward. I opened my eyes, and it was over. I was back in my normal body, but I was also changed—forever, I guess. A transfiguration."

I suggested she talk to Doug about it, seeing as how he has served as our resident spiritual advisor for the past couple thousand miles. "No one can make me understand that," she mused. "I'm the last person on earth to suddenly go all supernatural."

For me, this day was decidedly non-supernatural. It was tangible—an affirmation of friendship and fulfilled dreams, a fillip spurring me to discover more surprises about myself. Sky and I wandered out in the middle of the pack this morning. It never occurred to me how much adrenaline would course through my aortas and veins and lungs. I pushed hard all the way, and so did Sky. Jack and Jill pumping up that ol' hill.

Yay!

The greatest climb on the greatest mountain on the best day of the whole journey. All of us strung out over the Tableland toward Baxter Peak, where we saw Doug and Pollyanna waving like cheerleaders. The wind was a banshee. The sky blue as the Aegean Sea. After all the crappy weather, we got so lucky on our last day.

Baxter was in our sights for so long, and then, we were there. So many tears, so much whooping, all that hugging and kissing and exclaiming. Every little thing I had dreamed it might be, a finish for the ages, the watershed moment of my life. I used to wonder if the astronauts were let down when they stepped on the moon. Of course, they weren't.

Brave Phillie broke out paper cups and a bottle of Champagne—the genuine French article—given to him by Mark. He twisted the cork and edged out the final few millimeters with his thumbs. The cork popped, and foam spewed all over as he held the bottle at arm's length, and we cheered him on—high-class stuff.

By this time, the daily parade was beginning at the summit, including a lean, dark-haired fellow who stood grinning quietly. Brave Phillie emptied the last of the bottle into the remaining cup and handed it to him. "Okay, you old 'leave no trace' son of a gun. Drink this and enjoy it, but by God, you better pack out the cup," Brave Phillie hollered over the whistle of the wind.

Another amazing A.T. coincidence! It was Doodad, our mentor from Springer. He remembered who we were just as we suddenly remembered him. "So, you made it," he said. "After I saw you off down at Springer, I heard about your altercation in Tennessee. Let me be the first to congratulate you guys!" He noticed we had added Momma

Llama and that we were missing Bone. We told him those stories, and he nodded appreciatively. "I'm taking off from Springer next spring," he told us. "I'm ready for another one of these."

Sky Writer clutched my arm and hollered, "Attention everyone! I officially proclaim a field promotion. Hereafter, Captain Stupid is elevated in the eyes of all hikerdom. Henceforth, he shall be known simply as The Captain. No more 'Stupid' for the man I love." The summit crowd cheered as Sky kissed me.

Not to be outdone, Pollyanna cleared her throat dramatically. "I also have an announcement. Doug officially came up with a trail name. It is what we are."

"We are hikers. We are finished!" I hollered. "We're through. It's over. So, what's your trail name?"

Pollyanna looked at me encouragingly. "You said it. Say it again!"

"Oh, wait," I hollered. "Through. Thru! Your trail name is Thru! Woohoo!"

Thru hollered back: "You are correct, sir! You guys are finished, but I will always be . . . Thru." And we were!

Epilogue

The following Spring Equinox at the Len Foote Hike Inn

If the clouds have dissipated and a clear sunrise is imminent, a staffer at the Len Foote Hike Inn customarily walks around the bunkhouse just before dawn, gently beating a drum. Groggy guests emerge and grab coffee before catching a glimpse of an orange disc peeking over the horizon with a backdrop of slaty sky, sometimes mottled by pinkish orange clouds. Guests content to wait until the breakfast bell rings are excused if they settle in for extra sack time.

Today everyone is up and motivated. Ceremony awaits. Bridesmaids and groomsmen are spiffy in matching khaki shorts and navy blue A.T. tee shirts. Parkas are shed, as the morning air is pleasant for late March. The intended are dressed identically to the others, except their tee shirts are red.

The Hike Inn is sold-out to the wedding party for the vernal equinox. On this morning, a rite is observed at Star Base, a celestial calendar with large rocks configured to track the movement of the sun to mark the seasons. Two granite slabs form an inverted V aligned with the sun as it peeks over the horizon and projects a shadow onto the back wall of a tiny manmade grotto carved into the ridge. In the middle of the shadow, the sun directs a ray through a hole in the granite V, the first sign of spring—a fresh start.

A jovial group waits in the drab light before dawn, toasting with coffee to greet spring. Keeping its appointment, the first sliver of yellow-orange slides above the eastern foothills. Distant twinkling lights of Dahlonega, including the shimmering Super Walmart where the Captain purchased precious phar-maceuticals, begin to dim. Time does not stand still, but it creeps slowly as the crowd welcomes a new season.

A former Marine who gave up war in exchange for seminary does the honors for an old friend. "I'm a tired old Methodist, and I normally stick to tradition," he says in a Southern minister's drawl. "But my buddy convinced me to keep this simple. I feel a little peculiar—anything but traditional—presiding in a pair of shorts and a tee shirt, but these folks aren't conven-tional types. So, here goes: When people meet under unusual circumstances, it intensifies their feelings for each other. In times of war, we find that hate, devotion, brotherly love and a thousand other emotions are honed to a razor edge. Similarly, in nature, we see and feel elements of one another's souls we would not experience in ordinary circumstances. We stand here in sight of Springer Mtn., where some of those gathered today met for the first time. There they began friendships that will last as long as they draw breath and, God willing, well beyond."

He pauses. "Now we bring together those who came to Gainesville, not far from here, to make a life together. Friends and families join them in com-munion with God in nature during these first precious moments of spring." His words drift into more conventional observances, and take on a singsong cadence. When it is time to exchange rings and vows, all goes without a hitch as the groom kisses his new wife.

On cue, hiking sticks form an archway, lifted together with tips touching. Everyone applauds, laughs and cheers as the bride and groom take a dreamy stroll through a makeshift archway assembled by their best friends. Sky sings "Amazing Grace," while Bone Festival picks a refurbished "Twangin' Perry." Ultragrunge and Pollyanna glow with that ancient aura women still feel at weddings.

Sky segues into a few verses of "Amicalola," ending with:

> *Amicalooooooola,*
> *Seeing us home.*
> *In Springer's shadow*
> *finally done.*
>
> *We're the Northbounders,*
> *Stalwart and true.*
> *Amicalooooola*
> *All thruuuuuu!*

Music yields to a wedding breakfast prepared by Hike Inn cooks who relish an opportunity to do something different. A wedding cake topped by a hiking bride and groom, breakfast soufflé, green-dyed grits, gravy, bacon, sausage, fruit, biscuits, apple cornbread—even a ramen cheese dish enjoyed by all but the thru-hikers, who appreciate the intentional irony but resist the minimal temptation.

The sun edges well above the eastern horizon, as Thru and Pollyanna stand alone at Star Base enjoying unseasonably balmy weather. "Star Base," Pollyanna says. "It's from a George Lucas script." Thru's arm is around her shoulders as he admires North Georgia's Blue Ridge. "The Appalachians end out there just a little past Springer. SOBOs run out of mountains and have to find something else to do—the same as when we climbed Katahdin. So, what are we gonna do? If Momma Llama and Brave Phillie can do this, how about us?"

Pollyanna stares east, creating comic suspense. "Still not ready," she whispers. "Maybe someday. Maybe a wedding night on Springer. Maybe not. But unless you accept that I have other fish to fry, we got trouble big fella."

"Those fried fish'll clog your arteries," Thru mutters. "Oh well, it's not like I don't have plenty to keep me busy."

The newlyweds, Momma Llama and Brave Phillie, stroll up, sloshing coffee mugs of champagne. "Sky's for sure moving back to Boulder," whispers Momma. "Captain knows she's not coming back. He says Sky and the A.T. transformed him, and that'll have to be enough. He's had a life of low expectations, but gosh, this has to hurt."

Sky and the Captain walk up, joined soon by Blue Devil, Ultragrunge, and Bone Festival. Blue Devil squeezes Pollyanna and Thru in his long arms. The Captain, only six pounds more than when he summited Katahdin, joins the embrace, and soon an old-fashioned group hug is underway.

Brave Phillie extends his hands in a patriarchal gesture. "If muleheaded thru-hikers don't realize another damn thing, we know this: Adventure's always in the cards! You've just gotta want it!"

Thru recalls the world-weary dad in the Shenandoah minivan who had resigned himself to a life without adventure. "I wish I was you," he told Thru. "You don't know how lucky you are."

"Yes, I do," Thru thinks as he wraps his arms around his A.T. brothers and sisters. "I always will."

Slowly, the affectionate group strolls back to rejoin the jabbering reception, part of the A.T. love story that will never end. Stillness settles over Star Base, and a young copperhead travels upslope through dry weed stalks and fresh bloodroot just pushing through the soil. He breaks into the open, quickly thinks better of it and doubles back to vanish beneath dried leaves and sticks—environs more to his liking. Spring is reborn in the North Georgia Blue Ridge.

Acknowledgments

As an epistolary novel with a linear plot (characters hike from south to north), *THRU*'s major elements came together easily for an old guy writing a first novel. Each character is a pastiche of real-life trail personalities. It only takes one day on the A.T. to discover that the path is a traveling circus peopled by colorful clowns, aerialists, beast tamers and ring masters. Little of what you read in this book was woven from whole cloth out of my imagination. After four decades and thousands of miles, vivid trail memories and ones I've long forgotten leaked into this narrative.

I hope readers who have gone end to end appreciate the book's portrayal of the grit and splendor of the thru-life and understand the concept of one's body as a "leg support system" and the exquisite misery of the "last-mile distortion zone." And for those of you who sometimes stare off into space and wonder what a 2,000-mile mountain stroll is like, I trust I've provided clarity. *THRU* is dedicated to all of you.

Many deserve gratitude such as my seventh-grade teacher, Trecy Chandler, who said: "Ricky, you should write a book." Trecy has left us, but I think she knows her former student came through. Another teacher, Mary Lovings, deserves a shout out for admonishing me when I showed lack of confidence in my writing skills and analytical aptitude.

I salute my thru-hiker kids, Steady and Optimus Prime, who inspired me to hike the entire AT for a second time to do research for this tome.

And my wife, Mommy Hugs, who usually listens when I blather on about the wonders of wilderness.

Deepest gratitude to my good friend Larry Luxenberg, board president of the Appalachian Trail Museum, and his associates there. Their belief in *THRU* and their excitement about using it to create fund raising enthusiasm allowed me to fulfill a lifelong dream of giving back to the trail project. Larry's book, *Walking the Appalachian Trail*, is a classic in its genre, and his encouragement has been priceless.

Greatest gratitude is extended to Mark Yarm, a wonderful editor who helped me discover, among other things, that even though the book had the requisite number of commas, most of them needed to be relocated. And more kudos to Margaret Nelling Schmidt who donated consummate technical skills in design and formatting as well as essential wisdom about art and graphics.

Thanks to the Chandlers, Skinner, LeVert, Mileto, Lawrence, Loudermilk, Huntington, Boyer, Bowden, Holden, Giles, McKinley and others in my hiking, biking and canoeing posse over the years. A loving nod to the Brugmanns, Pod, Bustace, Shrek, Loot, Spork, Bean Sprout, Finn, Song, Single Track, Laz, Turtle, Driftwood Dog, Salamander, Red Dog, O.d. Coyote, Catfish, Bruce Lee, Hiscoe, Baltimore Jack, Bag o' Tricks and anyone who's suffered through the epic poem, *Duncan's Pies*.

Thanks to Brian King, Bob Almand and others at the ATC for their advice and kind words.

All my love to the staff and board of the Len Foote Hike Inn who keep my enthusiasm alive for sharing hiking and wilderness education—particularly with kids who might not otherwise experience the wonder of gasping uphill in a national forest wilderness.

Finally, I quote my hero, Benton MacKaye, from a letter he wrote to me in 1974: "The problems of the country rank with those of the major crises going back two centuries. To wait for the solution of these problems would be like waiting for hell to freeze over. What then in the meantime? What chance for anything resembling the good life? 'Fat chance,' say most people. But not say you nor your likes who walk the trail and think; you set the slow and proper pace for the thousands who tread the trail today, refusing to wait until hell freezes over."

—Richard Judy, the Peregrine
Roswell, Georgia—2014

About the Author

Richard Judy (trail name: Peregrine), a graduate of the University of Georgia, spent a long career in public relations. He thru-hiked the A.T. in 1973 and bicycled from Los Angeles to Savannah Beach in 1975. His son and daughter are also thru-hikers. He serves as board president of a not-for-profit group overseeing the Len Foote Hike Inn in the North Georgia mountains. He will soon complete a section hike of the A.T. which began in 2000. He lives in Roswell, Ga., with his wife who has hiked the entire width of the A.T.

CPSIA information can be obtained at www.ICGtesting.com
Printed in the USA
LVOW05s2101051214

417467LV00019B/119/P